MW00891293

SON
of the SEA

A Novel

ANDREW E. KAUFMAN

Published by Straightline Press

OTHER TITLES BY ANDREW E. KAUFMAN

For my father.

And the time came when the risk to remain tight in a bud was more painful than the risk it took to blossom.

—Anaïs Nin

PROLOGUE

I WATCH THE CHILDREN'S CAROUSEL go round and round, one wooden horse leaping ahead of the next as they surge forward. Their motion is wavelike, slowly rising and falling along the contours of a jubilant organ recital. A sea of tiny sneakers and chubby knees flow past me, children's giggles sounding from near and far.

Beyond this carousel, the fair plays out, a backdrop for memories that shine like silver. I'm there again, a kid, immersed in the summer of 1995. A time when the world was fresh and whole, in the place where it all began.

PART ONE: THE BEFORE

1

My sixth birthday was coming up, and my father asked where I wanted to celebrate it.

"The fair, Daddy. The fair!"

"Slow it down there, Champ," he said, laughing as he caught me on my second sprint around the kitchen island.

We took the scenic route, wheeling up the Pacific Coast Highway. Public beaches, RV parks, and miles of horizon flew past my window, broken only by an occasional surf shop or boho café. Ahead, far-reaching bluffs flanked the coastline, along with tall, arching palms shaped by the trade winds. Eventually, the landscape settled as the seashore pushed closer, unveiling the marriage between sand and sea. I imagined seeing it all better from high up in a Ferris wheel.

Dad's attention bounced between me and the road. "Whatcha doin', prune? Stewin'?"

"I'm thinking about the rides, Dad. I can't wait to go on the rides!"

"Soon, Champ. I promise."

My twin sister, Deena, and my mother had made their own birthday plans for the day, heading to the mall to buy my sister a bathing suit for summer.

The Del Mar Fair, San Diego's unofficial start to summer, came around each year from late June to early July. The all-day attractions were enough to send me into overdrive, never mind the promise of deep-fried euphoria: corn dogs, banana fritters, apple cider doughnuts, and funnel cake ice cream sandwiches. There were the giant slides and bumper cars, the animal exhibits with pigs, calves, and goats, and live country music.

"Look at all the colors, Daddy," I said as we breezed past the arcade's string of giant stuffed animals—pink pigs, purple gorillas, and blue bears—tethered by ropes. I could barely contain myself.

Alone time with Dad was special, but going to the fair made this birthday the best yet, better than even the year before when Mom and Dad had rented a bouncy house for Deena's and my party. We had a blast, thrashing our way into blissful exhaustion, which was fine until Bobby Kimmel barfed chocolate birthday cake all over Mary Jo Sorkin's brand-new white party shoes. In theory, it wasn't funny, but I had to turn around and laugh into my shirt. Poor Bobby. Poor Mary Jo. It was a safe bet they'd never attend our birthday celebrations again.

The day was broiling, but as night fell, the mercury began a gentle descent. My father and I roamed the causeway, cool air brushing the nape of my sunburned neck and cheeks. Mingling with the dust was the smell of fry grease and sugar, braided with the earthy tang of livestock. Arcade games pinged and ponged while neon-lit amusement park rides shot toward the heavens, painting the sky with dazzling colors.

"He's my little buddy. Da, DA, da, DA," my father sang as we got in the fried Oreo line for what had to be our sixth or seventh food stop.

My stomach was turning a little sour.

"He's my little buddy," Dad went on.

We had our own song—of course we did—and he always sang it when we were alone on our outings: trips to the hardware store with ice cream on the way back or to pick up a few last-minute grocery items that Mom needed for supper. But this, *this* was a whole day alone with Dad at the fair.

"Can we go there next?" I asked, pointing to the giant Ferris wheel as it twirled in the distance.

My father grinned, his sable hair glimmering in the midway lights. He was a tall man, shoulders strong and broad, his chest a barrel, but his towering presence had never felt intimidating to me.

"Let's see how your tummy holds up after the last food installment, Champ, okay? We don't want you getting sick."

My attention scattered. There was still so much to see, so much to explore, and I realized my birthday wouldn't last forever. As the day wore

4

on, my father's steps had slowed and dragged, and by the time we were closer to the Ferris wheel, his lids looked heavy.

"What do you say we take a break for a few minutes?" he asked, pointing to a bench several feet ahead.

We took a breather to let my stomach settle and give Dad a rest, then closed our distance to the Ferris wheel. When we got there, I gazed up in awe. It was massive, glorious. Each car was painted a different color, and when the ride went into a spin, it looked like a sky-high, mile-wide, spinning rainbow. When it was our turn to board, the attendant seated us in the purple car, which happened to be my favorite color—surely, Dad had planned it that way.

Our car climbed toward the top while they continued to load passengers, and I got a bird's-eye view of the park. Everything was so small, people scattered like blowing specks of dust. Outbuildings were no larger than my hand, and scores of tiny rides moved at different speeds and in different directions. Beyond that, the silvery coast shone up and down the shoreline. As I'd anticipated, it was a whole new perspective from what I'd seen while we drove here.

"Daddy?" I said.

"Yeah, Champ?"

"How did everything get so small?"

"It really didn't." He pulled me in and wrapped his arm around my shoulder while we shared the view. "Things just look different when you get farther away from them."

The answer seemed simple enough in the moment, but life wasn't lived atop a Ferris wheel, and I'd already learned that the view wasn't always sunny and bright. A year before, Mom had undergone surgery to remove a malignant tumor from her ovary. The doctors caught it early, her surgery went well, and the prognosis looked good, but it was a scare for us all. Looking back, I think the experience changed her perspective about our family so that how she loved us telegraphed a new fragility. But on that night, suspended high above the world, I knew that this evening would end, and as I looked into the darkening horizon, my premonition seemed to permeate everything. Still, I tried to hold on to this moment and believe in its permanence.

Mom and Dad met as kids in a Baldwin Park neighborhood outside of Los Angeles. He was fifteen, and she was thirteen. From the moment my father saw her, he knew she was the one, and Mom said it was the same when she saw him.

"I was practically born married to your mother," he once told me. "There was never anyone else, and there never will be."

They dated through their teens and got married as soon as Mom turned eighteen. Several years later, Dad graduated from the University of San Diego Law School, and they decided to stay in town and start a family. They wasted no time—that's not an exaggeration. Since Deena and I came into the world as twins, we joked about how my parents started their insta-family.

"Whaddya say, Champ?" my father asked, rattling my shoulder and bringing my attention back inside the Ferris wheel car. "Do you think Mom and Sister are having as much fun right now?"

I shrugged.

The wheel began to turn, and soon, my father and I were riding into the sky, then dropping to earth, over and over. My senses were heightened. I was flying. *We* were flying. As we ascended again, fireworks set the evening sky aflame, pushing my birthday further toward perfection. I swear, it felt like this day might go on forever after all. But then we were on our way toward the exits. It was all ending too fast. As we turned a corner, I spotted a stand loaded with handmade wooden toys.

"Can we, Dad?" I asked, desperate to stall.

He gave a quick nod. I blazed ahead.

They were the most amazing toys—shelves and shelves of them—with moving parts: animal wizards, astronauts, and wide-eyed kids playing ball. But one in particular stole my attention, a father and son running together, their dog trailing behind them. My father, noticing my interest, took the toy down from the shelf and handed it to me. The figures rested on a carousel, and when I spun it, round and round they went—Dad, son, and pup constantly joyous. I spun it several times.

"This is you, me, and Jimmy!"

My father laughed. "It does kind of resemble us, huh?"

He took the toy to the cashier, and a moment later, he handed me the bag. I peered inside for one more look. It was an amazing treasure to remember our amazing trip to the fair, and my dark thought from the Ferris wheel began to pale.

"This was the most perfect birthday I've ever had," I said when we got closer to the exit.

"Not perfect yet." My dad pointed to a photographer off to the side in a small studio, taking portraits. "Should we?"

"Yes!" I clapped. "YES!"

But when we entered, the photographer told us he couldn't take our portrait because he was closing down for the evening.

"Can't you make an exception just this once?" Dad looked at me, then back at the photographer. "It's my son's birthday, and this would make it the best."

Shaking his head, the man said, "I'm really sorry, but I've already shut down the register."

Dad looked into my tearful eyes. "Sorry, Champ," he said. "Maybe next summer."

I turned my gaze downward and nodded, surrendering. This was a once-in-a-year opportunity that would end when we left the park. In fact, it was probably already over.

We were about to walk toward the door when my dad stopped. He looked back at the man.

Pointing to floor equipment where several red and black wires were frayed and exposed, he said, "Hey, buddy, see that right there? That's extremely dangerous. It could start an electrical fire. Those things go off at alarming speed. I should know. I'm a lawyer."

The man looked at the wires, and his expression flattened.

Dad walked back toward him and made his voice confidential. "You seem like a really nice guy, but someone could report you, and then the fire department would have to get involved. They could shut you down for the rest of the season."

The photographer scrambled to unplug the equipment. After he finished, he turned to my father and said, "You know, maybe I can squeeze you in for a quick photo after all."

"Excellent!" my father said. "It'll mean so much to my boy!"

We got into position. Dad put his arms around me, and we gave the camera our biggest smiles, and then the flash went off, making time stand beautifully still.

"Thank you for making my son's birthday so special," my father said, handing over cash for the photos.

The photographer's smile looked a bit stilted, but I figured it had been a long day, and he was either tired or upset that his equipment had caused a hazard.

"That was fun today, Dad!" I said as we walked through the exit.

"It sure was," my father agreed. "What was your favorite part of the day?"

"Us!"

"Us?"

"Yeah, you know." I shrugged. "I love us."

His mouth curved into a smile, his head dropping as he looked into my eyes.

"I love us too, Champ," my father told me.

2

MY TWIN SISTER, DEENA, AND I were ten when our mother's cancer
came back.

I was too young to remember many of the details, but from what I
learned, Mom went in for her yearly scan to make sure it hadn't returned.

It had.

But there was hope—the malignancy didn't appear to have spread.
Just to make sure, the doctor ordered a PET scan.

The image lit up like a house on fire. The cancer had metastasized to
her liver, spleen, and brain. She only had a few months left.

I adored her. We all did. I remember one day, she lost her footing on
the staircase with a full laundry basket. Down she went, five or six steps.
The basket flew from her hands, clothes tumbling right along with her,
rear end bumping along each tread until she hit the floor at the bottom
of the staircase. My sister and I came running, terrified and trying to
remember who to call in an emergency.

It looked like the living room had rained clothes.

Mom glanced up at us, dazed. "Kids? I'm not sure which hurts
more—my pride or my ass."

There we were, crying so hard with laughter and relief that we were
soundless and breathless. Most people would never get away with some
of the stuff she said, especially around children, but her charm won her
certain allowances. It also won her a lot of friends, along with her looks.
She was fair-skinned and Irish-freckled with thick hair, brown with
shimmering copper highlights—and she didn't color it, she was quick to
say. Her pale green eyes drew attention and admiration, even as they

seemed to see right through you. She carried herself in a stately way, even in pajamas, but there were times when that beauty seemed hemmed with unease, perhaps a reflection of how the first bout of cancer had changed her in ways she couldn't yet understand. Something hanging over her— maybe fear for herself but also fear for our family.

In those years before her cancer, we didn't know how to read the omens. For example, there was a woman, Catherine, who took a bus to her job as a receptionist at a nearby doctor's office. My mother was replanting daffodils in our window box one morning and introduced herself. After that, each time Catherine passed our house after work, Mom would come out to chat and laugh with her. Catherine became a widow, she told us, after her husband had died from a stroke while the two were celebrating their fifteenth wedding anniversary in Maui.

"We were barely there for two days when it happened," Catherine said, shaking her head. "We'd been saving up for years to go on this trip. Neither of us had been there, and we were so excited to finally see the island. Then, it fell apart. All of it …"

My mother comforted her and turned the conversation to lighter notes. Catherine wore beautiful, expensive-looking clothes, and Mom asked her where she shopped.

Catherine peered down at her salmon-colored skirt and a crisp white button-down blouse and said, "Oh, I sew them all myself!"

Catherine's clothes looked designer-made, and each weekday after that, Mom seemed to look forward to studying her outfit. But despite the beautiful clothes, my mother suspected that Catherine had less money than her pride would allow her to admit; she didn't even have a car in a city where freeways ruled and most people were vehicle-dependent.

A few months later, Mom's birthday rolled around—though none of us realized it would be her last—and we threw a party for her. Catherine arrived with a special gift: a dress she'd sewn especially for my mother. It was gorgeous, a hand-embroidered, multicolored maxi dress. My mother threw her arms around Catherine, thanking her for such a beautiful, personalized gift.

Over time, the two women's mutual admiration continued to grow. It didn't matter that we lived in a large, luxury home and Catherine came from a small studio apartment across town. For Mom, money meant very little, and people were people.

"We're just borrowing what we have," she once told me. "We'll have to turn it all back in when it's our time to go, anyway." A sorrowful, unintended forewarning of things to come.

Mom often put guardrails around my father's ill-tempered side, and as it turned out, she was the only one who knew how to keep them there. One evening, while she and Catherine were having wine, Dad snapped at me for leaving my bike lying on the lawn for the umpteenth time.

"Now, Sam," she told him, a hint of sternness in her tone, "things could be a lot worse. He could be stealing bikes instead of leaving them on the grass for someone else to take."

Reflecting on my mother's emotional subtlety during that moment, I realized that she wasn't just a brassy and cheery person—she was perceptive as well. Sometimes, she got a laugh out of Dad, but other times, he just shook his head with exasperation, exuding a faint buzz of discomfort. I had nothing to prove this, but it was during those times that I wondered if she recognized a more understated side to my father that nobody else did, and trenched beneath her good humor was a gradation of concern.

When death approached, Catherine came over to spend time with my mother. I remember standing in the corner of the room and seeing the joy in Mom's eyes the second her friend walked in. It left me wordless as the radio on the nightstand played her favorite music in the background.

Catherine took a seat on the bed, then placed a hand over my mother's. Neither spoke, but I could feel the energy between them, loaded with sadness and love.

Being so young, I couldn't visualize what the end of her life would look like. I remember wishing Mom would get better, then feeling deep resentment toward Catherine because her saying goodbye seemed like giving up. Peering back through the eyes of an adult, I'm staggered by how much strength it must have taken for Catherine to bid farewell to her best friend, knowing the end was near.

"Catherine?" Mom said, voice battered by sadness and disease. "I wish I could feel happy again, even if only for a moment."

Catherine studied my mother with intent, then stood up and went to the closet. She pulled out the dress she'd made and held it up, the silky tapestry of brilliant reds, purples, and greens, sending new warmth throughout the room. A hollow-cheeked smile blossomed across my mother's face.

Catherine came back to the bed and, with the utmost care, swung Mom's legs around to the mattress's edge. She raised my mother's wasted arms into the air, then held them up while lowering the dress over her. After finishing, Catherine dragged a full-length mirror from the corner of the room and placed it in front of Mom; tears filled her eyes, but this time, they were tears of happiness, of fulfillment.

In one of those odd coincidences that so often seem to accompany death, my mom's favorite song—"Heaven can Wait"—came on the radio.

If only we could dance through the dark.
Heaven can wait while we gaze at the stars.

My mother closed her eyes and breathed in deep, swaying to the haunting melody and soothing echoes.

"I want to dance, Catherine," she said. "I want to dance as though my life has just begun."

Catherine lifted Mom's delicate body from the bed, wrapped her arms around her, and the two women twirled and twirled in slow motion, moving to the swelling violins and crashing cymbals. A gust of wind spilled through an open window, blowing the drapes apart and sending shafts of sunlight through the fabric of her dress that revealed her wiry frame. Overpowered by the sight, I remember thinking she looked beautiful because her bliss shone brighter than sunlight, but the vision was complicated by my tears because she looked like a dancing skeleton, which made the burden of losing her seem heavier than ever.

When Mom passed away, it was as if someone had flipped a switch and cut the lights. She was our everything, and without her, our lives tumbled. At my age, death was such an opaque concept.

"How can a person just disappear?" I asked my father at the funeral, tears running down my cheeks.

He didn't have an answer. There wasn't one.

A few days later, Catherine came by the house to deliver a gift to our family, a kelly-green blanket she'd embroidered with the phrase, *Motherhood: all love begins and ends there.*

Days after Mom passed, my father moved the ten-year anniversary vase he'd given her to a more prominent place in the living room. For a moment, he seemed to second-guess himself as if there were a possibility that he might accidentally knock it over with a sweep of his hand. He reached out and readjusted it in the center of the coffee table.

"Griffin," he'd said with tears in his eyes, "a woman hasn't been born yet who could replace your mother."

A truth that would stir echoes through my life for years.

PART TWO: INTERSECT

3

THIRTY YEARS LATER, THE FIRST thing I heard were screeching tires, and the first thing I felt was a neck-breaking *slam*.

My body lunged sideways, then forward. With a forceful *poof*, hot plastic snapped against the side of my face. A strange chemical odor I'd never before smelled now permeated the vehicle.

Next came thickheaded awareness*: An accident?*

And yet my body felt nothing. Maybe it meant I was injured. Dead? Everything around me seemed stock-still, and then I heard a scream. *Oh God. Did that come from me?*

The world began moving in wavy circles and in triple time, and I could not grasp the mechanics of this awful event.

I'm just trying to get home. I've got things to do. Trish will be waiting for me. Oh, shit. Did I remember to close the garage door after I left this morning? Where am I, anyway?

Beating on my window. I startled.

A San Diego firefighter stared back at me. He'd been talking, but I hadn't heard a word of it. He made an exaggerated gesture for me to open my window, but when I hit the button, it wouldn't work.

Trapped. No way out? My heart hammered against my rib cage. I was hot, dripping wet. My face hurt. My eyes burned. All sensations were returning, along with the awareness that I could not move. *Paralyzed by fear or paralyzed from the accident?*

The road tilted and swayed in a veil of light smoke. Next, I saw things I shouldn't. Shiny gold trim on a slick cherrywood casket, perched over a shadowy hole. People wearing dark attire and vacant expressions. I felt, more than saw, my father collapsing at my mother's graveside with silent, racking sobs.

The earth tilted again, and I glimpsed a nebulous figure of the firefighter, making another gesture, this time for me to turn my head away from the window. I did, then heard crackling safety glass.

"Are you all right, sir?" he said through the new jagged hole in my window. "Sir?"

I nodded, then forgot what I'd agreed to.

What felt like seconds later, I was out of my Jeep and staring at the inside of an ambulance, although I couldn't remember how I had gotten there. A paramedic crouched beside me.

"My name is Julie," this new stranger said, warm and friendly. "Are you able to tell me yours?"

"Grif—" My voice sounded as though it had been dragged through gravel. "It's Griffin."

"Great, Griffin. We're going to take good care of you."

She asked a few questions: Did I know where I was? What day it was? Who was the president? It took longer than it should have, but I provided the correct answers. She nodded with teacherly encouragement.

But when I tried to move, my shoulder delivered a ferocious objection. Pain knifed at my knee, and the skin on my face burned— from the airbag maybe. I was shaking from the agony.

Julie probed and assessed. "Just a few injuries. We'll get you checked out at the hospital."

I was in no position to argue. As my world started to regain shape and focus, I peered out through the back of the ambulance. Several yards away, I saw a fire truck, a crowd of onlookers, and a little farther on, the other car—a brown sedan, its front end smashed in, its windshield shattered.

"Did I …"

"No, you didn't hit him. He ran a red light and hit you. Side impact. The police already have a bunch of witnesses."

Rescue crews pulled the driver from his car. I looked up and saw what I thought was a hallucination. A nightmare. I froze, trying to swallow what felt like a golf ball lodged deep in my throat. I tasted blood, then realized I'd bitten my bottom lip.

No way. It can't be. It cannot.

A new wave of shock shimmied through me. A new fear. I believed I was just getting my bearings, but somehow, I'd been knocked to the hub where all evil intersected. *Hallucinating*, I again tried to assure myself. A CT scan at the hospital would clear all this up—a quick peek to confirm that my reasoning was wooly, and it would improve after a few days of rest. And yet, the surrealness of this moment felt physical. My body throbbed with pain, and my limbs were jumpy with fear.

I tried to stare through the apparition, willing it to go away. Yet the bone-deep familiarity of the figure being hauled onto a stretcher was more than just a menacing specter from my past. The resemblance did not fade; instead, it expanded, lingering like a night terror.

My father's cheeks had hollowed, but injured prey never forgets the huntsman's face: those defiantly pursed lips, that set jaw. I would have recognized him anywhere.

At a maximum of ten yards away, I was looking at a villain, one who incited terror in me for so long that my instincts went on alert, urging me to run as fast and far as I could. How many times had those hardened, bloodshot eyes seared holes through mine? How many times had he broken me?

I told myself to calm down, that I wasn't that kid anymore. That he couldn't hurt me. But as the Monster lay across the stretcher, all I could think was, *Keep that man the fuck away from me.*

"Griffin? Still doing okay?"

My attention swerved. Julie observed me with the kind of expression I suppose paramedics are required to have in situations like this: a sufficient degree of detached professionalism, seasoned with a touch of emotional investment.

"Griffin?" she again asked.

"I don't know," I replied, splitting my cagey attention between her and the Monster.

The other team of paramedics unlocked the stretcher wheels and began rolling him this way. A glance to my left revealed another ambulance alongside the one I was in. My body shook. Razor-edged fright sliced through me, and I tried to gulp down the metal taste in my mouth. I didn't want to look at him, didn't want him looking at me.

When paramedics rolled the Monster past me, I wrenched my head to the right as if it might make me invisible, but that never worked when I was a kid, and it wasn't doing anything for me now. It was a futile attempt, more a survival instinct than a tactical one.

At a few feet apart, our gazes locked, anyway, but his reaction was nothing like what I'd expected. His eyes darted back and forth between mine like dancing blue flames—they were begging, dumb with fear. *Does he even recognize me?* It was hard to tell. Then, my father disappeared into the neighboring ambulance before I could attach logic to this freak accident, this stroke of ugly, bad luck.

"You look a little out of it, Griffin," Julie said. "You okay?"

After losing sight of him, anger replaced fear, and then outrage came streaking in. I'd thought I was done with that abomination. But as life had shown me many times over, dents in the psyche never leave; the pain just migrates to different places.

New sounds jolted through me, the rattle of the tow truck chain snapping taut, the groan of my wrecked Jeep being dragged onto the flatbed; both sounded louder than they should have. I stared at the crater over the driver's side door that looked big enough to kill a man. But somehow, against the odds, I was still here to tell the story.

"I don't know what I am," I told her.

4

In my world, there is a divide.

There's the Before and the After.

One is about a life of happiness, the other, about a life come undone.

My father, Samuel McCabe, was the great-grandchild of Irish immigrants, Ewan and Johanna, who came to the US in the mid-1940s. Their son, Landon, and his wife, Bedelia, gave birth to my father in 1964, raising him in a modest two-bedroom bungalow just outside of Los Angeles.

All three men were alcoholics.

Don't blame our Irish blood—it can affect anyone—just blame it, as I do, for the devastation that would become my childhood. Because on that unseasonably cold autumn day when my mother left this world, the father I once knew left, too. After that, my sister and I essentially became orphans.

There was no steady progression toward evil, no warning of what was to come. The guillotine hit the block, cutting a clean break between past and present—after that, it was impossible to fuse the two back together.

At first, my father made me invisible, placing most of his attention on Michter's bourbon. Then, as his grief hardened into anger, the target on my back got bigger. The man who crawled out of his bottle was a stranger, an imposter. And soon, a man who could strike terror in me when he entered a room. Dad remained a successful lawyer, but he became a failure as a father. No longer did he adore me. No longer did he delight at the sight of me.

He hated me. Or, seeing it with the benefit of hindsight, he hated what I represented. I'm pretty sure that each time he looked at my face, all he saw was the beautiful life that had expired, along with my mother. I became the epitaph on her tombstone, the symbol of absence. He probably saw the same in Deena because she resembled Mom so much.

Oh, I occasionally got mercurial glimpses of someone different when he was off the bottle, but it never lasted, and when the Monster returned, he was fiercer than before.

It was as though I'd been plucked from one planet, then dumped onto a rocky, lifeless other. I can barely recall the good father anymore. Today, he's a marshy recollection that's lost context and meaning. What I *do* remember is feeling tormented by dread—a raw, fleshy fear that still chafes at me—and hiding from him before our paths crossed. But most of all, I remember feeling insignificant and left out in the cold until something inside me warped. And those awful words that still loop through my head like a broken tape, my father's voice, telling me that happily ever after was the biggest lie ever told.

5

IT HAD BEEN A FEW days since the car wreck.

I emerged with injuries the doctor classified as "minor," but they sure didn't feel that way, more like someone had chucked a white-hot dagger between my shoulder blades. I was convinced I could still smell the acrid chemical odor that came off the airbags, and the skin on my forehead felt like it had suffered a nasty sunburn; but those echoes from the accident felt more like penalties than injuries, holding me close to the most vulnerable parts of my childhood trauma.

My Jeep hadn't done much better. It had survived—well, relatively speaking—but the passenger's side had a lion-sized crater that kept the door from opening. In the meantime, I decided to splurge on a sporty black Mustang convertible rental. I was hardly that kind of guy, and when I'd made my choice, the counter clerk looked at me like I was struggling through a midlife crisis. But after what I'd been through, I decided to lean into form over function.

My fiancée, Trish, and I drove the rental to Ocean Beach—or, OB, as we locals called it—to meet Ryan, my best friend since childhood, and his wife, Ashley. Trish placed a hand on my leg but kept her gaze aimed ahead. No words, but her touch provided a necessary anchor to the present moment. I stole a quick glance at her and tried to smile.

"You sure you're up for this, babe?" She knew me all too well, could read my body language and the look in my eyes as if she were a mind reader.

"Oh, yeah," I said, trying to convince myself more than her. "This is fine."

She went back to staring out through the windshield. Clearly, neither of us was buying my attempt to smooth out this latest bombshell in our lives.

About two years ago, Trish's brother, Cam, was in a boating accident. He and his best friend, both newbies, were sailing off the coast of Newport Beach when a pop-up storm caught them by surprise and capsized their boat. The friend died instantly, and Cam suffered a traumatic brain injury. Trish spent months driving him to and from rehab while he tried to recover, but he was never the same after that, intellectually or emotionally. He'd lost his best friend and part of his own mind. Trish was the one who found him when she came to pick him up for physical therapy, hanging from a beam in the garage.

To this day, I could still hear her voice. And her pain. "It might as well have happened to me," she said through agonizing sobs when he died. "Cam and I were like the same person. I can't see a world without him in it."

It was the year of tragedy: after the funeral, her parents' marriage fell apart, and they decided to get a divorce. This sort of thing often happens when parents bury their children, but as Trish said, she never dreamed that would be the case for her mom and dad. Their love had seemed sturdy, indestructible, the sort that could weather anything.

I loved Trish, and I learned to love the breaks that ended up becoming a permanent part of her. But after those losses, her perception about what it meant to love someone was different.

"I was wrong," she'd told me. "Going all in on love just means suffering."

She worked through those doubts as best she could, seeing a therapist, but there were times when I sensed fear still living in the shadowy corners of her mind, forcing her to feel unending grief. She loved me differently; I tried to feel that it wasn't *less*. I tried to assure her we'd be okay, but if I was being honest, I didn't do a great job of it. I had my own issues. Childhood pain lurked, leaving me too afraid to fully invest emotionally. Our individual traumas sometimes seemed to cross paths, infringing on thoughts about a future together. But we did our best not to let them get in our way, instead telling each other that working through them might be an opportunity for intimacy and to strengthen our bond before marriage. I tried to believe that, but I secretly worried that executing the idea might be more challenging than it looked.

Ryan and I were at the beach, flying our drones. It was a new thing we'd taken up. As a kid, I'd lie on my back in the cool, fresh-cut grass, staring up at the sky, and imagine myself floating in a dark blue outer space where my problems didn't exist. In truth, there was no such place. Trouble was like a constant, gathering tornado ready to touch ground at any moment. Staring up at the sky was as close as I had ever gotten to breaking away from my problems and leaving reality behind. Years later, I'd taken that plan of escape a step further and considered becoming a pilot, perhaps as another way to continue my search for balance. But like many of my dreams, that one had never made it off the ground.

"You can barely put one foot in front of the other," my father once said, laughing after he got a good buzz on. "What makes you think you'd be able to fly a plane?"

When I started flying my drone, I took videos of the earth and felt soothed while looking down. After the car crash, I wanted nothing else today.

Ryan and I now stood at our usual spot, the Ocean Beach Pier, thumbing the controls to steer our drones out over the water. I'd hoped we could go to Sunset Cliffs today, just a few miles south, thinking it would make a beautiful shot, zooming in on the shallows from above, then pulling out to reveal rough sandstone bluffs that dropped into a lathered sea. But Ryan had his own idea, which entailed the same old thing: a stultifying, redundant hour of watching surfers rise, drop, and wipe out. I did love Ryan, but I didn't love his sometimes-unyielding personality. Still, he had a good side. He was the friend who always showed up. He'd seen me through some difficult times—romantic breakups, financial troubles after college, and problems with work—so I tried to ignore any resentments as best I could.

"I really like coming here," he said, agreeing with himself, as if trying to justify his strong will while we set up at the same old spot.

Ashley and Trish walked down by the shoreline, probably discussing whatever novel their book club was reading.

Ashley was the one who'd gotten Trish and me together. They'd been friends since college, and Ashley decided to fix us up on a blind date. When Trish had walked out onto the patio at the Poseidon in Del Mar, the sun bent downward over the ocean behind her and ignited the chestnut highlights in her brown ringlets. And that smile—that dimply smile—set off a fire inside my heart. I was stupid with nervousness, and she laughed when I later told her what a wreck I'd been the moment I saw her. But I was sure she'd figured that out after I knocked my silverware off the table and sent it clanging and scattering across the floor. The heat of humiliation flushed my cheeks, but to her credit—and to my benefit—she pretended not to notice.

Today was a great day for the beach. A cloudless sky had turned the ocean the color of polished turquoise. I took a whiff of the rich, briny air. It reminded me of my surfing days. I could still see them all in my mind's eye, those golden summers when I ran around on the beach, wearing nothing but longboard shorts, my body fit, my skin bronzed. The hot sand on my bare feet. The cool ocean spray at my back. The water, dancing and flashing like fire and ice as I raced to catch that last wave before sunset. This was my real home, but it was always better on days when the catering trucks weren't around to send off hints of fried grease. The smell reminded me of funnel cakes, Ferris wheels, and fetid memories.

"Seriously, Griff," Ryan said. "It's a one-in-a-million shot, running into your dad again, right?"

I kept my gaze on the drone. "Something like that."

"Hey," he said, glimpsing at my screen as I tried to zoom in on the Point Loma Lighthouse, resting on a lush green knoll, "remember what I told you about those reveal shots. Introduce the subject slowly, and don't be afraid to experiment by varying your height. Now, where were we?"

"Never mind," I said.

Ryan shrugged.

We brought our drones in for a soft landing on the beach, then ran to retrieve them.

"But being at the same intersection at the exact same moment?" Ryan said, deciding it was time to restart the conversation he'd interrupted. "Then crashing into each other? That's a huge coincidence. Literally, what are the odds?"

"Unfortunately, the odds have never been in my favor, Ry."

He didn't say anything, just looked down at his feet as they broke through the damp, ribbed sand. The act felt like an objection of some sort.

The underlying message had always seemed to be that Ryan didn't like my "negativity," as he called it, but that was only because he couldn't tolerate anything that threatened to dismantle the snow-globe world in which he'd always lived. His favorite phrase was, "Think positive!" as if the mere act of saying this could solve all of humankind's problems.

Trish and Ashley caught up with us, and with them came the worry that their presence might change the tenor of a conversation Ryan and I had barely started. It wasn't that I minded them joining in, but Ryan had been present for my childhood. And flying drones was almost the only time I had him to myself for a little while, even though what he believed he saw in our home decades ago didn't always seem to be an accurate portrayal of how things had been. My dad was always on his best behavior when Ryan visited. Only when nobody was looking did the Monster appear. So, Ryan—Mr. Think Positive—had never seen a lot of the rough stuff my father did to me, and he'd downplayed anything he *had* learned from me secondhand, which had a tendency to dull the sharp edge of trauma.

Over time, I came to suspect that Ryan harbored an unspoken belief that my life wasn't always as bad as I'd said and that I was ungrateful. He even tried to justify my father's bad behavior.

"Being a single dad has gotta be hard for the guy," he'd said so many times that the phrase practically lost its meaning.

I fantasized about telling him that the last I'd checked, being a widower wasn't a license to torture your kid, but I could never summon the courage, and Ryan didn't seem to care much about that kind of pain, not really.

"What a day!" Ashley breathlessly said, cupping a hand against her forehead and looking out at the leapfrogging waves. "This never gets old, does it?"

Ashley was a San Diego transplant by way of Chicago. She'd moved to Southern California about five years ago, so her admiration for this city appeared fresher than it did for us natives.

"So, you haven't seen him in how long?" Ryan said, again restarting our conversation. "Your dad?"

"Enough that I was finally starting to move past what had happened between us."

"How'd he look?"

"Pasty-faced. Rattle-boned. I haven't checked with the cops yet, but I'm willing to bet he was drunk when he slammed into me."

I stole a glance at Ryan. His hesitation seemed guarded.

"Well," he said, "I'm surprised he's lived this long."

I offered no response.

I caught Trish watching me. With haste, I pulled my focus away from her and averted my gaze to the sky. "I just can't reconcile the man I once knew with the man I saw. And that expression on his face. So defenseless. Vulnerable." I gave pause, allowing the weight of my statement to settle. "Scared, even."

"Words I never thought I'd hear you use to describe your dad."

"And hard as I try, I can't unsee it. It's like … haunting me, and I don't know what—"

"Holy shit!" Ryan said, peering over the top of his Ray-Bans and pointing toward the water. "Dude! Did you see that guy just eat it? Epic wipeout!"

I saw nothing more than a flipped surfboard, bucking over a wave by itself. All at once, like the whir of my drone, a blur of sensations and sounds buzzed through me. Crunching metal. The intolerable shove of gravity, bulldozing my body from side to side. My father's submissive expression. For a few seconds, the ground tilted, and I thought we were having an earthquake, but when I looked around, nobody blinked or flinched. It wasn't the tectonic plates shifting beneath my feet; it was that same sensation I'd felt after the accident.

"You okay there, bud?" Ryan's question anchored me a little. I was standing on the beach yet lost at sea.

"Fine," I replied with a half-smile that faded. "I'm fine."

Trish was watching me again, now with a creased brow.

Ryan said, "Look, if this is bugging you that much, why not just see him and get it over with? You know, if only to satisfy your curiosity and stop this craziness you're feeling. I wouldn't mind seeing the guy myself. C'mon, we'll go together. I'll pick you up and—"

"That's a hard no, Ryan." Aggravation strained my voice.

The tone—and my words—made him stop to stare at me as if it might give him a better grasp on my frame of mind. No longer paying him the benefit of my attention, I took my gaze away and stared at the water, irritation bubbling beneath my skin.

"Fine," he said. "I was just trying to be helpful."

Ashley shot Ryan a warning look. Trish squeezed my hand but didn't say anything. So, that left a gap of silence. And it felt awkward. Everyone was waiting for me to say something, but all I wanted to do was run off to Sunset Cliffs by myself, where I'd wanted to go in the first place.

This wasn't the only time Ryan had pushed a little too hard, nor was it the only time I'd been troubled by it. We had a history—or *he* did. I should have put an end to his sometimes-overbearing behavior long ago, but as a kid, I had been a different person, too insecure and scared to confront anyone. Ryan was blessed with the kind of features most women fell for and most guys envied. He looked like a *Men's Health* cover model with his flax-blond hair and gray-blue eyes. But I'd always felt like he used those advantages to slide through life and even push his agendas when nothing else worked. And the longer I allowed that habit to persist, along with his continued denial about my father's bad behavior, the harder it had become to push back. Today, it was a dynamic that felt so ingrained in our relationship that I felt as helpless as ever to make it stop.

"It's okay, Griffin," Ashley offered, regarding her husband with a quick side-eye. "This is your story. You don't have to do anything you don't want to."

But it wasn't okay, nor was that old ache I felt so many times as a kid, rising to the surface like a bad stink and refusing to leave whenever Ryan pushed me toward my father.

6

It was the weekend.

Ryan and I decided to have a sleepover. It was the only chance to get away from the Monster and the closest I could get to finding a taste of happiness. Real joy was that long-ago day at the fair, but after my mother died, the father I had known died, too. In his place was this sour, other creature who waited at home, sharpening his knives for the next attack and who made everyone as miserable as he was.

Ryan's family was nothing like that. At his place, I could pretend his parents were my own: a loving couple who encouraged and nurtured their children. The old life. The good life. A life with humor.

When Ryan's dad got angry over little things, he would sigh or try to make himself laugh, saying something like, "Don't worry about cleaning your room, son. The magic fairies will be stopping by later, and they always do a great job, so if you want to mess it up more, go ahead!"

I wished I could have moved into his house.

"Maybe we can order a pizza!" I said that Friday afternoon on our way home from school, walking backward and facing him. "Your parents could rent a movie and let us stay up late like last time. I've saved some allowance money. My treat!"

Ryan made a sour face.

"What's wrong?" I asked.

"We always stay at my house." He took a slight tone with me. "Can't we stay at yours once in a while?"

His comment felt like an uppercut to the flank, although I knew he didn't mean for it to hit so hard.

"I don't want to do this at my house," I said, tension rushing my speech.

"Why not?"

I sighed and looked away. "You know why."

Because it was my rare chance for a reprieve. Because as brief as it was, I looked forward to it. I *needed* it. But at the same time, I wondered whether sleeping at his house would provide the real relief I wanted or just suspend my pain. Whenever I got home after a visit with Ryan and his family, things felt worse than when I'd left. But having the sleepover at my house created a different kind of worry. There would be no transitioning into that misery—it would just be a constant, seamless state.

"It'll be fine," Ryan said. "Your dad and I get along great."

Try being me and staying alone with him for a few hours, then see how much you like him.

"Please?" he pleaded. "I'm *so* tired of my place!"

The comment came packed with so much irony that I couldn't come up with a response.

"If we go to my place," he said, "it'll be boring, and we won't have any fun."

This sleepover was starting to sound like a bad idea. But telling him I didn't want to do it would just make him more persistent, and in that moment, both places looked hellish. My only hope was that my father might nix the idea, and we'd have to go back to Ryan's. At least then, I wouldn't be the bad guy, and Ryan couldn't be as mad.

So, we trudged to my house to ask my father. My mistake was bringing Ryan along. I wanted my dad to give us a definitive no, but since he was less inclined to go on one of his angry diatribes in front of a guest, the chance of that no was slimmer than I would have liked it to be.

"Sure!" my dad said with a hulking smile. I could smell the booze on his breath. "That would be fun! Maybe I'll order out Chinese for you guys. Should we rent a movie?"

Ryan's grin was so wide, I could have slid a roasting pan through it—and I kind of wanted to try.

At first, my father drank enough to be obnoxiously happy and overbearing—just staggering around and telling stupid jokes—though not bad enough to unleash the ugly. But the more ice cubes I heard clinking into glasses and cocktails pouring, the more anxious I became. He wasn't abusive and vile, not yet, but I felt the threat mount and spent the whole evening worrying that things could go sideways in a hurry.

Meanwhile, Ryan enjoyed himself immensely, sinking into the couch and stuffing his face with Cheez-Its while he watched a Lord of the Rings marathon.

The next morning, Ryan went home, and by afternoon, Dad was all in on his weekend drinking binge. I tried my best to stay out of his way, but he could sift through every square foot of our huge house in a matter of minutes and find me.

I was on my bed, reading with the door closed. Without so much as a knock, my father barged in and leveled a poisonous glower at me. He staggered deeper into the bedroom, lost his footing, regained it, then kept going until he stood directly in my personal space, polluting the air with his 80-proof breath.

"What did I tell you before the sleepover?" he demanded. "What was the ONE thing I asked of you?"

I shook my head, my physical reaction so stupefying that I couldn't think.

"I told you to clean up!" He let out a sick, gurgling burp, then wiped his mouth with the back of his hand. "DIDN'T I?"

He'd never mentioned anything about cleaning up, but arguing with him would make everything worse. I couldn't present logic to a drunk man who could barely stand up straight, let alone follow a coherent line of reasoning.

"But Ryan only left a little while ago. I was—"

"What does CLEAN UP mean to you?"

I said nothing. Instead, I sat quietly and listened while he relished in berating me.

"Did it mean laaaaazily go about your way and do a shiiiiitty job of it afterward, or did it mean clean as you go?" My father moved in closer until he stood directly over me, hawkish and wheezy. The gust of booze was heavy and oppressive, and I had to blink a few times to clear it.

"No, it didn't mean that, Dad."

He paused, body swaying. No further comment, but the silence was unbearable. He was an atomic bomb about to blow. All I could do was wait, biting my cheek until he unleashed the rest of his fury, hoping the collateral damage wouldn't hurt too hard.

"So unappreciative!" he said, flailing his hands about. "I do so damned much for you and your friends. SO much! And all you do is take, take, take, never once giving back. NOT ONCE!" Whispering his words now, he added, "Why do you hate me so much? Why?" Tears filled his eyes as if he believed his own bullshit, as though I'd broken him beyond repair instead of the other way around.

There was no point in answering. All I could think was that none of this would have happened had Ryan not begged me to have the sleepover at my house.

Then, the bomb blew.

"You have no redeeming qualities, Griffin! Not one!" My father wagged his head, voice crackling with contempt. "Shit … you're barely human."

He slammed the door on his way out, and for this, I would blame Ryan for years.

7

TRISH AND I LAY NAKED on our backs in bed. A thin sheet covered our bodies from the waist down, yet it felt unreasonably heavy. The ceiling fan sent cool gusts against my damp skin. I stared at the blades while they made their rounds, trying to make sense of the last few days. Ryan had gotten one part right. The improbability of my father and me occupying the same patch of earth at the same moment—and colliding—was sort of mind-blowing.

Trish shifted in bed, and I came back to the now.

I'd practically phoned in my part during sex. There used to be passion in our lovemaking, but lately, something was missing—something that felt imminent, even within reach, but nevertheless, absent. It wasn't Trish's fault. I was still very attracted to her, yet just as her suffering and losses sometimes caused her to retreat from me, I could feel an unspecified part of me peeling away from her. The situation with my father added to the unspoken tension that ruled me these days, and I had a waking sense that Trish felt the deficit, too. But I was afraid to bring it up, worried that pointing at thin ice would only shine a light on my inadequacies and make them look worse.

Before my father literally crashed into me, my biggest worry was deciding if I wanted to be a dad. Trish wanted kids someday, and that had sounded like a great future. We'd even been putting money away for a big destination wedding in Hawaii. But when I pictured having a child—a son, if I'm being honest—Trish slipped from my vision. I couldn't see or even feel her, which made me question if I was really in love enough with her or if what we had was called "love" at all.

Admittedly, I figured this vision of the future just had a glitch, caused by my old emotional damage. Still, marrying her and having children sounded much more appealing than re-creating my screwed-up family life.

I could see myself as a conscientious father, but would I be a loving one? I'd said before that I wasn't crazy about kids, but was that simply because I was hiding behind a secret fear that I might end up being a bad father just like my dad? Did I fear fatherhood the same way I feared alcoholism?

"How's your shoulder?" Trish asked.

"Still hurts but better."

Trish was probably waiting for me to bring up my uncomfortable conversation with Ryan. The topic felt heavy, but I tried, anyway.

"So … how about that Ryan, huh? Loads of fun there, yes?"

Trish tamed her smile. "He can be a little difficult at times, but he means well." She curled onto her side and rested her head on my shoulder, watching her fingers while she walked them across my chest. "But maybe he had a point."

I turned to look at her.

She placed a hand on my forearm. "Just hear me out. You said that seeing your dad at the accident did a number on you because he was so different from how you remembered him, right? I mean, he was more frightened than you were. With his history, that says a lot. I know you're still reeling—it would knock anyone off-balance—but if you see him, maybe you'll find an explanation for this abrupt personality change. If it gives you some answers, relieves some of your tension, it may be worth the trip. I think that's what Ryan was trying to tell you."

The idea of seeing my father sounded absurd. It made the hairs on my neck bristle. The years of exhaustive abuse had left me with this lingering fight-or-flight reaction. With that came more memories, forcing me to relive the sickness of my past: cleaning up a vomit-covered toilet just so I could use it after one of my father's all-day weekend drinking benders. The time he unexpectedly showed up at my high school track meet drunk, cursing and hollering from the bleachers and trying to instruct my coach on how to win the meet.

I broke free from the memory and said, "How can I possibly stand in front of that man when the only thing I'd want to do is tell him what a total failure of a father he was?"

Trish didn't answer. She knew I had a point. I trusted her to empathize with me from both an emotional and professional standpoint. She was a lawyer at the District Attorney's Office, prosecuting people who abused children. That irony hadn't slipped past me; it was one of the reasons why I felt so comfortable opening up to her about my past.

"You entered my life about thirty years too late," I'd half-joked when we became a couple.

But between her job experience and knowing me well, she was the only person who truly understood what my ghosts looked like and how they affected me.

"There's just too much bad history between my father and me," I told her now.

"Look, I get how difficult it'll be to see him again, and I also get that it could bring up all kinds of awful memories. I do. But if you decide to see him, you won't have to stay long, just enough to get rid of this anxiety. Then, you can be done."

"What would I even say to him?" I made an attempt to squelch my disdain, which only added unwanted tension to my voice. "*Hey, Dad. How's your hateful self been all these years?*"

"Maybe just enough to figure out why he was scared of you?"

I bit back a sarcastic reply about my father but didn't offer Trish an immediate response; instead, I stared at the ceiling fan again as it carved circles above me. She wasn't wrong. My old man's vulnerability—his fear—after the crash continued to haunt me.

"I just don't want him to think I'm coming for a friendly father-son visit," I said. "Or to rescue him from his medical and financial concerns."

She gave me a doubtful smile. "You know that's not what this is about."

"Then, what is it about?"

"This wouldn't be for him—it would be for you. Griffin, you've been stuffing down your stress since the accident happened. He's all you can think or talk about. Look at what that's doing to you."

Trish didn't know everything about my abuse—I'd left out the worst because sharing it felt too dark, too unnecessary, and she already knew enough from her work to fill in the blanks. I assured her that it hadn't been sexual or physical—just years of psychological torture. But she did understand how, from the moment I saw him again, I was reduced to a child, slammed with flashbacks. And terror. I was back under my father's thumb again, screaming into my pillow. Wanting to die.

"Griffin?"

I swung back into the present and tried to collect myself. After considering her for a moment, I said, "You really think going to see him won't make me feel worse?"

"At first, yeah." She paused for a moment, then nodded as if agreeing with her thought. "It'll be hard, but you'll probably feel better once you get it done."

"I'm not so sure about that."

"Okay, then I guess you have your answer." She shrugged and smiled that way she often did as though saying, *Why ask if you know all the answers?*

I smiled back, then gave her a kiss.

"The point is," Trish said, "*you* get to make your own choice about this now. I can't speak for Ryan, but I hope you know that all I want is to help you make peace with the past."

I scoffed. "I thought I'd been doing that until my father threw a wrench in the works."

"Only if you let him."

I got up, then walked into the bathroom. "For all I know, he could already be out of the hospital by now, anyway." I hid myself in the bathroom for too long. When I came back, Trish looked at me briefly, turned off the lamp on her nightstand, then rolled onto her side.

I'd spent a few years doing therapy in my twenties, working to get over my past. It helped in many ways—but since my father crashed into my life, some of that progress slid off the rear end. All over again, I was the injured kid whose feelings had no edges or meaning. I didn't want it to be that way, but this regression felt biological, like the return of a cancer. Those years in therapy helped me to identify and reclaim those feelings. My ability to externalize them, however, was stunted.

Nothing more to say, nobody to say it to, so I sat up in the dark, staring at nothing while Trish fell asleep.

This from the man who made his living with words.

8

"OH NO! YOU'VE REALLY DONE it this time! What are we going to do *now*?"

"I don't know!" I screeched into the microphone. "I'm so scared!"

"Don't you play dead on me!"

"But … But I …"

"Let's ask Bandi! That wise owl knows everything!"

"Look! He's up in that tree!"

"And … CUT!" Brian, my director, said. "Nice work, both of you." He checked his watch. "We're coming up on lunchtime. Take a break for a few?"

I pulled off my headphones and nodded to Brian, then to Sherry, my costar in this cartoon series I'd been working on. I was Farris the 'Possum who, of course, played dead when he was scared. Farris and I had that in common. I was paralyzed by the idea of going to see my father. In the meantime, I'd been staving off dread by way of diversion, enjoying the rental car that I splurged on, taking rides up the coast with the top down and music blaring. Adding to my masterful avoidance technique, I made my escape to another city for work—admittedly, it was a relief, if only a temporary one. I didn't mind working up in Hollywood. Los Angeles is a crowded, messy place to live in, but for the occasional gig, it was an easy commute from San Diego—about two and a half hours without traffic but a lot more with. Then, I got to come home to America's Finest City.

But while driving through sections of my childhood that had been built up almost beyond recognition, I not only saw San Diego's past and present—I saw my own. When I was a kid, downtown was composed of a few moderately tall buildings. Today, it was one mirrored skyscraper upstaging the next. Was that me, too? As time went on, had the complexities of life become more overpowering and, like a mirror, more reflective of a life that had once been? After my accident, did that now look even more complicated and chaotic?

I enjoyed my job as a voice actor. I got to hide behind my words and be whomever I wanted—an astronaut, a cowboy, anything. It felt good to pretend for a little while. I also voiced audiobooks and commercials.

One job in particular had made me kind of famous. I'd gotten a voice-over gig for a clever TV and radio ad for Mobilife Insurance. My big line was, "Don't get caught with your pants down, Fred." To my surprise, the line went viral and became a popular meme on social media. The production company won multiple awards for the ad. I must have made an impact, too, because people often told me my voice sounded "so familiar!" When I explained why, they'd parrot the line back to me: "Don't get caught with your pants down, Fred!" and break into hysterical laughter as if they'd been the first to make that joke. I didn't mind the attention—it was great for my career, and I was pleased to be recognized for my work—but the novelty had worn off.

My career had been a matter of pure luck. I'd developed a rich, deep voice after coming out of puberty, and people started telling me I should try out for the school play or join the choir. I'd never given either serious thought because by then, I was too focused on surfing and keeping my body in top shape. Then, one day, while driving through Studio City in LA, I got a flat tire and stopped at a repair shop. When I finished talking to the cashier, some guy walked up to me.

"You've got a great speaking voice. Has anyone told you that?"

I laughed. "It's been said."

"I'm David Freeman, and I work as an agent." He stepped back to appraise me. "You're a great-looking guy. Have you thought about acting?"

"People have suggested that, but I'm kind of a private person."

"What about being a voice actor?"

I shook my head and turned to walk away. "Thanks, but I don't know. It's just not for me. I just …"

"Look," he said, pulling a business card from his wallet. "Give it some thought, and call me if you change your mind."

I took the card to be polite, figuring I'd never actually make that call. I'd heard about everyday people being discovered on the street but figured those were just flukes.

About a year later, I graduated from UC Berkeley with a business degree and landed my first job as a sales rep for a Jacuzzi company—not exactly what I'd envisioned for myself after spending four years in college, but at least it paid, and it felt like a decent place to start … until it ended with an abrupt layoff. I had eighteen dollars and sixty-eight cents in my checking account and needed to buy food. While I was paying the cashier, David's card fell out of my wallet. I'd forgotten all about our meeting. With zero career prospects and nearly zero in the bank, I reconsidered his offer and decided to give him a call.

"We'll need to get you to an acting coach," he told me, "but I have no doubts. You've got a career ahead of you."

It only took a few lessons to discover that I had skills I'd never known about. David started sending me off to auditions, and before long, I had a new career with plenty of job offers.

Whenever I talked about my work now, I could only say that I'd stumbled into a dream job. In truth, however, it also felt like a new existence. It was so far from what I'd imagined for myself as a child that I secretly thought of it as the beginning of my life—and the end of all those years of merely surviving.

Now, I stepped out of the recording booth and headed toward craft service for a quick bite. When I turned on my phone, a call came in straightaway, startling me. I looked at a number I didn't recognize and almost hit Ignore, then remembered I was waiting on a callback for the role in a full-length animated movie that had the potential to grow my career yet again.

Wingate Studios was making *Funland Falls*. They were relatively new to Hollywood but had already proven themselves as a serious competitor. A few years ago, three big execs from three major studios formed the company, so they brought experience and power to what would have been yet another start-up. Wingate had had a success earlier that year with *Mildred,* an historical drama that topped ninety-million dollars worldwide during its opening weekend and was up for five Oscar nods—one of them, the golden crown of achievement: Best Picture. *Funland Falls,* I hoped, could be a down payment for Trish's and my future, whatever it held: a destination wedding, a child, maybe even a new house for us down the road.

"Griffin McCabe," I answered.

"Griffin. Hi," said a man who did not sound like my agent. He sounded more like a jovial grandfather, phoning his grandkids. "It's Nolan Laseur, your dad's landlord."

Damn it. I should have let him go to voice mail.

"I'm calling about your dad."

"Okay … what about him?"

"I didn't see him the other night when I came to bring his supper. Naturally, a lot of us got worried."

"*A lot* of you?"

"Yeah, you know, me, plus other neighbors in the complex. Your father and I got to be friends over the years. We're close."

I was baffled on a few counts. One, that someone could tolerate my father long enough to maintain a friendship with him. Two, that anyone would be concerned about a nasty old drunk like him. And a whole group of people? None of this tracked.

The man was friendly and speaking in familiar terms, but there was a chance he knew about my father and me being estranged. On some level, I sensed a performance in his tone—after all, I worked in show business and knew how to spot one. A touch of instinct told me that he might have been affecting this familiarity on purpose, raising a red flag but maybe only halfway. Still, my instinct also told me I didn't have much to worry about with this man. And I could still hear Trish's plea to just get more information.

"So, we called the police," Nolan went on.

"*We?*"

"Out of worry, of course. The police came to check on his welfare, but when they got into the apartment, the place looked abandoned, so they called the department and gave them his name. They found out he'd been in a car accident, and that's how I got your number."

I wish I hadn't given it to the cops in the emergency room.

"But I'm just a little confused about what all this has to do with me," I said while getting into the food service line, comforted only by a familiar cacophony of silverware striking against plates. I eyed the Greek grilled chicken kabobs, drizzled with tzatziki sauce. Just reaching for one made my mouth water, the scent drawing me in more. Whatever this phone call was about, I could look forward to comfort food in less than five minutes.

"Well, as I mentioned," Nolan continued, "we're concerned about him. I found out he's still at Green Hospital in La Jolla. Have you gone to see him?"

I clawed my fingers into my leg. "I have not."

"Then, there's the matter of his rent. He hasn't paid it in months."

Because he spent it all on booze, I thought as I took my seat at a table but didn't bother giving a voice to the notion. I imagined his apartment fans would have figured that part out by now. Perhaps *they* could pitch in for his rent, even throw in a few bottles of bourbon while they were at it.

"To be honest," Nolan said, "I don't think it would be good for Sam to return to the apartment, anyway. We all love him, of course, but he's been having some really bad days, and I think it's best for his own safety. One time, he welcomed a bunch of strangers into his apartment. He even left the stove burner on and—"

"Okay, Nolan. I have to stop you right there. I'm not sure how any of this is my problem. He and I don't have a relationship of any kind. We haven't for years."

Nolan made a sound with his throat. He paused for a few seconds, then, "Well … you're the only next of kin to come forward."

"Come forward?" I laughed, but there wasn't an ounce of amusement in it. "He crashed into me at an intersection."

"Wait." Nolan stopped for a long moment. "*You're* the one he hit? Wow. Life's coincidences—they can be like signposts."

"Or just coincidences," I suggested, then glanced at my watch. "I actually don't have much time to talk right now. I really need to get back to work."

"Of course. But as I said, if he does leave his apartment, it will need to be cleared out as soon as possible so we can rent it to someone else."

"Fine. Do whatever you have to."

"I thought maybe you could—"

"Like I said," I interrupted, trying to sound cheery but failing miserably at it, "heading back to work now."

"Well, someone has to take care of this."

"*Really* going now, but thanks, anyway."

"Uh … well … can you at least come by?"

"No."

"All the same, I'll text you his address and leave the spare keys under the mat," Nolan added, "because you *will* want to come by." Then, just like that, he hung up on me.

I stared at my phone.

Why did I feel as though I was slowly—and involuntarily—getting roped back into my father's life because of a damned car accident?

9

NOLAN'S ABRUPT AND NEBULOUS COMMENT was doing one hell of a job taking up whatever space was left in my brain for matters outside the car accident and what it had stirred up. I was curious about why he felt it was important to visit my father's apartment. But instead of going there, I was in the Green Hospital parking lot, staring at the building through my windshield.

Just staring.

This Mustang didn't feel like freedom anymore. Even with the top down, it felt like it was making this visit inevitable. The hospital loomed over me, unobscured by a car roof.

"If it gives you some answers, relieves some of your tension, it may be worth the trip."

Tricia's words.

Yet I wondered how the Monster had managed to penetrate my life after I'd worked so hard to dump him off at the wayside. It was just like him to come back around and mess with my head. That was, after all, his favorite pastime.

But not squaring up with my father was like owing a fat check during tax time and avoiding a call from my accountant. It would have been much easier if a stranger had T-boned me in that intersection—it would have been a gift—because we would have exchanged insurance info, then never seen or heard from each other again. Now, this physical and emotional proximity to my father was niggling and nattering and yammering inside my head, screaming so loud that all I wanted to do was shout at the world to leave me the fuck alone.

I needed to go through this, even though it would make the pain hurt harder. Still, I wasn't convinced that now was the right time. Putting off our meeting a few more days would allow me enough leeway to pull myself together and prepare for whatever that fight-or-flight reaction triggered in me.

Yeah, that's what I should do.

I turned the engine over and seized the gearshift, but as I looked out my rear window for clearance, a father and son bustled past my car, holding hands and laughing. For a moment, the boy made eye contact with me. He looked to be about six and in a familiar way. It wasn't only because of his brown hair, the scattered freckles across his face, and light eyes; it was his demeanor. Carefree, buoyant.

Screw the universe and its signposts. And screw you, Nolan.

But my mind flashed back to a young Deena, dark tendrils of hair following her on the wind as I chased after her in the sand, our parents a few steps behind. A permanent part of me hungered to go back to those good times while another part ached with the knowledge that I'd never be able to.

Parking Lot Dad messed up Young Boy's hair and gave him a smile. The kid giggled, and then they disappeared from view through the hospital entrance.

I turned off the engine and shoved the gearshift back into park as if it had caused my sorrow. I gazed back at the hospital, and a sheen of sweat formed on my palms.

A few moments later, I was out of the car and heading toward the entrance.

As soon as I stepped out of the elevator, hospital smells assaulted my nose—a combination of antibacterial cleaner, commercially washed linens, with a touch of something acrid. The place reminded me of a movie set, construction seams thrown between each wall panel with ridiculously polished tiles that shined like glass and looked like nobody had walked over them.

When I reached the nurses' station, I identified myself as my father's next of kin, but saying the words felt like signing a contract with a cold gun barrel pressed against my cheek. This was how life had been going lately. No real choices, just a variety of bad options to choose from.

Before long, a doctor walked out with an electronic tablet tucked under one arm, moving like a man on an important mission. The teal embroidered name on his whiter-than-white coat told me he was Dr. Roger Still. The man looked to be around my age, tall with piercing blue eyes, the kind that seemed as though they could peer deep into your soul if you weren't careful. His badges clacked as he sat down across from me, and he affected a sincerity he probably used on all his patients' families.

"Your father managed to escape serious injury," Still began, "which is remarkable. Blunt force trauma like that can cause traumatic brain injuries, especially with people his age."

I offered a hollow smile, then made an awkward gesture with my hands.

"But he shouldn't be driving in his condition," the doctor added.

"How much was he drinking?"

He frowned and checked the tablet. "Come again?"

"His blood alcohol level. How high was it?"

He shrugged. "It was zero."

"But … I … that chart has to be wrong. My father's been an alcoholic for decades."

"That may be the case, but it wasn't a factor in this accident. His altered mental status was due to Alzheimer's."

The word, at first, seemed like one I had heard on another planet. Surely nothing to do with me and nothing that could touch the Monster. I drew a breath, and it was as though someone had slammed me against a wall. My skin flashed hot and cold, and everything around me disappeared. I couldn't make a reply; instead, I focused on the shiny stethoscope draped around his neck.

"You didn't know?" the doctor asked.

His words felt more like a judgment than a question. But I wasn't the bad son here. *He* was the bad father.

"We haven't seen each other in years," I tried to explain while attempting to pull my mind around a diagnosis I never saw coming.

"I'm very sorry … I just assumed that you knew."

I stared at him, trying to steady myself.

"Would you like to visit with him?" the doctor asked.

I shifted my weight, crossed my arms. I needed to see this for myself. Also, this might make it easier to stand in front of my father.

He probably can't keep his mind straight, anyway. I can do this, then leave. So, across the burning embers of childhood I go.

Barefoot and all.

It was indeed much like a fire walk as I moved down the hallway.

When I drew closer to his room, the door was wide-open. I stopped short of the entryway, far enough away so we couldn't see each other yet. The air felt viscous. My stomach tugged into a fist-sized knot, and a faint pounding went off in my ears. My miserable childhood, fresh as yesterday, awaited me on the other side of this threshold, and I would never be ready to see the man who destroyed it. For a moment, I wondered if, despite his illness, he still had the power to tear me down and unravel the progress I'd made.

Relax. He's got Alzheimer's, I told myself, trying to stop my mind from spinning. But I'd heard the disease could make nice people meaner. If that were the case, he was probably bathing in the glow of fire and brimstone.

I wanted to turn back, get out of here.

Run.

Or stand up to him. I hadn't come all this way to flee my fears. I wasn't that kid anymore. I had choices. After this, I could turn my back and never have to see my father again. Then, I could return to my life before the accident, reading over scripts and streaming shows on Netflix. Maybe even patch things up with Trish after our recent impasse by asking her to go on our first big vacation together. Or muse with her about wedding plans, sharing random suggestions and laughing about which of our friends might hook up at the reception after meeting each other for the first time.

Everything is fine.

One more step, and I'll be there.

Exposed. Assailable.

When I walked into the room, my father was fast asleep, oblivious to the *beep, beep, beep* of the bedside monitor that tracked his vitals. His unconsciousness brought a measure of relief, sparing me from having to interact with him.

I drew uneven breaths and took the opportunity to look him over.

The years had worn heavy on my father. The bed was inclined, and his head dropped forward, chin resting on his chest. His arms were reedy, and his papery skin clung to his joints. I looked at his scalp: bare, save for a few scattered birthmarks and grizzled strands of hair. A round purple bruise, the size of a half-dollar, marred the top of his forehead, probably from the accident; although, before now, I would have assumed it was from one of his drunken falls.

I questioned my perception. Could this frail, meager man really have been the Monster? The man who ruled my life with those insufferable fists of iron? My impulse was to touch his skin to see if he was real. I sidled a little closer, listened to his labored breathing, and watched his quivering hands. Before I could touch him, he let out a tiny murmur, and his head dropped off to one side. I recoiled. In an instant, I'd walked too far out on thin ice. I needed to find safety before it cracked beneath my feet. To find dry land. I hurried toward the door.

"Griffin?" he said through an infirm whisper.

The word stopped me, but I didn't dare turn back around.

Don't look at him. Do not.

So, instead, I kept my gaze leveled on the doorway as if my life depended on it, and in a way, it felt just like that.

"Champ?"

The nickname went through me with a jolt. At first, I was unearthed, then it felt good, and then I felt bad about feeling good. *Is that the ground I feel, slipping away from me again?* Once more, I was riding that seesaw: a confused ten-year-old boy, staring at my father's brokenness as my mother's casket sank into the cold, damp ground.

I turned and looked at him but said nothing—he didn't, either. His expression, however, displayed the same defenselessness he'd shown me after the accident. I took him in for a few more seconds, still dumbstruck.

Who is this man?

A stranger. That was the only thing I could be sure of. So, instead of engaging with him, panic took over, and I left the room, trying to put as much distance between that man and me as quickly as possible. But in telling myself he was just a stranger, I felt a jab of unexpected sympathy that I wasn't sure I could fully comprehend.

Then, a childhood memory swam to the surface, canceling the emotion before I could let myself believe the truth of it.

10

MY FATHER WAS AN ARMCHAIR alcoholic. He kept sober in court while cross-examining witnesses, but when he got home, the suit and tie came off, and he was ready to boot and rally. He'd scarf down supper, take pleasure in picking on me, then move his shit show into the family room, where his favorite recliner awaited him. The only time he left his throne was to refill drinks or hit the bathroom to piss or throw up. Getting slogged was his favorite destructive pleasure, but it was also my temporary shelter, assurance that he'd stay downstairs for a few hours and not come teetering into my orbit.

Although my father's drunken party of one kept him out of my way for a little while, it was one of the scariest times of day. When the night drew down, so did my reprieve. I never knew what he'd pull next. The anticipation, the wait, was terrifying because I knew he was becoming freshly volatile.

One evening, however, he changed his routine. At around seven thirty, he materialized in my bedroom doorway as I sat on the floor, studying for my algebra test, surrounded by textbooks, markers, and an assortment of papers.

Slurring enough to prove he was already inebriated, he said, "Take me to Liquor Emporium."

I blinked a few times and decided he was just testing me. "I'm only fourteen, Dad. You know I can't drive."

He braced both arms against the doorframe to keep his body from rocking and only said, "Do it."

So, he meant it. The last thing I wanted was to get into a car with my intoxicated father, let alone be in a confined space, where I'd have to inhale his astounding bourbon breath. I needed to figure out a way to say no without infuriating him.

"I can't, Dad," I tried. "I'm studying for a big algebra test tomorrow."

"Study after."

"I really can't."

"Come with me," he said, but this time, his tone dropped an octave, and I had a sick feeling this wouldn't end well.

"But I don't—"

"Fine, I'll drive myself, then," he said as if this were a logical choice, assuming I'd worry while he stumbled into reverse and zigzagged down the hallway.

Secretly, I hoped he would get on the road and kill himself in an accident. The only problem was, if he did, he might kill someone else, and I'd be complicit for letting it happen.

I jumped up and followed him as he started toward the stairway. "Please don't drive!"

"I'm fine," he muttered back, waggling toward the staircase like a drunk marionette.

I entertained the possibility that he might tumble down the stairs and injure himself, affording me an escape from an evening that would spell out disaster, but he reached the first floor.

"Just STOP!" I yelled.

He made his way toward the door that opened into our garage. "I have this!" he snarled.

"No, you *don't* have this!"

He spun around. "Then, just drive me! It's not a big goddamned deal."

I tried to weigh out my options. The liquor store was about a mile away, but my father was essentially a loaded missile. Could I risk letting him out on the road, hoping he'd make it there and back without taking lives? Or should I have grabbed the wheel myself? I had driven a car once. My uncle in rural Kentucky had let me drive his old Dodge in a dirt field one summer. I had done okay, but a bright field and a dark city street were different environments.

The jingle of car keys settled the debate. My father was holding up the fob, his grin shrouded by a thousand shades of darkness, half-teasing and half-challenging. I swear, he enjoyed seeing me squirm. My heart banged so hard that my shoulders shook.

A sound from above distracted me. When I looked up, Deena was leaning over the veranda, arms resting on the banister, staring at me. She'd heard the entire discussion, knew the predicament I was in, yet her expression was flat and void. What made it worse was that she continued to stare after I'd caught her. Our exchange made my breath catch. No, it chilled me. Here I was, about to risk my life, and she was viewing it all from overhead as if watching some boring TV show.

I broke away from the sight and decided to drive my father to the liquor store. If I did this right—driving slowly and cautiously—I'd have a better chance of avoiding an accident than he would. I'd be on the road for several minutes, but nobody seemed worried about me, not Deena, not my dad. And with that realization, I felt a part of myself giving up on me, too.

By the time I got behind the wheel of my dad's Mercedes, the sun was sinking on the horizon. It wasn't dark yet, but it would only be a matter of time before I'd be driving at night. I fumbled around for the headlights, knowing that they were somewhere on the left side of the wheel. But I kept activating the turn signals. Finally, I managed to turn them on. My father smirked.

I'm not sure why it happened—and of all times, now—but a contrast hit me hard. This was the peak of summer, around the same time my father and I had visited the fair several years ago. Life had been so easy then, but on this day, with the setting sun in my eyes, it was as if I'd traveled from heaven to hell.

And I might die, too. But at least I found the headlights.

"Right side brakes, left side gas pedal," my father murmured, raising a tremulous index finger, oblivious that he had the order wrong. "Both hands on the wheel."

Driving advice from a drunk man was like asking a comatose person for directions to the Laundromat. I chewed the inside of my cheek and pulled into reverse, wheels faltering as they crisscrossed in and out of our driveway's concrete border. When I got to the end, I stopped, rotated my body, then glanced both ways through the rear window to check for oncoming cars. As I made it onto the road, I heard a tiny mewl that I recognized, after a moment, as my own voice.

As if negotiating a minefield, I idled along our sleepy, palm tree–lined streets. My dad had already passed out. He was snoring and probably dreaming about his next chug of bourbon, but at least he wasn't judging me. I could focus better on the road and needed every ounce of concentration I could get to push through this rolling nightmare.

A new wave of uneasiness spiraled through me when I reached an intersection that led to the main road. I hit the brakes too hard and jerked the car into a convulsive halt. My father gave a loud moan as I stared out at the cars, zipping and zooming before me. With only a Stop sign to govern the fast-moving traffic, I had no idea how I'd find a way in without getting slammed by an oncoming car. It was now dusk, and their headlights made it hard for me to see.

Nerves needled beneath my skin while I peered over the wheel, eyes shooting back and forth in both directions, watching traffic that showed no sign of slowing. Everyone was rushing home to beat nightfall— everyone except the fourteen-year-old driver who was trying to commandeer a car to the liquor store.

To my great relief, the traffic eventually eased up enough for me to turn onto the road, but I had to move fast if I was going to make it. I gunned the gas pedal, and the car took off with such force that my head wrenched back against the headrest.

But I didn't make my move fast enough. As I powered onto the road, a car came rocketing toward me. White-knuckled fear screamed through my nerves, telling me that death was near. The other vehicle's horn howled. I gritted my teeth, punched the gas harder, and managed to gain some speed—not enough, so I kept pushing the pedal, making the tires shriek.

The car swerved around, almost clipping me. For my effort, the driver delivered a steamy expression of rage and flipped his middle finger at me.

"Be careful, you idiot!" my father said, now awake. "Don't kill us both!"

All I could think about was how to pull myself out of this horrific road show before I did just that. An idea went through my head: if my father was that far gone, why not turn around and go home? I could have told him he'd passed out, wouldn't wake up, and the cashier refused to let me buy the booze. But the idea was a nonstarter. What if he wasn't that far gone and *did* remember what happened? He'd be more furious, which was something I couldn't afford. And I'd still have to find someplace to turn the car around. I was stuck. No way out.

Liquor Emporium was only another block up the road. The evening had surrendered to insistent darkness. I pulled over onto a side street and put the car in park. Grateful to be alive, I tried to steady my speeding breaths that had added a layer of fog to the windows' interior.

By the time we arrived, my father was awake and yelling at me for not parking close enough to the store's entrance, forcing him to make a short walk through the parking lot. When I failed to respond, he poured himself out of the car and duck-walked to the store. I was grateful for the break; it gave me time to regroup and anticipate the return trip.

All I have to do is make it home, I coached myself. *I got us here. I can get us back. I can do this.*

The return was quieter but no less frightening. I crept along gloomy, ill-defined streets, trying to sense my way through the night. Branches along the tree-lined route shifted and swayed overhead, urged on by the angry evening winds.

No one had taught me about using high beams or how to turn them on, so I forced myself to find my way with what I had: dull headlights, dim streetlights, and moving shadows.

By the time I reached the house, I was numb. Panic and anxiety had dissipated, leaving me with nothing.

My father staggered into the house with his comforting bag of booze, and I sat alone in the car for several minutes with no comfort of any sort.

Nothing here would calm me, so I returned to my soft, messy bedroom, which looked the same as I'd left it, study materials strewn across the floor. Before being forced from this house, it all looked like chaos; now, it felt familiar and had the appearance of safety. I needed this return to normal—or something like it—but the life-or-death responsibility that I'd taken behind the wheel of my father's car had washed the old comforts away.

11

CHAMP.

The affectionate nickname my father had given me came from my other life, the Before.

As much as I tried to resist, the name pushed happy memories to the foreground. Even though they would later turn rotten, an irrefutable part of me missed those days.

But not *him*.

I got into the elevator, mind twisting like a pretzel. Though it had never been my plan, I was already too involved in my father's life. I needed to fight my way out of it. Take a step back, find some ground, right myself. My father was a grown man—albeit a sick one—but I could walk out of his life, just as I did all those years ago. There were measures in place to take care of him. Realizing this, I drew what felt like my first real breath since I'd gotten here.

"Mr. McCabe?" The question met me as I stepped out of the elevator. A woman rushed toward me, winded.

A tilt of my head was the only response I offered her.

"Hi, Mr. McCabe. I'm the social worker for the hospital, Kayleigh Hartley. Dr. Still told me you were leaving. Glad I caught you in time."

Kayleigh held a tablet across her chest with both arms like Hermione Granger on her first day at Hogwarts. She looked to be in her late twenties, and her eager expression told me she wasn't the patient sort.

Kayleigh pulled me into a side room for privacy, and after closing the door, she said, "I want to have a chat about your father."

I nodded with reservation. "I'm technically his son, yes."

"After doing an assessment on him, we've determined he's unable to take care of himself on his own."

"Okay."

"So, at this point, you have two options for your dad."

"Just to be clear, I'm actually not a part of my father's life. We haven't had a relationship in years."

"But legally, you're the only next of kin."

"I have a sister. Don't you have any documentation about her?"

Deena and I had been estranged for years, but that didn't mean she was free of any responsibility.

Kayleigh pulled the tablet away from her chest, tapped the screen a few times, then looked up at me. "I don't see anything here about her, but regardless, decisions *do* need to be made about your father's care."

"As I mentioned before, other than blood, my father and I have no connection to each other. Isn't there something you do in situations like this?"

"There is …" Kayleigh said, stringing out her words, eyes searching mine. Judging. "In a case like this, the county could take conservatorship over him. Medicare will pay for a skilled nursing facility, but it tends to be a minimum standard of care. I mean, lower quality than he'd receive at a private establishment."

I fell off into rocky silence, exhaustion tugging at me, irritation looking for a target. For the first time, doubt clouded my resolve, urging me to walk straight out the door.

"Somewhere lousy, you mean?" I said, unsure why I bothered to ask.

"All I'm saying is that your father's an extremely sick man. If it's affordable, you could pay the difference to ensure he gets the proper care he needs." She shoved a sheet of paper at me, which sent me back a step. "Here's a list of facilities we have relationships with. No need to make any decisions right now, but he *is* due to be released in a few days, so we'll require a decision before then. Do you know if he has any other source of income that could help pay for a place?"

"Again, we're—"

"Not close, right." Kayleigh nodded irrelevantly.

This time, the irritation found its target: me. For a guy who was usually good at finding solutions—and worked professionally as a communicator—I sounded inept. As much as I hated the idea, it would probably make a lot of things easier if I just reached out to Nolan to see what he knew. I took the list, folded it over itself twice, and shoved it in my back pocket.

Kayleigh looked down at her tablet and gave it a few more taps. "So, I also don't see anything here about health insurance. Do you know if your dad has any?"

I could almost feel the weight of her foot on my neck, taking my stress to a new level.

"Mr. McCabe?"

I searched for an exit sign. "Look, I have your name, Kayleigh, and if I get more information, I'll share it with you." Before she could ask me for anything else, I made my escape.

In the rental car, I checked my texts: only one, and it was from Nolan. I didn't need to open the app to know he was sending along my father's address, as promised. I tossed the phone and Kayleigh's information sheet onto the passenger's seat, then drove off.

12

I HAD MY OWN WAY of coping with stress.

I worked out.

Hard.

I made myself so exhausted that I no longer had the energy left to worry. This ritual had roots that ran wide and deep, going as far back as my junior varsity years. I was short for my age—a plus with the girls because they thought I was "too cute!" but not so much with the boys because it made me an easy target. When the school bell rang, I was an anxious wreck. Most times, nothing happened, but sometimes, the captain of the baseball team and his buddies were there, waiting to shove me around on my way home. Even when nothing happened, my fear of the unknown felt as tormenting.

Things changed the summer before my sophomore year. I had an accelerated growth spurt and started working out at the nearby Y. The scrawny frame I once saw in the mirror was becoming more substantive and solid, muscles gradually rising beneath skin. This metamorphosis felt like a miracle. The stronger I got, the more encouraged I was, and the more I continued to work out.

By the time September came, I was *that* kid. The one who transforms over the summer from a meager little nerd to a taller, athletic teen. My features changed, too, going from that weird prepubescent stage when everything looks out of proportion to filling out and finding symmetry. For the first time in my life, I walked into the new school year with a sense of confidence. I'd gone from barely being noticed to turning a few heads. Some even wondered who the new student was and where he'd transferred from. Never before had a girl noticed me—let alone smile at me—but there they were, making eye contact. And it wasn't just the girls who treated me better. Looking fit and muscular earned me respect from the guys, too, and when I joined the track team, my popularity grew more. At last, I was in a place I never knew I could be, and all the abuse came to an astounding and welcome stop.

But only at school.

Because all the muscle on this earth couldn't stop my father from continuing his verbal beatings. With him, it was never a battle of the brawn, and I didn't stand a chance when it came to his psychological arsenal.

"What are you doing, anyway?" he snarked from his recliner one evening when I came home from the gym. "Taking those steroids or something?"

"Just lifting weights, Dad."

"You know they can teach a chimp how to do that," he added, speaking around the handful of peanuts he'd stuffed into his mouth. "You're not special."

But it didn't matter which barb he threw my way. This was one thing he couldn't steal from me. Unlike my self-esteem, this change was physical, visible, and all I had to do was look into a mirror to find validation. And being on the track team also meant freedom. My father would start in on me, then out the door I'd go for a run, depriving him of a target. Soon, running became my respite from pain, and I could feel myself lifting away from the negative emotions that had pulled me down. By the time I got home, I'd exhausted myself to a point where nothing bothered me, not even him. So, I kept running harder and faster each day, building my physical and emotional endurance.

But the physical payoff wasn't always in my favor. I often limped around school, dogged by pulled muscles and inflamed tendons. I'd ice the injury, down some ibuprofen, then off I went again.

These decades later, it still didn't take much stress to launch me into one of my mini marathons. The recent run-in with my father certainly qualified, but other incidents did, too. Sometimes, my job got to be too much—personality conflicts, last-minute disappointments. Even being stuck in LA traffic could send me to the gym. During those times, I'd feel like a limping sixteen-year-old all over again.

I'd been on the treadmill for over an hour when it let out a punitive *beep*, a fitness club warning to indicate it was almost time to let someone else have their turn. In spite of that, I glanced at the screen and punched the key to increase my incline and speed. It was fine. My injuries from the car accident were almost healed; I said *almost* because my shoulder sometimes burned a little during overhead presses and a third set of pullups, but that was nothing a little Aleve and ice couldn't handle.

Trish disagreed. She used words like *compulsion*, saying they disrupted regular life. I couldn't argue the point, despite *regular* being relative. When I alleviated stress this way, I had to cancel social engagements with friends, and I'd shown up late for work, sometimes even calling in sick because of those nagging injuries from adolescence. She half-joked about me being late to my own wedding after working out to calm the prenuptial jitters.

It was easy to justify shirking certain responsibilities when I needed the freedom that running gave me. One time, I'd committed to a role I later regretted so much that I disappeared into an hours-long workout every evening for weeks until I had to drag myself to the studio each day. It was for an audiobook entitled *Strange Places,* about a vet who'd served in the Gulf War, then came back home, feeling like a stranger in the neighborhood where he'd grown up. I liked the material—and I could even identify because that's how I felt, growing up in mine—but the war part was completely unfamiliar to me, making it difficult to get in character.

I was fit, but it came at a high cost where intimate relationships were concerned. Trish had been my longest, about four years.

Another word she used was *addiction*. Her suggestion was that with so much alcohol filling the family gene pool—and since I'd made a conscious decision never to drink—it was possible that I'd traded alcohol for exercise.

"It's like you jump into these workouts whenever you feel powerless," Trish had said one evening when she walked into the bedroom and found me doing multiple sit-up reps. Earlier in the day, I'd had a disagreement with my director. The same thing happened when her brother died and her parents broke up. I wanted to help but felt so damned ineffective that I started intensifying my workouts.

"Keeping fit is just self-care," I'd replied. "Is that so wrong?"

"I'm just worried that you can't be happy unless you exercise."

Even though I'd gone on the defensive, I couldn't say she was wrong. But working out had become such a big part of me that I no longer knew how to separate from it. I needed the gym like a junkie needs his fix kit.

Tonight, by the time I finished running, the gym crowd had cycled several times, shifting from the lunch-break athletes to the after-school crowd and then to the after-work crowd.

I arrived home from my workout, my shirt, my shorts, even my sneakers drenched in sweat. The moment I walked through the kitchen, something tomatoey and spicy pervaded the air. It took one look at the tinfoil-covered plate on the stove to tell me I'd missed another dinner. I wasn't sure yet if this was an annoyed meal offering or a neutral one, and I couldn't see Trish nearby to get a good read on her. She was probably in bed, reading on her laptop or doing work.

Measured steps took me to the bedroom door. I peered inside. Trish looked over her laptop, and her expression said everything I needed to know. Not annoyance, more a touch of compassion, wrapped in a fragile layer of dismay.

"Hey, Twiz," I said. "What's up?"

It was my nickname for her.

On one of our dates, she noticed a billboard advertising Twizzlers candy and said, "I'm so obsessed with those things. It's kind of crazy. And only the cherry."

Without a second thought, I made a beeline to the nearest convenience store, then bought her a package of cherry Twizzlers. When I came back to the car, the look on her face was priceless; her eyes lit up brightly, and so did her smile. A comforting, cozy smile that felt like warmed honey. And I realized I would have walked out of the store eight hundred times just to see it again and again. The truth was, by that point, I would have carried a washing machine on my back if she'd asked me to. That was how lovestruck I was by her. I couldn't believe my luck. I'd found this amazing, beautiful woman. A woman who loved me back with equal measure.

On our next date, when she opened her apartment door, I held up a package of her favorite cherry obsession and said, "Hey, Twiz! How's it going?"

She laughed and threw her arms around me. The name stuck, and I've been calling her that ever since.

Now, I entered the room and leaned over to kiss her forehead, but she pulled away.

"Ew! Griffin! You're all sweaty!"

With a playful grin, I tried to go in for another kiss.

This time, she blocked me with her hands and said, "Go take a shower!" But she was laughing.

"Thanks for leaving dinner out for me," I said, lifting the wet T-shirt over my head, then tossing it into the hamper.

"Feel better now?"

"Yeah. I think."

"Are you sure you should be running with your injuries from the accident? Won't it exacerbate them?"

"Nah, the shoulder isn't bothering me much anymore."

"*Much?*"

I laughed it off. "I'm fine, really."

"So, what happened today?" Trish asked, her tone telling me she knew there was a reason for my impromptu long-distance race. There was always a reason, but I was sure she already knew what this one had been about.

I took a seat on the edge of the bed, kicked off my sneakers, and said, "I went to see my father."

Trish closed her laptop and gave me her full attention. "How did it go?"

I puffed my cheeks full of air, then let it out slowly. "That's a loaded question."

"Did he recognize you?"

"He did. But it was weird—*really* weird." I gazed down at my bare feet and shook my head. "He seemed like a complete stranger."

"Well, it's been a few years."

I looked up at her and said, "My father wasn't drinking when he hit me."

"That's a relief." She sounded more neutral and inviting.

I made myself tell her the news about my father's Alzheimer's— speaking about it breathed more life into the story but also made it more real—how it was likely the reason why he'd slammed into me at the intersection and why the social worker recommended I pay for a higher level of care because he'd need it.

"Wow," Trish said. "Talk about a plot twist."

"Adding to that, I got a call from his landlord."

"What did *he* want?"

"Not much," I said through a mild laugh. "Just everything. He expects me to get my father's apartment cleared out."

"What's your thought about paying for a better facility?"

My mind had continuously grazed over this while working out, and I now sensed an evolving idea. I just needed to figure out how to put it into words.

"I don't feel like I owe him that much," I said.

Trish didn't speak.

"What? Do you think I do?" I asked.

She pushed a loose thatch of hair away from her face. "I guess I'm trying to gauge where you're at with all this. If I'm going to be honest, it's been kind of hard to read you lately. You haven't really said much about him for a few days."

"Because I've needed a break. You probably needed one, too."

She shook her head. "I don't think that's it at all."

"Then, what is it?"

"Avoiding the inevitable isn't healthy. Like we talked about."

I could always tell when something became more about our relationship, and this was it. I rose from the bed, gathered my sneakers, then placed them neatly against the wall.

"Griffin."

I turned around. "Yeah?"

"You've been working out for hours, and we both know what that means."

She was right, yet all I could think about was how much better I felt now.

"Look," she said, "the accident with your dad was extremely stressful, probably the worst thing that's happened to you in a long time. Add to that your history of abuse, and it's going to knock you off-center. I get that. You know I do. But you don't need to keep running off to the gym to process everything. I'm right here, and I'm on your side."

I walked into the bathroom, turned on the shower, and said, "I know that."

"Griffin, can you please come back here? I wasn't finished."

I let out a lengthy sigh, came out of the bathroom, then stood before her.

She said, "There's no detour around this. Your problems are still going to be there when you get off the treadmill."

Again, she was right, but I didn't want her to be.

"I'll try harder," I told her. "I swear."

I leaned in toward her, went for another kiss, and this time, she let me.

13

I HAD A REASON FOR not bringing my sister in to discuss our father's health care. We hadn't spoken in years. After making my escape from the house and going off to college, I had deliberately lost touch with her and my dad.

My history with Deena wasn't stellar—truthfully, it was complicated. *We* were complicated. Unlike many twins, we weren't close, and even though we had many of the same experiences at home, it always felt like we went through them separately. Because of problems with my birth, she was about fifteen minutes older than I. It made sense that I resisted entering a world I'd later learn to fear, and I used to joke about sending her out to test the waters before me.

After Mom died, Dad treated Deena as though she were the golden child, me, the bastard son. I held a lot of resentment toward my sister because of it. She could have been there for me, maybe used her better standing with him to defend me when my father went on the attack. But she didn't. Instead, she made herself scarce, hiding behind shadows or staying at a friend's house so she could act as though my abuse wasn't happening.

Deena had made a few scarce attempts to reach out while we were in college, but she was smart enough to take the hint that I wasn't interested. I rejected her calls, unable to lose the bitter taste in my mouth from her and my father. Since she and I had never been close to begin with, it wasn't difficult to scrub her from my life.

But now, because I was being forced to deal with our father, it seemed fair that she should, too. I hadn't convinced myself that I needed to help him at all, but I decided I might not be as resistant to the idea if Deena agreed to cover part of the cost.

I brewed a fresh cup of coffee, then placed it beside me on the desktop in my office at home. After Trish and I moved in, we'd put a wall down the middle of a spare bedroom so we could each have our own workspace. The coffee's smooth and earthy smell helped me focus.

I opened my laptop and found Deena's professional Facebook page. The cover photo featured a family portrait taken on the beach, backlit by a brilliant blood-orange sunset, with one ridiculously handsome husband and three beautiful kids, a boy and two girls. They were the flawless suburban family, everyone happy, everyone smiling. I guessed she rewrote her history.

I read on. Golden Child had become a pediatrician. Of course she had. Perfect family, perfect job, perfect Deena. But to my advantage, there was plenty to glean from her page. She had never left San Diego. It was kind of funny—well, not *funny*, funny—that the three of us had been living in the same city after all this time and had never known it. But our family was all about withholding, so that shouldn't have come as a huge surprise.

She looked good, too, still the cute, petite brunette she'd always been. When we were younger, people told her she looked a lot like Reese Witherspoon with dark hair, and I had to admit, the comparison wasn't unwarranted.

I went deeper into the internet, searching for her phone number. It didn't take long to find one: her name and cell were listed on the website for a volunteer group that provided medical aid to kids in underprivileged neighborhoods.

I looked over my laptop but saw nothing of the view beyond my desk. My head was too busy with a heavy debate. Surely, I was the last person she wanted to hear from, but I was determined to try this, anyway. I had no other choice. My savings account was earmarked for a future with Trish and whatever else came along with it—not for supporting the moribund ghoul from childhood. I could afford to help him a little bit, but I wasn't going to drain my accounts over this. I rubbed a notch of tension in my neck as I dialed my sister's number.

"This is Deena," she said, sounding all businesslike.

I tried to speak but hadn't anticipated the words getting stuck on their way out.

"Hello?"

"Deena," I managed to say, "it's Griffin."

Dead quiet.

I pulled the phone away to be sure we were still connected, then said, "You there?"

"Griffin," she said, her tone going from perfunctory to mistrust in a matter of seconds, making it clear that she was not happy to hear from her twin brother. "Why are you calling me?"

I took a micro break to reevaluate. I might not have thought this all the way through. The hospital didn't even know that Deena existed. My mind rewound further back in time: Nolan had never mentioned her on the phone, either. Was it possible that, much like me, she hadn't been in touch with our father for years? If this were true, I'd need to switch up my plan. It wouldn't be smart to give her too many details—doing that would put me at a disadvantage and make it easier for her to bow out or hang up on me.

So, all I said was, "I need to see you."

"You've *got* to be kidding me, Griffin."

"I'm serious."

"Yeah. So am I. No."

The guardedness in her tone sounded a lot like mine, and the emotion that came with it felt familiar—an innate expectation of trouble that accompanies alcohol-related family problems.

I wrapped my legs so tight around the leg of the chair that my shins burned with pain. But I didn't dislodge them. In an odd way, the discomfort anchored me, chasing off the jumpiness that tried to occupy me.

"It's urgent," I tried again.

"I'll be the judge of that. Tell me."

"*Dammit*, Deena. It's not like I'm stalking you." Although it occurred to me that *stalking* was exactly what I'd been doing. "I'm not some creeper. I'm your brother."

"A brother I haven't seen or spoken to in more than two decades," she reminded me. "For God's sake, Griffin, I don't have time for this. Just tell me!"

I surrendered. "It's about Dad."

"What, is he, like, dead or something?"

"Dying, or close to it."

That rendered her soundless for a few moments, and then she said, "Look, I haven't seen him for almost as long as I haven't seen you, and to be honest, I've got no desire."

That answered one question but led to another. What could have happened that was horrible enough to make Deena abandon our father?

"I think you should see me, Deena," I said, knowing those words were nothing more than a desperate attempt to keep her from hanging up on me. "It would be a big mistake if you don't."

"What the hell's *that* supposed to mean?"

I didn't know, either, but I pushed back harder. "Can you just meet with me, please? I promise, it won't take long."

Quieter, as though she might have been considering it, then, "Do you even still live in town?"

"Yeah. So does Dad."

All I could hear were her soft, bothered breaths, but I hoped that meant she was giving this more thought.

About three seconds later, she said, "Crystal Pier. Five o'clock, Wednesday evening. I'll meet you between the time I get off from work and the time I come home for dinner. Five minutes, Griffin. That's all you get from me. That's it."

14

MY PHONE WENT OFF WHILE I drove down the I-5. I glanced at the screen. It was my agent, David Freeman, calling from Los Angeles. David and I had been working together for years. We often joked about how I got discovered in the tire aisle. Not exactly the case but good enough for an occasional laugh.

One of the things I appreciated most about him was that he wasn't your typical Hollywood agent. With many, you had to find your own opportunities, then call them in to do the deal. Not David. He worked hard for me. I wasn't a commodity—I was human, and he was always as thrilled about my successes as I was. He was damned good at what he did, too. With his help, I'd made a name for myself in the industry. I had two Emmys sitting on a shelf at home, plus a few other awards to prove it. I often got early consideration when jobs became available, and a lot of those perks were because of David.

But a call from him could be a toss-up: sometimes, it was about problems with a current job, but other times, it was about new work. These past few weeks had been a dumpster fire, and I worried that more bad news could send me back to the gym for another punishing workout and more friction with Trish. On the flip side, I'd been waiting to hear about that new film job.

My finger hovered over the car's Answer button for a few seconds. *Which will it be? Good news or bad?* I pressed it.

"Hey, David," I said, a hint of uncertainty saddling my voice.

"Griffin, hi. Got some news for you."

I was unable to reply. I just didn't trust it yet.

"Great news, in fact. I got a call from the folks at Wingate."

"Go on," I said, trying to keep as calm as I could. There was no gun-jumping when it came to deals this big.

"Congratulations, Griffin! Wingate wants you for the lead role in *Funland Falls!* I mean, they *really* want you!"

"Holy …" I took in a deep breath, held it, then let it out fast. "Damn, David, you don't know how much I needed this."

"You've earned it, Griffin. So, they'd like you to come up here for an audition, but that's more a formality than anything else. I'll email all the details, but from what they've told me, they're very enthusiastic about you."

The more David spoke, the more adrenaline kicklined up my spine—the good kind. Was this really happening? My mind was already cycling through what this meant. I thought about taking my career to the next level. I thought about all the money I'd be making. The stability.

"Production starts next month," David added.

"Not a problem," I said, then thought about how I couldn't wait to tell Trish.

She was always excited whenever I got new roles and loved to ask all kinds of questions about them. But this … this was huge. *Finally, something good.* I thanked David, hung up, and let out a whoop over the Mustang's windshield, letting the wind carry it all the way back to Hollywood.

I burst through the garage doorway that led to our family room and yelled out, "Hey, Twiz! Are you there? I've got great news!"

Trish rushed into the living room, and I told her everything. How Wingate had practically already cast me as the lead role in that major motion picture I'd been talking about. What this could do for my career, for us.

"Oh, Griff!" Trish let out a squeal of delight. "This is amazing!" She threw her arms around me, then pulled back to take me in again as if not wanting to miss a second of my exhilaration.

We dropped onto the couch, and I recounted the rest of the details.

"I'm so happy for you!" she said once I finished, then gave me a long kiss on the lips.

My heart got jumpy against my chest but in a good way. The wonderful way.

She went on, "I absolutely cannot wait to see this when it comes out!"

I hadn't looked that far ahead, but yeah, the thought was enticing.

"Hey," I said, "what do you think about going out to celebrate? We can go to Juniper and Ivy."

She put a hand on my arm and gave me a melty gaze. "My absolute favorite. I think I just fell in love with you all over again."

Before I could laugh, my phone went off, and I checked the screen. The call was from Green Hospital in La Jolla, where my father had been staying. I held up the phone, rolled my eyes.

"Who is it?" Trish asked.

"The hospital. Let me just deal with it really quick."

I answered the call.

"Mr. McCabe? Kayleigh Hartley calling. From Green Hospital."

"Hi. What's up, Kayleigh?"

"So, I'm just circling back to see if you've made a decision about your father."

"Not yet. I'm waiting to talk to my sister about it."

"Do you have any idea when you might know something?"

"I'll be seeing her tomorrow evening."

"I don't want to rush you"—what people say when they're doing exactly that—"but we *will* need a decision from you before we're able to discharge your father from the hospital."

"I get it, Kayleigh, but I don't have one for you yet."

"How about a ballpark?"

"My *ballpark* is, I don't *know* yet. I just told you I'm seeing my sister tomorrow night. I'll be in touch after that." I hung up on her, but when I looked back at Trish, her mouth was half-open, her head angled at me. "Right?" I said. "Can you believe these people?"

She didn't respond, not unless you counted her crinkled brow.

"What is it?"

"You were very rude to her, Griffin. What's going on with you?"

"Nothing. I didn't mean to be—it's that whole situation, and I was preoccupied about the movie deal."

"I know there's a lot going on, but she was just trying to do her job."

I closed my eyes, took in a deep, cleansing breath. "You're right. I'll apologize the next time I see her."

Trish slowly nodded, tucking away her last snag of discomfort.

The atmosphere at Juniper and Ivy was electric with bounding activity. Servers burst through swinging kitchen doors, balancing plates on their arms and drinks in their hands before swooping in and out between tables. The crowd was spirited, a mix of conversation, laughter, and a few shrieks here and there, the noise bouncing off an open ceiling with crisscrossing wooden beams. But the food—damn, it was our favorite for a reason. Smelling the sourdough bread, smoked fish, and roasted veggies was enough to send me off into a spiritual experience before even putting my hand on a fork.

Trish and I sat at the bar, waiting for our table, and I could not stop staring at her. She wore the silky black-and-red floral-print dress I'd bought her. This was the first time she had it on. About a month before, she had fallen in love with it while we were shopping but said it cost way too much, so as soon as she wandered off into a different department, I snatched it off the rack and put it on layaway. I'll never forget the look of shock when she saw the white gift box with a giant red bow on the bed. Her mouth fell open, and her eyes sparkled in that special way whenever she felt dear to my heart.

But when the server brought her second glass of wine, that snag of discomfort showed up again at the edge of her smile.

"Is something wrong?" I asked.

"Kinda … I'm just wondering, when did you talk to Deena?"

"Oh, that. It was yesterday."

She let out a mirthless laugh.

"I planned on telling you tonight, but with all this excitement about the movie …"

"The movie was today. What about last night?"

"I got home late."

"But I was up when you came in."

"I know. I was too exhausted. I should have mentioned it then. I'm sorry."

"Talking to your estranged sister after almost twenty years is kind of a huge deal, Griffin. It's not something you stick in a folder for the next day."

"Again, I'm sorry. Please, don't be angry."

"I'm not angry." She paused, as if deciding if that were true. "Just a little disappointed. I don't want to sound overcritical because you *have* been going through a lot, but this is starting to feel like a pattern. Can you see how it might bother me? I'm just getting to a place where I can think about our future again and not feel like every minute of every day, something terrible might happen and ruin everything. It's been a hell of a few years—you know that—and I know we've had this conversation before, but I need to believe you actually hear me. The more you hide, the more fragile *we* feel."

"I *do* hear you. I didn't mean for it to sound like I hadn't. I'll try harder next time."

"But you said that the other night when I tried to help."

"I'll do better, I promise."

The hostess arrived to escort us to our table, but the heft of Trish's mood was hard to ignore.

Once we got seated, I reached across the table for her hand and said, "Things are finally looking up for me. Can't we just focus on that tonight? Let's have fun and celebrate, okay?"

"Of course," she said, but I couldn't help noticing the chunk of happiness missing from her smile.

15

THE CRYSTAL PIER IN PACIFIC Beach wasn't the most private spot for a conversation with my sister after all these years, but it *had* always been one of her favorite places to hang out. I liked it here, too. The pier was central to all the places where I loved to surf and where most of my friends hung out.

Built in the 1920s, it had been an amusement park above the water with colorful, flashing arcade lights and the Crystal ballroom, where couples danced their evenings away. But all that was gone now. What remained was the Crystal Pier Hotel with its string of refurbished 1930s-style cottages that featured seaside sun decks and great views of the water.

When we were young, Deena had spent every summer on this beach, running through hot sand, splashing in the ocean, and teasing boys. When she got older, her activities had shifted to better suit a teenager's life. During the day, she lay out in the sunshine, flirted with the surfers, and laughed it up with friends. Once evening came, she'd show off her expertly honed tan while partying on the beach.

I had liked it there, too, but my activities were more focused on the unending pursuit of physical perfection. I surfed all through high school and split my time between the water and running. By all appearances, I was just another resplendent Southern California beach boy. It was my greatest charade. Or I thought it was.

Since Deena and I often went to the beach at the same time, it was hard to avoid her. So, we awkwardly greeted each other as any school acquaintances would. To everyone else, it probably didn't look strange, even though it was. I had my friends. She had hers.

Deena was waiting at the foot of the pier when I arrived. I was early, but she had gotten here sooner. Odd, considering that she didn't want to see me, but I attributed it to the possibility that she came to enjoy her favorite beach before our meeting, hoping it might give her the fortitude to deal with me.

But the closer I got, the more disorientation dropped over me, tension and uncertainty amassing into disbelief. I was looking at my mother at this age, and it shook me down so much that my chest quaked. I hadn't noticed the resemblance online, but Deena's movements and subtle mannerisms made it unmistakable.

I had to stop and catch my breath before proceeding any farther. Aware that a heavy conversation awaited me, I used everything I had to pull myself together, instead focusing on her unexpected clothing choice for the day. She wore a pair of light-blue shorts that stopped above her knees and a mid-sleeved button-down shirt with matching stripes. This was a complete reversal of the girl I once knew: never once would she have been caught looking so conservative. It had always been bikinis and flip-flops by day, then revealing tops and sandals by evening. But a lot had changed over the years. Mother and physician: presto chango, the new Deena had arrived.

When I reached her, she gave me the up-and-down as though judging my own look. I wore a T-shirt, loose shorts, and a backward baseball cap.

She probably thought, *For crying out loud, Griffin, you're in your thirties. Don't you think it's time to stop dressing like a skater?*

For a moment, even *I* felt a little dodgy about my clothing choice. Then, I wrote it off, telling myself we *were* at the beach after all. Still, the discomfort raging between us was vast. Oppressive.

"Let's walk," she said, but it came out more like a command. "We should be done by the time we return to this spot."

"All righty then," I said with sarcastic cheeriness. "Guess you weren't kidding about the five-minute rule."

Deena ignored my comment and started walking ahead of me.

We proceeded up the weathered and boarded pier, both silent, both keeping our eyes aimed ahead as if we were each on our own—and it felt just like that.

"You look good, Deena," I offered, holding out the olive branch in an attempt to cut through the frosty uneasiness jammed between us.

"Thanks," she said with zero affect. "You, too."

Not exactly a proclamation of sisterly love, but it was more than I'd expected. I nodded modestly because I didn't know what else to do. When Deena stopped and turned to look at me, a gust of ocean air blew strands of hair across her face. She pushed them away.

"So, what's the story with Dad?" she demanded.

"You really haven't seen him for years?"

"Nope."

Judging by her unsettled expression, there was plenty more to that story. I was dying to ask, but we weren't on firm ground, and I couldn't afford to shake things up if I wanted her to help out with our father. So, I spilled about Dad crashing into me, how I'd seen him at the hospital, and—the final shocker—that he had Alzheimer's.

"Wow." Deena started walking again. She gazed up the pier, and her long brown lashes fluttered. "Didn't see *that* one coming."

"I know. Neither did I."

"Was he hurt badly?"

I was surprised she cared. "Bumps and bruises, but he did better than I did."

Deena didn't bother to ask how I felt after the accident, which told me she was still trying to preserve that wall between us. To be fair, I was walking and talking just fine, and her allotted time allowance was running out.

"I'll just get straight to it," I said. "I've been forced to handle Dad's affairs, and it's getting harder to do it by myself. I was wondering if you might be willing to help out."

I got an eye-to-eye deadpan for that one.

Deena said, "The man does not deserve my time and effort."

How the hell do you think I feel, Golden Child?

With nothing to lose, I went ahead and asked, "Did something happen between the two of you?"

"That's not any of your business, Griffin."

Message received. The only sounds now were waves, crashing beneath us as they collided against the pier's pile caps.

"You know I shouldn't be the one who has to take care of him."

She snapped back. "Well, I shouldn't, either."

"You're kidding me, right?"

She gave me the cut-eye. "I'm absolutely *not* kidding."

I looked at her, then away, then back at her with utter disbelief. "This is so classic of you, Deena. I'm the one who suffered all his abuse, and you got the hall pass. Now, *you're* playing the victim?"

"That's not true!"

"Really?"

"Things weren't always what you thought, Griffin."

"Then, tell me, *Deena*. What *were* they like?"

Her affect was flat, a mirror image of the heartless spectatorship she'd shown that strange evening when I drove our father to the liquor store.

She took her gaze from me and dismissively said, "Oh, screw it. Never mind."

"Wow," I said in an angry whisper, no longer able to bridle my indignation. "It's *so* like you to turn your head the other way. I guess some things never change."

She threw a hand onto her hip. "What's *that* supposed to mean? Look, I didn't come here for you to insult me!"

"Well, you sure didn't come here for the truth."

"And now, you just want to fight with me."

"No, but that's fine. I'll take care of Dad. You just go back to your perfect life with your perfect family and pretend like I never called. My *God,* Deena! It's the same damned story with you, isn't it?"

I didn't wait for her response, choosing instead to walk away and leave her standing there. She'd goaded me into taking full responsibility for our father, and I wasn't going to stay here for it.

Deena shouted after me, "You only know half of the story between Dad and me, Griffin!"

I stomped off. I couldn't take another minute of it.

The years hadn't changed her one bit.

16

IT WAS HALLOWEEN, AND MY high school was having a contest for the best costume. After hearing the first prize was a new surfboard, I was all in. My own board had seen better days. I'd picked it up at a garage sale and added a few more creases and dings while learning how to use it. By sophomore year, I wasn't the best surfer yet, but I wanted to be, and a new board would help.

Although the prize was enough to catch my interest, something else excited me. When Mom was around, Halloween had been one of the highlights of our year. She'd make a major event of it, starting preparations days before the 31st. She baked frosted cupcakes that looked like little pumpkins and cookies shaped like ghosts—and then her mischievous sense of humor crept in. Each year, she'd make us wait with anticipation, trying to figure out what creepy concoction she'd been scaring up in the kitchen. One year, it was a blood-red velvet cake with a leg sticking out from the top; the next, her cookies with big, bloodshot eyeballs lodged in the middle, staring up at us. Our favorite of all time was her brain cake, made of red Jell-O and God knew what else.

Mom loved to wear costumes when she took us trick-or-treating, and we always had a group theme. One time, she dressed up as an axe-wielding camp counselor, and Deena and I were her bloody, terrorized campers. She chased us all over the neighborhood as we went from house to house, screaming our heads off and laughing. We got a lot of strange looks from the neighbors who didn't know Mom well enough, but for those who did, we always got extra candy.

After she'd passed, Dad was too busy working or drinking to care about Halloween, and since Mom wasn't around, nobody else took us trick-or-treating. This school contest was a chance to recover some lost joy—if only for a day.

After great deliberation, I decided to be a tiger: ferocious, self-sufficient, and badass enough to not take shit from anyone. I'd put away a few dollars from mowing lawns all summer, so I used some of the money to buy materials for my costume. I went out and got a tiger-print shirt and sweatpants, plus orange and black makeup for my face. I even found remnant materials at a fabric store for a tail to pin onto the back of my pants.

On the morning of the contest, I woke up a few hours earlier than normal, in the zone and ready to make a surfboard-winning costume. After putting it on, I started the makeup process, which I worked with great creativity and precision to get just right. Once everything was done, I stood before a full-length mirror to inspect my work and couldn't get the tigerish grin off my face.

This looks great! I thought, straightening my posture. *I could win this. That surfboard is mine!*

I hadn't felt this excited about something in a long time and couldn't wait to see what the other kids would be wearing at the school spirit rally. I took off into the hallway and downstairs, but as I made it to the door, my father stumbled into my path, looking like he had a killer hangover. He had this instinct for sniffing me out at the worst times, and the second my father flicked his attention at me, his expression turned sour. But why? Had I forgotten to do something he'd asked of me? To put something away where it belonged?

With that disapproving, boot-faced scowl I'd come to know, he gestured up and down with a hand at my costume and said, "What the hell is *this?*"

"It's for school, Dad. A Halloween costume," I said with forced enthusiasm, trying to sell him on the idea. "They're having a contest."

Instead, he glowered at my costume, brows snapping together, jaw set, as if I were some dog who'd shit the rug.

I distractedly walked past him, but he snared my arm and tugged me back. Deena was coming down the staircase and froze about halfway when she caught the scene playing out. My father let go of my arm, shoved me forward, then glared at me some more.

"What kind of ... *boy* does this?" he said, voice dripping with venom.

"But all the kids are doing it, Dad."

I got a quick glance at Deena, still on the staircase, still watching us. I tried to read her expression, hoping to see concern, outrage ... *something,* but she had nothing for me.

"You little pansy," my father said, throwing enough fiery contempt to burn down our house. His cheeks flushed with disgust, and beneath them hung a poisonous leer.

How could being a normal teenager make him that furious?

Then, he went right in with his teeth.

"Get upstairs, get out of that ridiculous outfit, and put your dress back on."

Tears were coming, but I fought like hell to hold them back. Then, cold reality clocked me: this used to be my best friend, the father who would have done anything to see me smile—who *used* to do everything— and now, all he wanted was to lacerate me. I had no idea who this man was, this imposter pretending to be my father.

I looked up the staircase. Deena was gone.

I ran upstairs, then closed my bedroom door. Sitting up in bed, I stared ahead into the abundant nothingness, breaths heaving so fast that it seemed almost impossible to control them. Next came the heartbeats—thundering, driving heartbeats—slamming hard enough to make my clavicle, my rib cage, even my belly, shake with each punishing stroke. There was no way out of this bottomless suffering, and I wanted to put an end to it.

So, I slammed the back of my head into the hard, unforgiving headboard, indifferent to whether I passed out or died: physical pain was my only escape from the emotional anguish that now controlled me. Slow at first, one, two, harder and a little faster on three, I rhythmically racked my head against the dense wood. *Bang, bang, bang.* My head throbbed and ached, but that was nothing compared to what I still felt inside.

I didn't pass out or die. I only felt worse, so instead, I buried my face into the pillow and let out the most frightening, violent scream I'd ever made. It was then that I knew it couldn't be sadness I was feeling.

It was unadulterated rage.

17

"I DIDN'T PLAN TO GO off on Deena," I told Trish, a little short of breath as we hiked a steep embankment at Cuyamaca Rancho State Park.

This was our favorite adult playground. About forty miles east of San Diego in the Laguna Mountains, the area was blanketed with fir, pine, and oak forests, divided by undulating meadows and fast-moving streams.

"I let my frustration get the best of me," I said, "but Deena wouldn't budge about helping out with our dad."

Trish's only response was to look up at the trail ahead and nod. I got a sense that her frustration over the other night was still simmering, but I was trying to fill her in on my meeting with Deena because I didn't want to shut her out again.

In an attempt to hit the reset button, I said, "I do want to make you a part of this conversation, even though I didn't at first. I'm truly sorry about that."

"Fair enough," she conceded with a single downward nod and a budding smile, "and I'm sorry things went that way with Deena."

"It's fine, I guess," I said. "I wasn't hoping for much, and I didn't get much."

"Weird, though, that she broke ties with your dad and refused to explain why."

"She told me to mind my own business."

"Subtle."

"Like a jackhammer, but that's apparently the new Deena. She was meek as a kitten when we were kids, but now, she's frosty, closed off, and she doesn't hesitate to bite back."

"Do you think it might have something to do with what she won't say about your dad?"

"The thought occurred to me," I said, dry leaves crackling and snapping beneath my hiking boots as I increased my speed to tackle the next incline. "But from what I saw, he treated her fine. Never once did I see him give her trouble about anything. She got to live her normal, carefree life."

Trish shrugged. "Maybe there was something you *didn't* see." She stopped walking to think. "It also could have had something to do with her being female. I see different shades of sexism in my abuse cases. The boys get picked on, and the girls get ignored. It's still abuse, just more subtle."

"I'd never thought about that. She always tried so hard to avoid me, so it was difficult to tell." We worked to keep up our walking speed on the incline. "I wonder if she found out something about my dad that nobody else knew."

At last, we stood at a vista, overlooking Cuyamaca Lake. The air was rich with the damp smell of sun-warmed soil. The lake looked like mercury under the day's bright white sky, ringed with muted green foothills that were stippled with caramel-colored patches of dry earth. I took it all in, and for a few seconds, I almost forgot my worries.

We moved on, but I was still stuck on something.

"You know what I resent most right now? She's living on her big doctor's salary. I mean, you should see the huge house she and her husband have in Del Mar. I saw it on her Instagram—it's ridiculous, right on the beach—and yet she won't contribute a penny. Money obviously isn't the issue for her."

But it looked as though one decision had already been made for my father. Earlier that morning, I'd told Trish that Kayleigh had called from the hospital to let me know that my dad was well enough to be discharged. Since I hadn't given her an answer, they'd be placing him in a standard skilled nursing facility, and she again reminded me that he would only be getting a minimum standard of care. Trish told me I should have acted more quickly, which added another stress divot to our relationship. She had well-defined opinions about how an ill relative should be cared for, probably because she had been her brother's caregiver until his suicide.

Trying to strike a reasonable note, I said, "I'm hoping that just means the place they chose won't be as nice or comfortable as a more expensive facility."

Trish gave me a look that was hard to read.

"It's like this, Griff," she said, her smile taxed by a whisper of impatience. "Everyone keeps telling you the same thing, and you keep hitting the same note. That's not what Kayleigh meant. You've never been to one of these low-end places. I have. My grandmother's sister got stuck in one. They're shitholes, and they're dumping grounds for the indigent."

I gazed at her with quick focus. "But you've only been to that one place, right? Do you think it's enough to make that judgment?"

"Griffin, I'm not judging at all. You haven't had time to think about these things, but it's pretty well-known that most state-run, low-cost facilities have a myriad of problems, and the care can be … well, awful. I'm not saying they mean any harm, but budgets have to be maintained. It's about better beds, better equipment, and a larger staff to take care of patients."

We walked on in loaded silence while I processed what she'd said. Perhaps her discomfort recalled those hard days after her brother's death when she blamed herself and wouldn't think otherwise. But a small part of me was bothered that she wasn't seeing the whole picture: spending a large amount of time and money on a man I hated was infuriating.

"I don't want to sound unreasonable about this," I said.

"Look, Griffin. This has nothing to do with being unreasonable and everything to do with saving yourself from a future of constant headaches. Getting him into a better place will put your mind at ease because they're more equipped to handle problems when they come up. I mean, do you really want to be getting phone calls at all hours of the day and night whenever something goes wrong?"

"That's the problem. I don't want *anything* to do with the man at all, and yet here I am. And the idea of spending money on him only makes it worse. He hit *me* in that accident; now, somehow, I'm stuck with all the bills to cover the rest of his life?"

"We could figure out a way. We'll just have to make a few sacrifices."

All I could do was sigh. Making sacrifices for Trish was one thing because I loved her and it felt great to make her happy. Making sacrifices for a man I'd despised for most of my life was another, like pouring gasoline with a lit match in the same hand. I didn't want to spend any part of my wedding savings on him. Even if I made a lot of money from the Wingate job, he didn't deserve any of that, either.

More walking. More silence. Nothing resolved.

Trish didn't say anything else about the subject, but I didn't know if I wanted her to. She came from a different place than I had: a loving, stable home environment, while I was a prime example of what came from the other side of the tracks. Not financially—we had plenty of money—but in the emotional sense. Once upon a time, I would have given up every object I owned to feel loved by my father. Trish didn't know what that felt like. She'd received unconditional love her whole life, not only from her parents, but from her brother, too. Her family wasn't perfect—none is—but it was as close-knit as any could be before Cam died. Back then, the biggest problems they had were when her dad spent too much money restoring old, broken-down cars or her mother spent too much time with friends. But those were more irritants than issues. Because of this, Trish was well-adjusted while growing up and unscarred, which often made me wonder how I must have looked to her. Could she see how damaged I was—or worse, did she think I was beyond repair?

Before the accident, Trish and I had had a more lighthearted relationship. We'd joke and make each other laugh to let off pressure. Like when she used to poke fun at my loud, multicolored socks, which I insisted on wearing. It was her thing. One morning, while we got dressed for work, she smirked at my selection for the day—a pair with purple and red stripes.

"I'm almost afraid to ask which side of the rainbow those slid off of," she said.

I pretended to be insulted, and then, while she wasn't looking, I stuffed those and five other ridiculous pairs into her briefcase. Later on, I got a call from her at work after a board meeting—or I assumed it was her because all I could hear were the tiny squeaks coming from her laughter. I made fun of that, and then we cracked up even more.

"I pulled a report from my briefcase, and out came the socks!" she said, still hyperventilating from laughter. "There I was, in front of fifteen people, with your obnoxious socks flopped out on the conference table! Doughnut socks! And those hot-pink ones with tacos? And really? You had to include the polar bear ones?"

I couldn't help but giggle. When I'd ordered that particular pair, I'd innocently thought the polar bear couples were adorable, until I realized they were making mad love and displaying other lewd poses.

"You should have seen their faces!" she added. "I'd never witnessed so many faces blush at one time." But her laugh outdid any embarrassment she felt.

This new snag with my father, however, pushed us in an ugly direction, toward a place where there was no room for humor or symmetry or sense of order. Because of that, it was difficult to tell her why, these days, I was again running from myself and back toward my childhood where I was unloved. Where fear used to crawl inside me like a prickly weed. At the same time, I was firming up the divider that had been rising between us—much like Deena was doing to me—and failing to give Trish what I'd promised her after Cam died and her parents divorced: security.

My guilt over that made me want to disappear on Trish just as I'd done when my father ruled my life, cornering me with his cruelty and trapping me in my own panic.

18

ONCE A MONTH, MY FATHER attended his men's club meetings, but they were just another opportunity to get hammered with his drinking pals. Each time, he'd arrive back to the house, smashed and struggling to make it through the door. I wondered how he managed to drive himself home without taking down a few street signs or worse, a few pedestrians. His Mercedes had all the telltale signs of a drunk driver. Deep scratches ran the length of his car from brushing against hell-if-I-knew-what. It was hard to tell which thing he'd hit at which time. One day, his passenger-side mirror had even done a mysterious disappearing act.

As a widower, my father turned to these men for company. Of course, it was about the drinking, but they were all married and miserable, always bitching about what pains in the asses their wives were. This felt like a contradiction since he'd loved my mother so much. Maybe, in his own sad and warped way, he wanted to connect with married life in any way he could. Or trick himself into thinking he was better off single.

The men's meetings were conducted at a different member's house each month. On this evening, it was my dad's turn to play host. Other than the partying, I had no idea what else went on during a gathering.

"Evaporate once people start showing up," my father snarled through one corner of his mouth as he stocked the bar with armfuls of liquor bottles.

His dismissal was a gift. The last thing I wanted was to hang with his band of belching drunks. That wasn't to say I couldn't tell what was happening downstairs. From the sound of it, the drinks were pouring, and the livers were screaming for mercy. As the laughter grew louder and the language got worse, I knew it wouldn't be long before these men would be stupidly smashing into each other and making bigger fools of themselves. I was just relieved to sequester myself and get some homework done.

Until my father flung open my bedroom door. My head shot up from my homework, and his glassy, bloodshot eyes stared back at me. He had a strange grin splashed across his face—one part gremlin, one part predator—which raised the hairs on the back of my neck.

"Hey," he said through a weird and silly giggle, "why don't you come downstairs and meet the guys?"

I gave him a wary look.

"Come on!" he pressed, giggles now morphing into smarmy laughter. He aimed a thumb toward the door and added, "I just want to introduce you to everyone!"

My father had made it clear he didn't want me anywhere near his friends, so this sudden reversal felt ominous and full of wrong signals. Was he setting me up?

"I'm tired, Dad," I said, "and I have three more chapters to read if I want to get to bed on time."

"It'll only take a few damned minutes!" he said, practically barking at me.

The choice was no longer mine. When I got downstairs, the crowd appeared amiable, even mellow. I saw drooping heads and hooded eyes. The night was drawing to a close.

"Hey, guys!" my dad said, slapping my back hard enough to make my lungs burn. "This is my boy! Griffin! Say hi to everyone, Griffin!"

I wrestled up a cardboard smile and nodded my greeting.

"He's a good kid … well, most of the time."

Laughter from the group.

Most of the time? He had never allowed me to defy him.

"Man, I know how that is," one of the men spoke up, confiding to my father. "Boys can be a real pain in the ass at that age. Gotta keep 'em in line. Right?"

"Oh, trust me, I do," my dad agreed. "He gives me his share of grief. I swear, they should slap this kid's picture on every box of condoms in the country as a warning."

The group roared.

My father managed to make it worse when he broke into hysterical laughter, eyes tearing up as he bent over and hugged his stomach. He was so proud of himself for what he thought was terribly clever instead of terribly heartless. The other men joined in, too, laughing harder, a few even howling.

I didn't laugh, didn't play along. Everything in the room disappeared, and all that remained was my searing misery. I bowed my head and concentrated on the carpet. I was trapped, wanted to dig a hole in the floor and crawl through it. But there was no escaping this kind of humiliation, no getaway car to take me off to a better place, and running from the room would just give them more fuel.

It was the worst thing my father had ever said to me, but what took my pain to the next level was seeing the men in hysterics. Not once had any of them considered how much this brief moment of entertainment would cost me.

Screw them. Without further thought, I grabbed my running shoes and pulled them on while the men filed out through the front door, continuing to laugh it up.

"Good one, Sam!" one of them said, sniggering like any of the teenaged assholes in my high school's hallways.

While tying my laces, I turned my head toward the kitchen where Deena stood, casually scooping ice cream into a bowl. Apparently, my father's warning to evaporate hadn't applied to her. She snapped the lid back on the ice cream container, but when she opened the fridge, our gazes met, and she froze, eyes big and round, probably because she'd been licking her spoon and listening to every word while our father tortured me in front of a live audience.

Her expression changed. She didn't look alarmed anymore; she looked—I don't know what it was, but it felt like the room's temperature had dropped about ten degrees.

What had I just seen?

I needed to get out of that house before it sucked the life from me.

I ran through a trench of darkness and past the cluster of inebriated men, fumbling for keys and stumbling into their cars.

When I reached the road, I took off, racing myself for freedom. I kept pushing myself harder—ramping up the pace and surging across the sidewalks and intersections—moving so fast that the slightest misstep could have sent me flying across the pitted asphalt. My lungs felt like a blast furnace, sending flames up my windpipe, but I didn't care. I'd dropped into some numb, altered state where nothing felt real anymore, not even my pain.

The sound of roaring motors grew louder as the men from my father's party came up behind me. Normally, my instinct would be to run faster and get off the road to keep safe. But I didn't do either. I allowed my feet to slow until pulling to a stop. I walked into the middle of the road, then turned around to face oncoming traffic, spreading my arms out like wings and daring them to hit me.

Darkened windshields rushed toward me, brakes squealed, and high beams flicked up. Horns yowled in protestation, mounting in intensity. When the first car got close, I locked myself into place, then stepped to one side as it zoomed past me. Another car came fast on its heels, and I did the same thing. Two more cars approached, but this time I didn't move. I kept my arms extended while they squealed and girdled around me. The vehicles kept coming, and I kept playing my deadly game of chicken.

Eventually, another car came my way, but this one skidded onto the shoulder just before slamming into me. The street snapped from chaos to stillness, the dissonance snaring me. I remained in place. The car's engine turned off, and the door yawned open. The high beams stayed on, leaving me unable to make out the vehicle or driver.

My father zigzagged toward me, loose gravel crunching beneath his loafers. Someone had probably called to let him know that his son had lost his mind and was up the road, dancing with death. The whites of his eyes were so red, they looked as though they were bleeding from their sockets. Not a muscle on his face moved. He didn't speak—not at first—the only thing coming from him, the sickening, squeaky sound of teeth gnashing. I kept my gaze locked into his, holding to the gritty silence.

"You fucking bastard," he whispered.

I gave no response, but I had a sense that he was more wary of me than angry after I'd acted like an out-of-control lunatic in public. Then, his expression changed. I had no way of knowing then that the exact look would come back to haunt me decades later—the same look I'd see after he hit me with his car. But having nearly died loosened something in me, maybe my temper or maybe an overlooked truth that he didn't have as much power over me as I'd thought.

He broke his gaze, got back into his car, and drove away.

The road was calm, thick with darkness, and it was easy to imagine I was the only person left on earth. I walked home, the shock over what I'd just done at last pouring into my mind from whichever place I'd stuffed it—with that came a piercing sense of dread. I'd never done anything like this before and, until tonight, never imagined I could. But something had woken up within me, something commanding, more powerful than my will. Something that frightened me because I'd never experienced such power and strength. Would it come back again now that I'd unleashed it?

My father had broken me in front of his friends.

Had I just done the same to him?

19

I WISHED I COULD PULL the tapes, hit the reset button, and do things right.

I wouldn't have blown up at Deena or pushed Trish away when she offered to help. I'd walked myself into the same tight spot I was trying to avoid. Like sticky, poisonous sap, my family drama had seeped into our relationship. I needed to figure out how to keep my past from destroying the present along with all the progress I'd made since leaving my father's house years ago.

Do you really want to be getting phone calls at all hours of the day and night whenever something goes wrong?

The benefit of time had me reconsidering what Trish had said. Whether I liked it or not, wherever my father ended up, I'd be his only family contact, and they'd never leave me alone. Could paying for a better facility keep him out of my life for good? I thought about that some more. My father had been a successful partner in his law firm, making boatloads of money. He'd probably blown a good part of that on booze, but did he lose *all* of it? He must have had assets at one point, an IRA, 401(k), or a pension plan. The idea was a moonshot but worth investigating.

A few other possibilities: my father was just old enough to start getting Social Security. I'd have to see if those funds were available. Also, did he have health insurance? If he did, was it enough to combine with Medicare to cover a better facility? According to Nolan, my father had been paying his rent up to a point—that money had to come from somewhere. True, it was nothing close to those lion-sized mortgage payments on the McMansion I'd grown up in, but it was something. Looking at Nolan's text, the apartment was in North Park, now in the midst of a gentrification upswing, but there was no telling which end of that seesaw he ended up on.

You should stop by.

As promised, Nolan left a key under my dad's doormat.

One thing was certain. This place hadn't received word about North Park's upswing. Dark bands of rust trailed down cracked, washed-out stucco, and the splintering gray roof shakes should have been replaced a while ago. I gazed up at the dusty, tattered window screens and shook my head. My father's income wasn't what I'd hoped.

More questions. This apartment building was a good thirty minutes from where he and I had crashed. What was he doing so close to the coast? Trying to visit our old house? With his dementia, did *he* even understand why he'd gone there?

The moment I entered his apartment, the stench of spoiled food and other nasty and nonspecific odors assaulted my senses. A clutter of junk spread out before me like some gaudy swap meet. A sad metaphor for my father's crash-and-burn life.

I did my best to maneuver through the piles, eyeing a few as I progressed. I was looking at a semi-organized mess. Each clump seemed separated from the next and organized by category. A pile of alarm clocks, a pile of highlighter markers, a pile of calendars, wristwatches, rulers, and other peculiar items.

What did he buy, like, ten of everything?

I stepped into the kitchen, sink piled high with so many dishes that more had to be pushed off to one side and stacked on the countertop. I blocked my nose with the inside of my elbow as I opened the refrigerator door, preparing for the wave of putrefaction likely to follow. But when the light flickered on, there was no food, just rows of water bottles, each precisely lined up on the shelf, each with a Band-Aid stuck to its side.

What in the world?

I closed the fridge. When I opened his pantry door, the mystery of where that horrid odor had been coming from was solved. Scattered across the shelves were a slew of opened canned goods, lids curled up, many with spoons sticking out of them. Some had only a few smears of food while others were partially full. Flies buzzed in and out. Ants crawled from the cans, then formed a perfect single-file line up the pantry wall.

Who is this man?

Nobody I knew. The thought of my father standing in the middle of the pantry and eating food from a can was not only terribly sad; it was oppositional to the father I had grown up with, a man who enjoyed fine meals and a certain amount of ceremony while eating them. A man who wore custom suits and scoffed at the idea of flying coach. But even while smashed, he'd never resorted to this. I could almost call it poetic justice, but as much as I wanted to, I couldn't. I wouldn't have wished this squalor on any human.

I was about to close the pantry, but a sparkling object on the top shelf caught my eye. When I pulled it down, an elusive memory came with it. This was Deena's elementary school Father's Day gift project, a clay paperweight, covered in silver glitter except for the one spot where she'd scratched in, *The world's best father.*

I must have missed that day.

I was surprised that he'd held on to this, but I guess even the pawn shop had standards.

Down the hall, a spare bedroom looked as though it had been made into a makeshift office space. Nothing on the walls, not unless you counted the filmy smudges around the light switch and doorknob. I would have described the furniture as less than minimalist: a tiny, no-drawers aluminum desk sat crammed against the wall. A mismatched filing cabinet was parked beside it. I opened the top drawer to have a look but didn't find any files; instead, it was crammed with laundry. Filthy socks, filthy underwear, and filthy shirts, all covered in stains.

I sighed.

The bottom drawer wasn't any better, loaded with dirty silverware, and lots of it, so full that a few utensils fell out and tumbled onto the mustard-colored carpet. In his confused state, had my father mistaken the filing cabinet for a washing machine and dishwasher? I closed the drawer, then searched the desktop, but there was nothing of interest. No paperwork. No laptop. Zilch. If my father had any savings put away, he hadn't been doing much to keep track of it.

As expected, the bedroom was also a mess. The bedsheets looked as though they hadn't been washed in months, stained by food and other things I did not want to know about.

This place is a petri dish.

Anyone living in these conditions deserved pity. It wasn't my father I felt sorry for, I kept telling myself. It was the situation. A shred of intuition protested the notion, but I pushed it away.

A framed photo of my mother sat on top of the dresser, which I remembered watching Dad take sometime during the Before. He'd surprised Mom with the car of her dreams: a fully restored cherry-red 1965 Mustang with a cream-colored ragtop, just like her father had once owned. Having been raised by a mechanic, he had been able to bring it up from the dust and make it like new again. Some of Mom's fondest memories were cruising up the Malibu Coast with her father, the radio blasting while they sang along to "Everybody Wants to Rule the World" by Tears for Fears. Now, here she sat in her own Mustang, top down and waving at the camera with one of the biggest smiles I'd seen on her. My breath caught. In that moment, I missed her more than ever.

I left the picture—and the painful memory—on the dresser.

When I entered the hallway, what I saw made me flinch. A framed photo of me stared back at me. It was from an edition of *The Hollywood Report Magazine* a few years back. They'd interviewed me after I'd won my second Primetime Emmy, this one for Outstanding Character Voice-Over Performance. I had the recurring role of Ben in an adult animated program called *Meeting the Francos.*

I stared at my reflection superimposed over the picture glass. The disconnect between my father's place and my new life felt so disorienting that, for a few seconds, I forgot where I was standing. *The Hollywood Report* didn't exactly sit on grocery store shelves near the checkout line. It was a trade magazine, so I wondered how my father knew about this article. Had he been following my career for all these years? I felt a burn in my chest. He didn't get to enjoy my success. He didn't deserve it.

I'd seen enough here. All I wanted to do now was leave. But farther down the hallway, I stumbled upon another shitty memory. Displayed on a little table was a frame—that was it, nothing else—that held a photo I hadn't seen in years but knew all too well. It was the portrait my father and I took that long-ago summer day on our way out of the Del Mar Fairgrounds. My mind swelled with more cottony disorientation, now mixed with more sadness, more anger—probably many other things, too—and I couldn't gain traction on any of it.

What in the hell is with this place?

Had he still cared about that day? For a brief moment, so did I, and then I forced the feeling away. I lifted the picture and brought it in closer. As the details got sharper, the memories did too, along with a hitch of sadness over having to let them go so I could survive the years that would follow. Tears formed, but I wiped them away before they had a chance to fall. Not only did I remember us taking that photo—I could feel the moment: bliss and innocence now polluted by hate and resentment. Something deep within me gave way. A sensation in my body I couldn't identify that felt almost ugly, like a half-healed wound tearing open. As I tried to get a handle on it, I kept staring at the photo in my hand, and that's when I noted the frame. Clowns and balloons surrounded the picture with the words, *HAPPY BIRTHDAY, STEVEN!* written in blue cursive across the bottom. Could my father recognize the absurdity? Was this the juvenile encapsulation of a mind turned inside out?

Familiar anger slid in again, a relief. First came his love, and then he cut it away with his sharp-edged abuse. Could this have been the real reason why Nolan urged me to come here? Hoping I'd see those photos and shake off the long-established belief that my father had taken pleasure in breaking me? If he was trying to sell me that, I wasn't buying. Life didn't work that way. You can't scratch out the past with magazine covers and old photos.

Again, I looked at the picture.

I'm not taking it with me.

Even if it was physical proof that love once existed between my father and me, it also represented the loss of it.

With a spike of anger, I slammed it face down onto the table.

20

I WANTED TO RUN FOR the shower. Wash it all off.

A Griffin McCabe shrine? What was *that* all about?

My father had loathed me. I was a spoiled leftover from his life with the woman he'd loved. Walking into my father's place now was like stumbling into a funhouse—minus the fun—populated with a maze of distorted mirrors and no clear way out

Or was it a shrine of regret?

After all, the man had lost his entire family; that seemed to be his fault, but had he at last felt guilt over it?

I walked down the concrete stairwell and coughed, overwhelmed by the pong of an overcooked microwave dinner, knotted with strong perfume. As I neared the apartment courtyard, footsteps approached quickly from behind. I turned around. An older gentleman speed-walked my way, flailing his arms and trying to flag me down.

Nolan Laseur was a tall, slender man, older, likely approaching his seventies. He sported a button-down shirt with a tiny plaid pattern of tan and red. His silvery hair was parted to one side with such precision that it almost looked as though it was sliced into place, and his nose was one step shy of aquiline.

"Griffin! Hi!" he yelled, coming at me. "I knew it was you. Seen the photos."

Photos? I'd only seen one of me as an adult. Were there more that I'd missed? All I could think was, *How much does this man know about the history between my father and me?*

Nolan added, "And he spoke of you a lot, too."

There was no time to be suspicious. This man probably had some information I needed. Namely, how I could wrangle enough cash to be done with my father.

Before I could respond, a female neighbor about the same age as Nolan waved solidly at me. "Hi there, Griffin!" She changed direction, then fast-tracked it my way. The woman was beaming and staring, and I wanted her to go away right now. "I'm Suzy!" she said, sounding weirdly excited, considering we'd never met. "Your dad and I are good friends!"

A snick of disgust tugged through me. None of these people had ever seen the real Sam McCabe. I thought back to his celebrated career as a passionate, smooth-talking lawyer who could convince anyone— including Ryan—that he was the good guy.

Suzy got way too close, then smiled into my face. Suzy was a space hog. I retreated back a few steps to take in her long, wolfish features and narrow, almond-shaped eyes. She was tall: I was a hair over six feet, and she could almost look me in the eye.

Nolan must have sensed my uneasiness. "Your father is very well-liked around here, Griffin."

"Did he give away lots of free legal advice or something?" My comment shot out so fast, it bypassed better judgment, and as expected, the joke flatlined.

Nolan cleared his throat. They were both staring, but this time, nobody was grinning. Suzy tilted her head almost completely sideways.

"So awful, what's happening with your dad," she said with a big, sad face. "Such a sweet man."

Who were these people? Acolytes from some cheerfully menacing cult? The Cult of Sam?

"It's nice to meet you, Suzy," I told her, then turned to Nolan. "Would you mind if we chat? I have a few questions I'd like to ask about my father."

"Certainly." Nolan pointed to a picnic table near the stairwell. "We can sit right over there."

Suzy headed off, and Nolan and I walked to the table.

"Oh, before I forget," Nolan said once we settled into our seats. "I found a guy who can clean and clear out your dad's apartment if it comes to that. There will be a fee, and you'll need to figure out where to store or donate his belongings. I can get you the estimate, if you want."

"That would be wonderful," I said, thankful it would free me from having to come back here again. "So …" I rested my hands on the table. "I'm a little confused about something."

Nolan raised his chin, giving me his full attention.

"When I went through my father's apartment, I saw a few strange items—several of them. For one, there were all these water bottles in the fridge, and each had a Band-Aid stuck to it."

"Oh, yes. That …" he said with a fraught expression. "The more your father's dementia progressed, the more time he kept losing. I think the bottles were some kind of system he'd devised, using the decreasing water levels with Band-Aids to mark the days, or the hours, or whatever."

"Did it work?"

"I doubt it." Nolan shook his head and scratched his temple a few times. "It was more a desperate thing."

"Which also explains the piles of clocks, wristwatches, and calendars?"

Nolan's smile was sad. "Probably."

Do not get sucked into feeling sorry for the Monster. Don't do it. Nolan only knows one side of him.

A change of topic was the best way to avoid that trap. "So, it looks like my father will need to be transferred into a memory care facility."

"I was kind of hoping for that."

"I'm just wondering, do you know if he had any sources of income that could help pay the cost?"

"I'm afraid that all went dry. Blew most of his pension. The drinking, you know."

"Health insurance?"

"He stopped paying the premiums a few years back."

"What about Medicare or Social Security?"

"He told me that because of his pension and the way his firm set things up, he wouldn't be getting much from Medicare. As for Social Security payments, he decided to wait for seventy. It's sad. For the first time in seven years, he started falling short on rent a few times, but each time, I covered it." Nolan paused, giving his comment further consideration. "Please don't mention that to anyone, though. I could lose my job."

"Of course."

"About the money." Nolan stopped for a moment. "There may be one thing that could help. Your dad paid cash for his Mercedes when he had the money, so it's free and clear and sitting down in his carport. It *is* a few years old, but you may get several thousand dollars for it."

"What about the accident damage?"

"Got it taken care of. It wasn't as major as I'd expected, just a lot of external damage, and my son-in-law owns a body shop. He did me a favor and fixed it up. I've been starting it up once a week to keep the battery from dying. I knew your father wouldn't be capable of driving again, but I figured I could at least help him sell it."

Nolan was probably the only true friend my father had left. But it looked as though any hope I had for coming up with the money to pay for health care was shrinking. By the look on his face, he and I both knew that the old Mercedes would only be a temporary solution to a permanent problem.

I offered him a weak smile before jumping to the next topic. "Do you know when my father stopped drinking?"

"That's a bit complicated." Nolan leaned back a few inches, then gazed past me, as though searching for a thought. "So ... I'm a recovering alcoholic myself. Been sober for twenty years. That's why your dad and I hit it off well."

I thought about the car accident and how my father had no alcohol in his system. "Was he in recovery, too?"

Nolan spoke through his sigh. "It's not that simple, Griffin. Your father tried to get sober several times before the Alzheimer's started. Even came with me to a few AA meetings."

"Did it work?"

"Oh, for a little while, but then he'd relapse. Sam wanted to stop, and we all wanted that for him. It was sad, seeing him cycle over and over, but that's not so uncommon. I've sponsored several people through the years and seen this happen more times than I can count. But during those breaks when the other residents and I got to know your dad, we could see that beneath all the alcohol was a good man. A different person."

I shifted my weight in the chair but kept my remarks to myself.

"I know you won't believe me, but he cared about everyone here. You know how people can be in this city with their pretty faces and fake smiles, but if you stumble on the pavement? They'll turn their heads in an instant. Griffin, I'm telling you, he wasn't like that. If you casually mentioned a problem you were having, he'd come back a few days later with a solution. Need milk? He'd drop it off at your door that night without a word."

Resentment prodded at me. Where had that guy been twenty years ago? Had he even once thought about getting sober back then?

"We all became your father's friends." Nolan's comment touched down in the middle of my thought. "This apartment complex is a tight community of old codgers like me. We take care of each other. Regardless of whether he was drinking or not, we did the same for him. As I'm sure you know, your father is a complicated man, but in the final count, he was trying hard to escape his suffering. He wanted to do better."

"But he kept drinking, you said."

"No, he *did* eventually stop."

"But you—"

"Just not the way most people do." He paused for a long time before looking me in the eye. "It's like this. He forgot he drank."

For a few seconds, I thought I'd misheard him. My father never forgot to do anything when it came to his drinking. He would have brushed his teeth with bourbon if he could.

"You have to understand," Nolan continued. "I'm talking about years. First, it was the small things, like leaving his apartment door open with the keys still in it, then, eventually, the memory loss got bigger and bigger. He'd forget that he ran out of booze or where he'd stashed his emergency bottle. As the dementia progressed, he'd get lost on his way to the liquor store. Often, when he did find one, they were already closed. Your father's drinking rituals were interrupted by his own failing mind."

I shifted in my seat. Memories of driving my father to Liquor Emporium in the middle of the night clouded my mind with dark fright, but I abandoned the recollection as best I could. "What about alcohol withdrawal?"

"Nope. None. It was a slow process."

"An unconventional way to get off the bottle."

"But it worked. It was like someone took him by the hand and led him away from addiction." Nolan drew a long, deep breath, and it came out just as slow. "If only he'd found his way back sooner. It would have been great to see him rally and find the happiness in life he'd wanted, but the dementia didn't do his sobriety any good. It was all too late."

Too late by more than twenty years.

"That Alzheimer's was a blessing and a curse," Nolan told me. "A giver and a thief. It made him sober, but in the end, he was worse off than when he'd begun."

My father loved everybody here, and everybody loved him. My father had stayed sober long enough to develop meaningful relationships with people. My father showed everyone a kinder, more affable side of himself.

But all I'd gotten from him was the bloody end of the stick.

21

IT WAS ONE OF THE few occasions when I saw my father sober.

He'd invited his coworkers to the house for a holiday dinner party. Since my dad had never seen the inside of an oven, he hired caterers to cook and serve dinner, and, man, did he go all out. He ordered the baked ham, the turkey, the delicious side dishes—heirloom zucchini with fresh herbs, cheese smashed potatoes—and much more. Our house hadn't smelled so good since my mother was around.

In an odd twist, my father wanted Deena and me to attend. It was likely just for appearances, but since he couldn't afford to get tanked-up in front of coworkers, I felt safe venturing downstairs to enjoy the delicious food. With him on his best behavior, I hoped to get a rare glimpse of the old dad I'd loved. And I did. When the guests arrived, he was as charming as could be, making them laugh and smile.

"Oh, Corrine," he said to one of his coworkers, "I can see why everyone at work loves you so much!"

And, "Vic, how did you get to be so smart?"

"Hey, Sal, can I get them to fix a plate to take home with you? No, it's no trouble at all!"

Seeing him like this made me miss the Before. And for once, I enjoyed the After. Thick, creamy eggnog poured into glass mugs, Christmas music played in the background, and the rich smell of roasted turkey and sweet potatoes—along with the perfect hint of nutmeg—made our house feel more like a home than it had in years.

But, as they say, some things never change. As the evening progressed, so did his "social" drinking. He wasn't sloshed enough to cause any problems—not yet—but he was on his way. My father was a pro at this game. He knew how to pace himself and keep from making a scene in front of people he needed to impress. Since he'd been priming the pump all evening long, he wouldn't have to play catch-up on his drinking once everyone left—a skill I never wanted to master.

As the conversation loosened up after dinner, my father's coworkers were thrilled to meet his children, and several came up to me to start conversations. A paralegal in her mid-twenties, named Jen Stevens, was especially sweet. I also felt the stirrings of an immediate crush: she was a striking brunette with long hair and high cheekbones in a sparkling midnight-blue evening dress. Jen was a sight for a boy my age and judging by my father's reaction, she was a sight for him, too. He spent the evening circling back to her, chatting it up and trying hard not to allow his eyes to wander down toward her breasts; although, those eyes got away from him a few times.

As the evening wore on, the crowd grew more serene, most of them full and happy, carrying on quiet conversations with each other. I was finishing my pumpkin pie when Jen materialized in the empty chair beside me.

"You must be Griffin," she said with a kind smile. "Your father talks about you and your sister often."

For a moment, I thought she was putting me on or just trying to make pleasant conversation, but her earnest expression told me she was serious. If my father was talking about me at work, I couldn't imagine him doing anything other than bitching about what a pain in the ass I was.

"Really?" I leaned in to make sure I could hear her well. "What does he say?"

"Oh, you know, how proud he is of you and all."

In what solar system did my father have anything nice to say about me? There was none, so I decided he'd been grandstanding to impress Jen and look like the awesome father he wasn't.

In a fog of confusion, my vision zoomed across the room to my dad who had been observing Jen and me with a keen eye. But he didn't appear amused—not at all. It was a look of disapproval, shadowed by an undertone of resentment, which flagged potential danger. I felt a hint of dread coming on.

"So, what do you do for fun, Griffin?"

I bounced back to Jen. Despite my bewilderment, I did my best to be conversational. I told her about school, the track team, and surfing.

"Oh, wow!" she said. "I used to surf all the time!"

Now, she'd recaptured my attention. Through the years, I'd known a few female surfers. While some of the guys dismissed and marginalized the girls, I loved hanging out with them. They seemed more laid-back, less competitive, and were a lot of fun to be around. Some were better surfers than the guys, although none of them bragged about it.

"I loved going down to Windansea Beach." Jen laughed. "It was my favorite place to surf."

"Mine, too!"

"Oh, the stories I could tell you, Griffin." She raised her hands in the air, palms out, and rolled her eyes. "But I'm sure you have plenty of your own. I bet we could talk about it all night long."

I was sure we could. Jen was super cool, and as we continued to talk, I found out she knew a lot about surfing technique and that we both knew the same pro surfers. Talk about an oppositional shift. For the first time in a while, I was having fun in my own house. It was awesome.

Until it wasn't.

Through the crowd, I spotted my father vulturing around us. It was creepy the way he kept materializing in different parts of the room, always with those hooded, bloodshot eyes trained on us. Since his alcohol level was on the rise, I knew he was on the verge of getting unpredictable.

Why does he have to ruin everything?

I turned back to continue my discussion with Jen, creating more distance between us, fearing that anything less might inspire the vulture to swoop in.

A minute or so later, my father's head popped up between Jen and me like a carnival Whack-A-Mole. My knee-jerk response was to jump out of his way. But as I observed him talking it up with Jen, the truth crystalized: it ate at him to see his teenage son getting more attention from a beautiful, young woman than he could.

He took a step back and started dancing to the music.

Good Lord. No, he is not.

Holding the drink almost completely overhead, his body moved out of sync against the kicky beat. I wanted to scratch my eyes out so I wouldn't have to look at it any longer, and then he stepped up his jam, almost showering us with bourbon as it swirled over the glass's rim.

"Come on, Jen!" he said, out of breath. "It's Christmas! Don't be afraid to have a little fun!"

Jen forced a compliant smile, but her eyes were shifting from side to side as if searching for the closest window to crawl out of. It was the most pitiable thing I'd ever seen. This fleshy, middle-aged man had barged in and made a total ass of himself, trying to impress a woman half his age. Not only did he embarrass himself—he embarrassed Jen and me, too.

"Hey, son," he said, still dancing with a strange mix of put-on humility and cheer. "The caterers are cleaning up in the kitchen. Would you mind helping them out? I'd really appreciate it!"

My dinner repeated on me when I thought about leaving poor Jen alone with my idiot dad. But I had no choice: the idiot had spoken, and I'd suffer later if I didn't obey.

I retreated, but as I gained distance from my father, his motivations became clearer. Although my socializing with Jen was innocent, my drunk, insecure father saw me as a threat to his masculinity. He'd gotten angry at me on more occasions than I could count, but this? This moved the goalpost miles off-center, catching me off guard.

So, too, did the swift knock I got to the side of my head after the last guest left. And this: "Get out of my sight. I can't stand to look at you."

I complied, trying to put as much distance between us as possible.

"You were so far out of that woman's league, it wasn't even funny!" he shouted as I began climbing the staircase. "And you don't even have enough fucking brains to realize how badly you embarrassed yourself in front of everyone!"

When I looked back at him, something dark moved through those eyes. Something scornful and unforgiving.

Something that told me my life might be even worse after this.

22

IT HAD BEEN ABOUT A week since Ryan's name had come up or my father's living circumstances, but it almost felt as though Trish was steering away from those topics to maintain peace between us. We pretended as if everything were okay, but she appeared a bit more closed off, less engaging, and when we spoke, it seemed as if she'd already left the room. It was like surfing with noodle arms, an aggressive curl at my back, ready to swallow me up.

Meanwhile, I'd been trying to prepare for my upcoming audition for *Funland Falls,* spending hours on the internet and trying to find out everything about Wingate and the project. I also got my copy of the script with director's notes. The story was about a young man named Jack, who befriends a wise old polar bear named Peechya—that was to be me—at the city zoo. Jack and Peechya take off on an imaginary journey, exploring the vast rivers and waterfalls of Antarctica. Along the way, Peechya teaches Jack about the challenges and thrills in life. It was a beautiful, heartwarming story, and I couldn't wait to dig into the role. I practiced my lines, and I thought of how the gig could be a windfall. We hadn't talked money yet, but the studio had plenty of cash, and I knew what roles like this fetched. That could help pay for my father's care.

I crossed San Clemente on the way back from LA when my cell rang. As soon as I recognized Deena's number, my nerves bristled. I wasn't only shocked she was calling; I questioned *why* she was calling. After the way we'd left things, she likely wasn't reaching out with an invitation to come over to paint rocks and have a buoyant brother-sister chitchat. I didn't know if I had enough energy left to defend myself if she wanted to give me a piece of her mind after having more time to think about my temperamental exit from the pier. The call could go to voice mail, but since I'd wished for a do-over and since our father was broke, this could be a last chance.

"Hi, Deena," I said, using the most generous tone I could summon.

"Hi, Griffin," she said, sounding less guarded than before. "I was wondering if we could meet somewhere to talk."

"I don't want to fight with you anymore, Deena."

"I don't want that, either."

At least we agreed on one thing. Best to get this over with. Spending another day thinking what she was up to would only bring more uncertainty. I checked my watch and glimpsed the GPS. Traffic looked light for this hour, so I told her I was almost back in San Diego and could see her in about an hour.

We met at Baja Beach Cafe in Pacific Beach, a seashore bar that served casual California cuisine: carne asada fries, quesadillas, and fish tacos. But you didn't have to look at a menu to know that: the mouthwatering smell of grilled chipotle and onions sailed on the ocean breeze along the boardwalk like an invitation.

Deena had arrived early again. She sat on the outdoor patio, sipping iced tea and looking out at swollen tides as they poured across the shoreline. She'd never been early while growing up, but she was a lot of things today that she hadn't been then: more confident, more buttoned-up.

She greeted me with a penciled-in smile, but this time it didn't register as icy, more with a hint of uncertainty—a difference from our last encounter when she could barely stand to look at me. Also different: her outfit was more casual than before, distressed skinny jeans with holes above the knees, an untucked pink button-down oxford, and a pair of white slip-on Vans sneakers. This was the Deena I used to know. Yet, in spite of that, she remained as much a stranger as ever. With her firewall lowered, her hostility less biting, it was easier to see that Deena had grown up to be radiant. She had always gotten attention from her classmates, but now she'd developed self-assurance and poise.

The waiter stopped to take my order.

"You still drink those, huh?" she said when my Diet Mountain Dew arrived.

I took a sip and swirled the sweet yellowy liquid inside for her to see. "Old habits and all that."

A mother, father, and their two children passed by on the sand. The boy threw an arm around his sister's shoulder, and then they giggled and acted silly while the parents smiled.

I turned to my sister. "Deena, I feel like I owe you an apology. I shouldn't have gotten so angry at you last time. I know we've had our differences, but that's no excuse for my shitty behavior."

She kept her eyes on her glass while turning it in place. The confidence behind her expression faded, hinting at the sister I recognized from childhood.

"About all that. There's something I need to tell you, Griffin."

Her distressed tone of voice made it evident that she hadn't called me here to impart anything good. I braced myself for it.

"What I mentioned at the pier?" she said, repeatedly stroking the inside of her arm, an old, nervous habit I'd forgotten about until just now. "How you only know half of the story about Dad and me?" She locked her gaze onto mine. "You weren't the only one he abused, Griffin."

I heard the words, but they refused to land. My mind felt swampy, my reasoning out of whack, and it took a few beats to say, "I ... I don't underst—"

"It happened to me, too," she restated.

"But ..." I paused and shook my head, and in a near whisper, I said, "How come I never saw anything?"

"Because my abuse was a secret."

"I don't like where this is going, Deena. Did he—"

"No, not that."

I felt an ounce of relief. "Okay. But tell me. Please."

Deena locked her fingers together and looked out at the ocean. When she came back to me, she struggled to find words, and I saw the same girl who stared at me from the kitchen that night during my father's men's club meeting with the same unreadable expression. Only this time, I read it.

Fear.

"You always thought I was his favorite because you never saw how he treated me," Deena said, "and from your perspective, it probably looked that way. But you and I spent so much time apart, and his behavior was so cunning that you missed a lot of what *did* happen."

"I'm not sure I—"

"What I'm telling you is that I wasn't his favorite at all. I was his *nothing*."

I squared my shoulders and leveled my gaze on her. "What does that mean?"

"He bought me whatever I wanted, occasionally spoke to me, but that was it. As far as he was concerned, I was invisible. He'd literally walk out of the room while I was mid-sentence, and he never looked me in the eyes. It was like I was this soulless ghost, wandering through that house." She stopped herself as if experiencing the powerful force of that agony all over again. "I remember one time, I was in the family room. Without even looking my way, he took a seat in his recliner, then pointed toward the door, ordering me out. I guess I didn't deserve any words. But he *was* more aggressive at times, too. I remember when he purposely shoved a hip into my side while trying to get past me. I know how weird this is going to sound, Griffin, but I was actually envious of you sometimes. At least he acknowledged you. I guess in the mind of a screwed-up kid, it can feel like getting any attention, good or bad, is better than feeling nonexistent."

Something in me fluttered with unease. And shock. I couldn't find my next words—they were buried somewhere deep inside with no way to grasp them. How had I missed the tells? Deena was right. Most of the time, we'd barely spent more than a few minutes around each other. And I was so busy trying to survive my own abuse, it was possible that, much like my father, I'd never paid enough attention to her. Trish had been right when she'd said that dysfunctional families often missed a lot of cues while looking in the other direction whether intentionally or not.

"We never got a chance to defend each other," I said.

"It wouldn't have made a difference. I couldn't get him to look at me, let alone listen or take anything I said seriously. But, Griffin, I did try. Do you remember that one day when Dad was going off on you in the backyard? I think we were about twelve. You'd just gotten home, and you were all excited about some project at school."

"That rocket I'd made … yeah." The memory surfaced. I could almost smell the model glue that was starting to dry, its strong, acerbic smell melding with the odor of fresh red spray paint.

"Dad went on the attack, yelling at you for talking too loudly or being too excited or whatever the hell it was."

My hands closed around the arm of my chair.

Deena went on, "I walked into the yard and saw the whole thing happen. When you ran inside, all I could think was that you weren't doing anything wrong. It made me so angry that I decided to speak up. Well, that was the one time he *did* pay attention to me, but it wasn't the kind I wanted. Not at all. For the rest of the afternoon, he kept fixating on me. It was creepy, Griffin. And frightening. Those cold, piercing blue eyes …"

The skin on my back turned frigid. I knew the look she was describing. Flinty. Heartless. I just never had any idea that she'd experienced it, too.

"That evening, he came into my bedroom, clenching something in his fist." Deena stopped. She stared vacantly ahead, lost in the retelling of her story. "At first, I thought it was a piece of cardboard, but when he got closer, I saw that it was a curled-up newspaper. He took a seat on the edge of my bed and told me to come closer. At first, I didn't move—I couldn't—scared about what he'd planned to do to me. But then he got angry and demanding. When I had enough courage to get closer, the heavy smell of booze nearly knocked me over. I'd never been so terrified in my life. He opened the paper to one page and pointed to a photo. It … I …" She stopped to find her breath. "It was absolutely horrifying, Griffin, the picture of a body that looked like it had been tossed onto the side of the road … and that headline … that awful headline. It read, 'Young Girl Found Murdered.' "

Deena's hands shook hard enough to make the table vibrate. She opened her mouth, but nothing came out, and then she said, "I … I … looked up at him, afraid he might tell me he was the killer or—I don't know the hell what. He didn't say that, but what came next was more terrifying. He told me, 'This is what happens to little girls who open their mouths too much.' "

The patio curled around me. My vision got soupy. My jaw locked. I could barely draw air. This was the stuff of nightmares—dark, revolting, unspeakable.

Sure, my father had abused me, but never once had I imagined that he'd been victimizing Deena at the same time, pitting us squarely against each other. Family resentments are difficult to break away from once they've been established, and my father knew that. It was probably his deepest hope that Deena and I would remain estranged and never figure out that we'd been played. He might have been a drunk, but he wasn't stupid. He'd engineered the entire relationship between his children, doing whatever he could to ensure those effects would be long-lasting.

I traveled back in time. When had the Monster truly come into being? I thought about that day at the fair when we had our portrait taken.

"You seem like a really nice guy, but someone could report you."

I hadn't had the depth of field to see it then, but now, the invisible ink had risen through the parchment. My father's intimidation tactics were right in front of me from the start, but I was so enamored with him and so young that I'd missed them. He had threatened to shut the photographer down if he didn't take our picture.

What else had I missed? Was my whole childhood a lie? Was the Before any different from the After?

"I never got between you guys again," Deena said with a defeated shrug. "I know how it looked, like I didn't care about what he did to you, but that was all an act. I was too afraid he might kill me." She stopped to take an uneven breath. "After that, I spent each day literally trying to stay alive. I became an actor—and a good one. Before long, my life started to feel like a performance, and I didn't know who I was anymore."

"My God, Deena."

It was one hell of a role for such a young girl to be forced to take on, let alone to keep it going for years. I was too young to recognize the real dynamics between Deena and me, but through the lens of an adult, it was clear. I'd also been an actor. And much like Deena, I'd been doing it all my life, first as a way to hide the fear from my father, then from the world. Now, I did it for a living: so well that, until this moment, I had believed my career was a fluke, a clean break from my former life and not just an extension of it.

"Of course," Deena said, "now, I know it was all his drunken attempt to scare and manipulate me. He wasn't a killer, and he wasn't going to murder me." Not a tear fell from my sister's eyes. Her lips were an angry red slash. "That … that goddamned *scumbag!*"

"The worst kind."

"It was why I tried to reach out to you once we left that house. I wanted to tell you what happened. Why I always seemed detached and kept my distance from you while growing up."

I looked skyward and shook my head, and my eyes got watery. "But I ignored you." Shame was all I could feel. Deep shame for adding another layer of pain to trauma that didn't need any more. I knew this wasn't my fault, but the effect was the same. I hurt her, and I hated it. "That's why you were so mad when I got back in touch with you."

"Not mad, more trying not to get hurt again." She sagged back into her chair and seemed to reflect on something. "The real anger was toward myself. I made you believe what I wanted you to believe. I destroyed us."

"You did nothing of the sort, Deena. *He* destroyed us."

She smiled with sorrow. Sorrow I could feel, so deep that it could cut through marrow.

"You had every right to be angry with me," I said. "*Damn it!* Then, I asked you for money to support him just to get him out of my own hair. I'm sorry, Deena. I'm sorry for not recognizing your pain. I should have noticed it. I should have seen *something*."

"You had no way of knowing. He made sure of it."

She was right about that, but I should have recognized her look of anguish that night in the kitchen. Anguish that spoke what she was too scared to say. But I was so busy being angry at her that I didn't take heed.

We were both running from my father, only in opposite directions.

23

I DROVE HOME, MY HEART heavy, my spirit shattered.

My sister had shown a side of herself I'd never before seen or even known existed. The real Deena. The one who, all along, had real feelings and real pain but who had been too terrified to show them. And even though my father had abused her in different ways, the results were the same: two damaged kids who were emotionally left for dead.

I had an inkling that my mother knew both sides of my father, but for the sake of her children, she had done everything she could to keep the darker one away from us. Once she'd died, there was nobody left to extinguish it.

And the drinking … Dad always drank, but looking back now, there were hints that my mother had seen him really drunk. I remember overhearing a conversation where Mom sternly told my father that there was room for only one love in his life, and she would not be second to the alcohol.

Deena also told me that our father had tried to reach out to her a few years after her college graduation. She'd torn into him, saying she never wanted to see him again. He was furious. Might that have been a reason why he never tried to contact me? In any case, it was definitely one of Deena's reasons for saying she wasn't willing to help pay for his care, nor was she open to having any kind of relationship with him. After hearing their history, I couldn't say I blamed her. I felt the same. Fortunately for Deena, the man hadn't slammed into her car, which afforded her the gift of staying away from him. For me, not so much. I'd been sawed into his life, and the only way out was to pay someone to take him off my hands.

My fists clenched the wheel.

I'd have to marry him into my finances, but I remained hopeful that *Funland Falls* might alleviate those worries, providing the cash flow to pay his expenses.

My cell went off, splitting me from my thoughts. I glanced at the screen. It was David, probably calling to firm up plans for *Funland Falls*. At last, a twinkle of light.

"Hey, what's up, David?"

He cleared his throat. "So, I got a call from Wingate. There have been a few changes I want to let you know about. It looks like the studio has decided to go in a different direction."

Different direction: the death knell in this industry.

"But you said it was practically a done deal."

"That's what they told me, Griffin. Word for word, but you know how Hollywood is. They said they love your work but, ultimately, didn't feel you'd be a good fit for this project."

"So, the Tinseltown kiss and kick. *Funland Falls* doesn't sound very fun anymore. I guess it was flattering to be considered, but it looks like Wingate fell out of love with me in short order."

David managed to scrape up a sympathetic laugh. "Maybe not. They did mention they may be interested in casting you for another animated feature. It may not be as big a role as *Funland Falls*, and the project is in development, but they sounded excited about it."

"I won't hold my breath—not unless asphyxiation is my new professional goal."

"But here's the thing, Griffin. Wingate *did* take notice of you. Coming from them, that's a pretty big deal. It may only be a case of delayed gratification, okay? Take whatever part they offer, then let them get to know you. You'll be laying the groundwork for something bigger down the road."

He was right. I'd seen it happen many times. It was just that, after all the muck with my father, then Deena, this was something I had wanted to look forward to. And to add to the insult, the chance to pay for my father's upgrade was gone, too.

"It'll be okay, Griffin. You know I've got your back."

I hung up, and dejection wrapped its arms around me.
Not like a hug.
Like the jaws of a vise grip.

24

TRISH'S FATHER, HUGH, WAS THE CEO of a major Southern California bank. The man had lots of money and a forty-foot yacht to prove it. He was a nice guy, just neurotic, and it surfaced in his very rigid ideas concerning ways of being around the ocean. He was insistent about participating in events near or on the water at one p.m.—not an hour earlier than that, even if the seas were quieter and the sun cooler—and he expected everyone else to go by those rules. He claimed it was the best part of the day because the coastal marine layer usually burned off by then, affording more sunshine to enjoy activities.

I never understood what the man was talking about. I'd been on the ocean my whole life, and the marine layer never had any effect on how much fun I or anyone else had. I knew from my surfer days that when you lived near the water, you learned to live by its terms. Besides, a little cloud cover never hurt anyone. But that was Hugh, always wanting to be in control, even over rival Neptune himself. In truth, I wondered if he just liked to be noticed near the water during mid-afternoon, when a larger crowd was out, enjoying the height of their day; although, it was hard to miss him in his yacht.

Hugh threw himself a birthday party each year aboard that boat, which never went anywhere for the occasion. He merely kept it docked at the marina while he entertained onboard with a wet bar, caterers, and waiters. The event wasn't my favorite, and it had felt forced ever since Trish's brother died and the subsequent divorce, but he insisted that "traditions are healthy!"

So, when the time came for this year's celebration, I cringed inwardly. Call it *my* personal tradition. What I liked least of all was what these events did to Trish. Maybe that was why I hadn't yet told her about losing the Wingate job. I worried it would only add to her stress at the party.

She insisted that we arrive at the parking lot fifteen minutes early so we'd be ready to board the boat by one p.m. In no other part of her life did she ever automatically do what she was told, but this was her father's world, and in it, the bylaws were different. Trish's dad had run the show her whole life, so the pattern was ingrained in her, and I didn't think she knew of any other way to be around him. For the most part, they had a great relationship, but I often wondered if she kept it that way by catering to his quirky needs and how much of that harmony came at her emotional expense.

The moment we went aboard, Trish spotted her dad and ran ahead toward him, leaving me behind. She threw her arms around him, and then they started talking. When I caught up with them, Trish turned to me, then enthusiastically smiled as if urging me to enter a conversation that I hadn't been privy to in the first place.

Still, I swallowed any feelings of awkwardness and cheerfully said, "Happy birthday, Hugh! What a great day it is to celebrate!"

Hugh looked up at the sky as if he'd painted it himself, then at me. "Great to see you, too, Griffin!"

That was all I got from him before he and Trish continued on with their conversation.

Throughout the event, Trish spent time with her father and cousins but barely said more than a few words to me. So, I tried to stay out of everyone's way and found my own entertainment by scrolling through my Instagram feed, watching adorable skateboarding bulldogs and blooper reels from comedy shows. I understood that she had to share responsibilities as a host—especially with her brother and mom absent. But all of this left me feeling as though I had no reason to attend. Losing the Wingate job only compounded my insecurities, making me wonder if I even *deserved* to be there. Besides that, Trish always seemed to be on around her dad in a way that never quite included me. And as I stood by myself, listening to the bouncy, upbeat music and watching the colorful streamers dance on the wind, I wondered if I'd ever be able to speak their family's language—or if I even wanted to try. On one hand, the whole happy event made my family look infinitely more broken than Trish's, but on the other, persisting with my father felt more real to me than the time I spent trying to assimilate into this other family. Playing the cheerful fiancé to both parents after their divorce had also become an escalating source of stress—it made me feel as thin and fake as the party tablecloth protecting his teak saloon table.

"I don't know how to be anyone's son," I had told Trish, exasperated after we'd met her father for dinner one evening. She'd reminded me that I was a professional actor but didn't seem to understand how sad that irony was. It had been so long since I'd played that role in real life, anyway, and all I could muster was a very basic, sanitized parent-son relationship.

"How's it going, babe?" she said about an hour into the party, finally getting some time to talk with me. "Having fun?"

I wasn't sure how honest to be. Should I have said this wasn't even close to being fun? That it made me feel like jumping overboard, then swimming far enough from the marina to get lost at sea? Or was I being too intolerant because of what I'd been going through lately? Instead, I pushed a smile onto my face and changed the topic.

"Hey, you're getting a really nasty sunburn on your shoulders."

"Damn it!" Trish turned her head to examine the blotchy, pinkish skin. "I forgot to put sunscreen there! Ugh! I'll be paying for that one tonight."

"Why don't I just run out and pick up some after-sun gel so it isn't as bad later?"

"Oh, that's really sweet! Would you mind?"

"Not at all." Not only did I not mind, but I also craved the perfect escape from this floating netherworld, which would eat up more time until we were finally able to head home.

But on my way to the drugstore, my anxiety kept mounting. The thought of having to go back and keep pretending that I belonged there made my jaw tighten and my toes curl. That feeling was so intense, I thought I might have a panic attack—as if all I'd been keeping back could break the dam. Off to my side, I noticed a jogging path in the park. People were walking, running, and chatting beneath an archway of purple and green jacarandas. The scene looked so inviting. If I could walk off my anxiety for just a few minutes, I might feel better, and then maybe I'd return to the party with a sound mind.

Aware of time but somehow numb to it, I let a few minutes turn into forty-five. I kept telling myself I needed to stop, but the thought only made me want to keep walking, even quickening my pace. Much like my other stress-induced workouts, time seemed to disappear, and the need to keep going took over. I started to jog unevenly in my sneakers, but for the first time all day, I felt like myself. The only reason I finally stopped after an hour was because with each slap of my shoe, the stress had dissipated, but my sense of impending trouble was piling up.

When I got back to the boat, Trish was chatting it up with her cousin and didn't seem to notice that I'd been gone for so long. But when she regarded me with a quick, irritated glance, I knew that I'd been caught. It was then I realized that I hadn't just abandoned the party—I'd also forgotten to pick up the lotion for her shoulders. Now, she'd be sunburned *and* angry. And rightfully so.

At first, the ride home was quiet—too quiet—and I had a good sense that Trish was thinking before speaking as she often did before confronting me. But the longer she took, the more jittery I got, and it became a different brand of torture. I had to end the silence before it swallowed me.

"So," I said, "I'm sorry for being away so long."

She shook her head. "What's that even supposed to mean? You made a conscious decision to stay gone, right? And where did you go, anyway?"

"I just needed to clear my head."

"About what?"

I felt another opportunity to tell her about the Wingate job, but my mouth wouldn't form the words, and there were more pressing matters at the moment. Instead, I said, "About the whole scene. Look, I get that you have an assumed responsibility at these gatherings. I also understand how much pressure your dad puts on you. But, Trish, you ran off to see him the minute we got on that boat, and then you barely said four words to me the whole time. I just wish you had included me more so I could feel like I actually belonged."

"I'm sorry about that. It's just that I hadn't seen my father in a while, and I missed him. I guess I was a little more on edge than I realized."

"But this happens *every* time we're around your family."

She gave me a silent stare. "You know, you talk about wanting to be married, but how can I trust you when you can't even stick around for a family get-together? This is what partners do. They support each other and each other's families. Even when things aren't perfect. You get that, right? Do you even *want* to get married?"

Again, I wasn't sure how honest to be. I'd spent the whole day biting back words.

I hesitated. "I don't know."

Trish had no reply for that—I wasn't even sure if there was one at the moment. She just kept her eyes pinned on me, her lips parted.

"Look, I didn't mean to say that," I quickly told her. "Of course, I *do* want to marry you. That was my anger speaking."

When we reached the house, she looked at me as if she were about to say something, then got out of the car and went inside, and I stood there, incapacitated by my frustration.

25

IT WAS TEN P.M. I'D been at the gym since earlier that evening after our disagreement. I grabbed my gym bag from the garage, then got right back in my car and drove away without saying goodbye. I'd done so many weight reps, squats, leg lifts, and crunches that I'd lost track, and I was still on the treadmill.

Again, running.

From whom? My father or myself?

Maybe both, but none of this was enough to fix the wrongness: the whole situation with my father, now the whole blurry horizon with Trish. Exercise used to be my drug. It had settled my mind and reduced anxiety. Yet I was having to do more of it to get those benefits, and there weren't enough hours in the day today to quiet my screaming mind.

Even before our last conversation, the tension between Trish and me had taken seed and was growing. We hadn't been arguing—not like we had in the car a few hours ago—but we weren't talking as much, and the mounting strain was like a third presence in the house. It was why I'd grabbed my gear and left. The anxiety felt like too much to handle, and I didn't know how to neutralize it. But even though this was a twenty-four-hour fitness center, I didn't see any cots lying around, so I'd eventually have to go home and figure out how to assure Trish that our relationship was fine. That we belonged together forever. That I could handle my father and my finances would be okay, even though I'd just lost the job opportunity of a lifetime.

A quaking spasm of pain shocked the center of my hamstring. By the time I hit the emergency stop, the muscle was knuckled with so much pain that I had to hang from the treadmill before shambling off. I massaged the injury with my palm, but that only made it worse.

I limped to a full-length mirror on the gym wall to examine the back of my leg. When I turned around, it wasn't a fit, well-defined body I saw—I saw gauntness, misery, and exhaustion.

I saw trouble.

When I arrived home, a familiar sight awaited me in the kitchen: a plate on the stove, covered with tinfoil. Then, I caught a glimpse of Trish in the bedroom. I lingered in the hallway, dreading what might come next but finally popped my head through the door to show face. She looked at me with effort.

Trouble.

But she seemed to relax some now that I'd finally come home.

I tried to cover up my limp but felt her eyes on me. "I pulled something. No big deal. Just needs a little ice."

"We have some packs in the freezer." Trish watched me hobble out, and she did the same upon my return. "Do you think you should have it looked at?"

"Nah. I'll be fine." I couldn't put any inflection in my voice at all.

After icing my leg for a bit, I jumped in for a quick shower, then put on sweats. When I came out of the bathroom, she had moved to the edge of the bed, her attention trained on the wall across from us. I took a seat beside her and stared ahead, too. I couldn't look into her eyes because I was afraid of what might come next. Afraid that this was it. That she'd had time to think and wanted to talk about our future. Or lack of one.

"Look at me, Griffin," she said.

I did, and her expression softened. She put a hand on my arm, but I was unsure if it was an attempt to dull an incoming blow.

"This isn't working," she said. "You know that, right?"

Here it comes. The goodbye.

"You mean us?"

"No. Yes." She sighed and flung her arm in a gesture at the whole house. "Wherever we're stuck right now with this situation your father put you in and your exercise addiction. You can't trick your body into not feeling things by exhausting it. You've already screwed up your leg, but you could be headed for something much worse. To be honest, it's hard to watch you self-destruct. It's destructive to *us,* too."

"I know."

"Then, *do* something," she begged.

I blew out a fast breath. A singular nod was all I could muster.

"Look at yourself," Trish said, pleading. "You're exhausted. And you're doing everything you can to avoid what you know is the inevitable. You can't hide from your father anymore. He's back in your life. There's no getting around it. And I won't let you take it out on me."

I'd been locking my hands together for so long that they were numb, yet I didn't release them because, once again, the pressure and pain were a comfort. I thought about my headbanging session as a teenager, drowning out pain and fear with more pain. At least I'd avoided a breakup, the one thing that I knew would crush me. The compassion on Trish's face offered assurance that we were safe for now if I confided to her. But part of me knew that we'd crossed some kind of line today, and no matter how justifiable my behavior seemed to me at the time, the fault for our conflict was mine.

So, I shared it all. That I didn't get the movie role, that Deena suffered horrible abuse from my father and subsequent shame that had plagued her since. That I'd waited a day to tell her about all this because I didn't want to spoil her dad's party.

Trish lowered her gaze, palms washing over the sheets on each side of her. "Wow. Absolutely catastrophic. All those years, she was suffering along with you."

"And I was blind to it. You were right about her holding back secrets."

Trish put a hand on my back and rubbed up and down as if trying to wipe away my pain. In a way, it worked. This had been the first time in days that I'd felt relief. But again, my guilt caught up.

"I'm sorry you didn't get the job, Griffin, but you've got plenty of years ahead to chase your dreams and all the talent to achieve them."

I nodded. "And then there's the situation with my father. I still can't decide what to do."

"Remember what I told you?"

"Yeah, that there's no detour around this."

She shrugged. "I guess I said something like that, but I meant what I mentioned in the car. That we have to be there for each other and for each other's families."

"*I* have to deal with him. You shouldn't have to. But I don't know how to face him again."

"It seems like a good first step to quit letting your anger get in the way."

"He doesn't deserve my kindness."

"Stop doing that. All this anger, all this guilt. You keep pushing yourself into reverse. You've got to remember you're doing this to heal, and please, let me in. I don't want to be one of those fiancées who has to constantly ask what's going on in your head, then drag it out of you. That's not who I am. And it's not who I want *us* to be as a couple."

Seeing my strained expression, Trish said, "What is it, Griffin?"

I shook my head. "I'm afraid that looking at him one more time will force me to go through the pain again."

"But you're not the scared little boy you used to be, and he's not the monster you once knew. He can't hurt you anymore. He's not even doing anything wrong right now. *You're* the one who's got all the power. Don't let him come between us. We're building a good life. A stable life. A really beautiful one."

How was it possible to forget that I'd taken control the second I walked out of my father's house for the last time? That I'd created the future *I* wanted. Yet the man crashed back into me, crushing my self-confidence, and here I was again, that scared kid.

"Griffin," she said, "I believe in you. And I believe in us."

"But I'm not—"

"Listen to me. I believe in you," she said once more.

I closed my eyes.

Trish covered both of my hands with hers and looked deep into my eyes. "If you can't believe in yourself right now, then believe me."

I took her into my arms, and as we embraced, heads resting on each other's shoulders, I felt something open up from within. Something like truth but more than that. A resurgence of something lost, now found. The start of something? I wasn't sure yet, but it kept intensifying. Maybe the things I'd been protecting didn't need protection anymore. At least not from this woman who I loved so profoundly.

I'd been there for Trish during her darkest time, so maybe there was a shared reservoir between us? The sort of strength that makes it possible for people to get through tough times together?

My father wasn't the only one dragging me back into that house— I'd been doing it to myself, and I was the only one who could pave another escape through those doors.

As Trish said, there was just one way out.

26

BY THE NEXT DAY, IT was clear that I'd pulled my hamstring.

At least it wasn't torn—a more serious condition that I'd endured more than once—but I'd have to keep a compression bandage wrapped around my thigh and continue icing it. The good news: my limp wasn't as bad today, and I wouldn't have to stay off the leg. But workouts were out of the question until the muscle healed. Funny how the body had its way of sending out its soft warnings, as well as amplifying them if you didn't listen the first time. I hadn't listened, so there I was, clobbered and nursing my jacked-up leg. Still, I worried that taking too much time off might worsen my anxiety rather than alleviate it. Round and round I went, like a hamster in a damned wheel, even when I was laid up on the couch.

I stood in front of the nursing home. My legs wouldn't move, but it wasn't because of the injury.

I can do this.

I had to.

Just go.

My father had been released from the hospital to Bright Horizons Skilled Nursing, but the moment I opened the door, the name proved itself to be a harsh oxymoron. The lighting was poor, the carpets were stained and timeworn, and a bad funk hung around the lobby. As I waited for the receptionist to return, I tried to look casual while covering my nose and mouth with a hand. The odor was a commingling of starchy foods, stale air, and a hint of urine.

The receptionist's area provided a clear view of an elongated corridor. All up and down, elderly residents sat parked in wheelchairs outside their rooms like dimming porch lights, waiting to flicker out. A few of them were sleeping, heads dropped to varying degrees, while others stared ahead with glassy eyes that didn't see and mouths that hung open.

"Can I help you, sir?"

I reeled around toward the reception desk. A woman stared at me. In her mid-twenties, her skin was as pale as her off-white shirt. Her name tag said she was Tess, and her bright lipstick said she was more ready for a night out than a shift at a nursing home.

"I'm here to see my father," I told her.

"Name?"

"It's Sam ... Sam McCabe."

She looked at her computer monitor and gave the keys a few taps. "*Your* name?"

"Griffin McCabe."

She typed some more, then stopped. They must have had me listed as next of kin because she nodded at the screen.

"Room 154," she said, "or we can bring him to the sitting area. It's homier there."

"The sitting area would be fine." I wanted to ask why the sitting area would be homier than the room he was literally living in, but some guesses were already forming.

Tess pointed toward the hallway and said, "Down there. You'll see it on the right."

When I got there, homey and comfortable were not descriptors that came to mind. The sitting area had the same spotty carpet as the lobby and the same sickly lighting that threw shadows throughout the room. A threadbare, misshapen couch smelled like a mix of mothballs and dust. I started to laugh: it looked a lot like the couch my college roommate and I bought at a secondhand store at the start of our freshman year. Maybe if I combed enough thrift stores, I could still find the very same old sheet we'd thrown over it, and then it could have one last hurrah here in nursing home hell. It would have fit right in.

A framed picture hung on the wall that reminded me of motel art, the bland image of an unoccupied tractor, parked in an anemic-looking field. Inspiring, I supposed, if you were a farmer. And if you hated vivid colors.

Above me, a yellowing fluorescent bulb flickered, then met its death. Right on cue.

I took my mind away from the lousy decor, but a sick feeling skidded into its place when I remembered why I was here and whom I'd come to see. Trish's advice came back to me: I wasn't doing this for him. I was doing this to heal. So, I tried to put those feelings at bay. The anger. The fear. At times, so difficult to distinguish. As a kid, my emotions often ran close together, folding into a volatile blob.

Just then, a nurse pushed a wheelchair toward me, and my father gazed up with a degree of clarity that I wasn't at all expecting. His features were reactive, his eyes focused. And he was smiling. Not that leer I knew while growing up. It was warm and friendly, more like, *Hi. Good to see you!*

I was looking into the eyes of a stranger. Not only because his face had aged over the years. It was the unfamiliar demeanor he exhibited, so different that, for a few seconds, I questioned whether they'd rolled out the right patient. But it was him.

The nurse locked my father's wheelchair in place, then said, "You can wave one of us down whenever you're finished with your visit."

Being left alone with him brought a shock wave of old, goosey feelings back to life, reminding me of all the times I hid from him in different parts of the house to avoid this exact circumstance.

He can't hurt you anymore, I told myself.

His smile broadened. He looked at me with fondness, as if our reunion were a joyous one, just a father and son, separated by nothing other than time and distance. But I'd already made up my mind: he didn't get to come back into my life and act as though nothing bad ever happened between us. We could be cordial, but he didn't get to erase our history. It didn't work that way. Then, I walked back my scorn. His reaction did seem a little hollow, just a rickety scaffolding to hold it up.

"Hi, Sam," I started out because calling him Dad felt like handing something over to him that he didn't deserve.

"Hi, Champ. I've missed you so much. What a handsome young man you've turned out to be."

My fingers felt a little cold, a little numb. He knew who I was, with a compliment he never *ever* came within a fraction of giving me. With this revelation came another old, familiar emotion.

Panic.

There would be no avoidance today, no hiding from what was. He seemed agreeable, but what came next? How did I know he wouldn't go off the rails and turn back into the Monster? Either way, the truth was staring me down like a formidable enemy. I was vulnerable. Laid out on a cold rock with my chest opened up.

Face him. Get the visit over with, then heal. I won't have to come back here again.

I worked like hell to steady my voice when I said, "How … how have you been doing?"

"Fine … fine," he replied, head bobbing up and down with each word. "Very well, thank you."

Okay, so he was coherent but a tad sparse in the self-awareness department.

"Do you remember the accident?"

"What?" His expression slipped, eyes rounding with worry. "There's been an accident? Who was in an accident? Are they okay?"

"It's fine. Everyone's fine."

He leaned back into the wheelchair, threw a hand against his chest, and said, "Oh, thank goodness." He chuckled. "You had me worried!"

I gave him a wilted smile. I didn't know a lot about Alzheimer's, but I was getting a crash course. A broken mind moves in strange and unpredictable directions. A part of me wondered if the cheerful demeanor was just another of his performances—as if somewhere in his mind, he knew what was expected of him—and he was holding on to it to the point of absurdity, delivering a script in an attempt to seem lucid. But another part of me wondered if he had the mental capacity to pull it off.

Stillness broadened between us.

"Hi. Do we know each other?" he asked.

I wondered if my expression looked as shallow as his. "It's me, Griffin. Remember?"

"Oh, yes!" Huge nod. "Of course! What a handsome young man you've turned out to be."

I didn't know what I'd expected. No mutual understanding here, no therapeutic healing, and nothing close to it. I wasn't sure what to do with myself and didn't know why I should keep sitting there on that shabby couch, knee to knee with a person who wore my father's face with only a broken piece of his mind. There was no point in continuing this visit, but I *had* accomplished one thing: he indeed couldn't hurt me anymore because I was a different person now—so was he—and I didn't have to be scared of him.

That was something. And maybe it had to be enough.

"Hi. Have we met?" my father asked again.

"Yep. It's Griffin."

Which one of us is the broken record?

"Oh, yes! Of course!" he said. "What a handsome young man you've turned out to be."

Times three. I must be having a great hair day.

On my way out, I asked the nurse, "Is he always like this? So agreeable and enthusiastic?"

"He goes in and out, sometimes for longer periods, sometimes shorter. And it can all change quickly. You never know which way he'll go."

"Is that normal?"

"There's no recognizable pattern. Each Alzheimer's patient is different."

Outside, I flipped my hoodie all the way over my head, but it wasn't about keeping warm—it was exactly what I used to do as a teen when I wanted to hide from the world. I hunkered into the driver's seat of the

Mustang, then deliberately closed the top and shut my eyes, but the world got in, anyway.

27

I PICKED UP MY JEEP on the way back from Bright Horizons. It looked nearly new, just as it had before the accident, almost as if nothing had ever happened. *Almost.* They'd hammered out the mother of all dents—now, if only they could do that to my past. But since there were no therapist's couches swinging from rafters at the body shop, the rest was up to me.

I limped through the front door on time, home before Trish, which was a rare occasion. As I put my keys on the counter, though, she walked through the door, and I marveled at what I'd missed during all those days when my workouts ran late. Coming home at the same time was comforting in a way I hadn't imagined. She stood in the doorway, and I took her in: the brown whorls of hair, framing the smile that reached to her eyes. I grinned, and she grinned more. It was a much-needed moment. After many days of frayed emotions and heavy distress, this was warm solace.

She took off her shoes, chucked them by the door, then rushed to me, throwing her arms around my neck and pulling me in. Cradling both sides of her neck with my hands, I pressed my lips against hers and kissed her deeply. It felt like happiness and contentment and love and all other things I'd missed out on since the accident. The blossomy smell of her shampoo. The soft, warm skin behind her ears. She pulled back from our embrace to gaze at me. But I had to kiss her once more.

"How was your day, Twiz?" I asked.

"Better now."

We both laughed.

"The Jeep looks great, by the way," she said. "Glad to have it back?"

"Very. I should have realized I wasn't a Mustang convertible guy. Besides, did you really want to marry the biggest middle-aged cliché ever?"

"But I do love my cliché." She gave me a peck on the cheek, then headed for the bedroom to change out of her work clothes.

I sighed, invigorated by our reunion, and then I went into the kitchen to fix us a drink.

"What a damned day," she said. I heard a bedroom drawer open, then slam shut. "Too many cases and not enough lawyers."

"That bad, huh?"

"Put it this way, I need a good pair of running shoes to keep up with it all—an extra pair of arms would be nice, too."

Trish was already on the back patio when I came out, carrying the tray I'd made for us: a pitcher and two glasses filled with the iced tea we both loved, a mix of lavender with a hint of honey. Her best friend from college, Jules, had turned her on to the recipe while they shared a dorm room, and I later taught myself how to make it for Trish. Lavender was said to have calming properties, so they often drank it while studying for exams. I loved that she brought this ritual to our relationship—even more because she respected my decision not to drink and found other ways to keep me steady. Also nice was seeing her on the back patio, just as we used to do, settling on the old outdoor furniture and talking about our days.

We sat and got comfortable. Curling up next to me, she ran her hands through my hair, and then we toasted with tea.

"So? How did it go?" she asked once we had time to decompress from our day. "With your dad?"

"I'm not sure how to answer that, but I'll tell you one thing. That place—it's a dump. I'm glad I went through with it, though, Trish." I took a long drink of tea, leaving the glass half full. "I went there to face my fears. It felt like I did."

After a deep breath, I told her that my father was a vacant shell of the man I knew while growing up, how he appeared so benign, our conversations narrow and limited. How he knew who I was and how his delight in seeing me felt convincing at times yet toneless during others.

"I'm proud of you, Griff."

"You know, once I remembered everything you told me, it felt good to take control … but it also felt a little complicated."

She noticed my glass, then reached for the pitcher to fill it.

"Seeing a kinder version of him took away some of the sting," I said, "but I also knew the gentle man I saw wasn't real, and he wore a mask, created by illness. Nothing from today can scrub away my difficult memories of him. I'm not sure what to do with those." I pressed my hands together and stared at them. "It's this weird cycle I'm on these days. I have short spurts of sympathy, and then I remember how much I hate him, and then I get angry with myself for feeling bitter. But during the process, I see he's just a sad and pitiable old man whose mind is only halfway there."

Trish was playing with the ice in her glass, seeming to ponder over what I'd said. I expected her to say something about her brother; in fact, I felt certain she was thinking about him, maybe because Cam also lost a lot of cognitive function from the accident. But when she finally spoke, her voice was a little more guarded, a little more professional.

"Your confusion isn't unusual at all. I often see it at my work. No matter how much abuse kids suffer, they become conflicted, constantly hopping from one emotion to the next. Often, they defend their parents and blame themselves. I know this is an extreme example, but I once prosecuted a couple who abused their kid in a bad way. The poor girl was undernourished and had these horrible, terrifying scars running up and down her back from lashings. But she refused to offer any information about what she'd suffered through. When the psychologist asked why not, the kid said it was because she loved her mom and dad. Can you imagine? After all she went through? I knew that beneath those words was a lot of pain and anger. This pattern doesn't end after childhood. But a lot of the time, anger does end up winning."

"I never wanted to be angry—I mean, nobody does. I only wanted him to love me. But that doesn't mean I want anything to do with him now. We're way past that point. I just want to escape him."

"You've already escaped, Griffin. You're all grown up, and you showed amazing courage by facing what's been eating at you for all these days. It's a win."

"Yeah, I think I can finally be done with him."

My cell went off. I glanced down at the screen. The call was from Bright Horizons, and I couldn't hide my cringe.

"What?" Trish asked. "Who is it?"

I turned the phone screen toward her so she could see. With deep reservations, I answered.

"Mr. McCabe? This is Deborah Simpson, the nursing supervisor at Bright Horizons."

"What's up, Deborah?" I was cognizant of Trish's attention and made an effort to keep my voice friendly.

"I'm sorry to bother you, but there was an incident with your father this evening."

"What kind of incident?"

"He got a little out of hand."

"Define *out of hand*."

Hearing those words, Trish inched forward in her seat.

"He became combative."

"Violent?"

"Nobody got hurt, but it took a few people to restrain him."

"Restrain him? I just saw him a few hours ago. He was relaxed and happy."

"Those things can change. I'm afraid he won't calm down. Do you think you could come back here? Try talking to him?"

"But aren't you equipped to handle things like this?"

"We are, but there's a little more to the situation." She paused. "Your father is in tears. He's screaming for you."

We could already hear my father's cries echoing down the hallway.

Trish and I traded wary glances. A receptionist, one I hadn't met, didn't need to ask who I was. Evidently, she could identify me by my miasma of anxiety. She reached for the phone, and then a nurse arrived to escort us toward my father's room. As we neared the doorway, I no longer heard the cries—he was howling, a sound so pained and visceral that it could absorb through bone. Trish took hold of my hand and squeezed it. She was my anchor, holding me in place while my mind tried to run from me. By the pressure of her grip, however, she was as rattled as I was. We stepped into the doorway and faced the scene inside.

Through all his wailing, my father had been left by himself with nobody to help him. I moved in a few more feet. His arms and legs had been restrained. One look at Trish, and right away, I could tell we were thinking the same thing. She shook her head, lips pursed, brows pulled together: disgust. We both rushed in toward him and released the restraints. He wasn't some animal that had to be tied up. They could have just as easily given him sedatives, but I guessed they couldn't be bothered with that.

"NOOO! NO, NO, NOOO!" My father lamented to nobody, loud and terrified. "NOOOOOO!"

I put a hand on his shoulder, but he wouldn't stop howling.

"What the fuck?" Trish said, trying to compete with my father's nerve-grinding shrieks. "This is insane! Why isn't anyone helping him?" She marched to the door. "I'm getting someone."

My father let out a yelp, raw and primal, that made me lean in more. Tears streamed down his face. He was hyperventilating, arms wrapped around himself, rhythmically rocking forward and backward, forward and backward, like a hysterical, horror-stricken child.

I once looked like that.

It was as if I were staring into a mirror and wearing his pain. In a flare, I was there again, suffering at the hands of his abuse. I lowered my head, squeezed my eyes shut, and tried to keep my body from shaking, my mind from screaming, and every muscle in my body from jumping.

Trish returned, all but dragging a nurse's aide, followed by the nighttime head nurse. Reading from her phone, Trish cited the law to them, chapter by chapter, section by section, naming specific violations and wielding her legal expertise like a scalpel. I stepped away so the nurses could help my father.

"*AARRAAOOOH!*"

My attention shot back to him. I saw fear in his eyes. I saw veins beating a visible path beneath the skin on his forehead. A blaze of heat flushed the back of my neck, and all I could do was stand and watch him suffer. Through all the chaos, I heard a nurse order another to grab some medication. Trapped somewhere between the Before and After, I held back tears because I was afraid if I didn't, they'd never stop.

The room snapped into liquid silence. I looked at my father—he was staring at me. It was as though a lever was flipped inside his brain. No more screaming. No more tears.

"Champ?" he said, voice unstable, crippled. "Champ, come here."

That name.

Hearing it, especially during this charged moment, shook me down all over again. The steps I took toward him felt heavier and seemed farther than the few feet between us. The moment I reached him, he clutched my arm at the bend and struggled to pull me in closer, his eyes never leaving mine. I felt the warm perspiration in his grip, saw his stomach sucking in, sucking out. He didn't speak, but if feelings were physical, the room would have been a hornet's nest. Then, something moved through his eyes, changing them, along with an expression I'd come to recognize. The same one he'd shown me after the accident.

Defenselessness.

Vulnerability.

Raw anguish.

At last, I understood what drove those emotions because, this time, they felt as much a part of me as skin and bone. I also knew that I could no longer run or hide from them.

My father firmed his grip on my arm, then guided my hand toward him and pressed it against his weathered cheek. He held it there, and a single tear rolled down his face.

That was all I needed to see.

I looked at Trish. "He's so out of here. This place is a horror show."

28

I CAME HOME FROM SCHOOL one day to find my father's car parked in the driveway.

My feet stuck to the sidewalk. It was only three o'clock. He seldom got home before six. This meant three added hours of having to hide, to avoid getting picked on and put down. I was angry to lose that time to myself: it had been my only chance to unwind from school and pretend as though my life had a semblance of normalcy before he turned it inside out. I considered going somewhere else for a while to reduce my exposure to him, but that would open me up to more trouble. Since my father knew what time I came home from school, I was sure he'd grill me about where I'd gone and what I'd been up to. I forced a gulp of air past the nervous constriction in my throat.

Things were quiet as I entered the house. When I peeked into the family room, my father's recliner was empty. The rest of the downstairs area proved to be as vacant. Next, I took cautious steps up the staircase. Was I worried about seeing him? Hell yes, but sometimes, not knowing where he was could be just as menacing. I hated surprises, especially in this house.

At the top of the staircase, I heard movement inside Deena's room. I approached. The door was open, so I looked inside. She was doing homework, bobbing her head to whatever song was playing in her earphones. I waved to her with wide, sweeping motions, trying to get her attention. She looked up, pulled off an earphone, then gazed at me expectantly.

"Why's Dad home early?"

She shrugged. "Dunno."

I considered her for a few seconds, trying to figure out why the atmosphere in this house felt so off-kilter today. "Do you know where he is?"

"I think he went to his bedroom," she mindlessly said, then put the earphone back on, dismissing me.

Soft and slow, I approached my father's bedroom. When I got there, the door was closed, save for a tiny crack that wasn't wide enough to peer through. Curiosity and trepidation wrestled with each other. Should I open the door wider to see inside? I wanted to find him sleeping or already passed out, but I would be in a world of trouble if he caught me snooping on him.

With my mind divided and vacillating, I accidentally tapped the doorknob with my wrist. I squeezed my eyes shut and froze, fear marching through me. But no one jerked open the door from inside or barked a command to enter—so I opened my eyes, and he was seated on the bed, still with no idea I was there. I nudged the door a little wider to look in.

My father sat on the edge of his bed, sobbing, elbows resting on his knees, and in his open palms sat the photo of my mother in her Mustang. To his right, a half-filled bottle of bourbon lay on its side on the floor. Above it was a dent in the wall, liquid dripping down from it where he'd hurled the bottle.

"I can't win, Ruth," my father said, voice so broken that I almost couldn't make out his words.

He wiped his nose, sniffed away his tears.

I stood there for about a minute, trying to decide if I should go in; although, why I would, I didn't know. Maybe it was because he wore his sadness in a way I hadn't seen since Mom died. Maybe his grief felt closer to mine, almost as though we were mourning my mother's death together as we once had. But still, I had good reason to be terrified of my father and didn't want him to catch me snooping on him. I'd just seen his fury splashed in brown bourbon across the wall, so why would I expect him to return my kindness?

He sobbed once. "And the kids, Ruth … the kids … what have I done to them? *God*, Ruth, I miss you so much …"

I turned to go, unable to fathom what I'd just seen and heard. Who was the man in my father's bedroom? Another stranger, another broken piece of him I couldn't recognize? Through the years, I'd seen many of those, but this one shook me. I'd often felt the wrath of my father's fury, the teeth on his words, and the disgust in his sharp disapproval. But inextinguishable regret? Never.

The Monster had tumbled.

At least for now.

29

TRISH INSISTED ON DRIVING US home from Bright Horizons, but I told her it was okay, that sitting in the passenger seat and staring out the window would only force my mind to wander into darker places. With reluctance, she took the passenger's seat but kept her attention on me the whole way back—still, I felt guarded, even though she tried to be nonchalant. I faked a smile, but it didn't work. She knew me too well.

We drove on in reflective quiet as the darkened road unfolded before us. Freeway lights swam overhead, one after the other, like soaring beacons leading to nowhere. No movie deal, no supplemental income for my father. How could I afford to get him out of that place? I thought I'd taken control of this situation, but I'd been telling myself a lie. I was still trapped beneath that yoke and, by the way things looked, might not get out from under it anytime soon.

No. He doesn't get to do this again, dammnit. He doesn't get to come back into my life and throw more rot into it.

But there I was, and the situation called for immediate action. Nolan had mentioned that my father's Mercedes was all he had that was worth anything. I could get a few thousand out of it to put my dad in a decent place for a month or two—it would buy time to figure out a more permanent situation. But if his Alzheimer's was that severe, how long was permanent, really?

I'd been biting down so hard that my jaw hurt, yet I didn't stop. Again, much like when I'd wrapped my legs around my office chair, it was a peculiar kind of ache, pain relieving pain. Shades from my past crept back in when I recalled banging my head against the headboard as a teenager, and I wondered if this could be the restart of an old, buried compulsion.

God, I'm so screwed up.

"You doing okay there?" Trish asked.

"Yeah, just thinking …" I wasn't up for another discussion about how I'd found new ways to abuse my body.

Things got quiet again. When I spared Trish a glance, she was still observing me, only this time, thick with intent.

"I'm just trying to process everything," I said.

"I'm worried, is all."

"I know."

"That you may be falling into your old habit of suffering in silence. You get that way when you're all stressed out."

Why does her concern feel intrusive right now?

I took my eyes off the road and gave her a look. My hands gripped the wheel tighter, sweat gathering between fingers.

Trish took in a long breath. She let it out slowly.

More quiet, but this time, it was weighty; anything I said from here on would either force me into a discussion I didn't want to have—or worse, start an argument. I was stuck. I was tangled. I took a sustaining breath, trying to figure out how to yank myself from this mess.

"Look, Trish," I began, "I appreciate everything you've done. I do. I just need a little space to sort through my thoughts."

"*Space*. Right," she said as if the word had an unpleasant taste to it.

She took me in for a good ten seconds, then turned her attention out through the window. But I could see her face reflecting in the glass: she wasn't looking at much.

"I'm sorry," I said. "I didn't mean for it to sound like that. I'm obviously overwhelmed, and my mind isn't clear enough to process how I feel."

"It's fine. I get it."

I could tell she was injured.

"Damn, it's hot in here," I said, reaching for the panel to turn up the airflow.

Her smile didn't look approving; it looked obligatory.

Trish did love me. I felt it. Just as I'd loved her through the loss of Cam, then when her parents' marriage fell apart; after that, she saw everything—even our love—through the distorted lens of doubt. Now, it was my turn to be on the receiving end for that same kind of attention. After all, we were supposed to be here for each other, no matter what … forever. But was this what our forever would look like? One of us always in crisis? Or would it be me, always demanding this difficult love from her? At times, healing felt impossible, like there were places in my heart that weren't just wounded but actually deformed by my childhood, and our life together would always remind me of it.

"Can we talk for a few?" I asked the following morning, poking my head through the patio door.

Trish sat on the outdoor couch, reading while drinking her morning coffee. She closed the book and looked up at me. I took a seat next to her and picked at a hole in the battered wicker, trying to order my thoughts. I'd brought this furniture into the relationship from my old place. The cushions were sun-faded orange and shredded at the corners. Before the accident, Trish and I had talked about replacing them, maybe even redoing the whole patio to make it more relaxing and modern, but that light conversation felt like years ago.

"I'm sorry for shutting you out on our way back from seeing my father last night," I said. "Everything got intense, and I wasn't coping with it well. I love you, and I absolutely hate upsetting you."

Trish placed her coffee cup on the end table with concentration, then came back to me and said, "Thank you for saying that." But a trace of apprehension played across her face. "You're good at apologizing, Griff, but then you go back to the thing you always do. You get defensive and irritable. You disappear on me, and it seems impossible to find you. It's starting to get really old."

"I know. I've been doing it since I was a kid. It's instinctual. I guess I'm discovering that a lot of things I did then don't work today."

"But you're not making enough effort to change that, and we keep getting caught in the same snag—me feeling hurt and you feeling frustrated. You're carrying your past like a rope around your neck, and it gets in the way of *us*."

Now, we were both worrying about this pattern and what it would mean for our future.

"I don't want that. I mean it," I said. "So, now that I've had more time to think about what happened last night, I'd like to try again. How about if I tell you what I left out, how I felt?"

Trish nodded.

I took a drawn-out breath before opening up to her. "First off ... I saw a side of my father I haven't seen since I was a kid. He was different from when I visited him earlier in the day. This time, it wasn't some illness-induced behavior. It was real. I could feel it. What I saw in his eyes, it was powerful. That doesn't change anything he did to me in the past or how I feel about him now, but it did make him seem more human. Also, after seeing how poorly they treated him, I agree with you. Leaving him there will just make things harder on me, so I'm more open to the idea of moving him to a better place."

"I think that sounds good."

"At the same time, my mind is in a tug-of-war. I've told you that all I wanted was to feel loved by my father. Last night was the closest I've come to it. But a few good minutes can't take away the years of abuse, so I'm working on that part, but it's going to take time. Will you stay with me for that?"

She smiled. "Griff, I'm still here."

"No, I don't mean it like that. I mean, will you be patient until I figure all this out?"

"I've always been patient, but you've got to stop going back to your old habits."

Her voice and feelings seemed sincere, but there was a reserve behind it, a backstop to her generosity that scared me a little.

"You have to know I'm making an effort."

"I do know that."

"It's just that, sometimes, it's hard, letting go of those feelings. The anger. The sadness. The loss."

"See? This is exactly what I'm talking about. I love this from you." She pushed a lock of hair away from my eyes. "Telling me these things makes me want to keep being patient." She smirked. "But for future reference? If you come between me and my coffee again, I'm coming after *you*."

I winked. Don't you dare threaten me with a good time."

Trish laughed, relieving me of my previous worries. Since my father's problems had become my own, I'd been thrown backward, putting a damper on all the intimacy we'd achieved. But regardless of what my father had done to me, it was because of Trish that I was able to feel loved again.

30

RYAN AND I HADN'T SPOKEN since that day at the beach.

The situation was awkward but familiar. Ryan was a delicate one. He would rather avoid a confrontation than talk about things. It then became my responsibility to reach out again. When I did, he acted as if nothing happened and we'd been good all along. I suspected that when his feelings were hurt, he didn't quite know where to lash out or how to ask for more information. Maybe it was because of his family's diversion tactics while growing up. They did a lot of hiding and ignoring when the threat of pain flew anywhere close.

Comparing my abusive home life to Ryan's, it was easier to view his as idyllic, but like most families, it wasn't, so I hadn't recognized how weird and over the top their positivity was. His parents whitewashed over the messy parts of life—serial affairs and some financial creativity that came to bite them in an IRS audit a few years ago, if I'd correctly pieced together Ryan's subtle hints and some later gossip—and I now believed that was how they dismissed the hard truths.

When Ryan failed tests at school, his dad would say, "It's okay, buddy. You'll do better next time."

When his sister, Gretta, didn't get along with other kids, their mom would jump to her side and say, "Don't let those girls get to you, sweetheart. They're just jealous because you have so much going for you."

Never did their parents face problems head-on; instead, they waltzed in loose circles around them. As a result, both kids developed into know-it-alls, thinking they could do no wrong and using their big personalities to drown out the harsh sounds in life. But understanding Ryan didn't make it any easier to deal with him. He could be exhausting at times.

Then, there was the other matter—for me, the biggest—that weird chemistry between my father and him; Ryan looked up to him, something I never understood and even resented.

I was tired after driving to and from LA these last two days to work on a few voice-overs, but I had the next three off. So, I decided to invite Ryan to lunch at his favorite restaurant, the Water Bar in Mission Beach, to see if I could smooth things over with him.

He was sitting on a barstool, eating French fries when I walked in, and with a broad grin, he waved me down.

"Hey, Ry," I said, pulling out a chair to take my seat. "How's it going?"

"Great! I've missed seeing you, Griff!" This was the Ryan reboot, and just like that, it made our arduous encounter go away. In *his* mind, at least.

"Yeah, missed you, too."

The truth was, with all my father trouble, I hadn't had time to miss Ryan at all, but I didn't dare betray that his feelings were anything less than completely mutual because, as I said, he was delicate.

I also wanted to avoid a detailed conversation about my father. Ryan had already forced his unsolicited opinions and advice on me once. Bringing up the matter again was a surefire way to restart our dance of dysfunction. But I had no doubt he'd bring it up. My only strategy would be to nod and grin a lot and imagine him as a cute and fuzzy panda bear.

"So," Ryan said, leaning in over the table and toward me, "did you end up going to see your dad?"

And here we go.

Seizing the glass of water in front of me, I tossed the cool liquid down my bone-dry throat, then answered, "I did."

"And?"

"It wasn't for very long." I smiled. The first visit *was* short; I just left out the other.

He made his head drop sideways and pressed his lips together. "Why was it short?"

"There wasn't much to say. And he was barely coherent."

"Ahh …" He looked down at the table, nodded, then looked back up to me and said, "Well, glad you finally took my advice."

"So, how's Ashley doing?" I enthusiastically replied, trying to pivot.

"She's fine. Do you feel any better after seeing him? Your dad?"

This conversation was a one-way street, and I knew where it was headed.

"Well, I don't know if I'd say that …"

"Why not?"

"Because it's complicated," I said, trying to temper my irritation by thinking about the adorable panda bear.

"Then, maybe you should see him again, right? Figure things out?"

There wasn't a snowball's chance in hell that I was going to tell him the truth and risk setting myself up for more of his opinions, so I only said, "I don't think I will right now."

"But why not?"

"Because, Ryan"—I closed my eyes so I could secretly roll them—"I … can we just leave this alone? I'm not in the mood to discuss it."

"I just think there were a lot of misunderstandings between you two."

"Misunderstandings?"

"Yeah." He nodded emphatically. "And seeing him could fix them."

My temper was bobbing up toward a place where I might not be able to retrieve it. Pressing back at it, I said, "It's not that simple. And I'd rather sort this one out on my own."

"You know, Griff, maybe it's time to stop being so mopey and feeling sorry for yourself and get on with it. Your father wasn't always *that* bad."

And there it was.

After all those years, Ryan had finally verbalized what I suspected he'd been thinking all along, and this time, I could not hold back. Anger I'd buried for years rose and expanded. I stood up and, in the process, knocked over my glass; it spilled, then hit the floor with a *thwack*, rolling several inches before coming to a stop. Ryan plunged back into his chair with broad eyes. Everyone in the restaurant looked our way.

But I didn't care.

"Let me tell you something, Ryan," I said, trying to control the quiver in my voice. "What you pretended to see and what really happened? Those were two vastly different things. But you were too busy looking the other way to notice. You cared more about kissing up to my dad than being the friend I needed."

"I did not—"

"No. Stop right there. No more excuses. No more denial. I was in pain, Ryan, and you just ... just *stood* there, watching it all happen, never once considering anyone other than yourself. But not anymore. That ends right here. All of it! I'm so ..." My next words stopped on their way up, so I walked away and left Ryan by himself, gaping jaw and all.

I walked into the house. Trish was working from her home office, her desktop covered in paperwork while she stared at her laptop through horn-rimmed computer glasses.

When I barged in, her head shot up. "Um, hello to you too."

"Sorry," I said, a bit out of breath. "I'm a little worked up right now."

"Apparently." She removed her glasses, set them on the desktop, then swiveled her chair around to give me her attention.

After I finished telling her what had happened with Ryan, she said, "But are you really sure you want to end things with him? Especially like that? I mean, you guys have been friends since you were little."

"I'm just so pissed at him right now." I stood up and began pacing the floor. "I've been putting up with him for years. Long friendships don't always mean good ones, and this one was problematic from the start. I only tolerated his nonsense because I had nobody else to turn to as a kid." I stopped pacing. "You know what? Maybe this is a part of my healing process, letting go of him, right? It'll probably help me feel better. Besides, he's been this way all his life. People don't change after that long."

Trish didn't say anything, but she was making strong eye contact.

"What?" I asked.

"You're all wound up, Griff. Why don't you sit back down so we can talk?"

I sat.

"Look." She tried to give me a patient smile. "I really want to help you with this. I do. It's just that I'm backed up on my work right now, and I'm extremely tired."

I worried that her need for urgency was an attempt to calm me down because I was one of many crises she needed to get out of her way today.

"But here's the thing, Griffin. Weren't we just talking last night about how you want to change? If it's possible for you, why can't it be possible for Ryan? Shouldn't you give him the same chance? Or at the least, smooth things out so the friendship doesn't end with all this anger?"

"I've been giving him chances all my life." I leaned over and buried my face in my hands. "I don't know. I just don't. I'm too … *angry* to talk about this anymore."

"Okay," she said. "Then, I'm sorry I couldn't help you."

It was a surrender on her part, and it also felt like a dismissal. But I understood that she needed to get back to work.

I left the house so Trish could finish, but I also needed the time to calm myself down. Once I did, my perspective shifted. I'd barged into the house with guns loaded, interrupting Trish, and never taken the time to listen to what she had to say. I wasn't sure what to do about that now. My apologies were getting old and redundant, and these days, it seemed little came of them, anyway.

I parked myself at a sandy beach tucked just beneath Sunset Cliffs. No answers waiting for me there, but I wasn't looking for any. I just wanted to *be.* To watch the softening currents come in, heaving sand over my toes. To see pods of pelicans wing and glide over the water before lifting toward the skies. It could get lonely here, but maybe sometimes, lonely was okay. I could pull a curtain across the world and process things, especially when so much seemed to be going wrong and I couldn't figure out life.

31

THE NEXT DAY, I WAS about to turn onto Pacific Beach Drive when my phone rang. For a moment, I suspected it might be Ryan, but he'd never been the first to reach out after our disagreements. I glanced at the screen but didn't recognize the number. There was a time when I didn't pick up for unknown callers, but these days, with my father in the nursing home and my career prospects adrift, I could no longer afford to be selective.

"Hello?"

"Is this Griffin McCabe?" a woman asked.

"It is."

"Hi, Griffin. I don't know if you remember me. My name is Marcella Goodwin. I was a friend of your mom's."

"Remember you? How could I forget you?" I laughed, relieved someone wasn't calling to tell me my nonexistent car warranty had expired.

Marcella was an old family friend. She used to come to the house while Deena and I were young, bearing gifts—silly little things, like squirt guns, party string, and bubble toys. Marcella didn't have any children, so I suspected that this was why she enjoyed spoiling us. And like Mom, she relished in having fun. I had fond memories of the four of us chasing each other across the front lawn, screaming and giggling. My mother adored her. Unfortunately, Marcella had lost touch with the family after Mom passed. Most people had. My father wasn't exactly rolling out the welcome mat once he began drinking. He wouldn't even answer the phone or open the door when friends dropped by to check on him.

Before long, it was like this: *message received*, and we never heard from old friends again.

"What on earth have you been up to, Marcella?"

"Oh, you know, little of this, a little of that." She giggled. "How are my two favorite, gorgeous kids?"

"All grown up!" I said, forcing buoyancy to avoid our shit sandwich of a life. I pulled a quick change on the subject. "Still live near the old neighborhood?"

"I do, but it hasn't changed much. Lots of young, upwardly mobile couples with a few kids, a dog, and plenty of money."

"Still a real estate agent?"

"I am, which is why I'm calling … well, besides wanting to hear your wonderful voice again. I just found out that the house you grew up in went up on the market this week. The last couple who bought it went to Splitsville. Oh, sorry—was that just out loud?" She laughed.

I laughed, too, but the news didn't shock me. It seemed as though everything inside that house was destined to wither and die.

"Anyway," Marcella went on, "I had another client who bought his childhood home not too far away from yours a few weeks ago, so I thought I'd—you know—run it up the flagpole, as they say. See if you have an interest?"

She probably didn't understand that our house ended up being a depository for sour memories. While my mother was alive, Marcella always saw our home as a happy place, filled with love—and it had been. She never knew how bad life got, so it made sense that she'd check in to see if I had an interest in buying the place, even though I would have rather put a nail through my eye.

"You know, Marcella, I think I'll pass on that, but thanks for offering me the opportunity."

"Sure! Like I said, I thought I'd check before other buyers get interested. Maybe mention it to Deena, too? Just in case?"

"Sure will! Great hearing from you!"

"You bet. Say hi to your dad, too."

"I'll do that!"

Too bad my father wouldn't know who Marcella was even if she had her name tattooed across her forehead. As for Deena, that house was the last place she would want to revisit. Nothing would make her happier than hearing that it had burned to the ground.

I hung up. I breathed in and breathed out.

Trish was busy sorting through mail when I walked in. I'd barely taken two steps when my cell went off again.

"Hi. This is Deborah, the nursing supervisor from Bright Horizons. Unfortunately, we've had another situation with your father this evening."

"What? Again?"

Trish looked up from the mail to give me a questioning look.

"I'm afraid so," Deborah said. "He refused to eat his dinner. He got aggressive, and when we tried to control him, he became more combative."

"*Control* him?" I gave Trish an exasperated look and shook my head. "I'm not sure why you're calling me. It isn't like I can make him eat from here."

"It's actually our policy. We're required to let you know. Part of the problem is that your father is sundowning."

"Sun *what?*"

"It happens late in the day with Alzheimer's patients. They can become agitated. We can't help that."

"But you *can* help by dealing with it, right?"

"I assure you, we're committed to giving your father the best care possible," she said as if reading from a script.

"I'm sorry." I laughed, but there wasn't a fraction of humor in it. "I saw how you handled my father the last time this happened. Leaving him all by himself in restraints like some animal? Even though he was clearly still in crisis? That's not the best possible care."

"We do try to—"

"You know what? This is the second time he's gotten himself worked up, which makes me think that the way you're treating him is part of the problem."

"Some situations become more difficult regardless of what we try."

"Again, you left him all by himself. It was awful."

"I'm sorry you feel that way."

"Please, take responsibility for your actions."

"I *am* taking—"

I hung up before she could feed me another of her stupid, standard lines.

"What was *that* all about?" Trish asked.

I shook my head. "Those people at Bright Horizons are completely incompetent. Any word yet about a new place for my dad?"

"It's taking a little longer than I'd hoped, but I'm still talking to coworkers about it. Apparently, there aren't a lot of available beds in town. Nobody's come up with anything yet, but there are plenty of others to ask. We'll get this done soon. I promise."

"I know," I said, surprised by my sense of urgency.

PART THREE: CONNECT

32

TRISH'S FEELERS EVENTUALLY RETURNED SOME leads. She had a few friends who worked in the Family Protection Division at the District Attorney's Office, and they made a few solid recommendations. Then, we pored over the list that Kayleigh gave me. Using both sources, we were able to find a good facility in Solana Beach, called Oceanview Memory Care. Trish also informed her coworkers about the code violations she'd witnessed at Bright Horizons, and they offered to look into the company. She told them to do whatever they felt was necessary but leave us out of it. We didn't have the time or energy to start a war.

Being the only living relative willing to take care of my dad, I was able to secure a power of attorney from a lawyer to handle my father's affairs. I then managed to sell his Mercedes for about nine thousand dollars, which would cover his stay for two months while I worked out a budget for the rest. I figured I could take on a few extra commercial voice-overs. My finances would be tight, but I decided I could make it work if I used some of my savings. Trish even offered to pitch in with more money if I came up short, which I greatly appreciated. Neither of us would say in so many words that we'd be digging into our wedding money.

Nolan called to let me know that he had gotten my father's apartment cleared out and would send the bill. Since I hadn't expressed a desire to keep any of my dad's belongings, he donated what was still useful—the desk, the bed frame—and put the rest into his storage in case I changed my mind. I doubted that would happen. I was trying to let go of the past, and holding on to idiosyncratic reminders of it wasn't helpful.

Never had I imagined I'd have to take care of an aging parent because, essentially, I didn't have any parents left—or so I'd thought. But I was trying to open myself up. Widen my perspective on the world. Nothing could change what my father had done, but I didn't have it in me to see *any* human suffer. I never had. The biggest question on my mind: did feeling one thing and doing another make me a liar? Did helping him make me a traitor to all the justifiable anger I'd felt? And what would my future look like now that my father was going to be in it? The person I pictured myself to be in that vision of the future was never the person I'd wanted to become.

My dad had been at the new facility for about a week. I was leery of visiting—my presence had made him go berserk the last time—but I'd built a career of doing things the right way and seeing them through. Since I was responsible for the extra cost, I needed to check out the place and make sure they were providing better care: these were all the things I told myself while I was driving to the facility, the only thing I'd wanted to do since I'd woken up that morning.

Inside was a big change from not-so-Bright Horizons. The walls were covered in beautiful splashes of blues, greens, and purples. The waiting room was well-appointed, the furniture current and attractive, not a stain anywhere. It looked as though they were vigilant about keeping the place clean, too. I could see vacuum tracks and deep footprints through the carpet pile. Another bonus: the artwork featured no sick, broken-down tractors in a pile of weeds—only beautiful, abstract, and comforting paintings. A few caught my attention: side by side, giclee prints of Haynes Worth's *Kindness*. I was well-acquainted with his work—I often admired it while passing through UC Berkeley's student commons, and looking at it always brought me a stayed presence of peace. The canvas pulsed with effervescent shades of blues and greens, layered with texture, light, and movement.

"Can I help you?"

I reeled around. The receptionist, a middle-aged woman with carroty hair and pretty green eyes, gazed at me with watchful interest.

"Oh, yeah. My father lives here. I just wanted to have a look around."

"Wonderful! Let me call our patient relations supervisor," she said, pressing the phone against her ear as she dialed the number.

"That won't be necessary," I said, trying to intercept. "I don't plan on staying long."

She held up a hand, shook her head, then said into the phone, "We have a new family member up front. Are you free to come down? Uh-huh. Okay. Thanks." The receptionist turned back to me and explained, "It's actually a requirement for first-time family visits." She beamed. "We enjoy getting to know you as much as our patients. Elena will be right with you."

Couldn't fault them for being diligent.

"Thank you." I took a seat in the waiting area.

The receptionist rearranged a bouquet of white lilies in a clear vase on the countertop, and then she stopped to look at me.

"You know, your voice sounds very familiar. Has anyone told you that?"

"They have. I'm a voice actor."

"Oh! Anything I'd know?"

"Mobilife Insurance?"

"Oh my God! YES!" She pointed to me. Making her voice deep, she said, "Don't get caught with your pants down, Fred." Then, with a bubbly giggle, she added, "I LOVE that commercial! I laugh every time it comes on!"

I repeated the line back to her.

Her laugh opened up more, and then she said, "I can't believe we have a *real* celebrity in the building!"

"Nah, I'm just common folk," I said with a grin—I couldn't help it. In some way, the calming atmosphere there softened this repetitious exchange. Plus, I'd managed to make someone smile today.

"Mr. McCabe?" The question came from behind me, soft and welcoming.

I turned. A tall, attractive woman stood before me with sculptured, honey-colored hair and a stylish, tailored wardrobe with sharp lines.

"Elena Martinez," she said, holding out her hand for me to shake. "So nice to meet you, Mr. McCabe." I returned the pleasantry, and she said, "Before I show you around, do you have any questions you'd like to ask?"

"Well, the main reason I placed my father here is because the last facility was below par."

"Oh, I'm sorry to hear that."

"They weren't able to properly care for him. I'd even go as far as saying they were negligent."

She leaned in a few inches, turned an ear toward me, and made her voice secretive. "Where exactly was this?"

When I gave Elena the name, her mouth tugged to one side, and she nodded with certainty, showing me she knew about the poor care offered at Bright Horizons. She said, "I can absolutely assure you, you won't have to worry about that here at Oceanview. Your father will receive the best care possible. I also encourage you to visit him as often as you'd like since that will be an important component in his care and well-being."

She was reading me as a concerned family member. That bar felt a little high.

"Well, here's the thing, Elena. My father and I aren't close. In fact, we hadn't seen each other in many years. I just want to make sure he's well-cared for, but I prefer to stay in the background as much as possible."

"Oh, okay, then," Elena said. "That's fine, too. We encounter all sorts of different family dynamics here at Oceanview. Our goal is always to make patients and families our top priority and adapt to their individual needs."

A relief. There were probably other family members in my situation, and she wasn't judging me as another lousy kid who was using this place as a dumping ground for an ill and aging parent.

"Shall I give you the tour of our facility?" Elena asked.

I obliged. My intention was to get a quick look at the place to make sure it was acceptable, then take off, but the *quick* part started to deteriorate once I'd arrived. I couldn't blame them for caring so much since that was what I'd wanted for my father.

Elena took me through a long breezeway that led to where the residents lived. To the left were floor-to-ceiling windows, showing off a vast, open view of the ocean. This was my kind of place—though sequestered by glass, I could almost smell and taste the dry, dusty sand, driven by beachy wind gusts, a sensation that always grounded me back to the earth.

After showing me the place, Elena turned and said, "Would you like to visit your father and see his room?"

A carryover memory interceded. I could almost hear my father's labored groans, feel the stiff pain in my arm while his grip tore at my skin.

"Mr. McCabe?"

I flinched at the sound of her voice, then tried to throw off the twitch in my hand. With perhaps the most forced smile I'd ever marshalled, I said, "I'm afraid I've got an upcoming commitment, and I haven't budgeted enough time, but I looked into the rooms while you were showing me around, and they're beautiful. I think I'll be good for now."

Elena's phone went off, and she took the call. "Oh, okay. All right. Be right there." She ended the conversation, then said, "I'm sorry to stop this so abruptly, but it looks as though I'll have to. I'm needed somewhere else."

"I understand." Not only did I understand, but I also welcomed the chance to make my departure without too much fuss.

"The exit isn't far," she advised. "Will you be okay, or would you prefer I call someone to help you find your way out?"

"No, I'll be fine."

"Great." Her phone rang again, but before answering, she hurriedly told me, "Take a right up ahead, then a left, and that'll lead you back to the reception area." She brought the phone to her ear and, in an all-business tone, said, "I'm on my way."

Elena hurried down the hallway, and I ran for the exit.

But about halfway there, I'd somehow mixed up the directions. I was about to circle back when I heard voices just ahead of me. I followed the sound to a recreation room with residents chatting, playing games, and generally seeming to enjoy themselves.

Except for my father. He sat in a wheelchair parked in the corner of the room, watching the other residents have fun.

None of them was paying any attention to him, but he didn't seem to mind too much. He wore the smile of a child, but it had an opaque, vacuous quality to it. They'd dressed him for the day, although in a manner that looked a bit rushed. I frowned when I noticed his tan pants, the elastic waist pulled too high over his hips, with a colorful and festive Hawaiian print shirt sloppily tucked into them. And his zipper was open. I didn't hold it against the staff. It was an effort in the right direction, but I again remembered my father, the lawyer, in his high-end suits and power ties. The dissimilarity was jarring.

A stray crayon rolled my father's way, and a female resident chased after it. My father strained to lean forward to pick it up, unable to bend a few inches from the back of his chair because the safety belt across his waist forbade it. The woman beat him to the crayon, anyway. For a moment, their eyes met. He smiled big and waved to her. She didn't acknowledge him. The woman greedily took the crayon back to her group at the table. My father resumed observing all that surrounded him, still with that smile, yet this time, I sensed a trace of sadness behind it. He sat in a roomful of people yet seemed alone.

Unwelcome familiarity hit me. I could almost identify with the way he was partitioned off from the crowd. I used to feel the same at most places I went. Many people I knew had such normal home lives, and I had the opposite, which left me feeling like a square peg crammed into a triangular hole. Maybe I still felt that way.

My father turned his head in my direction with eyes that didn't find me. But on the chance they might have, I worried that looking at him for one more second would just make me hurt harder. So, I turned to leave.

But not fast enough because my father's voice called out to me, "Champ? Is that you?"

I froze.

But when I peered over my shoulder, he was flipping through the pages of a picture book that a staff member must have given him, unaware of my presence.

The voice didn't come from him; it was from inside my head. A Siberian chill smacked the nape of my neck. I rubbed my eyes, trying to clear out the brain fog. Could his dementia have been playing tricks on *my* mind as well? Luring me into a place where I was now questioning my own perceptions? Or was it my own voice inside my head, telling me that my need to recover from him was more compelling than my need to dislike him?

"Champ?" I heard again.

I placed both hands against my ears and closed my eyes.

I took off down the road at a speed that was neither safe nor legal, but I didn't care. I had to get away. The more distance I put between my father and me, the easier it would be to separate from my knotty mind and scrambling thoughts—that worked when I was a kid. I'd run from our house and jog for miles, but today, my leg was still injured, and disappearing acts didn't solve my problems anymore. Not when it came to Trish and not with my father, either. Now, he wasn't only back in my life; he was in my head.

Why was I feeling anything for him? Did seeing him in such a sad state make it more difficult to envision the cruel man he'd once been? More questions in search of answers, more confusion. Would I ever escape the man?

You've already escaped, Griffin. You're all grown up.

There came Trish again with her wisdom and another lesson not yet learned.

Rain began to fall, the smell of hot, wet asphalt filling the air. A shiv of lightning split the sky in two, followed by a sharp *crack* of thunder. Outside my car, people scattered, putting purses or briefcases—or whatever they had handy—over their heads to shield themselves. The road went from gray and dull to black and shiny, much like a mirror, reflecting the unsettled earth that hung beneath it.

It rarely rained in Southern California during summer, especially so heavily, yet here it was, as though life were serving a harsh challenge to what we knew—to what *I* knew. The driving rain pushed down harder. I flicked on my windshield wipers, but they displaced the water more than cleared it.

After a while, the storm let up some, going from heavy to moderate, enough for me to see where I was. The first thing to catch my eye was a corner bar. Not once in my life had I had the urge to drink, but in this moment, unfamiliar curiosity picked at me. Could alcohol numb my constant, consuming unrest? It had worked for my father at a price that was more severe than the feelings he tried to bury. But immediate escape was the name of this game, and I was ready to play. Besides, it would only be this one time, a short-lived, well-deserved escape.

But will I like it too much?

Not an unreasonable question. Yet, as if independent of my mind, my hands steered the car around the corner and into the bar's parking lot. I pulled into a spot, then ran to the entrance, rain soaking my hair and clothes in the short distance I'd traveled.

Inside, I found shelter from the rain but not from my dismay. I headed for the bar, but when I got there, I didn't even know what to order.

"Bourbon," I told the bartender, thinking maybe I'd understand why he was so drawn to the drink.

As soon as he placed the glass in front of me, the too-familiar, sickening smell hit me hard, and it all came back to me: the image of my father idiotically stumbling into doors and knocking into walls as he tried to make his way through the house. His vomit on the carpet.

My utter disgust.

Then, I thought, *What if it turns me into an asshole, too? Into the Monster?*

The sound of a glass slamming onto the bar counter, followed by a large belch, demanded my attention. When I searched to my right, I found an older guy with salt-and-pepper hair, eyes narrow slits, body undulating from left to right. For a split second, I saw my father, and then my stomach soured with revulsion. I stumbled back a few feet.

Why the fuck did I come here?

Then, my mind found clarity.

I knew where my next stop needed to be.

33

"LET'S GET YOU OUT OF this rain," Nolan said when he opened his door and saw me soaking wet and agitated. After ushering me inside, he led me to a small kitchenette table.

I tentatively lowered myself into the chair. Nolan retrieved a few towels and eyed me with worry. But since he'd been an AA sponsor, I suspected he wasn't too rattled to find trouble on his doorstep.

"I was heating up tea when you came," Nolan said, pouring liquid from the kettle to cup by the stove. He brought the cup to me, took a seat across the table, and said, "So, let's hear it, Griffin. Tell me all about what's wrong."

I took one of the towels and pressed it against my face. The relief was instant. I appreciated this side of the man. His welcoming manner, his warmth, offered assurance and safety, yet all I could do was shake my head.

"Sip a little tea," he said, gesturing to my cup. "It'll help."

I did, then told him everything that happened: my disorientation at Oceanview, my pitiable father, the vivid sound memory of his old nickname in my ears, and especially the way I'd fled to a bar.

When I finished, he said, "No wonder you're in a state, Griffin. You're under a lot of pressure, and seeing your father in such a sad state shook you up. But you already knew that bar was the last place you needed to go before you even walked into it."

I swatted a wet lock of hair away from my forehead. "I tried to sabotage myself. I feel like I'm losing my mind."

"Desperation drove you inside. Wisdom drew you out. You knew drinking wasn't your answer—you saw your dad try and fail at it for years—and it would only steer you into another disaster."

I put both hands around my cup and stared into the dark tea. The smell was something herbal, spicy.

"You will be better for this in time, Griffin."

I looked up at him. "How can you know that?"

"Because I've lived long enough. That's how I learned." An insightful smile. "You'll grow from this, and then you'll move on."

I stared at him, considering what he said.

"These cheap chairs are about as comfortable as road asphalt," Nolan said. "What do you say we move into the living room?"

From the couch, I studied his apartment: neat as could be, everything stored in its proper place—remote controls in a basket on the coffee table, a stack of crocheted drink coasters next to him. I looked at the dark mahogany bookshelf, filled with titles, all kinds of them, organized by author and size. One in particular caught my eye, *Frankenstein* by Mary Shelley. I remember reading it in high school; even more, one passage that stuck to me: *I am an unfortunate and deserted creature, I look around and I have no relation or friend upon earth. These amiable people to whom I go have never seen me and know little of me. I am full of fears, for if I fail there, I am an outcast in the world forever.*

I pulled my attention away from the book, and it landed on the opposite wall where a beautiful, elaborate metal compass hung, encased in glass.

"A gift from my sponsor a long time ago," he said, noticing my interest, "so I wouldn't lose my way."

"Did it help?"

He laughed. "If only life were that simple. But I guess symbolically, yes. It reminded me to stop getting in my own way. We all tend to do that sometimes, don't we?"

"Truth."

"Indeed." He leaned back and stared out his window, falling into a state of easy reflection.

I allowed my gaze to rove further into Nolan's place, and my vision settled on a round table, displaying an array of framed photos. I focused on a few, and it became evident that Nolan hadn't always lived a solitary life. He was once surrounded by people who loved him—kids, grandkids, and …

"Is that your wife?" I asked, pointing to one of the pictures.

He took his attention from window to table. "Yes, my Elaine," he said, the drag of sorrow settling across his features. "That picture was before life got hard."

I considered the photo again; the beautiful woman stood on a beach, waving to the camera with a bright red bathing suit and a satisfied grin. I always held the theory that people are closer to their true selves in how they react to the wind, sand, and mercurial water—through that lens, I could see this woman as relaxed and content.

"What happened?" I asked.

Nolan looked downward and squeezed the bridge of his nose. "She was only in her thirties when cancer took her from me. By the time they found the tumor in her brain, it was too late. I watched the love of my life suffer, then die."

My head felt like it weighed a few hundred pounds, and the effort to sit up straight seemed like too much. Resting my elbows on my knees, I said, "Nolan … I … I'm so, so sorry. My father must have really related."

"He did. When Elaine died, it felt like I did, too. That was when my heavy drinking started. A life without her wasn't a life worth living. The only reason I didn't end things was because of my children. They'd just lost their mother. How could I leave them fatherless, too? I'd been sentenced to a lifetime of suffering, and the only way I knew how to relieve my pain was to keep drinking. I didn't care what the alcohol did to me—all I wanted was to stop … feeling."

"How long did that go on?"

"Years. But then one evening, I left the bar, as usual, with too many drinks in me. I got on the road and ran a red light. You can probably guess what happened next."

Flash bang. Once again, I saw myself driving my drunk father to the liquor store, trying to prevent what I knew Nolan was about to tell me.

"Yeah, ran right into another car. Luckily, I'd just pulled out of the lot and I wasn't going too fast, but I smacked into them pretty hard. I jumped out of my car and ran to the other vehicle to check on the occupants. There sat a mother and father in the front, two little girls in the back." Nolan stopped and held up a hand. He closed his eyes, breathed in deep, and shook his head. His voice faltered when he said, "What I did to that family … I'll never forget the looks on their faces. They were strangely quiet. One of the kids, a little girl, looked into my eyes. I was stunned. Unable to speak or move. That's when it all felt real. Her terror became a part of me."

"I'm glad no one was injured."

"I was lucky, and I never took another drink. After I got sober, something occurred to me."

I leaned in toward him.

"I learned the value of time and suffering. Losing my wife, surviving the accident, and seeing that family alive—all of it forced me into an understanding that time is the most valuable thing we've got, and there's not a second to waste. Nothing lasts forever, but that's the most beautiful part of life. Now, when I see pictures of my wife, I can smile. I remember the love she gave me instead of the pain of losing her. Our time together was too short, but what a lucky, *lucky* man I was to have it at all. To experience that kind of love."

"And the suffering part?"

"What I did when I got into my car that night was unforgivable. I deeply regret it, but it's not about the pain. Tragic moments are hard lessons that still have to be learned, and I'd learned mine."

I wasn't sure what my own suffering could teach me—it was as if my thoughts jumped the track to every bad memory my father had put there. The only rationalization I had for this was how different Nolan's situation and mine were.

I said, "I assume you know about the past with my father and me."

"I do."

"You loved your wife, but I can't see the value in growing up with a father who abused me daily. Time after time, all he did was hit and run. The man didn't learn a thing."

Nolan settled back deeper into the sofa and said, "Don't be so sure of that."

I gave him a sidelong look. I was tired, and I didn't feel like debating the matter.

"There's a lot you don't know about your dad. Don't believe for a minute that he wasn't aware of his mistakes and didn't regret them. I know this because we talked about it many, many times. But he was beginning to learn his lessons before the Alzheimer's. And most of those lessons were because of you, Griffin."

Never once had I seen my father show the slightest sign of regret—a thousand shades of anger and hostility were all he ever had for me.

Nolan went on, "I can't tell you the number of times he picked up the phone to call you but never had the courage to dial your number."

My expression dulled. "What did he want to say?"

"He wanted to apologize."

"Yeah? So, what stopped him?"

"He couldn't forgive himself for what he did to you and Deena and figured you wouldn't want to hear it, anyway. I urged him to call in spite of that, but he told me he wouldn't do it unless he got sober and stayed sober. Otherwise, he'd look like a hypocrite."

I was starting to see Nolan in a different light. He seemed like an excellent manager—he'd managed the mess in my father's apartment, and now, he was handling the emotional cleanup here, too.

"Alzheimer's got your dad off the bottle, but in all the wrong ways," he said. "That disease took away his chance to finally make amends to you."

"I never thought my father could take responsibility for anything. I didn't even think remorse was something he was capable of feeling, certainly not love." But as I spoke, my words fell hard on that memory of my father, weeping in the bedroom and speaking of his regret.

"Your dad *did* love you, Griffin. During the times he was sober, I got a rare chance to meet the real Sam McCabe. Beneath his alcoholism was kindness and, believe it or not, great fondness for you."

I closed my eyes, trying to make sense of the senseless. All those years, I longed to feel love from my father and never got it, but finding out it had been there all along still couldn't change my outlook. Not even if he had my pictures on the wall to prove it. Facts were facts, and the pain my father caused was as real as the day he'd inflicted it.

"I don't know if I can forgive him," I said.

I wasn't sure if I had enough goodwill to show up for it. But then I looked back at my own emotional landscape. I had a whole decade of living on the cusp of my inability to admit I was wrong. Not until Trish—and lately, Deena—had I realized that there was no shame in saying I was sorry. Now, with Ryan, I was burning unnecessary anger on our unfinished business. Whether or not we stayed friends, forgiveness would make it easier on us both.

"Maybe try to see it this way." Nolan looked toward the ceiling and breathed in deeply through his nose. "Your father never wanted to cause you pain. He just couldn't figure out how to stop his life from going up in flames, so he reached for the gasoline can instead of the water hose."

The value of time and suffering.

I wondered if that was *my* lesson, too. If there was an uncovered truth that adversity wanted to teach me.

Outside Nolan's window, the rain began to let up, and I thought about what he'd said. My father might not have meant to cause me pain, but he still did. It was *his* choice to reach for the gasoline instead of the water hose.

34

I SAT ON A ROCK at Windansea Beach in La Jolla, where two sandstone points reached toward the sea on both sides of me like protective arms. The storm had passed. In its wake, a bruised and battered sky moved overhead, casting gray-brown hues across a seamless ocean. Waves crashed hard as if in protest of the squall that had muddied their waters. I breathed in fresh air cleansed by the storm. I gazed at the sky, my safe place when I was younger, then at the water, my safe place when I got older. It can get lonely loving a place that doesn't even know you're there, yet you keep returning to it anyway because it's beautiful. I guess that's what people mean about being a loner in nature.

This also used to be one of my favorite surfing spots because the waves were usually pumping. Back then, all I needed was a board and a barrel to find a pocket of happiness. But not anymore. I'd emptied out all of my old coping equipment, and it seemed the only thing left at the bottom of the toolbox was a moonless void.

So much to absorb. So many circumstances and events to sort through. What Nolan told me went against everything I thought I'd known. My father had acted deplorably cruel, but could it really be possible that life pushed him into a new understanding of his destructive actions? That he felt actual regret? I still wasn't so sure yet, but if I turned the magnifying glass around toward myself, I could see that I'd had my own share of weakness and damage to overcome, and I wasn't done yet. Looking into the past, Deena was a prime example of my imperfections. The signs of her abuse were right in front of me, yet I had been too focused on myself to notice, instead choosing to paint her as an adversary. All people make mistakes on their evolution through life—that's how we learn and grow, as Nolan had said.

Something else was on my mind, too. While I'd wanted to feel loved by my father, had he become sober enough to hope for the same from me? Did he even have the right to ask for it? And if he did, was I strong enough to forgive him and love him back? It was a big ask, the kind of challenge that made everything else look trivial. Just a few weeks ago, I wondered if I had the courage to step into my father's room for the first time. Now, in comparison, that paled into insignificance.

Maybe sometimes it feels good to just let go.

Like water breaking through a narrow stream, the notion came rushing in: I might have been able to move on with life if I could just let go of the resentment toward my father.

I learned the value of time.

Now, Nolan spoke to me. I could, if I chose, use my time to seek wisdom from my pain instead of allowing it to embitter and consume me. Each day, the disease stole more of my father's mind. If finding forgiveness was the key to finding happiness, my only chance was sliding away with each minute.

As if holding up a compass, I saw where I needed to travel.

And it pointed in one direction.

In a chair near his window, my father stared out at the fountain garden. A spray of sunlight washed across his features. I wasn't sure if the light was playing tricks on me, but he looked more at peace than before. No hollow smile varnished across his face, just a tangible air of calm about him.

Until he turned to me. The shadowy dints reappeared on his face, as did deep lines like rough-hewn roadways where alcohol and heartache had carved their paths.

My father's face brightened at the sight of me, and my two conflicting impressions merged, anchoring me firmly in the present. I grabbed a chair and dragged it close to his. He observed me for a beat, then directed his focus back out through the window. I shared the view with him, and we admired the courtyard fountain in the midst of a profusion of flowers: purples, pinks, yellows, and oranges. Bordering the courtyard was an array of robust, tropical greenery. I spared another glance at my father, who appeared entranced by the view, eyes going from one spot to the next. Again, I saw a stranger, but for the first time, I was able to appreciate the experience as an open door, not a cause for resentment.

Everything is different now, but does different have to be worse?

My father turned to me, his eyes clouded by time and illness, and said, "It's a beautiful day, isn't it?"

"It is," I said, looking back out through the window. "It's very beautiful. Do you know who I am?"

"Yes," he said, nodding. "It's wonderful to see you again."

He was aware of his surroundings, even me, which put a lump into my throat. My chest swelled in the place where that old nickname Champ still lived. This feeling was an awakening, a fresh start. Was it the start of forgiveness? My father and I turned to each other. He reached out to put a hand on my face, but it didn't come across as a gesture of love. More, it came across as exploratory.

"You," he said.

"Yeah, it's me."

My father's eyelids became heavy, and his head drooped. I checked my watch.

It was getting late, so I told him, "I have to go now, okay? But I'll come back to see you again. I promise."

I turned to leave. Halfway to the door, I heard, "That would be wonderful, Nolan. Just wonderful."

35

I WAS RUNNING AGAIN.

I'd started at five p.m., and it was now six thirty.

The doctor told me to avoid exercise for another week, yet there I was, and I couldn't stop. Addiction ran deep in my family, and I was no better off than the others; I'd just chosen a different fix. At least it was a healthy one—in some respects maybe but not in others. I'd already jacked up my leg. What came next? Another injury? An eating disorder? I wasn't stupid. I knew I was playing a dangerous game, but I kept working harder to destroy my body than to heal my pain. Pain that was literally becoming more difficult to outrun.

I'd expected too much from my father when I went to see him the day before, but my emotions were so ramped up after nearly discovering a new addiction—his addiction—that I'd already lost perspective. I came to him, ready to open a new door, only to see that it was double-padlocked from the outside with no key in sight. It didn't matter what my expectations were. Life doesn't always go the way we want. It doesn't wait for us. It operates on its own terms, yet we keep chasing the elusive glimmers, hoping that this time will be different. I couldn't even blame my father anymore; he'd been fighting his own war. This one was all on me.

Trish had been away on an overnight business trip to LA. When I arrived home, she took in my sweat-soaked body but did not say anything; she didn't have to.

In an effort to explain myself, I told her about the events from the day before but avoided the damning details, including how I had heard a nonexistent voice, then almost took my first swig of booze. I wanted to give her the whole truth, but I couldn't step up to it, too ashamed and afraid that she'd see how stuck I really was. So, instead, I only told her about seeing my father in the recreation room, then seeing Nolan, then going back to see my father. How we'd had this beautiful moment together, right before I'd found out that he didn't know who I was.

Trish's features softened with compassion. "It was just that one time. He may recognize you next time. He's done it before, right?"

I went into the kitchen, opened the fridge, and stared into it, but I didn't see a thing.

"Griffin?"

"It's fine," I said way too fast. "I'll deal with it."

Trish said nothing more. She vanished into her office. I supposed this was her way of letting me deal with it.

It had been hours.

Trish still hadn't come to bed, and I knew that her disengagement wasn't just her way of letting me deal with it—she was probably also taking care of her own frustration. Much like me, she'd chosen to do that by herself instead of talking it out, which threw another veil of distress over our already-tense lives.

Unable to fall asleep, I got out of bed. When I reached Trish's office, she was at her desk, thumbing through a pamphlet of some sort. I stood in the doorway, staring at her for several seconds, but she wouldn't look up.

"Okay, I get it," I told her, my words slow and measured. "You've made your point."

Trish looked up, but her expression did not welcome me. It was uncharitable. The resistance I'd felt on previous occasions—that backstop on her usual generosity—was again staring me in the face and pressing down on me. It was as if I were standing before a cold, blank wall.

"I'm tired, Griffin. Tired of caring for you more than you care about yourself."

"So, that's it? You're checking out on me?"

Her jaw went slack. "Really? *You're* the one who's checked out."

I froze, unsure what to say or do.

"You keep doing this," she said. "You make me stand on the sidelines where all I can do is watch you implode. For God's sake, you're back to overworking your body, and it hasn't even healed yet. And the worst part? You can't see that you're drowning."

I stepped deeper into the room. "That's not true."

"You can't be serious." She scoffed. "Quit lying to yourself, Griffin. Quit avoiding the obvious. You're in trouble. Serious trouble."

"I *know* I am!" I closed my eyes and clenched a lock of hair on each side of my head.

"Then … *do* something," she begged. "For God's sake, anything! Just try!"

I stopped myself from going further, afraid I'd regret what I said. My muscles burned. My overworked limbs were failing. I yanked a chair toward me, then crumpled into it. Seeing me collapse from fatigue only proved her point.

"I can't do this …" she said, her voice brittle and choked by emotion, her eyes watery. "I can't stand seeing you this way! I feel like I'm looking at our future, and it isn't what I want to see." She got up from her desk but refused to meet my pleading gaze. "You know I care about what you're going through. I really do." She reached for the pamphlet on her desk, then handed it to me as she left the room. "Maybe you'll find better advice from strangers."

I got up from the chair and looked at what she'd given me. It was about a support group for children of Alzheimer's patients. I thumbed through it, thinking she knew she couldn't fix me, so now, she was sending me off to a meeting instead, likely in some cold church basement with watery coffee and a tray filled with stale everything bagels.

Commotion called for my attention. I looked up and saw Trish unzipping a suitcase, so I raced inside.

"Hey! Where are you going?"

"I'm sorry," she said, folding a pair of jeans with haste, then shoving them into the suitcase. "I need to stay with my mom for a bit so I can clear my head." She finished stuffing clothes into her leaving-me bag, zipped it up, then wheeled it toward the door.

"Please don't go. Please." I shook my head. "I don't want this."

She spun around. "Do you think this is easy for me? *Damn it*, Griffin! I'm tired! I'm just …" She stopped herself as if there were no point in going on, then proceeded toward the door.

I reached for her shoulder, but she shrugged my hand away. She was leaving me. It was really happening. In the years we'd been together, and despite our challenges, neither of us had ever walked out.

I watched her go through the door. Out of my life. Then, I leaned against the wall, trying to steady myself as my body slid down it until I sat on the floor, tears stinging my eyes.

I brought my hands to my face, and one word went through my mind—so real, so commanding, I could almost hear it.

Alone.

36

MY FATHER DIDN'T MIND WHEN we sat in his family room as long as he wasn't there. When he left the house, Deena and I would take turns dominating the space, reclining in his chair, and watching the big screen TV.

On this evening, my father took off for the neighborhood bar to throw back a few with his buddies. Deena was out with friends, so I came downstairs to the family room, excited to catch up on some shows.

But about a half hour into the show, he startled me by wandering back through the room, then went straight for the wet bar to pour himself a drink. I'd heard his car leave the driveway, but after cranking up the TV speakers, I must have missed his return.

"Move out," he ordered, shooing me away as if I were some family pet who'd hopped onto the furniture.

When I got up, he shouldered me out of his way, then plummeted into the recliner. He yanked the lever and changed the channel to his favorite sportscast.

There were many occasions when he'd dressed me down so harshly that it brought tears. In those instances, I'd bite my tongue, then run off to my bedroom, but that only sharpened my feelings of isolation. Times like these were difficult, too. Being unseen, unheard, and unwanted brought a sting all its own.

Not this time.

This time felt different. The burden of rejection had been bearing down on me for so long that I thought I'd die if I had to suck one more breath from inside that house. So, I decided to run away. I tossed a bunch of clothes into my gym bag, then took off.

But as I gained distance from home, more distress shadowed me. I hadn't given much thought to where I'd go. I couldn't stay at Ryan's place. His parents would ask questions, and that would just lead me into more trouble, then right back to my father's house. I couldn't ask a family friend to take me in, either—most had disappeared after my father had started drinking. Even my mother's best friend, Catherine, couldn't stand being around him. She'd distanced herself at my and Deena's expense.

I'd thought I could escape the emptiness I felt inside that house, but there was more of it waiting outside. I had no place to run, and as nightfall arrived, the temperature got colder, hastened by the gathering wind of an oncoming squall. If that weren't bad enough, poor planning took my problems one step further because I hadn't even packed a blanket. All I had was a thin windbreaker from track that I wore while leaving the house, which wouldn't keep me warm.

Out of necessity, I found a bridge to camp out under until morning. As rain began to fall, I knew I'd left one bad situation and jumped straight into another; I spent a good part of that night sleeping and waking between the glaring headlights, shivering, and shaming myself for being careless.

When I woke up the next morning, the storm had passed. I was hungry with only a few bucks in my pocket, which, if I was lucky, would buy me nothing better than a candy bar. While trying to figure out my next move, a man came toward me—he looked to be somewhere in his sixties, but he was homeless and might have been younger. His hair fell past his shoulders in frazzled strands of black and gray that framed his leathery face. He wore shoes—if you could call them that—so depleted that he'd wrapped duct tape around them, and I couldn't tell where the shoe began and the tape ended.

Flap, flap, scrape, scrape.

The sound of his improvised shoes picked up momentum as they shuffled my way. He took a seat beside me on the curb, gazing ahead, as if we'd already known each other for years.

"Haven't seen you around," he said after a minute or so. "You a runaway?"

I nodded.

"Where'd you come in from?"

A fair enough question. A lot of homeless teens were drawn to Southern California because of the warm climate.

"I'm from here," I told him.

"I was one, too. A runaway."

I turned to look at him. "You've been on the streets for that long?"

He picked up a rock, flung it across the road. "On and off for years, yeah."

"That sounds like a hard life."

He locked an ugly gaze on me for about five seconds, then let out a cynical laugh, revealing a snaggletoothed smile with rotting brown teeth. "Where do you think you're headed, son?"

"I'm not sure yet. I'm trying to figure out—"

"I'm not talking about finding the next roof to get under, boy." He gave a flick of his hand. "I'm talking about the rest of your life because it looks like you're headed to the same damned place I'm at now!" The man jumped into a standing position, wildly flailing his hands, eyes pinging in every direction with abandon. "I'll tell you what!" He ducked and weaved as if trying to ward off a helicopter zooming around his head. "One day, you'll blink and wonder how the hell you got here and where you went wrong! Why you spent all those years going from one bridge to another, one dumpster to the next, lookin' for something to eat that won't make you retch it all back up on the sidewalk!"

My only reaction was to look for an escape route.

"And that's if you're lucky!" He spat twice at the sidewalk for emphasis, then went on, jabbing his index finger at me. "These streets here? All you gotta do is run into the wrong person. They'll knock the daylight outta you … or do something worse to your body, if you know what I mean!"

He came at me. I tried to jump out of his way, but he managed to catch my arm by the sleeve, pulling me back in. He tightened his grip on my arm until it hurt. I tried to endure the pain.

186

Looking me dead in the eyes, gnashing his teeth, he said, "Get your sorry ass outta here, kid! You got no business bein' here! Wherever you left's gonna look like a vacation compared to this."

He shoved me away by the arm, and I went running. On some level, I felt sympathy for him. He was obviously a mentally ill man, trying to exist in an insane world. He had no place to go—wandering from one overpass to the next, just trying to exist—but I had a home. Even with its own variant of pain, it had a roof and a kitchen full of food.

On my way back to the house, I passed a woman huddled in a storefront doorway. She shivered, then looked up at me, terrified. But when our eyes connected, something passed between us. An unspoken conversation. A connection. There we were, from two different places— me a wealthy neighborhood, she, the streets—but her dejection felt like my own. I handed her the few dollars in my pocket, and when I gave the woman my windbreaker, her fear transmuted to guarded gratitude.

It was late evening by the time I made it back to our front door. I stood there for a long time, trying to gather courage to step back into my private circle of hell and endure the ridicule for my botched runaway attempt.

My father was sitting in his usual spot in the family room when I entered. I thought about using an alternate route through the house to avoid him, but he was going to see me eventually, so I decided to trudge through and get it over with. I got some food from the fridge and shoved it down into my empty stomach, then chased it down with a big pull of milk.

I walked into the family room, dreading his retribution. Although my father damned well knew I was standing there, he ignored me, watching TV and sucking on his glass of bourbon. I was thankful he didn't lay into me, but then a new version of reality pushed through: I'd been missing for twenty-four hours, and my father hadn't even noticed—either that or he couldn't have cared less. The despair that fueled my departure in the first place had returned, only this time, tenfold. The hard truth was that a homeless stranger considered me more relevant than my own father did.

I'm not sure how I found the backbone to speak up—perhaps it came from a place where desperation and anger met.

"Why can't you just love me?" I blurted out.

He gave me the benefit of his attention, though with great annoyance because I'd interrupted his TV show.

"*What* and *what* now?" he said.

"Love me. Why can't you love me?"

He took a gulp from his glass, looked like he was thinking on it.

"Because, Griffin, you're unlovable," my father said very simply, then dismissed me from the room by taking another swig.

37

I WOKE UP THE NEXT morning in a world I barely recognized.

Ryan was gone. Deena was gone—although she'd never been there from the start—and now Trish, the person I leaned on the most, was gone, too. The most painful part of it all was that I recognized the real problem: I was doing a spectacular job at driving people away.

I would do anything to get Trish back, but she wouldn't welcome the effort. I was sinking, my nose just above the waterline. I had to fix myself; I just wasn't sure how yet. I considered the pamphlet Trish had given me. A lunchtime meeting began in about an hour in Kensington Heights. Maybe she just needed to see that I was serious about getting better. Those people might be strangers, but maybe they were strangers with stories similar to mine.

In an effort to reconstruct a bridge between Deena and me, I called to ask if she wanted to come along. A very quiet voice in my mind hoped that she'd say yes and even reconsider helping me pay for our father's care.

She swiftly, but diplomatically, turned down my offer.

I took a seat in the back row near the door. The meeting hadn't started yet, so I circled my vision through the room, observing the other occupants. A middle-aged couple sat up front, holding hands. A few rows back, a woman sat alone, keeping her eyes aimed straight ahead with no discernible expression. In her forties, she wore a black business suit that did not look cheap. She'd probably stopped here after a long day of work, and despite her effort to hide it, she looked lonely and sad.

"Hi."

I looked to my side. A woman about my age smiled at me. She had mid-length blonde hair and soft bangs across her forehead.

"I'm Kristine."

"Hello, Kristine. I'm Griffin."

"Nice to meet you. Is this your first time here?"

I laughed. "Is it that obvious?"

"I wasn't going to say so, but …"

The meeting began. People told compelling stories about their loved ones who had become lost within themselves. Others explained the struggle of trying to accept that parents or spouses who meant so much to them had practically walked away from their own bodies. An older man stood up to talk about the special love he had for his wife.

"We were very close. I've always gone to her when I needed someone to talk to, and she always knew what to say. Where will I go now?"

The woman in the black suit stood up but broke into tears before she could speak. A lady next to her got up and placed an arm around her shoulder. The group waited, but the woman in the black suit didn't talk; instead, she apologized to the group, then lowered herself back into her chair.

It was all so intense, but I struggled to connect to their stories. These people had close, adoring relationships with their suffering loved ones. They had lived a different story with years of happy memories to prove it. For those who spoke about parents, hearing them talk about their cheery upbringings made the hurt harder, stretching an already-exacerbated injury. Still, I tried to frame this in a way that might help instead of hinder me. If I removed our differences, would there be broken pieces left to connect us? I decided to wait this out, hoping I could adjust and discover meaning through others' experiences. My relationship with Trish might depend on it.

A man raised his hand, then got up to speak. "Loving someone with Alzheimer's is like going to a funeral every day. You mourn their death before it even happens."

One woman stood. "I grew up, left the house, and moved out of state with my own family to raise. For years, I lived thousands of miles away from them. Then, my dad died, and my mother was on her own. When the Alzheimer's came, there was nobody left to care for her, so I had to put her into a home. I couldn't afford to take time off from work, so there was no one on the outside to come see her. It's a shame that this is the American way. Nothing like other cultures, where generations of families live in the same house and take care of each other."

All around the room, people nodded, lamenting, probably because their parents felt stolen from them, too, and there was nothing they could do about it.

"I love my father so much," a man said. "We weren't just father and son. We were best friends." He wiped a tear away with his sleeve, then muttered, "*God*, I miss him."

His comment drove the knife blade in deeper: I wasn't a member of this club. My only comfort was knowing I could make a quick escape. When I stood, this Kristine woman looked up at me, but her expression was hard to unravel. Was she holding me responsible for trying to cut and run? My need to get out of there surpassed my need to figure out her impression, so I broke from her gaze, then tiptoed toward the exit.

An unpalatable mixture of separateness and guilt followed me through the front door—guilt for bailing on the meeting, separateness that sent me running in the first place. And despite being outside in the open, I remained trapped by those feelings. I lowered my body onto a brick ledge and kicked at dirt, trying to let the fresh air clear my lungs, my thoughts, too.

Unfortunately, the opportunity was short-lived. A group of people spilled out through the exit—among them, Kristine. She gave me a half-smile, complicated with something I couldn't quite decode.

I got up and went after her. "Hey," I said, jockeying beside her as she continued walking. "I know how it probably looked when I left, like I didn't care about what was going on, but it wasn't like that."

Keeping her gaze aimed ahead, she laughed. "I only met you a few minutes ago, Griffin, and we barely spoke. Why do you think that would be enough for me to have any meaningful impression of you at all?"

"Because I'm an approval junkie?"

That made her laugh. "Look, it was hard for me the first time, too."

I turned to look at her. "Does it get any easier?"

She stopped walking. "I'd even venture to say it gets better, but you'll have to stick around more than a few minutes to find out."

"I know. That was pretty chickenshit of me. It was just hard to relate to those people."

"Really?" She towed her head back a bit to appraise me. "You have a loved one with Alzheimer's. They have loved ones with Alzheimer's, right?"

"No, not a loved one." I paused and took a good breath. "Just a father. We've had nothing to do with each other for years. It seemed everyone in there had relationships that meant something. I had nothing like that."

"Wow," Kristine said, mouth widening around the word.

"What's wrong?"

"I know we've just met—so excuse me for being this blunt—but you're not special, and you aren't the only one who had a lousy relationship with their parent."

"I didn't hear anyone else talk about that."

She raised a brow.

"I know," I admitted, "left too soon. I can be a little impulsive."

"Just a tad," she said with a deliberate smile.

"Do you know anyone there who had a rough go with their parents?"

She raised her hand.

Now, it was my turn to say, "Wow."

"Look, Griffin, you've got a lot to learn if you're going to survive this."

"Can you help me?" I nodded toward the end of the street. "I know of a diner up on the corner there. It's not mama's cooking, but they serve a decent cup of coffee. My treat?"

"I don't know." She looked at her watch. "This is my lunch hour. I have to get back to work soon."

"We can make it quick. I promise."

She studied me for about five seconds, thinking about it, then agreed.

Someone I could talk to. A sense of belonging, of no longer feeling unmoored.

We sat in a booth at Fritzy's Restaurant, a classic greasy-spoon diner. The floor was covered in off-white tile with gold sparkles, the booths, upholstered in pumpkin-colored vinyl with brass tacks holding them in place. I breathed in the air, a combination of deep-battered this and baked that. To this day, the smell of fry grease still sent a wave of nausea arcing through me, memories of my sixth birthday at the fair. But I knew the coffee was good.

Kristine took a bite from her Danish—filled with walnuts, covered in thick white glaze, and the right amount of cinnamon sprinkled on top—then washed it down with a sip of coffee. "Wow," she said, "these are *really* good. You might want to order one."

I aimed a palm at the Danish and shook my head. "Just coffee for me."

"I suspected as much." She laughed. "You look way too fit to indulge."

"It's kind of my thing, staying fit."

"It suits you well."

I shrugged. She might not have thought so if she knew the full story.

"So," Kristine said, "about the meeting. Besides me, there are several people in the group who had lousy relationships with their parents. That's why they come there. To clean up all the garbage."

"Does it help?"

"Not sure about them, but it has for me."

"How long have you been going?"

"Let me see …" She looked up at the ceiling and moved her eyes back and forth as if a calendar were pasted to it. "My mom died about a year and a half ago, and I started going to the meetings soon after that."

"Oh, I didn't know she'd passed."

"Is your …"

"My father, and he's alive."

"Lucky for you."

"In principle, that should be the case."

"You *are* lucky. You still have time."

An elderly couple sat in the booth ahead of us. The woman firmed up a napkin in the neckline of her husband's shirt, then used another to dab the corners of his mouth. He raised his quivering head to look at her with loving eyes.

Kristine allowed me to finish watching, then said, "You asked for my advice? My suggestion would be to go back to the meetings, and instead of shutting people off, turn up the volume. Listen to their stories. Let them help. But most of all, flip the script from being a victim and open your mouth. You do have a voice, you know. Doing anything less will make you feel like more of an outsider, and it's too damned hard, trying to navigate this all by yourself."

"I've already paid a steep price for doing that." I sipped some coffee, placed it back on the table with care, then met her gaze. "Everyone who mattered to me is pulling back."

"I'm sorry, Griffin. That's a terrible place to be. But you *can* turn this around. I'd give anything to push time back and make things right with my mom. She and I were estranged for years. I spent so much time being angry at her for what she did to me that by the time I found out she had Alzheimer's, it was too late. She'd already passed. If I'd just swallowed my pride and forgiven her … but your father is still here."

"I don't know. I've tried to talk to him, but the last time was an epic fail."

"What happened?"

"We had this great moment together, and then I realized he didn't know who I was."

"So? Go again tomorrow. Your father could come back. They do that, drift in and out of awareness."

She wasn't the first person to recommend that I keep trying. When would I start paying attention to good advice?

"Look, nothing stays the same with this disease," Kristine said. "There's no pattern, and there will always be fits and starts, but you have to keep jumping in and trying. There may be visits when he *does* recognize you."

"He did, a few times before."

"Then, there you go."

"During the last visit when he didn't recognize me, the hard part was thinking we'd had a connection, then finding out there hadn't been one at all."

"Welcome to Alzheimer's," she said with a laugh. "But you've got one thing working in your favor."

I nodded for her to go on.

"Most patients can recall the distant past—they just can't tell you what they had for lunch a few minutes ago. So, you may get the chance to tell him how you feel about what happened between you, and he may be able to do the same. Don't give up on him. There may be moments when he's cognizant. If he is, dive into the past. You'll be surprised how lucid they can become."

"I didn't know all this. I guess I could have educated myself better."

"That's not what's important."

"What is?"

"That you don't end up in the same place I did. Alone and full of regret."

I read her as a teacher or some kind of professional group leader. There was a briskness in her manner that reminded me of some of my favorite professors in college, a mix of generosity and impersonality. I also sensed a clock on her advice—that she was an inscrutable and busy person who was only showing a part of herself, and her willingness to spend time here was nearing its end. I respected that, so I politely ended the conversation before she could. As we parted, I briefly thanked her for the good advice, then went my separate way.

I was grateful for our talk but noticed the smallest hint of chagrin. I didn't like having to ask for help like some flashing beacon of neediness. Still, in some ways, I felt more stable after our conversation. I'd come a long way but still had more to go before I could find forgiveness.

38

I PARKED MYSELF ON A seawall along the Pacific Beach boardwalk, eating a fish taco from Roberto's and watching people who many within the surfing culture referred to as *hodads*: people who hung out at the beach but didn't surf. Skateboarders, joggers, and tourists breezed by, the familiar and comforting smell of coconut suntan oil drifting across the air as they made the most of San Diego's agreeable climate and endless sunshine. The waves peeled perfectly, surfers shimmying back and forth atop them like dancers in the mist. Why hadn't I been out there in so long?

It was four days, and Trish still wasn't back. She wouldn't even pick up the phone or answer my texts. With each hour she was gone, the fissure between us widened, and I became more worried that she'd reached her saturation point and we were done.

They'd settled my father down in the TV room. He sat by himself in the front row. The place moved patients around a lot here—a good thing, I supposed, and much better than leaving them in their rooms—but I couldn't help but feel as though the staff was forced to play a challenging game of three-dimensional chess, switching one patient here, another there, in order to keep them from being stagnant.

I stood at the back of the room, observing my father with guarded interest. He gazed vacantly at a midday talk show on TV where a woman recounted her sad love story.

"He never came back!" the woman said through sobs and sniffles. "And *she's* the one who did this to me. *Her!*"

The host frowned and nodded, then offered the woman a box of tissues. From the look on my father's face, he'd might as well have been watching a deck of cards flip across the screen.

I walked to the front row and took a seat beside him. He regarded me mildly, as if I were just another resident.

"Hi, Dad," I said, realizing it was the first time I'd referred to him as my father.

"Oh, hi," he replied but didn't mention my name.

"What are you watching?" I asked for lack of a better topic.

"It's a documentary about the Battle of Normandy!" His face lit up. "Very interesting. Would you like to watch it with me?"

The talk show played on. I wondered if someone had switched the channel on him while he wasn't looking.

"Sure," I said, observing the talk show host who welcomed another woman on set to join the current guest. They must have loathed each other because Tearful Woman popped straight up like a jack-in-the-box when she saw New Woman, lips pursed into a straight magenta line, hands clamped onto her hips.

My father asked, "Did you know they had to delay the invasion of Normandy because of bad weather?"

"No, I didn't."

"They said it right there." He pointed to the screen. "Another interesting fact: D-Day doesn't stand for anything. It was just a placeholder we used to keep spies from knowing the real launch date. Can you imagine that?" He chuckled. "All this time, I thought it meant more."

I nodded and smiled. Although I enjoyed the history lesson, I was puzzled over which part of my father's fragmented brain was teaching him about D-Day. This visit felt like more of the same: a circular discussion headed for nowhere.

So, we sat, immersed in the lull—me watching the inane talk show, my father watching the Battle of Normandy. We were in two different worlds, but hadn't we always been?

"So," I said, "are they treating you well here?"

"Oh, yes … yes. Very much, thank you. They have pizza on Fridays! Who doesn't love a pizza?"

"You have to keep jumping in and trying."

I took Kristine's advice and said, "Hey, do you remember that summer when we vacationed at Catalina Island?"

His vision bounced from TV to floor. The creases between his eyes burrowed deeper. "No, can't say I do."

"We all went. Mom was still with us then. We rode our bikes."

Nothing. He went back to his TV watching. The five o'clock news came on, but his mind was probably now playing the talk show from earlier that he didn't see. I blew out my cheeks, released the air slowly. I checked my watch. Then, I thought about the surrealism of this situation: I kept hoping my father would return, but as whom? The man I least liked? A different, nicer man who remembered what he had done to me? A merger of both? Despite Kristine's advice, I had to question what I was doing here and where *he* was, other than falling through the cracks in his mind.

Long silence.

"How about the fair that one summer? On my birthday? Do you remember that?" A question that came more from a place of desperation than hope.

He scratched the back of his head. "I … I don't think so, but my memory has been terrible lately."

I looked out through the door and into the hallway, then back at him. The intermissions between us kept expanding, my hope for any progress shrinking. I didn't know what more I could do here.

I grasped for another attempt, random as it was, and said, "I love us, Dad." What I'd told him when we left the fair that day.

He didn't respond to that one, either.

But then something changed, something that, at first, was too vague to recognize but soon took shape before my eyes. Did I see confusion spreading across his face? No, it was more than that. Eyes, once without focus, widened and gained clarity. His expression, once vacuous, populated with signs of life.

We weren't in Normandy anymore.

My father had entered the room for the first time—or at the least some part of him had. I held my breath and chewed my bottom lip, hoping he wouldn't disappear on me again, that this might be what I'd been waiting for. Context. Recognition.

In a voice faint and breathless, he sang, "*He's my little buddy. Da, DA, da, DA.   He's my little buddy.* Oh what a day that was, Champ. One of the best."

Sensations of weightlessness rippled through me. And as we reminisced about our day in the sun, we were there again, walking hand in hand under a cloudless summer sky, smelling the churros as they fried in the distance, and feeling the happiness and camaraderie we shared as father and son. My heart filled with exhilaration. My eyes filled with tears.

"Don't be sad, Champ," my father told me. "How about some cotton candy? It's a wonderful day!"

Indeed, it was.

39

I STRODE THROUGH MY FRONT door and couldn't stop grinning. A breakthrough. An opening. Not only had my father recalled our summer day at the fair; he remembered me. Guardedly, I allowed hope to wander, weighing how much this might change our situation if just a little. As soon as I got inside, my first thought was how excited I was to call Trish and tell her about the progress with my father. She might dump me into voice mail, but I had to try.

The phone rang a few times, and to my surprise, she picked up. Also a surprise was her apathetic tone.

"What's up, Griffin?"

Excitement wilted. My heart deflated. She sounded like someone else or as if I were someone else, some irritating telemarketer pushing a free vacation escape.

"Hey, Twiz!" I said, realizing I hadn't called her that in a while—a bad omen I'd somehow missed, indicative that things had been going south for a long time. But saying her nickname didn't feel right anymore; it had lost its luster. Now, it was just a name. Nothing else. Flat. Meaningless. Coercing a return of enthusiasm in an effort to rekindle what she'd extinguished, I said, "I have great news, and I want to tell you about it!"

"What?" she said, but it sounded more like a demand to get it over with than a question.

"So, I took your advice and went to the support group you recommended, which I think is going to help me a lot. I even made a new friend who's been through a situation like mine, and we had a great talk."

I'm rambling. Rein it in.

"So, here's the big part," I continued. "I also went to see my dad today, and it was good. Well, not at first, but then he remembered me, Trish. He knew who I was!"

"That's great. I'm glad for you, Griffin," she said, voice flavorless.

Who is this woman, pretending to be my fiancée?

"Look, Trish, I know I messed up badly, and I didn't do a good job of letting you in. I've made a lot of mistakes, but I'm trying to change now. I'm trying very hard. Can you just give me a break?"

"Yes, Griffin. Of course."

"So, can we get together?" I asked. "Can we talk? I've missed you. I'd like to—"

"Look, I'm happy for you. I am, but you can't expect me to drop everything I'm doing right now."

"Why not?"

"Because I'm busy. I've got a caseload at work that's breaking my back, and my father's been sick with the flu." She paused. "And because I need a little more of a break from this."

"A break from *me?*"

She didn't answer.

"Wow …" I said.

"I'm sorry, but things have changed."

"So, our relationship has, like, what, timed out? I love you. Doesn't that matter? And you *do* love me, right?"

She began to say something, then stopped herself.

"Man, I don't like where this is going, Trish."

"That's the point. *We* haven't been going anywhere for a while."

"What are you even talking about? Have you've fallen out of love with me or something?"

"I'm not saying that."

"Then, what?"

"I just need some more time to think about us."

"But it almost sounds like you're not sure if there *is* an us anymore."

"Please, don't do this to me!"

"Do what? What am I doing? Telling you how much I love you? How much I miss you? Is that what I'm doing? And since when is that a bad thing?"

"Don't corner me, Griffin!"

"And now you're shouting."

"I … I'm sorry." Trish tempered her tone. "But you're putting words in my mouth, and I don't like it! I only said that I need to think things over."

"Just say it. Do you want to end this relationship?"

She paused, then said, "If you want to know the truth … I've given it some thought."

The floor opened beneath me, tension and uncertainty transmuting into ferocious heartache.

"I'm sorry, Griffin. But you forced an answer. I don't want to hurt you."

"I don't understand this. I thought you were coming back. What's changed?"

Trish didn't say anything more, but I wasn't sure if I wanted her to, afraid it would drive the hurt deeper. But I had to know.

"So, is this it?"

"I have to go," she said, and I felt her slip away.

Maybe this time, for good.

40

I WASN'T SURE WHY I'D come here.

But I'd been wandering through a thick fog for the last few days after the breakup, and Oceanview was where I'd landed. Maybe it was because my father was the only person who still smiled at me. He smiled a lot these days, and while I knew the expression could simply be the ripple of a failing mind, I wasn't sure if that mattered. I just needed to look at a friendly face today. And no, I hadn't missed the irony.

The staff told me it would be okay to wheel him out into the courtyard. We could both use the fresh air. He enjoyed looking at the garden through his window, so I hoped being near it might stimulate his mind. I settled onto the bench beside him. The garden air was cool and damp; a fountain flowed with inexhaustible, sunlit water, trickling from tier to tier until it reached the bottom basin.

My father took in his surroundings with wonder: a male hummingbird with its glossy, dark rose-red throat, flittering over an emerald Moon Boat leaf. The honeysuckle breeze. The sounds, first from the rippling fountain, then the warbling melody of birds farther off in the distance. If I squinted, I could almost rewind past the bad times and imagine that his pleasure now was a mere extension of what it had been like when his smile was real, his love sizable and openhanded.

I observed him, contemplating what was going on in that mind. Did the inside see what the outside world showed? Was it the garden before him, or as when he was watching TV the other day, was he hundreds of miles out in some oppositional universe? The mysteries of a shrinking mind—there were many. A mind on its way out, which led me to ask how long it would be before what was left of it was gone and communication became impossible. How long before Sam McCabe vanished? As Nolan said, the only thing a person could do was appreciate the value of time.

My father turned to me with an appraising gaze.

"What is it, Dad?" I asked. "What are you thinking about?"

He grinned. "It was a wonderful day, wasn't it?"

"You mean, the last time I saw you?"

"Yes. We had such a good time at the fair."

"It was, Dad," I said, trying to keep up with his pathless mind. There was no point in trying to correct him. Besides, he was the happiest I'd seen him. "An amazing day. My favorite."

"Oh, yes," he said, raising his chin. "The trees … those rocks. Had you ever seen any that big? So pretty, covered in the very, *very* green moss. And the streams. It was all so beautiful …" He smiled at what sounded like a make-believe memory. "Just *extremely* beautiful." He closed his eyes and breathed in deep through his nose. "The air smelled so very good."

In a matter of minutes, we'd traveled the city, going from his room, to the fair, and then on a hike we'd never taken together. This was a wild game, but since it had no rules, anyone could play.

"We walked very, *very* far," he went on. "Didn't we?"

"We did."

"It was a very special day. I'll always remember the wonderful time we had."

"Me, too, Dad," I said, indulging in my father's fantastical hike and how beautiful it could have been if we had it today. We would have had one of those special father-son talks where he imparted his wisdom about life.

"Just give Trish her time," he'd say. *"She'll come around. Be patient. When your mom and I had disagreements, my best plan was to take a few steps back and let her think."*

"I don't know, Dad. She seemed different when I called her the last time."

"Patience, son. Everything changes. Remember that."

I would have leaned far into the moment if it had happened. I would have loved him even more. Life could have been so different if he had been this carefree and open all along. Who would I be today? A better man, for sure, and a happier one, but how would that have shaped the life I saw? Would Trish have stayed with me? Would I need her the way I do? Instead, I was full of anger and regret, loneliness and loss.

"She's going to leave me, Dad," I blurted out.

My father nodded, but a glazed zombie look passed through his eyes.

Why was I telling him this? It wasn't as if he was capable of offering advice. I guess I needed to say these things out loud without feeling as though I was talking to myself.

"I don't know how I'm going to live without her, Dad. I … I did so many things wrong."

"Really …" He steadied his gaze on me, then stroked his chin a few times.

"I should have treated her better, so much better. I should have loved her more bravely." I looked down at my open, empty hands and shook my head. "You can't do that to people, you know? You can't just … just … act like their feelings don't matter. You need to do things right the first time because once the damage is done, it's done." My eyes brimmed with tears, warm tears, that rolled down my cheeks, dropping into open palms. "Because … because … you can never change what you've done, Dad, ever."

I looked up at my father. He was staring down into his own lap, mirroring me, brows heightened, eyes wide, as though he'd discovered a thousand bucks resting there.

Tears dripped off the edge of my nose. I sniffed, wiped the next one away with the back of a hand. "But here's the thing, Dad. You don't always see how badly you hurt someone while you're doing it. You can't, and … and … that makes it worse because you keep going at it, making them feel more alone." In a near whisper, I added, "So damned alone." I scrubbed my face with both palms, then raked them through my hair. I labored to take the words past my gravelly voice when I said, "You can't do that, Dad."

"Oh, yes …" he said, narrowing his eyes and tapping a finger on his temple.

"I was only a kid, Dad."

"I know," he said, probably irrelevantly. I couldn't tell.

I stood up to glare at him. "How could you do that to me, Dad? I … I don't understand how … I mean, you were supposed to love me, right? No kid should *ever* have to ask for that. It's supposed to come naturally. But all you did was starve me, Dad. You broke me—day after day, you did it—leaving me to feel worn down and hollow. And the worst part? What made it harder? You acted like you never thought twice about it, not for a minute. You couldn't have cared less." I gave in to my anger and in a low growl, I said, *"But I survived you, Dad."*

"That's good, son."

His reticence fed my anger.

"How *dare* you try to destroy me!" I said, spitting out my words. I gasped for air, once fragrant, now heavy with the fetor of resentment. Wrapping my arms around myself, I rocked my body as though the brutal sorrow had waited for this moment to own me. Sorrow that was raw, jagged, and as organic as my next breath. I battled for composure or something like it … anything to free me of the scalding wretchedness that wouldn't stop burning, throbbing.

I stopped rocking, looked up at him, and through my tears, I said, "Why, Dad? Why did you have to hurt me so much? Why couldn't you love me?"

He didn't answer.

"Please … say something," I murmured.

My father looked at me, stunned. A vein in his forehead swelled and pulsed, and it seemed like he was trying to respond but couldn't get the words out. Then, he opened his mouth, jaw juddering, breaths huffing, and shouted, "BECAUSE WE GET PIZZA ON FRIDAYS!"

41

THE NEXT DAY, I SAT in my car at the Oceanview Memory Care parking lot, staring long and hard at a text from Ryan:

Hey, Griff. What's up?

Weird for him to be the first to reach out after our argument. No apology, no invitation to discuss our differences, just a safe, benign message. Since I'd let things go this long without calling him, I suspected he was testing the climate.

I put the phone back into my sweatshirt pocket. He'd been wrong to say what he did, but my reaction had been wrong, too. It came from years of stuffing down my frustrations. And while I did miss Ryan in some ways, life was already guzzling my energy. I wasn't sure if letting him back in would invite more exhaustion, but Trish had put *me* on ignore, and I knew what it felt like to want another chance. If that were the case, I'd be a hypocrite to deny Ryan his.

Oh, and speaking of second chances, I went to an Alzheimer's support group yesterday after seeing my father. I needed it. But this time, I stayed for the whole thing. It was helpful. Much like with Kristine, I was getting a good education about the disease. After listening to the other group members' stories, I had a better idea of what to expect. I hoped that would help me feel less overwhelmed by my father's unreliable behavior.

It was hard, going back to see him since the previous visit—what I now preferred to call my emotional *breakthrough* instead of *breakdown*. I still felt guilty about screaming at a man whose mind was barely there. But after leaving the car, my resolve felt different in other ways. Maybe that was because I was walking in with more knowledge. Or maybe, after getting in my own way so many times, I'd worn myself out, and I was too drained to feel anxious.

Maybe I was just tired of being tired.

I decided to change things up this time, rolling him to the sitting area, which looked more like a comfortable family room in someone's house, along with a beautiful view of the ocean. The couch and matching love seat were fluffy and welcoming. An aquarium sat inside one wall full of pink, orange, and yellow saltwater fish, darting through bubbling blue water. Nolan had sent my father's clothing, and the staff dressed my father in a long-sleeved burgundy shirt with gray cotton pants. The ensemble looked nice on him; he came across more as a lovable grandfather than an abuser and a drunk. It forced me to recheck my perception of reality.

I wanted my father to enjoy our visit, but from his far-flung gaze and unoccupied expression, I read him as being mostly absent this afternoon. I wasn't even sure if he was tracking my continued presence with him in the sitting area. So, we sat steeped in quiet. And that was okay. I'd shed expectations. I was open.

Several minutes later, my father turned to me and said, "Oh. Hi," as if I'd just entered the room. He didn't speak my name, so I couldn't assume he remembered who I was, but who knew? His mind flipped fast.

"Hi, Dad," I said, using my usual strategy of calling him that, hoping it might make him aware that he was speaking to his son. "How are you doing today?"

"Fine, fine." He nodded affably. "Everything is wonderful."

Something else I'd learned from the meetings: Alzheimer's is often a disease of opposites. Hard personalities can turn soft while soft ones can turn hard—either way, patients have a potential to become confrontational and even violent. I'd already seen him make that change but, thankfully, not lately.

His smile faded. He stared into the empty, unlit fireplace, wringing his hands, and his awareness seemed more acute, almost as if he were zeroing in on a thought.

I waited.

He said, "You know, my father was a drinker."

Not a surprise. I knew all about the long line of alcoholics throughout my family tree—they went from the highest branch to the deepest roots—but this was the most lucid statement he'd made since I started visiting him.

"That's where I got it from, you know," he went on. "The drinking."

"I do."

"You were too young to remember much about your grandfather."

Not only lucid—he knew who I was. I held steady, trying not to show a strong reaction, afraid that anything more might take him from me.

"Your father could come back. They do that, drift in and out of awareness."

Remembering Kristine's comment, I waited for him to come forward on his own.

"My father was a mean bastard when he drank," he said.

"Really, Dad?"

He didn't answer, but his eyes glinted with tears. His troubled gaze dropped toward the floor, and then he brought an unsteady hand to his forehead. This reminded me of the time many years ago when I saw him sobbing behind his bedroom door. The affect was similar. Much like then, his anguish was convincing, so intense and palpable, that I could almost reach out and hold it in my hands.

He shook his head and began to mumble something.

"What is it, Dad?" I asked.

He raised his head. Stared at me. Then, in a soft, fissured voice, he said, "I was just a kid."

It was the same plea I'd made to him during our last visit. Was I looking into a mirror? I got a little wobbly. My mind fumbled for purchase while the nape of my neck gathered heat. My father's mouth opened and closed as if trying to form words that refused to come out.

"What happened, Dad?" I asked, leaning in toward him. "What did he do to you?"

He looked me dead in the eyes and said, "Everything."

A wicked chill ripped up my spine. My face stiffened with shock. And each muscle pulled tighter than a steel cable. I understood what he was telling me, and I believed him. Neither of us said anything more. I was trying to get my bearings. The blood had left my father's face.

I moved in closer. "Dad? Are you okay, Dad?"

He turned to me. He latched a hand on to my arm and said, "Ruthie, sweetheart. What a pleasant surprise. When did you get here?"

I didn't know how to respond. Correct him? No, what good would it do?

"Ruthie?"

"I just got here, Sam," I said in a thin, papery voice that sounded nothing like my own. I had no idea why, only that his story had pulled me under its stronghold, body immobile, thoughts fettered.

Everything ... everything ... everything.

Like haunting winds from a distant yet familiar place, the word howled through my mind.

42

THE SINS OF THE FATHER shall be visited upon the sons.

I had been the victim of a victim.

That verse was common enough in church. At the time, it didn't mean much to me. My mother had tried to be devout, and she brought Deena and me to Mass on occasion. I remembered sitting in those dark cherrywood pews, more inspired by the high-reaching, kaleidoscopic arches of stained glass than the actual idea of religion. Green, purple, and blue sunlight spilled through it and into the church, a kind of beaming beauty that lifted my spirits and quieted my boredom. The intermittent ritual seemed more like a product of my mother's upbringing—along with a fading sense of obligation—than an actual belief system, and after she died, it had been hard to believe in a god who took her away, then allowed me to suffer.

The verse, however, meant more to me today. I guess on some level, I should have recognized the possibility that my grandfather had been abusive, but I was too busy hating my father to consider it. With this wider perspective, however, the story was formed: in our family, cruelty was a malignancy, metastasizing from one generation to the next. Odd that the strongest connection to my father these days was our shared identity as victims. But if I could reach the other side of that, would it allow me to identify with what he went through and, yes, feel sympathy for him? Isn't that what healing is all about? I was talking about freedom from adversity. I was talking about moving on from things that had been holding me back.

I started to pull from the drive-through at the In-N-Out Burger near Garnet Avenue in Pacific Beach when my phone went off. I looked at the screen, flinched, and felt a banging pulse in my throat. It was Trish.

Without forethought, I tapped Accept, then tried to sound in good spirits despite my acute apprehension. "Hey. How are you?"

"I'm doing okay, Griffin." She sounded stiff and formal.

Once more, it was hard to ignore feeling as though I was talking to someone I didn't know.

"I was wondering if you might have time to talk," she said, tenuous uncertainty straddling her delivery.

"Sure. When do you want to meet?"

"Are you free right now? I can make it easy and come to your house."

Your house. No longer ours.

I split my attention between the bagged burger on the passenger seat and my watch. I was still coming off the intense visit with my father and was not at my best, physically tired and emotionally spent, but putting this off would just prolong the mounting anguish.

"I can do that," I said.

"Great. See you in about twenty."

Trish hung up before I could ask if she wanted me to pick up dinner for her while I was at the restaurant. I tried to remember what she usually got. No cheese, but onions? Pickles?

Wait. What am I doing?

Walking myself right into another pain trap, probably. She might not have even welcomed the gesture, instead seeing it as an overzealous need to please. I was overthinking again, but I did know one thing: I was starving, hadn't eaten all day, and I needed nourishment if I wanted to be present for whatever awaited me in this conversation. I skipped getting food for Trish and downed the burger and fries while driving home.

When I got there, her car was already idling in the driveway. Normally, it was about a thirty-minute drive on the 52 from her mother's place in

Rancho Peñasquitos to the beach area. Since she told me she'd be staying there, it looked like she'd made the trip in about twenty. Either that or she'd already been in the neighborhood when she called, hoping to get this done fast. With her frosty tone and need to rush this, I had a sinking feeling. I got out of my car, and Trish did the same. I tried to draw a sustaining breath, but it hitched halfway down my windpipe.

"Thanks for doing this without warning," she said while we walked toward the front door, but it felt more obligatory than grateful.

Inside, I took a seat on the couch. She sat across from me, hands folded stiffly in her lap and wearing a weak smile.

I offered her a drink, but she declined. Given that she wouldn't look me in the eye, I knew why she was here.

"You're breaking up with me," I said, stating what was undeniably obvious.

Trish's eyes glistened, and her nod was slow but deliberate.

I had nothing. I wasn't even sure if there was anything left to say. What should I have done? Told her she'd put my heart through the shredder? Begged for a second chance? All of that would have been futile.

"I'm sorry, Griffin, but you know where I came from. You were there when Cam died. It was hard to trust in love after my parents' marriage fell apart. I've tried to get through that fear. You know I have. But I needed assurance. I've given you so many chances, but I feel in my heart that you're not that person because you also can't trust me or this relationship. It feels like if I stay, I'll be setting myself up for another fall, and this one will finally destroy me."

"Do you have any idea how hard it is to hear you say that? To know that being with me is the thing that could ruin you?" Through clenched teeth, I said, "My *God,* Trish, that fucking hurts."

"I'm sorry. I never wanted to hurt you!" Her eyes were rimmed in red. She rubbed a palm across her neck, and her voice broke when she said, "I care so much about you. You have to know that."

It wasn't safe to believe her anymore.

I didn't look at her because I was afraid that if I did, I'd shatter across the floor. I refused to let her see me crumble. She didn't get to share in my pain anymore, didn't get to take any part in it, especially when she was the one bringing it on. It took every cell in my body to hold it together, but I clung to my resolve, turning my head away from her.

"Please, Griffin … look at me."

Meeting her eyes felt too difficult right now. It would just make this loss more real.

"Griffin, please."

I gathered enough courage to turn and look into her eyes.

"You've already suffered enough," she said, "and that's why this is killing me. I never wanted to be the one who piles more hurt on you."

"But you did."

"I know that," she said, then in a hushed voice, "and I hate it so much. But I don't know how to avoid this anymore. I love you. I always will. You have to believe that, but this relationship is too broken to continue."

Broken?

"We're not ready to be married. I don't know that we ever were. I think that came to the surface after the accident. I … I kept hoping you'd come around. But you haven't recovered from your father, and you can't be there for me until you do. Griffin, you're a wonderful, sweet, loving man. You have more going for you than any guy I've ever known. But you're not a husband."

That last part stung because it felt like an insult more than an explanation.

"Our timing was off," she went on. "I'm sure that if we met somewhere in the future, this would have worked. And it would have been amazing. But you *will* figure your life out—I know you will—and when you do, you'll find someone to love you back the way you deserve."

"Just not with you."

"I …" Her voice betrayed her, and it took a few seconds to reclaim it. "No, and I know I'll be missing out."

That last sentence hurt the most because I would be, too.

43

IT TOOK A LITTLE WHILE for the breakup to feel real, but when it did, it hit hard. Trish and I had been together for so long that I had no idea what a life without her would even look like. When you become a couple, you give up something, but you also gain something. No longer do you think of just yourself—you become part of each other, one entity. Before this, we were Trish and Griffin. But I'd forgotten how to just be Griffin. I wasn't even sure how to be alone anymore, to come home to an empty house with an even emptier heart. It was as if I'd been broken once more, but much like so many times lately, I could no longer bury my feelings about it.

It wasn't just hard letting go of Trish—it was also hard letting go of all my ideas about a future that had taken root. The idea of getting married, then becoming a family. At the same time, I wondered whether our wedding plans were meaningful to me at all or if I'd just gone along because Trish cared so much about them.

I drifted into the Alzheimer's meeting, rudderless. I just needed to throw myself into a group of people—it didn't matter who, as long as they populated my castaway world and empty heart.

The group was situated in a large circle so we all faced each other. The chairs had always been in rows, but with this new, uncharted setup, I could no longer camouflage myself behind the person in front of me. I'd have to get acclimated to it. And I'd stopped hiding, anyway.

Throughout the evening, I wanted to talk—I needed to—but each time, I lost my nerve and backed down. I'd been holding out since I began coming there, wary of telling strangers personal details of my life. But I was starting to see that my shyness was holding me back and prolonging my problems. Finally, the feeling in the group shifted toward conclusion.

"Does anyone else want to share before we wrap things up tonight?"

I sheepishly raised my hand.

As if recognizing my discomfort, Kristine tendered a nod of encouragement. I held my gaze on her. The members pivoted their attention my way, and I searched their faces. A sea of attentiveness looked back at me. It was an unfamiliar surprise to be seen before opening my mouth.

I cleared my throat. "Hi," I began, my hollow voice echoing back at me. "My name is Griffin."

Some gave me a collective, "Hello," while others nodded their welcomes.

"So … I … I've been coming here for around three weeks." A kind of stage fright pummeled me, and it sounded like someone else talking—strange for a man who made his living as a performer. I pushed on. "I've been shy about speaking up. I guess that's because a lot of times, I wasn't sure what to say or how to say it." I let out a nervous laugh. "Which is kind of funny because I'm an actor. My presentation should be a hell of a lot better."

The crowd laughed.

"Anyway, during the past month or so, I've lost everyone who mattered to me. That's my fault. I pushed them away. Not on purpose." I thought about Trish, how I'd rejected each attempt she'd made to help me after my accident. "It's because I've been in pain and refused to let them in. Either that or I failed them." I thought about Ryan and Deena and so much unfinished business. "Now, this is it. You're all I've got left, and the loneliness is hitting hard. The sting of loss. The isolation."

My gaze stumbled across the circle to a woman with a friendly face. She was tilting her head to one side, and she creased her brows with what I interpreted as compassion, as though she might have once felt the same way I did. I kept my focus on her for a moment because it helped me find the solidity I needed to continue.

"These days, it feels like I'm struggling just to … to … exist, and I'm not even sure if I'm doing *that* right. But I'm trying, trying really hard. This is such a lonely place to be. Don't get me wrong. I take full responsibility for putting myself here. I'm owning it. But where do I go from here? You know?"

A man sitting a few seats down held up his hand in agreement.

"I had a terrible relationship with my father. He was an alcoholic who abused me, and now he has Alzheimer's. Funny thing is, before I came here, I had this crazy idea that my experience was unique and I wouldn't have much in common with all of you. But I was wrong. So wrong. I guess I got in my own way. Again." I ran a hand across my damp forehead. "Man, I need to stop doing that."

A quiet, comforting laugh from the group.

"But I'm finding out that it doesn't matter how different our experiences are because many of the emotions can end up looking similar." I gazed at one person and said, "The loneliness." I looked at another. "The grief that never seems to end." Then, I looked at Kristine. "And the regret of missing out because avoiding a risk felt safer."

She closed her eyes and nodded.

Bringing up all this sorrow took me back to the exact moment when I first began to think that I didn't deserve to be loved and that the only way to protect myself was to build a callus around my heart to keep it from breaking. It was the day of my high school graduation when nobody came to see it. All the families had gathered, taking photos and celebrating. I was surrounded by all those people, yet I might as well have been standing alone in a swamp.

"But discovering what we have in common does help. I don't feel as alone anymore. I don't know … I guess what I'm trying to say is … thank you. Thank you for being in the place where nobody else stands anymore. For being here to hold me up at the exact time I need it most."

The entire crowd stood. Some clapped while others looked at me with admiration. A couple came over to shake my hand and introduce themselves. And all of it felt wonderful, like rubbing a soothing salve on an old, enduring wound. This was the place for which I'd been searching. My place. Where I could grow and move forward with life. It turned out, I *did* need people after all and that letting them in wasn't as scary as I'd once thought.

Kristine came up to me. She said, "I'm proud of you, Griffin."

"Thank you, Kristine. That means a lot to me."

As we walked toward the exit, she said, "I was going to ask if you had any interest in that Danish I saw you coveting a few weeks ago."

"You mean the place where Danishes go to heaven?"

She laughed. "Yeah, that one. But it's such a lovely evening. Feel like taking a walk instead?"

"I think I'd like that very much."

Kristine was right: Kensington was beautiful this evening. The temperature had slipped just a few degrees from daytime, thanks to the warm Santa Anas sweeping in from nearby inland valleys. Above the tree-lined street, branches tossed against each other, lifting and settling to the authority of a powerful yet gentle gale.

Kensington Heights defined quaint. Known for homes that resembled cute little dollhouses with expertly manicured lawns, the prices were anything but small: a 1,500-square-foot home would take you back as much as $1.5 million. Similar to many areas in San Diego, Kensington was a city within the city, showing off its own distinctive character. Known for its landmark—the large, colorful neon sign with its namesake stretched across Adams Avenue—it had also been home to the historic Ken Cinema, which showed classic revivals and cult films like *The Rocky Horror Picture Show*. Unfortunately, like many small movie houses across the country, the economy forced it to shut down a few years before.

"It's official," I said as we rounded a corner near Kensington Café. "My fiancée left me for good."

Kristine slowed down to look at me. "Oh, Griffin. I'm so sorry."

"I can't say it blew me back on my heels. I felt it coming." I stuck my hands in my pockets and shrugged. "All signs were pointing in the wrong direction."

"But that doesn't make it any easier."

"No, it doesn't. This will sting for a long time."

"And you were already carrying enough weight on your shoulders."

I peered into a darkened store window and saw my reflection staring back at me. "I've been doing that my whole life. Sometimes, it feels like my second job."

She laughed with a note of sympathy. "Speaking of jobs, I never asked what you do for a living."

"I'm a voice actor. I do cartoons, commercials, documentaries, and audiobooks—whatever's paying."

To her credit, she didn't spout off the pants-down line. It didn't seem to register.

I asked, "What about you?"

"I work for a nonprofit that helps at-risk youths. Changing the course of a kid's life for the better—nothing compares to it."

"It sounds awesome. What do you do there?"

"I'm a social worker."

I turned my head toward her. "Um … way to bury the lede."

"I know." She laughed. "I don't usually bring it up unless someone asks."

"Why not?"

"People tend to form opinions about mental health care professionals. They think we want to fix them, but that couldn't be further from the truth. I get paid to do that all day long, so why would I want to do it during my free time?"

"No wonder you're so insightful."

She laughed. "On a good day."

"No, you gave me so much great advice the day we met, Kristine. It's made a difference for me."

She asked about my abuse, and I gave her the whole story. How my father and I were like best friends, then after my mother died from cancer, he became abusive. I'd been trudging around in this territory so much during the past month that saying it all out loud—especially after speaking at the meeting—felt helpful.

"My God, Griffin." She looked into my eyes, shaking her head. "To lose both parents in different ways. I can see how that makes this much more complicated."

"You want complicated? After being estranged from my father for more than twenty years, he literally crashed into me on the road. That's how we reconnected."

"Shut up!" She stifled a laugh.

That made me laugh, too. "True story. Now, here I am. Stuck to him like Loctite glue." I picked up a fallen leaf that had blown onto the sidewalk, held it in my hand. "But you know what, Kristine? I'm working through it. At first, I thought this was a case of horrible luck, but now, I'm starting to wonder if there's more to it than that. Maybe someday, I'll be better for it, you know? Maybe these are the seeds for change. A chance to repair a break that I thought was permanent."

She looked at me with admiration. "The way you're already starting to recognize that? It's a big deal, Griffin."

A gap of quiet opened between us, an expectant pause. She hadn't told me the story about her mother, and the omission seemed to register with her, too.

"I haven't gone into what happened with my mother because it's so ugly," she started, "but now that you've told your story, I feel more comfortable about it." Kristine let out a long, heavy sigh. "She was barely home, always out with a different guy each night, and she had no boundaries—I mean, zero. She was super inappropriate around me and my friends and never acted like a mother. Then, she became a heavy user."

"Our parents were both addicts."

"It happens a lot. Kids like us end up in my office."

"Same situations," I said, "but it's interesting to see how different our experiences were. I had a loving mother, and you didn't. But we both lost them. What did she use? Your mom."

Kristine's laugh was cheerless. "Whatever she could get her hands on. Ugh, and those trashy men who came by. Total bottom-feeders."

"What that must have done to you …"

"It was a lot for a young girl. I never felt safe inside that apartment."

I thought about having that same feeling in my own home—but again, different circumstances. I asked, "Did the men ever—"

Her pace slowed, but she kept her gaze trained ahead, locking her hands in front of her, as if it might keep the memory from swallowing her up.

My chest felt heavy. "I'm so sorry, Kristine. I can't even imagine. That breaks my heart."

"Cost me years on the therapist's couch. And if that weren't enough, the situation got worse. She accused me of stealing her men and called me a slut. Can you imagine? Classic narcissist." She let out a long, exhausted sigh.

"It goes beyond detestable."

I thought I'd sensed a gradation of controlled guardedness the first time we'd met; it was subtle, hard to detect unless you peered deeper beneath her smile. It made sense now.

Kristine started again. "She got more confrontational. More violent. I was scared out of my mind every time she walked through the door, afraid she'd come after me. One day, she scored a bag of meth and left it on the coffee table before going to the bathroom for a minute. That was all it took. One of her tweeker friends took off with the drugs. Don't deprive an addict of their dope. They'll kill for the stuff when they're in withdrawal, and that's what she nearly did to me. She threw bleach into my face."

I jerked at the thought.

"My eyes felt like they were on fire, and although I could barely see what was in front of me, I ran outside. There I was, a fifteen-year-old girl, out on the street. You can probably figure out the rest of the story."

"You ran away?"

"Exactly."

At least I had a home to go back to after running off. Not the case for her.

"Where did you go?" I asked.

"At one point, I lived in a broken-down car, abandoned in a field. That was like moving into the Four Seasons after what I'd been through. But then the police discovered it, and there went my four-wheeled condo, riding into the sunset on the back of a tow truck. From there, I became another tragic street cliché. Not once could I have imagined I'd end up being *that* kid."

"Is that why you became a social worker?"

"One of the reasons, yeah, and probably the biggest. Forget the degrees and all the books I've read. I had something more valuable to teach. Real-life experiences that I could use to make a difference in kids' lives."

Night had come to fruition, the warm air giving in to its demands and dropping a few more degrees. The sky was a blanket of thick black velvet, covered in a spray of stars that winked like tiny pin lights. At that moment, something opened up within me. Connecting with Kristine felt new. Essential.

She got quiet, and I made no attempt to fill the space or interrupt it. But I started to think about a positive kind of inheritance: building a better me from the heavy cuts of life. I also thought about how the commonality of our abuse as kids had changed us in similar ways, infusing us with wisdom yet leaving us scarred.

I sensed a trailing edge of hope that I couldn't yet put into words. Was this my doorway into the learning part?

44

I STILL HADN'T RESPONDED TO Ryan's text, and the longer I waited, the harder it got. I'd reached for my phone a few times to call him, then shied away from the effort. I just didn't have enough attention to spare right now, but I had enough insight to recognize that I was *being* Ryan by repeating his exact behavior that drove me crazy.

Instead, over the last several days, I'd seen my father a few times. I was between jobs, so it was convenient to stop by while out running errands. Since Trish had left for good, the house felt empty and soulless. Getting out and keeping busy helped to chase away the loneliness. Not the loss—that would have to go away on its own terms—but I kept my days busy, dropping by the Alzheimer's meetings and making a few new friends. They joined Kristine and me afterward at the diner, where we laughed and talked. I called the group my new tribe. I was starting to understand what people meant when they said you get to choose your own families.

Lately, my father was spending more time in bed and sleeping for longer periods. I asked the doctor about that, and he told me it was part of the Alzheimer's progression through the later stages. During the times when my father was awake, he had more difficulty getting up and moving around. All this left me to again suspect that the time we had left together was getting short.

As for my father's mind, it was drifting in and out of the past, recalling events I either couldn't remember or viewed as trivial. I wasn't even sure if some of them happened, much like the camping trip or hike or whatever he'd meant when he'd talked about spending time with me in the woods.

So, on this day, I was pleasantly surprised he'd joined me in the moment. Another surprise, he'd gotten a new dog—or so he thought. It was actually an old dog. After about twenty-five years, Jimmy, our family's seventy-five-pound chocolate Lab, had risen from the dead and was taking up residency in my father's room despite the facility's strict no-pet policy. What the hell? I'd play along if it made him happy. According to my father, Jimmy liked to jump onto the bed and snuggle up next to him. He also barked too much at the nurses. But during his more peaceful times, Jimmy splayed himself out on the floor and found pleasure in decimating his favorite toy, my father's make-believe leather work shoe.

"Do you see Jimmy over there?" Dad carped, pointing to the floor. "He's looking right at you."

I considered the empty spot on the linoleum, looked back at my father, then gave him an unsubstantiated nod.

"He needs to go potty right now. Can you take him outside?"

"Sure. Come on, Jimmy," I said to no one as I walked to the door. When I reached the end of the hallway, I bought a granola bar from the machine, ate it, then headed back to my father's room.

"Did he go potty?" Dad asked upon my return, leaning forward with eagerness.

"He did!" I wiped my mouth in case there was a trace of granola left on it.

"Number one or two?"

"Both!"

"Good boy, Jimmy." He clapped. "That's a good boy!"

Not the most meaningful interaction we'd ever had, but it was entertaining and cheerful. And he did appear more alert today as if the Jimmy hallucination focused him. After what I'd been through lately— losing Trish, the recent revelations about his own abusive childhood, then hearing Kristine's tragic story—our banter felt easy, almost what normal could look like. It brought me back to earlier days when we loved to joke around. It was like stepping sideways into an old life that, in some ways, felt new again.

My father scratched at the stubble on his face.

"Itchy?" I asked.

He nodded.

I went to the sink to grab some shaving supplies, remembering how meticulous he used to be about keeping himself well-groomed. In his right mind, he would have hated seeing himself this way. With care, I spread shaving lotion across my father's face, and only then did I notice that I could not find my old fear. From that, I could almost see a millimeter of an opening toward forgiveness. I hadn't arrived there yet, but the prospect no longer felt like an impossibility.

Knowing that we'd both suffered at the hands of an abusive, alcoholic father connected us in a way I'd never imagined it could. It wasn't okay that he continued the cycle of abuse—people choose how they deal with crises, and his approach was lousy and destructive—but that didn't mean I couldn't get past it. Maybe the other part was that it was easier to feel sorry for my father than to hate him. Whatever worked. This part of my life was all about recovery. It was about at last claiming the peace I hungered for. I'd spent a long time despising and abusing myself after my father got done with me, so perhaps the time had come to start loving myself instead.

After finishing, I wiped the excess shaving lotion from my father's face with a warm, damp washcloth, then dabbed up the excess moisture with a towel.

He smiled up at me. I smiled back. I couldn't help it.

As he fell into peaceful slumber, I studied the planes of his face. Somewhere in there, I could almost see the good father I once knew, the one who had existed before my mother died. Who loved me fiercely, unconditionally, and who meant everything to me.

45

KRISTINE AND I HAD BEEN spending more time getting to know one another.

Between our great conversations, the Alzheimer's meetings, and discovering new ground with my father, I was gaining a better sense of self and becoming more hopeful about life. There were actually moments when I felt good inside my skin. I was less afraid to reveal the more fragile parts of myself that, for years, I'd kept out of view, wearing guardedness like a flak jacket. I was healing. I could feel it.

Kristine and I walked along Wipeout Beach, a sandy span of shoreline at the foot of Coast Boulevard in La Jolla. The name served it well: I'd spent many summers here doing just that when I was a surf rat.

"As much as losing Trish hurt," I told Kristine, "I'm starting to see that her breakup was for my own good. I think that, on some level, she did love me, but she let me go so I could learn how to grow and thrive on my own."

"It looks like that's what you're already doing," she said, kicking sand as we walked.

"I hope so. But I can appreciate her now instead of feeling injured, and I have no resentment toward her. What's the saying? You have to learn to love yourself before you can love others? Yeah, that's me."

She laughed. "That's everyone."

I was happy to find out that Kristine also ran track throughout high school and liked a good run, so we decided to go for one along the coast from La Jolla Shores to Torrey Pines State Beach. It was a great day for it. The temperature was in the high seventies, the sky clear as glass. The ocean breeze felt pure, washing over us like a warm, soothing rapid and adding speed to my legs before sneaking off to sea. Kristine seemed to feel it, too, and we pushed our pace on the inclines, delighting in a good run.

Everywhere I went, new transformations awaited. I couldn't remember the last time I was able to relax into a run instead of being ruled by it. Exercise had been my obsession; now, it was again becoming my peace. With each stride, I settled deeper into that new knowledge. Kristine must have sensed my happiness because she kept turning to look at me with a knowing grin.

"Man, I really needed this run," I told her as we started our cooldown on the south end of the beach.

"Me, too." She closed her eyes and aligned her face with an inviting beam of sunlight. "My stress levels are on the rise these days."

"What's been happening?"

"Nothing compared to what you're going through." She lifted a shell off the sand, then turned it in her hand, examining the blue-gray fan-shaped ridges. "It's just that I've been feeling more isolated from my girlfriends lately. Everyone has kids, and I don't. It's not like I feel this huge absence in my life because of that—more like I feel excluded when they talk about decorating nurseries or complain about their kids' annoying habits. I never have anything to add, which leaves me feeling like an outsider among the people I've identified with for years."

"Like you don't fit in anymore."

"Exactly." She looked ahead and jumped topics. "Gosh, I can't believe I've never gone running here after all these years in the city."

"Stick with me. I know all the good beaches in town."

"After seeing this place, I believe you. Surfer?"

"Guilty. I practically grew up in the Pacific."

"You look the part."

"Yeah? How's that?"

"The graphic logo tees, the strings around your wrist, and the worn sweaters with shorts? They scream SoCal surfer. Oh … and that surfboard tattoo on the back of your leg doesn't exactly hide the fact."

I checked the back of my calf. "Shit. I forgot about that. I suppose I'll eventually need to grow up and dress my age."

"Why would you want to do that?"

I laughed with an edge. "I don't want the young surfers looking at me like I'm an older guy who's trying too hard."

"But you pull it off well. I say, go with it."

I bobbed my head from side to side, weighing her comment.

"Were you good at it? Surfing?" she asked.

"I did okay." I picked up a sandstone and skipped it against the stirring waves. "Placed in a few competitions here and there."

"Sounds like you did more than okay. Do you go surfing now?"

"I haven't been out on the water in a long time."

"Why not?"

"You know, life. Work, relationships, and all the other stuff that comes with adulting …" I stopped walking to think. "Funny how we abandon the things that help us get through the hard times and instead double down on the stress."

"I think we get wired into that."

I considered the bounding blue-green swells off in the distance, massive and crestless.

"But now that my life is improving, I have thought about getting back to surfing."

"That's a great idea."

Without warning, Kristine kicked off her running shoes, then took off toward the water. I followed her lead, and we laughed and splashed our way along the shallow coastline. A few minutes later, Kristine grinned at me.

"What's up?" I asked, returning her expression.

"I was just thinking back to the first time we met at that meeting. Man, were you checked out. It was almost like someone had perp-walked you into the room, then shoved you into a chair for interrogation. I read you as angry and defiant, but I don't even know who that guy was anymore."

"He's a stranger to me, too."

"After seeing you smile and have fun, I can see this is the *real* Griffin, the guy I suspected was trapped within himself when he abandoned the meeting that day."

"I guess I'm seeing that opening myself up is an option after all."

Maybe it always was. Looking back, I wore standoffishness like a coat of armor to keep people at a safe distance. I'd been forced to act that way for so long that it migrated and became a part of my identity. Or had I forced it? But since the armor had come off, I was able to reveal the true me without fear or shame.

"I'm glad you figured that out, Griffin." Kristine took me out of my thoughts and back into the present. "I see people who never do. It's tragic."

I walked deeper into the surf until I was waist deep in water, then fell back into the current, letting it spill over me. It felt cleansing. It felt like renewal. There was once a time when I'd fly my drone from high above, looking down at the water, a mere observer. Now, there I was, immersing myself in new beginnings.

46

I STOPPED IN LA JOLLA to grab cash from an ATM, and on my way back, I saw how close I was to the old house where I grew up. For reasons I couldn't explain, I turned onto Muirlands Vista Way, the street that led there. Maybe finding out about my father's dark past made me more curious about my own. Maybe this was a part of my healing process. Maybe I was still a punishment junkie.

When I rounded the corner, an *open house* sign sat out front. It had been weeks since Marcella called to tell me that the place went up on the listings, yet it hadn't been sold. All up and down the Southern California coast, it was a seller's market, homes being snatched up as fast as they were listed, pitting one buyer against the other in a bidding war.

Too many demons roaming that place, I only half-joked. *They scared me— they probably scared the shit out of potential homebuyers.*

I'd read that upscale homes weren't moving as fast as the others. With ours listed at a whopping $5.2 million, that could have been the case here—either that or they needed to knock down the price.

Curiosity piqued. I stepped out of my car, walked through the open gate, then moved toward the house. Was this a bad idea—maybe the worst ever—to reenter a house with thousands of chilling memories? As I approached, I tried to see it with an objective eye.

This was the kind of home one often saw in Southern California: Spanish style, white stucco, and a tile roof the color of baked clay. Our house took that to the next level, though, an arrogant display of wealth with arched double doorways, tall and deep. Row after row of windows on all three levels. And hungry vines, worming across elaborate iron balconies. To top it off, a gaudy, dramatic fountain sat out front, the centerpiece of our circular driveway.

Impressive on the outside, rotten inside.

There were signs of passing time. The front doors' once-slick and golden finish were faded, chipped, and weathered by the years. Its ornate metalwork was corroded in spots. Even the front gate, once freshly painted with a slick black sheen, had grayed out from oxidation. More cracks in the driveway than I remembered, too. It was an open house, but no one was here. The real estate listing had used the words *in need of TLC*. I thought *terribly neglected* would have been a better choice.

I was surprised to find the house empty, and I meant that in every sense. It was desolate, void, not a stick of furniture anywhere. Even the windows were naked. Outside, the wind sent a branch scraping across the glass, causing an intolerably long, eerie *screech*.

I shivered.

Didn't they stage homes for sale these days? And where was the selling agent? That kind of freaked me out. Was her body stuffed into an attic crawl space? Probably not—although, it fit the mood and would have made one hell of a true crime podcast.

I had to make jokes; otherwise, I would have run, screaming for the door.

Maybe the agent had forgotten to take down the *open house* sign and lock things up after finishing. Trish's aunt worked in real estate and said it happened more often than people knew. She once told me the story of an agent who'd made that egregious mistake; neighborhood teens converted the home into their own overnight traveling house party. When the agent came back the next morning, the place was trashed, and he had to pay for cleanup and repairs out of his own pocket.

It was better that nobody was here, I decided. At least I didn't have to pretend I was interested in buying the godforsaken place.

I stepped deeper inside. One thing that came to mind was how much bigger it looked than I'd remembered: 6,000-plus square feet of dark hardwood floors and a darker history. When grown kids come back to visit their old houses, their perceptions are usually the opposite. They were small then, and everything looked bigger. But this house was already big—maybe that made it harder to experience the perception of shrinkage.

I looked into the living room.

If walls had eyes and ears, this house would be begging for mercy.

I moved on, my flip-flops slapping against the floor and sending off echoes throughout this hollow, tenantless space. As I got deeper toward the heart of the house, an odd sensation wriggled through me. This place felt more like a living, breathing thing than one made of stucco and tile. So many emotions, so many vile memories lingering in the corners.

I looked toward the family room, half-expecting my father to be in his recliner. The memory felt like an old movie reel, clattering behind my eyes. I could almost smell his bourbon invading the air. I looked away, but the view wasn't much better in that direction. Wary, I spotted the door leading into the garage, and all at once, I was that terrified fourteen-year-old boy, strong-armed into driving his drunk father to the liquor store. A reconstituted surge of panic warmed my chest.

I climbed the long, serpentine staircase that led to the upper floor. Each step felt like unhinging different parts of my past. But I'd already made it this far. Turning back now would be skirting a tumbledown childhood that refused to stay hidden, and I knew where that path led.

I reached the second-floor landing, also barren. A slew of family photos had once hung here, commemorating our happiest times, but all that remained today was a dull, exposed wall.

I glanced into my mom and dad's room. Nothing to see there. Most kids didn't spend much time in their parents' bedrooms while growing up, and that was the case for us, even more after Mom died. Next, I went past Deena's room but gave it a quicker look—I'd spent less time there—then headed for my bedroom, the place where I often tried to seek refuge from my father when he got drunk and belligerent.

Nothing had changed other than the paint color and a few extra shelves on one wall. I walked up to the window bench: I used to sit here and look out through the glass, watching other people's lives go by while mine stood stationary. I took in the Millers' place across the street, where they enjoyed a lot of their time in the front yard. In my mind's eye, the scenes played out like some idyllic family movie: the summer fun they used to have washing cars and spraying each other with the garden hose or running through sprinklers, laughing and screaming as they chased each other with water pistols. When they took a break from the fun, Mrs. Miller came out to deliver frozen slushies, and then they'd all drink and talk. I always wondered what they were discussing, but the window glass that separated us prohibited it, so I made up conversations, pretending as though I were a part of their family. With age, I'd come to see their situation—and many others—in a different light. Compared to mine, every other household looked perfect, and it was hard to discern between shades of gray. Only later in life did I learn that the family on the outside might have been different than the one within; nevertheless, I felt like an outlier, looking in.

I turned back, saw the closet, and flinched. I moved in closer, then opened the door to that awful night.

47

I ARRIVED HOME AFTER HAVING a blast all day at the beach with friends. The highlight was when Ben Kennedy came out of the water, and a big wave yanked his swimsuit straight down to his ankles, exposing his junk. Unfortunately, everyone knew it but him, and we all started rolling with laughter.

Sunburned and hollowed out by a day of exertion, I was happy but tired. In the bathroom, I checked the mirror—I'd developed a nice tan over the past weeks, and the sun had introduced golden highlights to my hair. The peak of summer was there. I stuck my leg in the tub to brush off a ribbon of dried sand, then tossed the damp towel over the shower bar.

My skin still tingled from sun and saltwater as I traveled down the hallway, but the day's excitement began to fade because my father would soon be home, so I'd need to eat fast downstairs.

I sat on the kitchen counter stool, snacking on chips, when Deena flitted in. As usual, she had nothing to say before disappearing upstairs to her bedroom. A little later, my father's car pulled up in the driveway, the daily warning sound to make myself scarce. I grabbed my snack and decided to dematerialize onto the back patio. But on my way through the living room, I got up too fast and slipped on the slick marble flooring. I don't remember much of what came next because my rear smacked into the hard tile and my mind fell into a jumble. All I *did* recall was banging my elbow against one of the side tables, and then the sound of glass shattering behind me.

When I got up, my ass hurt like hell, but it was nothing compared to the panic that rifled through me once I saw what I'd done. Pieces of *the* glass vase were scattered before me—the one my father had given my mother for their ten-year wedding anniversary. The one he'd carefully positioned in the center of the table after she died so it wouldn't break.

Just then, my father stomped through the living room. I knew that I was more than in trouble. I was as good as dead. He appeared in the archway and stopped when he saw the broken pieces of white, yellow, and green glass. His face turned red, veins protruding from his neck. I'd witnessed my father's fury, but it was never like this. I knew how much that vase meant to him. I'd seen him hold it many times with great care and admiration, as if it could bring back a part of my mother.

"I didn't mean to!" I yelled quickly, trying to explain myself. "It was an accident! I'm sorry!"

But his tight-lipped scowl told me that my apology would be about as useful as throwing myself onto the jagged pieces of glass, so I stood motionless, trying to prepare for his wrath. The collar of my T-shirt was wet with perspiration, and a hammering pulse hit the base of my jaw.

My father broke eye contact from me, then turned and left as if he were going to retrieve something. I didn't plan to wait and find out what that was. Fear sent me straight to my room. When I was younger, I'd hide in closets whenever my father went through the house on his tirades. At that age, huddling there helped me feel safer. I could make myself as small as possible with the added assurance that he wasn't lurking behind me. Though I was older now, my mind spun into a fast rewind. Call it an inherent survival instinct, but I dashed into my closet, yanked the door shut, then waited. The pitiful shame hadn't escaped me: there I was, a seventeen-year-old, regressing into a child.

Pipes banged and rattled downstairs, and my heart did the same. My father had turned on the kitchen sink, I reasoned, which assured me that he was far enough away. But when the sound stopped, I could no longer detect where he was. The silence was deafening.

Bang, bang, bang.

I heard footsteps coming up the staircase, slow and rhythmic, like a hammer beating down on a nail. My father let out a loud cough, making me aware that he was just a few feet away. I closed my eyes, expecting to hear my bedroom door crash open at any minute, but that didn't happen. I overheard him clunking around in his bedroom, maybe getting ready for bed. Maybe he was too drunk to execute a punishment? Maybe I could finally relax some?

Time passed. Exhaustion outweighed fear. I didn't know when I'd dozed off, but I woke up the next morning, lying across the closet floor. One thing was easy to define: the guilt over breaking that vase was sharp as ever.

But the guilt wasn't for *him*—it was for my mother.

Only after coming downstairs did those feelings change. My father sat at the kitchen table, an open tube of glue at his side, a sagging, drunkenly reassembled vase sitting before him.

48

I NEED TO GO OUTSIDE, get some fresh air.

Beyond the patio doors, the yard and another memory awaited. This was a much happier one, and I could use it. Nestled deep within the courtyard was the spot where my mother's garden once grew. Sadly, it had been replaced by a swimming pool. I gazed into the shimmering turquoise water and studied my reflection, but I didn't see myself as I was today. I saw the joyful, celebrant boy I'd once been. The boy who loved each day as much as the next. Who screamed and laughed while his twin sister chased after him with a garden hose. The boy who loved to sit on the back patio steps, eating cherry Popsicles in the midst of a balmy summer, lips, tongue, and fingers covered in bright red.

I missed that boy like I missed my mother.

49

IT WAS FALL WHEN MOM found out that her cancer had returned. The outside light was changing, the air taut and cool, and the oncoming winter felt more like an approaching shadow. I could sense that her thoughts about what was to come were troubling her, which seemed to manifest as life advice. Perhaps she found comfort in making sure that Deena and I would be okay once she was gone.

"Griffin," she told me that day as we stood in her garden, clearing it out. The annuals were drooping after their final summer song. "Don't waste a second doing anything that doesn't make you happy, and if you find yourself stuck in one of those situations, run like your ass is on fire."

She shuffled as she worked, dragging her clogs, covered in loud yellow daisies. She'd also put herself in a frilly sundress and floppy hat even though the weather had turned. It didn't dawn on me then that she was dressing for a spring garden season she would not live to see.

My mother liked to involve me in the work, although Deena was the natural since she and Mom usually paired up whenever Dad and I went off on our own. Still, gardening felt immensely satisfying when she included me, and I loved the beauty of it—but mostly, I was grateful that Mom was paying Deena and me equal attention during that last fall.

Gardening had always been her lifeblood, her oxygen. She loved to push her hands through the rich soil, nurture the burgeoning stalks, then see them flourish into a riot of color. Mom's floral displays were legend in our neighborhood, and each summer, people came by to marvel over the palette that blanketed our yard. My mother welcomed everyone in, and by the time they left, she'd turned them into friends, sending them home with bouquets.

Southern Californians joke about how their front and backyards are the size of postage stamps, but that wasn't the case for us. While our house was big, so, too, was the yard, which was more of a courtyard. Mom's garden occupied a big part of it with another large, flowing fountain at its center.

As a kid, I felt like standing at the foot of her garden was like staring into a rainbow—delphiniums the color of plum pie, hollyhocks with the most vibrant shades of fuchsia I'd ever seen, and primrose, yellow as the sun—all framed by vines of electric-blue wisteria and mandevilla. Looking back as an adult, though, I think my memories about her garden were more imprecise than I recalled, and grief later filled in the gaps with cotton candy. In doing so, I did myself a disservice because after realizing this, I wondered if that was how it felt to forget who you are.

Mom and I were similar in many ways, and we shared the same poetic view when it came to her garden. We'd spend hours over the weekends working and laughing. But we didn't just plant seeds; we talked about life, about people, and about … well, everything. I loved what she taught me about the world as much as what she taught me about growing. One spring, as we began our annual process of preparing the soil, she opened her hand to reveal a solitary seed.

"Holding this in your palm is like looking into the future right before it unfolds, Griffin. So much to look forward to, so much beauty yet to come."

I believed her then, unaware how chilling those words would later become. Besides that, I hadn't yet learned that beauty could be a facade. At the time, though, it felt as though that kind of joy was the course our lives were destined to take. But along the way, a detour dropped into our path, one paved with hooks and needles instead of firm, solid ground.

Before I knew it, my mother was gone, and in her wake, the alcohol demon took firm hold of my father, refusing to let go.

50

THERE WAS STILL ONE UNRESOLVED matter I needed to tend to, and her name was Deena.

I'd been thinking about my sister a lot lately. After hearing her story, my conscience felt heavy. I knew I hadn't hurt her on purpose—I'd been my father's tool—but that didn't change the outcome. That kind of pain endures like a deep, persistent bruise. With all the continuing problems I'd had lately, I didn't get much of a chance to deal with the fallout from what Deena had told me. But as I began to confront my own problems, my need to address hers grew exponentially.

I'd hoped there was a chance to make things right by my sister. If we could at least figure out a way to bury our differences, maybe we could strike enough of a balance to mend the rupture between us. I didn't know if she and I could reach a place where we'd feel close—we were cheated out of that opportunity years ago—but if I was going to be honest, a secret part of me wanted to be the cool uncle who dropped by his sister's house for Christmas dinner or showed up on the kids' birthdays, armed with gifts. I could have a new place to belong, a family life. Maybe Deena could eventually warm to the idea.

I must have picked up my phone to stare at it about fifteen times, trying to gather the guts to dial her number.

Call her already. Do it.

I took my advice, and while she picked up on the first ring, Deena's, "Hello," was on the heavier side of tentative.

I couldn't blame her; had the roles been reversed, I would have been as locked down.

I cleared my throat and got to the point. "Hey, Deena. I was wondering if you might have some time to meet again ... to talk."

"I don't know, Griffin," she said with a wilting tone. "I feel like we've already said enough."

"But that's the thing. We haven't. I've got more to tell you, Deena. A lot more. I promise, I'm not calling to cause you more pain. I'm calling because I want to make things right."

"It's a little too late for that, don't you think?"

"I don't know. Maybe. But I'm willing to find out. Are you?"

All I heard was punctuated silence while she wavered.

"Please," I tried again.

"I've moved on, Griffin. You should, too."

"I'm making every effort to do that, but I can only get so far."

Deena let out a long sigh.

"I promise," I persisted, "I'll stay out of your life for good if that's what you decide you want after this, but please, just give me one last chance."

More pause, more deliberation, then, "Okay. Fine."

Deena was meeting me at De Anza Cove along Mission Bay. Her choice. It seemed she preferred to conduct our meetings outdoors. Was that another of her built-in security measures to help her feel less trapped? Not that I could fault her. I had my defenses, and I guess she had hers.

Okay, Mr. Overthinker, how about giving it a rest?

Clearly, I was nervous. A simpler explanation probably existed, considering that we *did* both grow up surrounded by water, our preferred second home.

I decided to be the one who arrived early this time. Was that a product of my sports-minded, competitive side, always looking for the edge? Or was it my curious side that wanted to get a take on her mood as she approached me?

I sat on a park bench, watching jet-skiers and wind surfers slice crystalline white streaks across the bay. Deena drove into the parking lot in a large white Honda SUV, not cheap but not the luxury vehicle I'd envisioned for her, which told me I was hanging onto an old, enduring bias against her. Was she more about practicality? More interested in maintaining a modest appearance? But then there was her house …

Deena got out of her SUV, then addressed me with that muted smile I'd come to know. This time, its brittleness looked more like exhaustion than reserve. She took a seat beside me on the bench, leaving a safe distance between us, then gazed ahead at the bay.

"Honestly, Deena, I had no idea you were hurting all that time." This might have been my last chance to tell her how I felt, and there was no time to waste. But she wouldn't look at me, her eyelids fluttering a few times, as if flinching before an oncoming blow. "There were so many things I would have done differently if I'd known," I added. "I just … I wish there were something I could do to lessen your pain."

"But you can't, Griffin." Deena gripped the wooden bench planks with both hands, feet anchored to the ground, as if they'd become rooted.

"I know that." I looked down, shook my head. "It's hard to get rid of my own pain. I've been doing the work, and part of that means making amends. I guess I'm hoping that it might bring you some peace, too, even if in a small way. I do want that for you."

For the first time since our conversation began, Deena's expression softened. All this time, she'd worn her sorrow like an old fracture: invisible to the common eye, but under an X-ray, there it was, healed over but never again the same. My sister didn't comment, but the dew in her eyes spoke of vulnerability, occluded by fear for too long. Fear that looked a lot like mine.

"How different our lives could have been," I said, "if we'd known we were on the same side."

"Better …" Deena said as if she'd waited all these years for her sadness to land. "It would have been better." Then, in the frailest whisper I'd ever heard, she said, "So much better."

The grave truth of her words, heavy as iron, dropped straight through the deepest part of me, then opened me up. I said, "I wish we could go back and live our lives the way we were supposed to."

"But we can't," she said, shaking her head with regret.

"We cannot." An unexpected surge of anger fired through me. "*Damn it*, Deena. We deserved to be happy."

"I ..." She shook her head.

Only when I saw the muscle in her jaw twitch did I realize I was gritting my teeth, too, as if I were a mirror of her. I waited for her to meet my gaze. When she did, I saw everything. The unremitting despair. The sharp-edged ache. The naked desolation.

Sounding broken and defeated, my sister said, "It was hard, watching you suffer, Griffin."

This was the first time she'd acknowledged that my abuse was real. That my pain existed. A stab of grief plunged through me, laid me out. Grief that, before now, I'd never known could exist. A kind that infiltrated the deepest part of me, something rotten, turning inside out.

"So many times, I wished I could have come to your rescue," she said with wet, dull eyes, "but I was terrified of that man."

"Of course you were." I closed my eyes. I opened them. "To live like that. To fear for your life,"

"Yeah." She nodded. "Just like that."

Forgiveness that I'd been working hard to find for my father was like a fine mist, disappearing into the ether. But this time, it wasn't about what he'd done to me—it was about what he had done to my sister. Abuse that had been soundless and invisible to me, but for Deena, it was anything but—so tangible and ceaseless that her fear had taken on a life of its own, always waiting around the corner like some malicious predator.

"Deena, what can I do for you right now? How can I help?"

"Nothing," she said. "There's nothing."

There really *was* nothing I could do, which towed me into the sinking awareness that I might remain estranged from her forever. I thought about trying to open a door between us, but before I could, she stood and only slightly turned her head my way.

Deena's voice was so soft, I could barely make out her words. "I have to go, Griffin. I ... I can't ..."

After wiping away her final tear, my sister walked off, leaving me alone with my regret.

51

TWO STEPS FORWARD, SIX BACK.

The solid ground I thought I'd found wasn't crumbling—it had collapsed. I was just starting to forgive my father, never once anticipating that those threads would already wear thin. It was impossible to unhear Deena's story once she'd told it. How could I feel compassion toward my father after the reminder that what he'd done had ruined not only Deena, but poisoned her and my relationship forever?

In *Candide*, Voltaire wrote that we must cultivate our own garden. Figuratively, he was telling us to keep a safe distance from the world; in other words, we can't base our well-being on people who are navigating their own walks through life—it will just add another layer of confusion, and it's a great way to lose ourselves again.

I wanted to follow that advice with Deena but had to be truthful with myself: it was damned hard. She *was* navigating her own passage. As difficult and heartbreaking as it was to see her struggle through that, I couldn't take this trip with her. We'd been on separate pathways our whole lives. And as ever, she had to go onward by herself and look for her own way to heal. That wasn't to say I couldn't empathize or listen if she decided to talk about it someday, but I couldn't let this failure turn into yet another festering resentment against my father. I'd made real progress, and it had been feeling good. The work was for me. I had to keep reminding myself of that.

In the interest of advancing my new way of life—and making more time to enjoy it—I invited Kristine over for pizza and to see what was streaming on TV.

"Hey," I said while pulling a slice from the box. "You mentioned you like rom-coms. A new one just came out, something about a guy who doesn't know he married the same woman twice."

She laughed. "Not sure how he'd miss that one."

"It's a rom-com. Anything's possible in a rom-com. It's called, *I Do—Again?*"

"Clever. Let's give it a go!"

We settled back and into the movie. It turned out the guy fell and hit his head on the pavement after getting off a city bus. He woke up with amnesia, and his ex-wife used the opportunity to right her wrongs, romancing him, and they fell in love all over again.

While it wasn't what I'd normally choose to watch, I didn't hate it. When the credits rolled, I turned to face her. "It had a good message, I guess? That life is better if you can learn to forgive and forget."

Kristine said, "Or in his case, *forget* and forgive?"

I laughed. "Yeah, that, too. By the way, just so you know, I did *not* intend for this to be a theme that runs concurrent with our lives."

She held up both hands with a grin. "I swear, I wasn't going to say anything, but since you mentioned it first …" She paused to reflect, then added, "But do you think the sex was better the second time around?"

"I guess he'll never know."

We dissolved into laughter.

"So, I need to ask for a favor," she said.

"Sure. What's up?"

"I'm involved with a charity that raises money to build safe havens for at-risk teens. We're having our annual gala on Friday. No pressure at all, but would you mind being my plus-one so I don't walk around looking like a sad loner?"

"You couldn't do that if you tried, but of course. It'll be fun."

"Awesome! I have to warn you, though, it can be kind of dull, lots of handshakes and small talk, but the food is great. There's only one catch."

I laughed. "Hardly anything surprises me too much these days. Go ahead …"

"Nothing too bad, but it's black tie, so you'll have to rent a tux."

"I've already got that covered. Black tie is standard at the entertainment awards I attend from time to time. I'm good to go!"

"All that, and the man owns a tux." She pursed her lips and shook her head. "You're the complete package, Griffin."

Nobody had paid me a compliment like that for a while. I had to admit, it felt pretty good.

"I'm not the complete package yet," I said, "but I hope to be when I grow up."

"Who the hell wants to do that?"

"Right? My mind still thinks I'm in my twenties."

"Me, too"—she scratched her head—"except my body keeps saying, *Yeah, you wish!*"

"Mine keeps asking me where the car keys went."

We both laughed.

52

WITH MY TUX HANGING IN the back of my Jeep, I stopped to pick up a six-pack of the root beer my father used to love, hoping it might lift his spirits during our visit. It was possible he wouldn't recall that, but maybe the taste would jog some of his memory.

When I walked into the room, I thought a stranger was standing over my father before recognition took shape.

"Ryan?"

He turned around, swallowed hard, and I could see his Adam's apple rise and fall.

"Really, Ryan?" I said, unable to let go of my contempt. "First, you take his side, and then you have the nerve to come visit him behind my back?"

"No." He shook his head, stepping away from the bed. "This isn't what it looks like, Griff."

I gazed around the room. "How did you even know he was here?"

"Ashley spoke to Trish."

"I should have known."

"Dude, I tried to text first, but you wouldn't answer."

He had me there, but it was no excuse for showing up at my father's room, unannounced, especially since our argument had been *about* my father.

He said, "I've been here a few times, waiting for you to come."

"Okay, now you just sound serial-killer creepy, Ryan."

He laughed, and I let my guard down more.

Then, he shoved his hands in his pockets and said, "Griff, I need to give you the truth. I couldn't wait any longer."

I studied him for a moment, then turned to gaze at my father, asleep, but it didn't look like the restful kind. His cheeks were twitching, and every few seconds, his head jerked.

After a few hesitant steps toward Ryan, I chose a safe spot and said, "What kind of truth?"

"I didn't come here to see your dad. I came to see you."

"Why should that matt—"

"Just hear me out, okay?"

I set the root beer on top of the microwave but didn't offer Ryan one.

"Look, I know you thought I was in denial about what happened to you as a kid, but I wasn't—I mean, well, I was, but not for your dad. It was for you."

I shook my head. "What does that even mean?"

"You were my best friend, Griff. I cared about you. I know I didn't always show it, but I … I … didn't want to believe he was hurting you. You know what my family was like. The only way I learned to deal with the bad shit was to act like there wasn't any. I know that compared to your family, you thought mine looked great, but it totally sucked sometimes. My parents had their share of serious problems, but they wanted their world to be so perfect that they pretended away anything that threatened it. That affected me. It was all I knew." He stared at his feet. "Deep down, I knew damned well that it was wrong to pretend like your father wasn't treating you badly."

"Then, why didn't you just stop?"

"I guess I was too proud, or too stupid, or … whatever. But I was just a kid, Griff, like you."

"You weren't a kid at the Water Bar, Ryan."

"I was going to say all this, but you jumped on my ass before I could finish my sentence."

At the time, Ryan was being pushy and invasive. It didn't feel like an olive branch or even like a real conversation was possible. But he was right about one thing. I blew up, then stomped out of the restaurant before giving him a chance to explain himself. It was a bad habit of mine. Whenever he got abrasive, I got edgy, then up went that armor so I could ready myself for battle. That was also because of my father, but I could no longer blame him for it anymore. I was an adult now.

"You know, Ryan, what I don't get is why you constantly told me things weren't that bad with my father. Why did you gaslight me like that?"

"I swear, that wasn't it at all." He shook his head emphatically. "It was because you never remembered the good times with your dad. I was just trying to remind you. I thought it would help clear your head, help you get oriented as you dealt with all *this*." He waved his hand vaguely at the room, then at my sleeping father.

"*What* good times?"

Circumspection reeled across his face, then, after a questioning expression, he said, "Early on, after your mom was gone but before his drinking got really bad? We all used to have fun together. Don't you remember that camping trip he took us on at Anza-Borrego? We all sat around the campfire, telling dirty jokes and having fart contests to see whose was the loudest."

An unexpected laugh escaped me. I'd forgotten all about that, but it was coming back. I remembered thinking I had the coolest dad around.

Ryan said, "Then, your father told that joke about the revolving door? You laughed so hard, you peed your pants! It was the best night ever!"

"Oh God," I said, my smile building with recognition, "then *you* cracked up and fell off that log."

Buried memories kept coming as if the building pressure of holding them back sent them shooting up through the shallow. Not just the memories, the feelings. Joy. Excitement.

Love.

How could I have forgotten all that? Kids block traumatic memories while growing up, but why had I also emptied out the good ones? As if chasing away bounding shadows, I made every last one vanish, building opposition against my father until I'd reframed the narrative.

"And there were other times when I knew he loved you," Ryan said. "Special times."

My head flinched back slightly. "*Special?*"

"When that baseball hit you in the head during Little League and you got a concussion, your dad was a total wreck while we sat in the ER together. Then, he stayed by your bed all night long, watching you sleep, worried that something bad might happen."

I gazed at my father, sleeping soundly now, innocently, and suddenly, my eyes were wet. I tried to say something, but all that came out was a tiny, excruciating sound.

Ryan adopted a soft tone, rich with understanding. "*That's* what I was trying to tell you, Griff, when I said he *wasn't* always that bad. I didn't mean to ignore the worst of it, though—I'm sorry."

"I had it all wrong, Ry. I'm sorry, too."

He smiled warmly.

"Well?" I said, wiping away my tear with a final sniff. "Are you just going to stand halfway across the room, grinning at me?"

He rushed over and bear-hugged me so tightly and so perfectly. And in that moment, something big unlocked within me. Fondness for him that I'd also shuttered, now within reach. He hadn't been perfect, but I hadn't, either. And it was okay.

"I missed you, man," Ryan said into my shoulder.

"Me, too, Ry. Me, too."

And for the first time, it occurred to me that all along, forgiveness had been my passageway to happiness.

53

THE CHARITY EVENT WAS TONIGHT.

It would be my first chance to see where Kristine lived when I picked her up. She was in Coronado across the bay from downtown San Diego. The area is a tied island, attached to the mainland by Silver Strand State Beach—or as locals call it, the Strand—a seven-mile tombolo that stretches into Imperial Beach. The main way in or out is over the Coronado Bridge, a tall and winding 2.1-mile aqueduct that extends across the yawning blue bay. Not the most convenient location in the city, but since it was close to downtown where Kristine worked, I could understand why she'd chosen to live there. But there were plenty of other reasons to call Coronado home. It boasted one of the best beaches in the US, along with its crown jewel, the world-renowned Hotel Del Coronado, where dignitaries came to stay and where *Some Like It Hot* had been filmed with Marilyn Monroe.

I pulled up to her place—a cute little cottage, white with green trim— off Orange Avenue. Her front entryway was flanked by potted plants, all pleasingly colorful and vibrant, along with a sign hanging on the door that read, *Welcome all!*

I had a sign at my place, too. It said: *No soliciting, fundraising, sales, estimates, religion, or politics. Thank you!*

When Kristine opened the door, I about fell back a step. She was stunning in her off-the-shoulder black evening gown, a slit running up the side, complemented by diamond earrings that added the right amount of sparkle. I was used to seeing her in jeans and a T-shirt, but tonight, she looked like a different person. Elegant, glamorous, and beautiful.

"Wow!" I told her. "You look amazing."

"Thanks. You, too. You wear a tux well!"

I gazed down at myself. "This old thing?"

She giggled.

I could see why the event was black tie only: it exuded formality, from the prism-edged chandeliers, to the colorfully lit ice sculptures, to the expensive china and ornate silverware. Everywhere I looked, I saw money: women dressed in jewels that could blind you if you looked directly into them. Many of the men wore gold watches that flashed and twinkled, lighting the way to money management accounts, probably worth millions.

As for me, I skulked around like a born-and-bred cowboy at a garden party. I was out of their league, an outsider, acquainted only with Kristine. But for her sake, I bucked up and tried to fit in instead of stand out. My uneasiness must have been obvious, though, because when I looked at Kristine, she gave me a wink of encouragement. It wasn't that I couldn't handle events like this—I'd been to plenty of movie premieres—more, it felt like a powerful echo from my past that unnerved me. These were the same circles my father often traveled. Powerful people, accustomed to getting things their way.

A woman not far from us with a troubled expression motioned to Kristine, and my date for the night sighed. "That's Sharon, one of the event organizers. I'm sorry to leave you here like this, but it looks like there may be a fire I need to help put out somewhere. Will you be okay for a minute?"

"Absolutely," I said with a smile. "I'll be fine."

That might have been true, but only until I spotted Trish standing across the banquet hall.

Oh. Shit.

I jerked my head in the opposite direction and tugged at my collar, trying to reassemble my thoughts, now scattering like a thousand marbles across a glass floor. I should have considered the possibility that Trish might have been there. After all, she and Kristine both worked with troubled kids.

Why hadn't I realized that?

Maybe because I'd figured out how to step away from my past and felt like I was living in a new world. And somehow, because the mind plays tricks, I thought I *had* left everything behind, including my failed engagement with Trish.

I gave thought to hiding from her but recognized how ridiculous that would be. This reception hall was a sealed-off box, and she was going to see me eventually. I'd have to act normal and not get worked up. While I had no plans to walk up to her, she might come to me. If it happened, it happened.

It happened.

Trish came at me, her expression one part alarm, one part curious, and one part … I wasn't even sure. Territorial? I was, after all, on her turf after she'd told me she didn't want to see me anymore. The tan gown she wore brought out her eyes, sparkling like green sapphires. I once told her I could stare into those eyes forever, but we must have had different ideas about how long forever was.

"Hey," she said with a curious smile. "I didn't expect to see you here."

I told her I was with a date.

"Oh." She searched the room as though trying to figure out whom I was with.

"She had to run off for a bit," I said. "Work."

Trish mouthed—but did not say—the word, *Okay.*

There was something odd about reuniting with a person who once loved you. They might look the same, but they're not. Time alters perception, making the person look like both an insider and an outsider.

"Griffin?"

Trish had been talking, but I didn't catch much of it.

"Yeah?"

"I was asking how your dad is."

"Oh, sorry." When I finished telling her the news about my father's decline, I could see she was saddened by it.

"I'm so sorry, Griffin."

"Thank you, but I'll be okay. I'm finding new ways to deal with my past and making the best of the time we have left."

She looked at me appraisingly with a glint of wonder. "This is a change for you, Griffin."

Until now, I hadn't given myself the time to think about that, but with Trish holding up a mirror to me, it looked clearer. I *was* changing.

"And you seem surer of yourself," Trish added. "It's almost hard to remember the old you."

She was the second person to say that, which made the summation feel more solid, authentic.

"I've been working through a lot of stuff," I told her, careful not to expose too much of myself. We were no longer in that space.

"It shows." Then, she gave me the old smile I knew well, warm and approving, as if caught up in her own generosity. All at once, we were together again, a thought that felt evocative yet off-limits. "I love this for you, Griffin, and I'm so happy."

I tried to muscle away the feelings and remain steady. It had been a long time since Trish had paid me a compliment. As the threads of our relationship frayed, so, too, had our appreciation for each other. It wasn't that I wanted to get back with her. I'd moved on. I probably just missed the feeling of being loved more than I missed her. There was a difference, and something in her seemed to respond to my skepticism.

"It's great to see you again, Griffin," she said, starting to back away.

I believed her. One thing about Trish that hadn't changed, and never would, was she always meant what she said. Maybe she was realizing she should have been more patient instead of giving up. But the thought— and a whiff of resentment—imploded when Kristine came back. The two women smiled at each other, eyes broad with an unidentifiable tension.

"Kristine. Hi," said Trish.

"Hi …" Kristine replied, voice faltering.

Oh. Hell.

Not only did they work in similar fields—they knew each other, something else I should have thought about. I gulped down my discomfort, observing the weird energy boomeranging between the two women. Kristine wasn't my girlfriend, but Trish didn't know this, so I figured that accounted for a part of the uneasiness.

A woman called out to Kristine. When she turned to look, Trish gave Kristine the up-and-down, and then Kristine turned back and caught Trish inspecting her.

"Hey," Kristine said, riding the edge of uneasiness, "would you mind if I take Griffin away from you? There's someone I'd like him to meet."

"Oh, absolutely," Trish said. "Great to see you, Kristine. You, too, Griffin."

After Trish walked away, Kristine muttered, "Wow. Super awkward."

It was a wild understatement.

"Do you know Trish well?" I asked.

"Not very. We've run into each other on occasion, mostly when I'm asked to testify in court. But I've only known her as Patricia. I just never put it together."

Her professional name, I thought. "I'm sorry. I probably should have realized this weird encounter could happen."

"It's fine," she said with a smile. "These things happen."

My phone went off. The second I looked at the screen, I knew bad news was coming. Memory care facilities don't call at this hour with heartwarming news.

"It's your father," the nursing supervisor told me in a gentle tone. "There's been an accident, and they've taken him to Scripps Memorial by ambulance."

That was all I needed to hear. I ended the call before even listening to the details about what had happened, then looked at Kristine.

"I'm sorry to do this, but I have to go. My father is headed to the emergency room."

"Oh no! Do you want me to go with you?"

"No, no. Stay. I'll be fine."

Before I knew it, I was speeding toward the hospital.

PART FOUR: DESCEND

54

I SAT BY MYSELF IN the lounge area, fiddling with my hands and waiting for the doctor to come out. Once the son who wanted nothing to do with my father, I was now the son who'd become his closest ally, his advocate. The son who cared. For a moment, I'd considered inviting Nolan to come with me but decided against it. I was already stressed and sad and worried. Having him there might only escalate those feelings.

When the doctor arrived, he took a seat beside me, then explained what had happened. A physical therapist at Oceanview had gotten my dad out of bed and standing, and then he became unruly. He accidentally struck a nurse in the face, knocking her over, then lost his balance and went down with her.

"Your father came through the fall with only minor injuries," the doctor said.

"Thank God for that." I could breathe a little easier now.

"In one respect, yes, but I'm afraid the news isn't all good. A few irregularities came up on a CT of his lower abdomen that suggest the start of a malignancy in his liver, which hadn't shown yet when he came here after the accident. But because of your dad's rapidly declining condition and his inability to tolerate surgery, I don't see a need to confirm that diagnosis with a biopsy. He also has sepsis, a potentially deadly condition."

I shook my head. "I've heard of sepsis before, but what does it mean?"

"It happens when the body's response to an infection starts damaging its own tissue. We're giving him antibiotics, but as rapidly advancing as this is, I don't know if we'll be able to turn it around." He paused and offered a deep sigh. "If we can't, he'll go into septic shock, which leads to organ failure and death. As it is, his liver already shows signs of failing, which could partly be from the sepsis, but looking at the emergency room records after his accident, I saw he already had advanced cirrhosis, which is irreversible and will continue to progress."

"Cirrhosis caused by years of excessive drinking."

The doctor nodded. "On top of that, I'm afraid his Alzheimer's is only accelerating the deterioration process. I see this a lot in patients with the disease."

I stood quietly. No need to ask how long my father had to live; the answer was *not much*.

"It would probably be a good idea to make hospice arrangements fairly soon," the doctor said, resolving my thought. "Someone from the hospital will be in touch to help you with that."

Hospice. The mention of that word was like a snapshot from the past. First my mother, then my father, both stricken with cancers, both discovered by accident, both too late to do anything about it. I could remember when hospice came to the house for my mother. Even though I was young, I knew it signaled the end. My feelings toward my father might have been much more complex, but that didn't matter now. His life was ending. I used to beg for this every day—now I was begging for more time. Death had a way of redefining emotions. Circumstances looked different, and hopes shifted.

So, here we are.

I decided to call Deena. She might not care, but our father was dying, and I felt obligated to let her know. She could do with the news what she wanted.

"What's up, Griffin?" she said, tone the friendliest I'd heard since we'd reunited.

Relief gave me the fortitude to continue, even as I stumbled in my delivery. "Hey, Deena, I'm at Scripps. Things are changing for Dad. I mean … they're not good." There was no right way to say what I had to, so I just took a big breath and spit it out. "They're saying he doesn't have much time left."

"Wha … what's happening?" she said with a hint of distress I hadn't expected.

I gave her every detail.

"I see." Her voice wasn't cold, but it wasn't sad, either. More as though she'd been caught off guard, stunned even, which was weird because I'd already told her this was coming.

Had my return to Deena's life forced her to reexamine her trauma, causing mixed feelings to creep back in about our father? I didn't ask. I was staying in my own garden.

"Anyway, I just thought I'd let you know."

"I appreciate it. Thanks, Griffin," she said, then hung up.

And that's that.

When I entered my father's room, his arm was in a sling, a purple bruise marring the left side of his cheek. When he gazed up at me, the creases in his forehead smoothed some, and his eyes softened as if I were the only one who could lead him out of confusion. Maybe I was.

I stood at his bedside and said, "Hi, Dad. Do you know where you are?"

He seemed to search his mind, then gave me an empty stare.

"Do you remember falling?"

I got the same nonresponse.

His chest rose and fell like tides washing in and out to sea. I saw a man falling away, vanishing before me. For the first time in a long while, I felt an alliance with him. This was my father stripped down, his rough edges burnished, his entire person innocent and fearful, just as I had once been.

It seemed crazy to feel sorry for him after all he'd done to me, but maybe I was tired of hating him. Maybe it was more than that. Had I identified with him in ways I hadn't imagined I could? True, our pain came from different places, but maybe our suffering was the same.

"My arm hurts," he said.

"I know, Dad."

"What … happened?"

"Do you remember falling?" I asked again.

And again, he searched for an answer, and then with discouragement I could feel, he shook his head. I wondered how it felt to live in a mind imprisoned by walls and locked doors. A mind turning hollow. Emptying out.

It must have been so lonely there.

55

THE DAY HAD FINALLY COME.

I'd been waiting to head off to college for as long as I could remember. For most students, that meant looking forward to great parties, making new friends, and a little learning in between. For me, it was all of those things, plus more. This was that getaway car I'd always hoped for, emancipation from my father and his drunken cruelty. Even though he'd agreed to bankroll my tuition, I felt no loyalty to him and had no intention of seeing him again.

Deena and I had been sharing my dad's old Mercedes, so I had to leave it behind. Since my father couldn't afford to take time out of court, I'd make my way up the coast to UC Berkeley by train. Fine with me. A few minutes in the car with him while he drove me to the station was a small price for freedom.

It was a rare occasion when I felt comfortable enough to step into a car he was driving. After dropping me off, he had to go to work, so boozing it up at this hour wasn't an option. The climate between us was different. No insults, no rage-fueled attacks, no vitriol, just rigid tension.

"Got your ticket?" my father muttered, an obvious attempt to break through the awkward quiet. "Did you pack your laptop? The lamp you wanted to bring? Don't get all caught up in the social life there. Focus on your studies."

I stared out through the passenger's window, chin resting in my hand so he couldn't see me roll my eyes, but he probably felt the cynicism through my lack of response. His concern was probably an act, anyway. Or maybe his sober mind was going for a quick fix to allay the guilt he'd accumulated through the years. Had that been the case, the effort sank like lead, coming across as nothing more than a pathetic, last-ditch effort. It was too late for reparations. This relationship was over, had been for years.

It started to rain as we exited the car at the train station. My father grimaced while we hefted my luggage and boxes through the parking lot downfall, but it didn't bother me. The rain felt like an overdue cleansing to wash away all the bad energy that had accumulated between us for too long. I tried to dismiss my father with a simple goodbye, but he insisted on coming to the train's platform. As we entered the station, his presence felt cumbersome, but I was relieved to see the train waiting there so I could just get right on.

As I prepared to board, the strain between us got even more uncomfortable. Unlike many other kids at this milestone in life, there would be no father-son hug, no words of wisdom to impart on me before this exciting, new life adventure. Even though freedom and happiness waited on the other side of this moment, my resentment toward him only metastasized. With a glimpse at a better life, the contrast between the Before and After sharpened.

"Good luck, son," he said.

Was that a quiver in his voice?

I wrestled up a smile, raised my hand a few inches in a semi-wave. Then, I turned to walk away, leaving him alone on the platform, rain soaking his gray overcoat.

Boarding the train and settling in my seat felt like a celebration and a long-awaited start to a new life. A better *everything*. What would it feel like to go through a day without dreading his abuse? As the train started to pick up momentum, I looked out through the window and startled. My father hadn't moved an inch from his spot on the platform. The winds had picked up speed, and the downfall came harder, yet he appeared suspended in it—like a sagging mannequin left out in the rain—wearing the most forlorn expression I'd ever seen.

He spotted me through the train's window and began waving goodbye. A vicious gale forced his hand sideways. For reasons I couldn't explain, I waved back to him.

56

"Nolan …"

He kept quiet for a moment, then said, "It's about your dad."

"It is."

I gave him the details.

After I finished, he sighed and said, "I can't say I didn't see it coming but, damn, this is hard."

"They told me he doesn't have much time left. I just wanted to let you know in case you'd like to see him for the last time."

Nolan didn't talk, but the quiet spoke of his sorrow so profoundly. I waited, knowing there was nothing I could say to ease his pain. He loved my father, and from what I could tell, the feeling had been mutual. The two men had been through many of the same battles in life. They were friends and confidants.

"I'm very sorry, Griffin." Nolan was trying to sound strong, but he didn't quite get there. "I know the two of you were just beginning to make peace with the past. But I'm so, so happy you were able to see each other again. I just wish the circumstances had been better."

"Me, too, but I guess it's better than nothing."

"What can I do for you, Griffin? How can I help?"

"You're very kind, Nolan, but there's nothing. I just want to make the most of whatever time I've got left with him."

I hung up and considered what Nolan had once told me.

"I learned the value of time and suffering."

I sat at my father's bedside, observing him while he slept.

We were once connected by strong love, but in the end, we were connected by sorrow. A tragic story, an old one, but that truth, once obscure, had at last revealed itself. There's a lot to be said about truth—it can hurt, but it can also mend.

"I love us."

"I love us, too, Champ."

That memory, those words, touched a place in my heart that had been lying dormant for years. That special place where a freckled-faced kid and his father walked hand in hand down the causeway. Where purple gorillas and blue bears lived and Ferris wheels spun toward the heavens, dissolving all of our worries.

Something else that, until now, I hadn't recognized. Throughout the derision and mutual dislike between my father and me, throughout the pain, there was also a hidden and persistent unity. We both loved my mother fiercely and felt the same degree of heartache over losing her. So maybe we were alike in other ways I hadn't noticed.

I thought back to what my mother had once told me while we tended to the garden.

"Griffin," she'd said, pruning vines of cherry-red bougainvillea after my father and I had had a disagreement, "anger is like drinking arsenic and expecting the other person to die."

How different might my life have been if I'd let go of my anger earlier instead of waiting for the dumb luck of a car crash to bring change? Now, I sat on the back end of that anger, racing to make up for lost time as my father's illness chiseled deeper into it. Even if I did get the chance to tell him how I felt now, would he be able to absorb it? Kristine had told me she could have yelled at her mother all day long and it wouldn't matter one bit.

Because it's not for them. It's for us.

No need to yell anymore, but there was plenty left to say. Even if he couldn't understand me, it didn't mean I had to remain silent.

It felt as though my chest had caved in. I could practically see my father fading away. The lines on his face looked deeper, and his trembling hands shook harder, all symbolic of a life gone by, piled high with grief and regret.

We're all human. We make poor choices—those can't be undone—but in the final count, we all bleed the same. We all feel pain.

My father's eyes fluttered open and discovered mine. I reached over to put a hand on his arm, but before I could, he took hold of my wrist.

Through a tortured expression and a pale whisper, he asked, "What ... what's happening to me?"

A tear rolled down my cheek, and my voice cracked. "It's okay, Dad."

I turned my face away from him and toward the window to wipe my eyes. Fingers of sunlight reached through the pane, igniting dust particles, which looked like a thousand tiny, falling angels. I turned back toward him.

"Stay?" he asked, his voice wavering.

"I promise, Dad," I answered back, the weight of those words bearing down on my throat, my chest, everything.

He squeezed my wrist harder as if it might help him hang on to this moment a little longer. On to us.

"I'll take care of you, Dad," I said, remembering an old promise.

57

NOT LONG BEFORE MY MOTHER passed, she had a talk with me. We both knew she didn't have much time left, and a big part of me felt like it was slipping away with her.

Looking back, I wondered if she worried that nobody would be there to keep my father's dark side at bay once she was gone, and she'd felt an urgency to warn me when she said, "Try to keep your sense of humor when your father gets difficult. You and Deena will really need to be there for each other."

She had no idea how dark he'd get and that we would never be able to fulfill her wish.

"Griffin," she said, voice weak as I lay next to her on the bed, head resting on her chest. The room felt smaller, and the other noises in the house seemed farther away. It was as if I could feel the house changing as Mom prepared to leave it. "I'm always with you. Remember everything I've taught you about life."

I was too young to comprehend the nuance of what she'd said, but my mother was sending me off into the world as she prepared to leave it.

I lifted my head to look at her, eyes brimming with tears. "But I don't want you to go."

"I know, sweetheart. I know …" Staring up at the ceiling, she stroked the top of my head. "You won't be able to see me, but the most important part of me will always be with you. The beautiful memories we shared, my love for you. Those will never *ever* go away."

"But what about our talks, Mom?"

"You can have those anytime you want. You know exactly what I'd say."

I held my gaze on hers, shook my head, then began sobbing. And together, we sat. Nothing more said, but love poured into the empty silence of what we felt but couldn't say.

"And please, Griffin, take care of your father. He's not perfect, but he loves you every bit as much as I do."

Mom probably knew about my father's abusive past but shielded us from it. There was no purpose in bringing it up then—life was too good.

"I will. I promise," I'd said.

At the time, there was no reason to do otherwise. Each day, my father showed me what love was, and I had loved him back with equal measure. I had no idea that he was about to turn into the most unlovable person in my life.

I'd forgotten all about Mom's wish until now. My father and I were closing the loop on our lives, and with that came a fear of finality that I hadn't felt prepared for. Like folding down the corner of a page but never coming back to it.

58

MY FATHER WAS SURROUNDED BY a nest of machines and metal. A series of bags hung from each tier of an IV pole with a pump to drive them. A steel table sat bedside along with a vitals machine to track his dwindling existence. Like the pendulum on a clock, swinging back and forth, back and forth, each noise brought him closer to the end.

Drip, drip, drip, beep, beep, beep.

Dad's eyes opened but didn't find focus, and with that one restricted movement, his rapid deterioration became more apparent. He'd gotten even thinner, and jaundice had set in, turning the whites of his bloodshot eyes and skin a phosphoric, mustardy color. Yet another signpost, pointing to a dead-end street. A disappearing act, gaining momentum.

I felt compelled to reach for his hand and have a tactile connection with him. In mine, his touch felt insubstantial—thin and nearly weightless—his skin cold and loose like worn, shiny wax paper. As I held on, I tried to understand the impulse. Did I feel as though in doing so, I could, in some way, make time freeze, even if just for a few extra heartbeats? Or was it because the bond I craved with him for years had only met with emotional deprivation—and this was my final attempt to recapture a modicum of that overdue love? So many thoughts whipsawing through my mind, and it was difficult to focus and gain clarity on any of them.

Two hospital staff members entered the room to inform me that it was time for my father's physical therapy, but they advised that, in his weak condition, this might only entail sitting him up in bed.

Physical therapy for a dying man? My skepticism must have shown on my face.

"It's important to keep him moving," said one of the therapists, a woman with raven hair pulled into a high ponytail. "It helps control the symptoms and keep him comfortable. Also prohibits the development of more health issues from being sedentary."

I thought but didn't say, *I'm pretty sure he's got them all by now.*

Because of the incline on my father's bed, the sheets had slipped, pulling him downward, which left his head at an awkward angle.

The physical therapists moved to opposite sides of the bed, and in one quick, spontaneous motion, they yanked the sheets up. His expression void, my father's head flopped from side to side as his body jolted into an upright position.

"Mr. McCabe?" one of them said, raising her voice and overemphasizing each syllable. "We want to move you to the edge of the bed. Can we try that?"

It was all so hard to watch. His nod was insubstantial, his eyes narrow and hopeless.

"Okay. On the count of one, two … three!" One therapist held my father's back in place while the other attempted to swing his legs toward the edge of the bed.

In the process, the hospital gown slid off his narrow shoulders, revealing a skeletal figure, his rib cage protruding, his spindly arms hanging from his sides. One of the physical therapists pulled the gown back over his knobby shoulders while trying to hold him in place, but his toneless body started to slump.

"Okay, very good, Mr. McCabe. You did great!"

At what? Showing them what death looks like?

My heart felt like it weighed fifteen pounds. I was looking at a man, once so powerful—a viper in the courtroom and a wild boar at home—whittled down to nearly nothing.

I sagged back into the chair, pressure building against my breastbone from not breathing enough. I wasn't sure how much longer I could bear this agony.

Mine, but mostly his.

59

I DROVE AWAY FROM THE hospital and toward Kristine's place. I'd been running to her each time life tightened its grip on me, probably depending on her too much. Was it healthy to need her this way? At that point, I wasn't sure if I had a choice because she was just the one who happened to be standing there in the middle of my crisis.

Windansea Beach swept through my mind, my seaside sanctuary whenever life threw me to the waves. I'd solved a lot of problems there, both on sea and dry land. The familiar could be a smarter option rather than a new friend. I made an abrupt U-turn and drove toward the beach. Even as I did it, though, another thought flipped over the previous one. Would I be doing the same thing I'd done to other people close to me by not going to Kristine's? I was, after all, trying to change those old, broken patterns. I gazed into my sideview mirror and laughed at the picture of indecision staring back at me.

Maybe I *could* turn to Kristine, but this time I'd be outfitted with all the knowledge I'd gathered. Might that make the outcome even better?

Then, there was the added question: what did I want our relationship to be, anyway?

I checked my car's clock. It was six thirty p.m. Kristine should have been home from work by now, but to be sure, I pulled to the side of the road and picked up my phone for a quick text.

> Hey, Kristine. Saw my dad today and could use someone
> to talk to. Are you available for a drop-in? No pressure,
> of course.

I watched the cycling dots.

Sure. Come on over!

When Kristine opened her door, she looked at my expression and showed me inside. I must have been wearing my feelings on the outside a lot these days because Nolan had reacted the same way when I'd gone to see him.

She led me to her cushy leather couch, and then she went off into the kitchen. I didn't have a chance to walk into her place the last time—we were in a hurry to get to the benefit—but now that I was here, I could see her personality in it. The living room was well-decorated and appealing. Smart and cozy was the theme, each piece of furniture welcoming with soft lines. I took in the paintings on her walls, one a Renwil Corney botanical on canvas, whimsical, with warm brushstrokes of peach, fuchsia, and periwinkle, tossed across a light-pink background.

Kristine came back from the kitchen and handed me a glassful of ice water. Holding an observant eye on me, she sat and listened to my full account about the difficult visit with my father, plus the news that doctors had uncovered a series of additional life-threatening health complications.

When I finished, she took in a long breath and said, "I'm so sorry, Griffin. Unfortunately, this is the hard part."

"I knew this was coming, but I thought I'd been prepared. You should have seen him, Kristine. How could I not feel something for him? I'm just not sure if I can grasp what that is yet."

She scooted a little closer and folded a leg beneath herself, apparently trading her therapist's hat for a warm, friendly ear.

"Was it sadness I felt? Compassion?" I stopped to think. "Love?"

"That's a lot to unpack, but the compassion and love parts seem new … and pretty big."

"It's the first time I've felt anything like that toward him since I was a kid. Could it be possible that I loved him all along but couldn't see it through the years of alcohol and abuse?"

"You certainly wouldn't be alone with that. I bounced between love and hate toward my mother, never fully landing on the love part for long.

Just because I disliked her didn't mean I didn't want to feel that love from her. That's nature. And since you and your dad had such a strong relationship at the start, that might make it more true."

"Maybe it goes both ways. Maybe he never stopped loving *me*, either. That's what my father's friend, Nolan, told me. I had a hard time believing it then, but now, it seems possible. The only problem is, it would be hard to recover that love because his mind is so gone, and it's getting worse every day."

"They call Alzheimer's the 'long goodbye' for good reason. It's a different kind of grieving. You know the end is coming but have no idea how long it'll take."

"Maybe I need to see the time we have together as the gift I never thought I'd get, no matter how unproductive or short it may feel."

"That's it. I think you nailed it."

I *did* love my father. And I would miss him terribly once he was gone. Something hard and jagged dragged through my gut. I lowered my head and closed my eyes.

"What is it, Griffin?"

I didn't respond, just shook my head with a kind of regret that, before now, I hadn't known was possible—the kind that peeled away everything I'd once believed.

Kristine put an arm around my shoulder, and we fell together into an embrace. I pulled back some, and then without thinking, I moved in to kiss her.

She abruptly broke away.

"Oh God …" I said. "I … I'm so sorry. I just—"

"Griffin, it's okay. There's no need to apologize."

I threw a hand up to each side of my forehead. "I … I don't know what's wrong with me."

"There's nothing wrong with you," she said. "It's just that I'm not straight."

"Oh God. Leave it to me to make things more complicated."

She laughed.

I leaned in toward her, suddenly aware there was still so much we hadn't learned about each other. "How come you never told me that?"

"Because I don't feel like it's the first thing I need to announce to people. Heterosexuals don't introduce themselves that way, so why should I? I knew it would eventually come up, but in a more organic way, and that's how I prefer it. Besides, I've always felt like it's only one small part of me. There are so many other things that are much more interesting."

She was right. Sexuality had nothing to do with her being a kind and generous person, and her generosity had had nothing to do with attraction. Through the years, I'd had many gay friends, both through work and my personal life. They would have been the same important people to me regardless of who they loved.

"Even if I were straight," Kristine said, "you getting involved with someone from your support network right now would be a bad idea. And I'd be selfish. I'd be sending you right down the same rabbit hole all over again, enabling you to repeat the same pattern you had with Trish. You need more time to grow, Griffin."

I didn't like hearing that, but she was right. When life dealt me a blow, I forced love to happen in an attempt to make up for the part of me that had been hungering for it. But that didn't work. It never had. I was getting wise enough to recognize it.

"Griffin, you're still figuring out who you are. That's a hard thing, but it's a beautiful thing. Why would you want to sabotage yourself now? You've worked so hard to get here."

I did want to discover love, but that wouldn't happen if I kept falling over myself and dragging my partners down with me. I wanted real love, not the same broken version I'd been addicted to for years. Next time, I wanted to be with someone I could fully love, who could love me back the same way. I should have used what my parents modeled during the Before as my guide—not what happened in the After. As I'd learned, my father had a lot of demons, but somehow, my parents had managed to make their marriage work.

When did I forget that? *How* did I forget it?

Because I was rushed to process my mother's death, then the relationship with my father fell apart, then I dropped into the giant sinkhole they'd left behind.

Ever since, I was barely hanging on, not once figuring out what healthy love looked like.

But it had been right in front of me the whole time.

60

IN FOURTH GRADE, OUR CLASSROOM had a pet hamster named Algernon, and it was pet love at first sight. When nobody looked, I'd speak to him, and in my child's mind, I'd imagine what he'd tell me if he could talk.

"Algernon? Bologna or salami?"

"Oh, salami for sure."

"Hot dogs or hamburgers?"

"Duh, hamburgers!"

And on and on it went. It felt as though we had a close friendship, Algernon and I. When my teacher allowed it, I'd let him crawl up my arm, then onto my shoulders, and there he'd sit, my copilot. One day, I got an idea. How fun would it be if I took Algernon home? I made a plan. I'd stick around a little longer after everyone left, then swoop my little buddy into my backpack, and off we'd go.

My plan worked perfectly. Soon, Algernon the Great—as I called him—was racing around my bedroom. I created obstacle courses made of books, pencils, whatever else I could find, and then off he'd go, hurdling over them and racing to the finish.

I took a bathroom break and left Algernon in my bedroom, but when I returned, a not-so-pleasant revelation awaited me.

Algernon was gone.

I thought I'd closed the door all the way, but apparently not. I couldn't see him anywhere, but to be sure, I decided to explore the confines of my bedroom. I checked under my bed, under my dresser, and inside the closet, sifting through all the clothes I'd dropped onto the floor.

He wasn't anywhere.

My heart fluttered. Algernon the Great had made his great escape.

"AHHHHHHHH! OH MY GOD!" my mother shrieked from downstairs.

I took off out of my room, then down to the living room. When I hit the ground floor, my mother was frantically screaming and chasing Algernon around with a broom. Panic struck. Thoughts scattered. She was about to kill my new best rodent friend and, in the process, seal my doom at school.

In order to rescue Algernon from a most certain death, I'd have to confess my crime.

"Don't kill him, Mom. Please! Don't do it! He's our class pet!"

Mom looked at the hamster, looked at me, and then in a ragged voice, she said, "What … in … the …" Without missing a beat, she yelled upstairs, "Sam! Come down here right away. There's a … a … *rat* loose in the house!"

"He's not a rat!" I corrected. "Algernon is a hamster! Please don't hurt him!"

"I don't give a rat's ass what you want to call that *animal*! I want it out of my house!"

My father materialized at the foot of the staircase, and if there were a picture of confusion, he was it. Mom rapidly caught him up on the situation, asking him to capture—but not harm or kill—the hamster now hiding under the couch and shaking like a spring.

With effort and a lot of patience, Dad was able to snare Algernon without hurting him, but my own fate was uncertain. He gave me a stern look.

"I just wanted us to have a sleepover!" I tried to plead my case. "I was gonna bring him back to the classroom tomorrow!"

"That's not the point, Griffin," Mom said. "You knew it was wrong to remove him from the classroom. He's not just yours. He belongs to your classmates, too."

"But I didn't think anyone would notice!"

"*Damn it, Griffin!*" my dad shouted. "Did you hear what your mother just said?"

Mom placed a hand on Dad's shoulder.

Dad said, "You're going back to school tomorrow to tell the teacher what you did and apologize."

Mom's eyes lingered on Dad, and then to me, she said, "We're disappointed in you, Griffin. They make rules for a reason. You can't just take something that doesn't belong to you because you want it."

"You made a bad decision," Dad added, ill temper still trailing his voice, "and you'll have to pay for it. Besides apologizing in front of your class, you're grounded for a week. Straight home after school, and you don't leave the house until it's time to go back."

Mom shot Dad another look, her eyes wide with a pop of irritation. Dad returned one of confusion. Mine probably looked more so because it was hard to read the unspoken conversation bouncing back and forth between my parents.

"Can you excuse us for a few minutes, Griffin?" Mom said, still eyeing my father.

They left the room, then went into the study, closing the door behind them, but it opened back up a sliver. I couldn't make out what they were saying, so I sidled up closer and peered inside to eavesdrop.

"What was that all about, Sam?"

"I was angry."

"But that's not how we speak to our children. You know that."

Dad looked away, shook his head, then let out a huff. "I guess I just got overwhelmed."

"Then, you decided his punishment without discussing it with me first."

"I thought you'd be okay with it."

"That's not the point, Sam. This isn't the Wild West. You don't get to deliver whatever brand of justice you think is right whenever you feel like it. We always talk to each other before making decisions about the kids. You know that. What were you thinking?"

"But he had it coming, Ruth. You know he did," Dad said with an unfamiliar snap of vengeance in his voice.

"*Samuel McCabe!*" My mother took a step back.

"*What?*"

A bothered silence invaded the room. Mom's response was less than generous; she stared coldly at him for a few seconds.

"Come on, Ruth!" he said, reading her annoyance. "You know what I meant."

"Do I?"

"Look, I'm sorry. I don't know what got into me. Work is making me edgy."

She relaxed some.

I'd never seen my parents disagree over anything before, but looking back, I understood why. In order to create a stable home environment, they wouldn't argue in front of my sister and me.

Dad said, "Do you forgive me?"

Mom softened her stance a little more. With defiance, she crossed her arms over her chest, and with the slightest grin, she said, "I don't know. I'll have to think about it."

"Would a kiss help?" Dad asked.

"I suppose …"

Dad pulled her into a hug and kissed her all over—her cheeks, her forehead, her neck, her chin, everywhere.

"*Sam*! Stop!" she said through her familiar giggle. "Enough already!"

"Penny for your hamster, dear?"

Now, they were both laughing.

I was too young to understand the full thrust of their exchange, but I do today. The roadmap to a loving and successful marriage had always been laid out before me. My parents were modeling what a loving relationship between two adults looked like. Not shutting each other out when life got difficult, but instead being open and having a good sense of humor that traveled in both directions between them. Mom put guardrails around my father's disagreeable side, much as she kept her garden from growing out of control.

Once my father started drinking, I learned all the wrong lessons—chiefly, to lock my feelings in the vault as an act of self-preservation. It was my loss, not figuring out until so much later how to carry their wisdom into my own life. The good news: I didn't have to keep living like that. I was allowed to fix my broken ways.

61

IT WAS MY BIRTHDAY.

With Trish gone, I wasn't sure what to do with myself. Splurge on some cheap, over-frosted grocery store cake with enough sugar to plunge me into a mood disorder? Become one of those people who tells everyone that birthdays aren't a big deal anymore because getting old sucks? That wasn't me. My father didn't even know what day it was, and Kristine didn't feel like a doable option, either. Although we'd talked things through after I clumsily tried to make out with her, it made me cringe to think about it, even days later. We'd be fine, but I decided to give her some room and let life settle before asking for her time again.

I thought about Deena. The internal debate began while I sat at my kitchen counter, staring at scrambled eggs that had gone cold ten minutes ago. Should I get in touch with my twin to wish her a happy birthday? Harmless enough, I thought. It was the biggest thing we had in common—coming from the same mother and all—but then I reminded myself that, as usual, it wasn't that simple. Would I be doing this more to soothe my loneliness than as an act of goodwill? Maybe a little, but would that be so horrible? I could make it look casual, say I was in the neighborhood and thought I'd drop by to wish her a happy birthday.

But how would I explain that I figured out her address by checking online without looking like a total creeper? She'd insisted on keeping a divider between us, but part of me wanted to poke at it. Call it a normal sibling impulse or call it hope. We'd cleared up a lot of our sooty past, and she *had* been friendlier the last time I'd called. Maybe she wanted us to be closer, too, but didn't know how to ask for it. Maybe I was telling myself happy lies. But I was so damned lonely and craved a connection with her.

So, now, I sat in my car, looking up at Deena's massive mid-century modern home, a boxy conglomeration of blazing white stucco, pencil-sharp lines, and floor-to-ceiling windows on each level, mirroring the bluer-than-blue ocean laid out before it. I looked down at the birthday gift in my lap and felt a landslide of inferiority. Why in the world did I think this broke-assed sand candle was a good gift idea for someone swimming in money? I could have at least gift-wrapped it instead of leaving it in this bag the gift shop clerk shoved at me. If Trish were here, she would have shot down my idea before it had a chance to grow legs.

I thought about leaving, but I'd come this far. The more I sat and deliberated, the more insubstantial I felt, a fear that would probably expand with each mile I traveled in the other direction. I gathered up the bag with my sister's stupid candle, then stepped out of the car.

Walking up to her house felt like trespassing. When I stopped at an archway, leading to the backyard, classical music filled the air, and I got a whiff of something that had to be absolutely delicious. A large group of people gathered poolside, accepting appetizers from servers with one hand while balancing their beverages in the other. I got a glimpse of Deena, crossing the yard to approach some new guests. She wore a white dress, accented by a bright red sash, her hair hoisted into a high ponytail. I barely recognized her: it seemed like a lifetime ago when I'd last seen my sister smile. A moment later, her little girls wove into the picture like radiant blonde butterflies, giggling as they ran circles around their mother. They wore matching dresses and hairstyles. It was like a scene from the most wholesome movie ever.

Deena had landed everything we'd missed out on in adolescence: close friends, a loving family. A full life. Good for her; she deserved it, yet I couldn't stop the knot of heartsickness tugging through me or the isolation that dropped like a steel plate. I longed for what she had—I hungered for it—but I no longer knew where to find it. But our circumstances were different, and there was no comparison. I was busy taking care of our father by myself, had just ended a relationship, and was wrestling with a multitude of regrets.

I looked down at my tattered blue sneakers, my holey jeans, and faded black T-shirt with *Sam's Sports Grill* splashed across it, which I'd worn to support my lie about just happening to be in the neighborhood. Not once had I considered that Deena might be throwing a birthday party or that my clothing choice would probably net me dozens of wide-eyed looks of reprobation.

This was a horrible, misguided idea. When I turned to leave, their large front door groaned open. Behind it stood a tall, good-looking man with broad shoulders, a great tan, and a gold Rolex Presidential that left me seeing white spots in the afternoon sunlight. I'd seen the photo of Deena's husband on her web page, but in real life, he had the imposing presence of a professional athlete. He stared at the shopping bag, my sloppy attire, and I felt like I'd dropped about ten inches closer toward the ground.

"Grubhub!" was all I could come up with on such short notice. I held up the shopping bag as evidence of my lie and gave a mortified grin. "Sorry, wrong house!"

I didn't get to see his response because I was already half down the walkway. When I reached the end, I dared to turn, but her husband was no longer there. Deena, however, stood in the window, staring at me, and for the first time, I noticed the resemblance between us, faint, but still visible, even at a distance. Same nose, same round, upturned eyes. My steps locked—so did our gazes. It was hard to read her reaction, but I could feel mine: full-bodied embarrassment. Anything I did would have only compounded the problem. Talking to her now would throw me in deeper because how would I explain why she caught me running from her house? And lying to her husband?

I was about to take off when Deena's expression shifted.

What is that?

Then, I got it.

It was the same look she used to give when my father went off on me.

She didn't know what to do, either.

When I got home, as an effort to walk back my embarrassment after creating the fiasco at Deena's, I decided to text her with a neutralizing message. I typed and deleted several times, trying to figure out what to say, then settled for, *So sorry for dropping by unannounced. Just came by to wish you a happy birthday!*

I watched the three dots bounce for a good twenty seconds, but then they stopped. A few minutes later, she sent a quick, *Happy birthday to you, too!*

More awkward.

62

MY FATHER WAS WELL ENOUGH to move back into Oceanview. Their palliative care unit would keep him comfortable, and then when the time came, he'd transfer downstairs to the hospice wing.

It was as simple as that and as difficult. We were nearing the final scene. I accepted it better than I would have thought even just a few days ago. I was waiting for something to happen or not to happen, never sure of which would come. All I could do now, I realized, was work on saying goodbye without regrets. There was no date marked on the calendar to tell me when my father's life would be over, but he was showing a few signs of improvement. The blood transfusions were tackling the anemia, and his sepsis was more stable but remained a grave threat. The doctor cautioned that these improvements would only be temporary; treatments couldn't address the more serious, underlying health challenges.

"I'm afraid it'll be a difficult road going forward," he told me before discharging my father from the hospital. "Likely, there will be ups and downs. He may come around at times and seem perceptive. If he does, that may come and go quickly. Your father's brain is shutting down, which is the body's conductor. When this happens, it's not just the mind that fails; the organs do, too."

With all that in mind, I took a leave of absence from work. Although I'd spent more hours than I could count watching my father sleep, our close physical proximity gave me a rare opportunity to reflect on both the good and the bad, make my peace with the past, and at last create distance from it.

I entered my father's room with a paper coffee cup in hand. I hadn't been sleeping well and wanted to stay alert for the short time we had left. As the steam wafted toward his bed, he took a deeper breath, relishing in the coffee aroma, but I wondered if he even knew what he was smelling.

In the thin, shapeless voice I'd come to know, he said, "You look tired."

Last time, he could barely form words. Was familiarity pulling him out of his loose-fitting universe? It was a nice surprise but also cautionary. This must have been what the doctor meant about the ups and downs. I had no expectations, no worries. This was me and my father, together, with a chance to communicate, and that was enough.

"Yeah, I'm a little tired, Dad," I said, dragging a guest chair toward the bed. "You look better today, but how do you feel?"

"Tired …" he said, fighting to keep his eyes open.

"I know you are, Dad."

"Gone … gone," he said in a trailing whisper.

I studied him for a few seconds, unsure of what to make of that. Was death's approach something he could feel in his bones the way an old injury aches before a storm? Or could this have been my own misperception, and his obscure stream of consciousness had been flowing in a completely different direction?

I wasn't sure whether to address the comment or let it go. It was hard deciding how to respond and be present for a man who was hardly here. And indeed, my father slipped into that faraway gaze of departure.

Selfishly, I wanted to call him back to the front, keep him alert, and connect with him more.

"Dad?"

He jerked back, and the cords in his neck strained. "Why are you calling me that? Who the hell are you?"

"It's me, Griffin."

He looked off to one side, mouthed the word, then said, "Griffin who?"

"I'm your son, Dad."

His hazy eyes opened wider. "Oh, yes, of course. Griffin." He laughed. "I didn't see you come in." Then, he added, "How have you been?"

Backward and forward, on and off he went.

I watched him closely. If I followed his movements and facial expressions, I could almost tap into his shifting mind. The way his eyes broadened with awareness of his surroundings and who I was. How he tightly shook his head and pinched his lips together when logic failed and confusion ruled. The way his gaze followed me when he was present and stood still when he wasn't. This was the new language between my father and me. At this stage, it was more about what he didn't say than what he did. A kind of rhythm between the lines. During his more responsive moments, I could jump back in and get the most lucidity out of him as possible.

He grinned at me, so I decided to jump back in. Maybe, if I mentioned something good from his past, he'd stick with me.

"Dad, do you remember what you loved most about Mom?"

He faded away again, and I feared I'd lost my chance.

Then, he said, "How much she loved you."

63

THE PHONE RANG AT 6:33 A.M., bumping me out of sleep.

I fumbled for the phone on my nightstand—knocking over my alarm clock and a few other things I couldn't identify—then turned the screen toward me. The call was coming in from Oceanview.

"Mr. McCabe?" a man said.

"What is it? What happened?"

"Your father's condition is stable."

My shoulders loosened. My pulse steadied.

"But there *is* a problem," he went on. "He's extremely agitated and upset."

"What happened?" I asked, rubbing my eyes.

"He's been distressed since you left last night, and it's just gotten worse. He keeps calling out for you. I thought we'd let you know."

My mind spooled back to that day at Bright Horizons: the same thing happened, but life had taken on a new shape, making the dissimilarities between then and now oppositional. This time, I *did* care. No, it was more than that. I was upset—so much that I got out of bed, threw on clothes, then jumped into my car.

I sped toward Oceanview, my vision dopey, my mind spinning faster than the wheels beneath me. What could have made him so distressed? Was he again distraught because I'd left him alone, or was his mind screaming for a lifeline as it fell through the pitted recesses of Alzheimer's? Then, my chronic worry returned. Would this be our last visit?

When I got to the room, my father was inconsolable, bawling, bottom lip continuously puffing in and out. I rushed to his side, but when his bleary eyes found mine, he only wept harder.

"What is it, Dad? Tell me."

He let out a yelp so primal and grievous that it tugged my muscles into stiff commiseration. I took his hand into mine, limp and callous, then squeezed it, and he squeezed back harder.

"It's okay, Dad," I said, trying to fight back the rift in my voice but failing at it. "I'm here now."

His eyes pleaded with mine. "I … I …" Then, he stopped and let out a defeated mewl, unable to finish what he needed to say.

I waited.

Weeping harder now, hungry for air, he said, "I … I did it all wrong."

"What, Dad?" I leaned in closer. I was here for this. "What did you do wrong?"

His head sagged to one side as if the weight of his torment was too heavy to bear, along with that faraway stare. He was slipping away again.

"Don't leave me, Dad, please," I begged, trying to call him back from whatever depths he'd collapsed into. "Don't go away again, not yet."

He wouldn't look up. I was tethered to his suffering but held steady—I had to. This might have been the most important thing he'd tell me since our lives collided. I had to do something before his mind checked out for good. Curling both arms over my head, hands in fists, and knuckling hard into the back of my neck, I surrendered to despair, ready to give up.

But then he lifted his head, his mouth opened, and with surprising resolve, he said, "I … I … I ruined you."

And there it was. The truth, laid out for me to see. Admission, coupled with regret. A gateway, once bolted shut, blew wide open, and with it came a small aperture for love to pass through. I didn't know how my father had managed to have such acute insight, but I was damned grateful for it. At the same time, the word *ruined* felt so permanent and irreversible. Had I been ruined or broken open enough to see what lay inside?

"Griffin?" my father said in a tiny, childlike voice, his milky-blue eyes searching the room. "Griffin? Are you there?"

"I'm right here, Dad," I said, looking for a foothold in his attention.

"I … I … wish … I wanted to know you better."

My head dropped to my chest. An almost-silent sob shook me under its hold. I closed my eyes, but tears squeezed through in spite of it.

My father would never have the chance to know me better. And with that irrevocable truth, something inside me withered, then perished because I'd been craving that for most of my life. I tried to answer him but didn't know what to say, and even if I did, I wasn't sure if I had the stamina to get everything out.

I rubbed my father's shoulder while he shook and moaned—tears swimming down his cheeks, one after another—and then I curled up beside him and rested my head across his thin chest, listening to his quiet whimpers and his soft, shallow breaths.

It was a new beginning but one that would end too soon. I wanted to take hold of time, to never let go of it. I wanted to love my father harder and longer. And I wanted him to love me back in the fierce, imperishable way he once had.

PART FIVE: DISCONNECT

64

TIME WAS CLOSING IN ON us.

My father's mind and body were on an accelerated decline. His brain kept lying to him, bending reality and distorting perceptions. Sometimes, he believed he was in Ireland—although he'd never been there—and other times, he didn't know where he was or even who *I* was. It seemed like torture for us both.

"My son is coming to visit today," he told me one morning. "His name is Griffin." He lowered his head and scratched his temple. "But I can't remember if you two have met."

My nod and smile were noncommittal, fractures of grief spreading through me, the junction between us pulling away. We were just a few feet apart, yet he was alone, and I was alone; and as the gap between us opened wider, the definition of *us* got hazier.

Other times, he told me stories from his past but spoke in third person as if they no longer belonged to him.

"Sam cherished his wife ..." he'd say, or, "He loved Griffin very much." And while the comments were true and stirring, his voice was colorless.

Alzheimer's flips time. The past becomes the freshest memory while the present gets lost in a distant fog. Life becomes a continuous one-dimensional route, backing into reverse. When he did make sense of the past, I listened with intent. These would be my father's final words to me, the stories he told, the foundation for my own new memories of him. I heard snippets of my own history I'd never known, stories about Deena and me when we were young and still close. I wanted to lean into it, learn from it, and make sure to never repeat the mistakes my father had made when my own children came along.

My own children.

I was shocked that the idea sounded agreeable to me. Something inside me had changed, as if getting the bitterness with my father out of the way had cleared the path to a vision of myself inside a future snapshot.

My father gazed out through his window, taking in the beautiful patio garden, and I wondered what he saw. Was it the sunlit fountain, flowing unencumbered? The abundant greenery, shifting to the suggestion of a gentle breeze? Or was it the hike we didn't get to take together? Even as I tried to envision our time in that garden, the memory felt flat, and I could no longer see him there.

The days moved on, and my father's rootless life continued to fall away.

On this afternoon, he lay in bed, his gaze empty, his lips inflamed and cracked, no matter how often I dabbed ointment on them. A prickly pink rash had risen along his neck. He shivered, so I placed a washcloth, wet and warm, across his forehead, then rubbed more ointment onto his lips.

"Does that help, Dad?" I asked, pulling the washcloth away, then soaking it in the basin of water.

He acknowledged the question by raising his head a few inches. My father was tired, so tired—everything about him was—telling me that his ability to fight had come to a finish. He looked up at me, didn't speak, but I could see it all. He was ready.

"I know, Dad," I told him. "I know."

He fell into sleep.

A nurse came in. Noticing how tired I looked, she offered to bring me food and coffee. How oddly natural it felt to be treated like the distraught son with his father and how oddly comforting.

Later, he woke up. Like a fragile nestling with eyes closed and mouth open, he told me he was parched. I scooped ice chips from a plastic cup, then tilted the spoon into his mouth. It was fine. All of this. I was keeping a promise to both my mother and father. I was taking care of him but no longer out of obligation. I was doing it because I wanted to.

For years, I'd kept him out of my life. I wondered about my compulsion to stay at his bedside. Was it a reflection of my needing him as much as he did me? If that were the case, I was no longer naive enough to believe that after he was gone, I could go back to the same kind of solitude I had felt before when we were merely estranged. For that matter, *how* would I miss him? Nolan had said that he could smile instead of cry, but I wasn't sure if either felt quite right. Our relationship was complex in its own way.

The day was late, and my father needed his rest. I got out of my chair, but when I turned to leave, the shadowy figure of a woman appeared in the doorway. With a jolt of recognition, I stopped.

"Hi, Griffin," said my sister.

65

DEENA TOOK SLOW, CAUTIOUS STEPS across the floor.

I was a little wobbly myself. My eyes and mind were in disagreement. Never had I thought I'd see my father and her in the same room together again.

"He's asleep," I told her. "He goes in and out."

Deena proceeded toward the bed but stopped short of it, just close enough to take him in, then said, "I can't believe this is him. It almost seems—"

"Impossible?"

Deena studied me for a few seconds, almost as if it might help her comprehend the strange new cosmos spiraling around her. She proceeded toward his bed, then checked his vitals on the monitor. After pushing a thatch of hair from her face, she punched a few buttons to change the screen. She shook her head, but it didn't look like pity, more like an expression of abandon.

Her attention wandered to my backpack on the chair, then to the empty coffee cups stacked on a nearby table, and she said, "How much time have you been spending here?"

"Every day."

The skin tightened around her eyes when she said, "I … I didn't know you were that involved with him."

"We haven't spoken enough for me to tell you."

She held me in her irresolute gaze. "Have you two talked much?"

"It hasn't been easy with the Alzheimer's, but we did our best."

Deena looked back at our father. She laid a hand across her breastbone and fingered a tiny gold cross that hung from her neck—a cross that, until now, I'd never seen her wear.

Who is this person?

She could have been anyone from anywhere, not my sister, my twin. We were never religious growing up. Had something happened in life to send her on that trajectory? Maybe she wore the cross to give herself the strength to see our father. More mysteries, but Deena was full of those. It seemed we were destined to remain siblings and strangers. Maybe we always would.

"He looks so harmless," she said.

The same thought I'd had after seeing him for the first time. How far I'd come. How far Deena had to go on her road to healing if she chose it. She eased closer toward our father. I kept quiet. The situation was delicate, and I didn't want to complicate it by opening my mouth—or worse, saying the wrong thing.

"Do you want me to leave you alone with him?" I asked.

With eyes fixed on our father, she flagged a hand toward me, shook her head, and said, "No, stay here."

Was she still afraid to be alone with him, even in his current state? No, I could see it now. There was something else. I might not have known a lot about my sister, but I recognized her expression. Much like I had, Deena was confronting her fear after years of avoiding it. I was probably the last person she'd look to for assurance, but I was all she had right now.

I pulled a chair to the bed for her, but she waved off the gesture as though she had no intention of staying long enough to need it. I took the chair back to a corner of the room. I sat, but even at that distance, I felt as though I were eavesdropping on a moment that was meant to be private.

With her back toward me, pushing her hair behind each ear again, Deena said to me, "So, this is how it ends."

I didn't respond. The comment felt rhetorical, more an effort to acclimate herself to a situation in which she hadn't planned to find herself.

After a long moment, her shoulders shook, slight at first, then more noticeable.

Deena let out a tiny whimper, then soft choking sounds. On instinct, I rose from my chair but had difficulty attaching purpose to it. What was I supposed to do? Join my estranged sister and place an uninvited arm around her? Tell her I understood how this felt? She and I never had that kind of relationship, and this didn't feel like the time to start. I deliberated, then decided there was nothing to do except wait.

Deena sniffed and wiped her cheek. When she turned back to me, I saw it all: the penetrating stab of sorrow. The deprivation. The fallout. I knew those feelings because I'd experienced them myself, but unlike me, she was just beginning to let them in. Deena nodded to me as if knowing these feelings were one of the few things we had in common. A miserable bond but, nevertheless, true. Our story.

"I'm not crying about him," Deena protested, busying herself by pulling a tissue from her purse. "I'm crying for myself."

How many times had I had the same sentiment toward my father? It was a reflection of how different life might have been if our mother hadn't died—an alternative history, pressing close. One thing seemed certain, the Before and After would have been the Now.

I'd been able to gain a semblance of peace while my father was alive. Deena wouldn't have that opportunity. Sad, but like many other things, I had to let go of that.

My sister stood in a different garden.

I walked Deena to the elevator. She was quiet, but I couldn't fault her. My sister was as much of a victim of our father as I'd been. Her damage didn't have to be permanent—I was sad she couldn't see that yet—but she'd faced her fears today, and it was a step on a long road toward healing.

We walked side by side. I could sense our emotional distance, yet some inexplicable part of me was still consumed by the need for closeness. It might have been the voice of nature speaking; she was my twin. We had grown together in the same womb, and then our father groomed us apart. Now, it appeared as though we would remain distant, and I didn't know how to change it. When we reached the elevator, the air around us felt thick with apprehension. I wasn't sure what to say—I didn't know if she'd want to hear it, anyway.

Deena stepped toward the elevator door, turned back toward me, and said, "I wish things could have been different for us, Griffin."

"Yeah," I said through the painful lump in my throat. "Me, too, Deena."

To hear that she felt the same regrets reduced the distance between us by a fraction of an inch. I wanted more, and she started to talk but then stopped herself. Instead, she let out a doleful sigh that spoke what she couldn't seem to say. She hit the elevator button.

"Deena?"

"Yeah?"

"Can ... would it be okay if I gave you a hug?"

Her eyes flooded with tears. "Of course, Griffin."

For the first time since childhood, my sister and I embraced. We continued holding on to each other for longer than I could have expected. She cried quietly into my shoulder, and I got it. She was releasing years of pain.

The elevator dinged, and by the time we pulled apart, it felt as though we had a new understanding of each other.

The door opened, and my sister walked through.

"Deena?" I again said once she was inside the elevator. "Maybe we can see each other again sometime? A walk on the beach with your kids or something?"

She wavered, and then with the slightest nod, she said, "That sounds very nice," but I wasn't sure if she really meant it. It seemed that Deena's habitual resistance was still holding me at a distance—not as far as before, but she was still keeping that divider up to protect her vulnerability.

"Hey, no big deal," I said. "Take care of yourself, okay?"

"You, too, Griffin." But this time, I believed she meant it.

The elevator door closed, and once again, my sister disappeared.

66

THE PHONE RANG, AND I jumped from sleep to answer.

"Mr. McCabe?"

"Yeah," I said through a heavy yawn that sounded more like a groan.

"It's Dr. Norwell from Oceanview Hospice Care. I'm afraid your father is declining rather quickly. You may want to come soon if you want to tell him goodbye."

Goodbye.

Hearing that word made the oncoming loss more immediate. I lowered my face into both hands and closed my eyes.

We're here.

The hospice doctor and a few nurses gathered around my father's bed. Noticing my arrival, the group parted to reveal my father. His eyes were closed, and other than the rise and fall of his chest, he wasn't moving. My legs became weak, my arms suddenly so heavy that I had to grab on to the chair beside me.

The doctor turned around to look at me. "I'm so sorry. Your father is nearing the end of life."

I nodded, then studied the doctor's face as if it might give me the resolve I needed to stand over my father. The hospital staff exited the room, allowing me this final, private moment.

I stepped toward him. His eyes were dull and unfocused, hazy with detachment beneath heavy lids. Unplugged from the world. His jaw fell open, but nothing more than inconsistent, strained gasps came out. The doctor didn't have to tell me my father was about to die; the truth played like some sad, discordant sound, the whimper of an oncoming exit.

If I could, I'd have told him that, while our communication was often flatlined by his confined mind and snarled logic, I'd finally found my way toward forgiveness and reawakened the love we once shared. That I now understood we were both held hostage by a generational pattern of addiction, cruelty, and abuse. And when I thought of him, I would choose to dwell on love, not anger.

I cupped a hand over his as if it might mend the chasm that Alzheimer's had placed between us, stimulating a more powerful connection. "I'm right here, Dad."

He didn't respond, his only movement the slightest tremor that moved through his body like a soft, fading hum. I tried to guess at what he was feeling right now. His mind had been shutting down for a long time, long before his body did. Could he comprehend the immensity of a moment brought on by impending physical death? I gazed out through the window at the garden—*our* garden—where regret paled and splendor flourished, but it looked different now, emptier, sapped of all the warm hues.

My father's eyes opened, and his hand twitched. I looked back at him and saw a man begging to be freed from his suffering. A man tired of the fight, ready to be done.

"I know, Dad," I told him, words catching on their way up as I fought against a kind of heartache that, before now, I hadn't known. Different from when my mother died, more complicated yet impactful in other ways. "I'll be right here with you."

With each blink, my father's eyes gathered tears, and I felt the full thrust of grief clawing through my chest, my throat, all over. Grief in its most primitive form. Grief that had at last unearthed a place to settle.

"I love you, Dad," I said, surprising myself. Although I hadn't told him that since my mom died, it came out effortlessly and genuine.

My father's mouth quavered for one second, two, and then in a tone, sickly and feeble, he said, "Champ, I … love …"

"I know you do, Dad," I said, voice breaking.

Tears of sadness, loss, and gratitude warmed my cheeks. My mind whisked me away to the place where amusement rides danced and his love felt eternal. Where I was his Champ. What a beautiful, imperfect road we'd traveled together.

My father closed his eyes. He opened them. But he did not speak. Instead, he sluggishly moved an unsteady hand up and down, up and down, an inch or two off the bed, reminding me of that stormy day when he sent me off to college, fighting wind and rain while he waved goodbye from the train's platform. I indulged in the memory, waving back at him just as I had through the train's window.

Then, his eyes closed for the last time.

The heart monitor slowed, then flattened. Within seconds, the doctor was back in the room. He stood bedside, placed a stethoscope on my father's chest, and listened. With a sad, sympathetic expression, he looked up at me and nodded.

This was it.

Like a bosun's gentle whistle, fading into a distant night, came an end to the long goodbye.

67

A MONTH LATER, NOLAN CALLED to ask if we could meet at his apartment. When he opened the door, he frowned, allowing quietude to speak his sorrow. I threw my arms around him, and he let out a squeaking sound, as if bereavement had engraved a path into his heart. I held on to him as he let out gasping sobs. Seeing him torn up over the loss of my father spoke to the six-year-old place in me.

When Nolan pulled back, he held his watery gaze on mine. This was the only true friend my dad had left. He'd listened to him intently and accepted his shortcomings. Above all, he offered respect when my father had little left for himself. Now, I considered Nolan family, and I felt grateful to know him.

We sat in his living room, tearfully laughing while Nolan told funny stories about my dad. When the conversation stopped, he studied me for a moment, then stood to leave the room, and I observed with curious interest. He came back, holding a tattered white shoebox. He took a seat at my side on the couch and looked at it one last time before passing it to me.

"Your father gave me this when he found out he had Alzheimer's. He didn't think he'd see you again, so he asked me to give it to you after he was gone."

Nolan handed me the box. Struck by apprehensive curiosity, I lifted the lid, and it took me a few seconds to register what I saw.

I pulled out the wooden toy my father had bought me at the fair—with the dad and son running together, a dog trailing behind. I thought

I'd lost it long ago—probably left it behind on purpose—but my father had been hanging on to it.

I raised the toy to admire it, gave it a spin, then traveled back in time. My father and I were at the fair again, sunshine on my neck, joyous sights, sounds, and emotions following us throughout the day.

I smiled and teared up.

This would be a part of my father that I could hold in my hands, taking me back to that happy day and freezing it in time, just as I'd hoped when he gave it to me.

Nolan looked down at his folded hands, his face serious. I didn't ask what was wrong, partly because I wasn't sure if I was ready to hear what was coming, partly because I knew it would come, anyway.

"There's something I need to tell you, Griffin, something I'm ashamed of because I've kept it from you since we met. I hope you can forgive me."

I was right. I wasn't ready for this.

"When you and your dad crashed that day, it was only partly coincidence."

I froze, jarred and confused. "What? What are you talking about?"

"Your father was on his way to your house when he crashed."

"But that doesn't make any sense at all. How could he …"

Nolan cleared his throat. "I lost count of how many times he drove around your neighborhood, looking for you, but the search went on for years."

A memory dropped before me, a long-ago summer evening when I was eight years old. I'd gone out to ride my bike and lost track of time. When I didn't arrive home for supper, my father got into his car and drove all over the neighborhood, frantically searching for me, worried that something horrible had happened. He eventually discovered me riding circles in the junior high school parking lot, and he was too relieved to be angry. That was in the Before, and this was the After, but the sharp divide that once ran between them now merged into one. In both instances it had been about my father's love.

I was about to ask how my dad knew what neighborhood I lived in, but I guessed at the answer. "That framed interview he had on the wall mentioned that I lived in Pacific Beach."

Nolan nodded. "He found the story online and begged me to locate the magazine. But we could never find your exact address."

"I'd made it undiscoverable. It kind of goes with the job."

"Of course. This was during the time when he got sober and before the dementia."

"And after?"

"After that, he kept saying that he wanted to see you, wanted to see you, over and over. It didn't stop, but with all his confusion, I couldn't imagine he'd actually try to find your house anymore, especially since I'd taken his car keys away. Well, one day, he wandered into my apartment and stole them while I was out in the courtyard, speaking to a resident. He was gone by the time I noticed the keys were missing. I was beside myself with worry. I know I told you I called the police after seeing his apartment empty the next day, but it was much sooner than that. I called after he disappeared."

"So, why didn't you just tell me all this?"

He looked down and pressed his fingers against his temples. "I was afraid to give you the truth. The first time I called, you were so adamant about not wanting anything to do with your dad. I figured the last thing you wanted to hear was that your dad was trying to find you. So, I kept my mouth shut, but as time went on and we got closer, the subject became harder to bring up. I'm sorry, Griffin. I should have told you the truth from the start. Please don't be angry with me."

"Nolan, how can I be mad at the man who's done so much for me? For my father? Who took good care of him when nobody else would? Besides, he and I wouldn't have had the chance to heal if he hadn't gone out looking for me that day. I guess for once, I'm thankful for bad luck."

"There are many things your father never got the chance to tell you." Nolan laughed with a note of sadness. "I swear, he must have told them to *me* about a hundred times. But the most important thing was, the day you were born was the day that would change his life forever. He had what he'd always wanted—a son he could love. He remembered feeling so much of that love, his heart actually hurt." Nolan looked out his window and shook his head. "If only he could have told you that."

He had. Not in so many words, but in so many ways.

68

IT HAD BEEN SIX MONTHS since my father passed.

I didn't hold a funeral. Besides Nolan and me, nobody was left in his life when it reached the end. I called Deena to give her the news. She thanked me for letting her know, and that was that.

Fair enough, I supposed.

Since I'd already made one attempt to make a date with my sister for an outing, I allowed a space for her to bring it up, but it didn't come. The absence left an empty chamber in my heart, one I realized I might never have the chance to fill. Maybe someday, we'd see each other again, if she could mend the wounds our father inflicted.

I struggled over not knowing what my dad's final wishes were. Since Ryan knew him pretty well, I decided to ask him what he thought. He told me that he had the impression of my father as someone whose dignity would have been injured by a funeral with practically nobody there, so I decided against it.

I opted instead to have him cremated, then chartered a boat to scatter the ashes off the San Diego coast. My father was never a big fan of the ocean, not like Deena and I, but it seemed like a beautiful way to set him free. At least for me.

What's the phrase? *Grief only exists for the living.* Something like that.

I stood at the stern of a thirty-eight-foot yacht, an endless, sloping horizon before me, a heavy wind at my back. Rippling pockets of silvery sunlight danced across the gentle tide, and the waves made a whispering sound against the bow. The breadth of view from where I stood lulled me into a solitary state where nothing existed except me and this massive body of water.

I leaned over the railing, then folded my father's ashes into tides of indigo, letting them ride off into the wind, twisting into a gray mist that dispersed, then faded over the swells.

In that moment, it felt as though I was letting go not just of my father's body, but also of a part of me—the wounds of my past.

"Goodbye, Dad."

I grew up a son of the sea when there was no one else to raise me. Someday, if my turn came, I'd continue to repair my past by being a dad who could guide his children through life with my love.

I could at last see myself as a father. A good one.

I was at peace with what being Sam McCabe's son had taught me. We'd traveled a thorny path, lost each other, but in the end, we found our way back. That doesn't always happen between an estranged parent and child. Unresolved trauma is like falling into a fire that never stops burning.

That wouldn't be my story.

No, mine began on the fateful day when our cars collided and our worlds converged. I had no way of knowing how much would change between us and within myself. And while our remaining time together was brief and fogged over by his collapsing mind, we were able to reawaken the profound and powerful love we'd once shared.

The boat moved on. In its wake, a trail of regret washed out to sea, followed by hope for new beginnings.

EPILOGUE

THE MUSIC STOPS, THE CAROUSEL slows to a halt, and then the most beautiful child I've ever seen gets off his tiny horse. He bounds toward me, and I fall in love with him all over again because seeing my son's happiness is like a forever-blooming sunflower.

My son, Braden, and I walk down the causeway, his small fingers wrapped around two of mine, his eyes dancing in all directions. Amusement park rides cycle fast while music and kicked-up dust rise through the air. The scene is noisy, chaotic, and in its own way, mesmerizing, a delightful rhythm of life. Looking at him is like seeing myself during my first visit to the fair. This child, this beautiful boy, is my bliss. Waking up to see him each day is another opportunity to create amazing memories and delight him. Nothing brings me more joy than this tiny human, this dark-haired, freckle-faced kid, with his big, toothy grin. Never had I believed I could love anyone this much or that he could love me back with equal measure, but so much has changed in me. I've become the father I wished I'd had.

The cycle of pain stops with me. I made a promise to do this right. To break the generations-long abuse that plagued our family. My affection won't be short-lived or interrupted by addictions of my own; it will last a lifetime, and my son won't know what it feels like to be starved of love. I'll nurture his spirit. I'll protect his life above my own and tell him he can be whoever he wants. He is my everything, and he will never want for anything. I'll give it all to him, no sacrifice too large, no affection spared, nothing but love and more love. And if he faces troubles of his own, I'll never give up on him.

Revisiting the fair with Braden is like pulling away an old, tattered bandage that I'd thought had been holding me together since childhood, then finding fresh, clean skin underneath. Although my childhood held many painful memories, there were also good ones. It's been my decision to embrace joy instead of sorrow.

"Daddy! Look!" my boy says, stabbing at the air as he points across the causeway. "Look at all the pretty balloons!"

"They *are* pretty. Which one is your favorite?"

He puts a pinkie finger against his lips to analyze the options. After inspecting the bouquet of colors, he says, "The purple. I like the purple!"

"Great choice, buddy." I grin. "It's my favorite, too."

"We're just like that, right?"

"Like what?"

"Like the balloons, Daddy. We're beautiful."

"We are, buddy. We're just like that."

I surprise him with a purple balloon.

He beams with excitement. "Thank you, Daddy!"

"You're welcome, kiddo." I check my watch. "Hey, do you know what would make this day even better? If we took some balloons home for Mom to enjoy. Why don't you pick out a few you think she might like?"

With big, bright eyes, Braden wastes no time selecting from the bouquet of balloons.

"And do you know what else?" I ask after our balloon-finding mission is done. "Do you remember what Mom said would be waiting for us if we hurried back?"

"Pizza!" Braden says. "And she said I can help! I put the cheese on real good!"

"You do, bud. You do a great job."

We walk toward the exits—well, I walk. He hops, leapfrogging from one pavement stone to the next.

"Daddy, look. They're taking pictures!" he alerts me when we reach the edge of the park.

I turn to see where he's looking. After narrowing my gaze, I feel soft drumming against my chest, and I can't contain my smile.

Braden looks at the man. Pressing his palms against his cheeks, he looks at me.

"Should we?" I ask.

"Yes!" he says. "Yes, yes, YES!" Then, he rockets toward the photographer.

When our turn comes, I hoist Braden onto my knee.

"Ready?" the photographer asks.

We both nod. Braden throws himself against my chest, and I snuggle him.

"Big smiles!" he says. "One … two … and … THREE!"

The moment the shutter opens, Braden looks up at me and reaches for my cheek, and then the flash goes off, capturing our picture-perfect moment together, one of thousands more to come.

ACKNOWLEDGMENTS

THIS IS THE BOOK I'VE always wanted to write.

Though quite a departure from my psychological thrillers, I wanted to write a story that, on several levels, dealt with the emotional aspects of familial relationships and all their complexities. I was also especially happy to write a story that took place in my hometown of San Diego.

And that's what drew me into this particular story—its characters and the trauma that many of us experience as we navigate the multifaceted pathways of growing up. Of becoming whole again after a fractured childhood. But I wouldn't have been able to portray this experience without the help of many people.

I'd like to thank the exceptional folks I met at Alzheimer's San Diego Care Partners Support Group: Diana Macis, Ron Bueno, Silka Kurth, and Chantal Fernandez. I am so grateful to you for sharing your trials, worries, heartbreaks, and even brief moments of laughter after watching your dear loved ones fall away from the world. You breathed life into my characters and gave them the emotional depth I needed to effectively show the devastation this disease often causes. I'm also thankful for Patricia Devlin for offering multiple resources during my research.

Thomas Cullinan shared his insights about watching his mother suffer through Alzheimer's and also read the manuscript to offer his valuable input so I could make this story even stronger.

Sarah Cypher, my editor, was also my teacher, showing me how to make the transition from thrillers to literary fiction. I'm pretty sure I had it all wrong at first, but through our work together, we created a novel of which I can be very proud.

Jovana Shirley proofread my manuscript and also created the beautiful interior formatting for this novel and did an excellent job in both cases. My good friend, Linda Boulanger, created the gorgeous book cover and would not be satisfied until I fell in love with it, which I did. She also headed my street team, keeping them engaged and excited about release day.

Stephen Jay Schwartz and Jay Ratner shared their experiences in Hollywood so I could accurately portray Griffin's work life in a manner that felt realistic. Peter Kern helped me with the nautical terminology for this story, and Stanley Wiley taught me about surfing and made sure that Griffin's lingo about the sport was current and accurate. Bob Sparks helped me with the real estate aspects of the story.

On a personal level, I'd like to thank my dear friends who talked me off the ledge on several occasions when I struggled to tell this story while simultaneously pulling the hair out of my head.

Deb Brada-Pitts, my dear friend and vacation buddy, has been there for me since our college years, and our bond has only gotten stronger since then. Thank you for coming into my life, for making it more beautiful, and for adding much-needed laughter.

LJ Sellers and I had more phone talks than I can count. She's the kind of friend who dropped everything whenever I was in need, even hopping onto a plane when things got really rough. I am so thankful for your loyal friendship.

Heidi Becker, my surrogate family member, thank you for jumping into action whenever I needed it and for doing so more times than I can count. Your kindness has meant the world to me.

Dana Lerner, Barbara Richards, and Suzanne Dana, three of my oldest friends, you have brought so much love and hilarity into my life, and I'll be forever grateful.

My dear friend, Jessica Park, thank you for being there for me an infinite number of times. And thanks for reading and rereading my manuscript and offering your valuable insights. I'm one hundred percent sure that this book would not have been the same without you. Thanks also for believing in this novel, even when I had a hard time doing it myself. And thanks for gently pushing me to keep writing when I wasn't sure if I could.

Finally, to you, my readers. I'm grateful to you beyond measure for staying with me after all these years and for giving me a place to tell my stories. Without you, this amazing career I always dreamed of would never have existed. I owe you everything.

ABOUT THE AUTHOR

ANDREW E. KAUFMAN LIVES IN Southern California with his chocolate Lab who thinks he owns the place.

After receiving his broadcast Journalism degree from San Diego State University, he began his writing career as an Emmy-nominated writer/producer, working at the CBS affiliate in San Diego, then at CBS/KCAL in Los Angeles. For more than ten years, he produced special series and covered many nationally known stories, including the O.J. Simpson Trial. He eventually realized that writing about reality wasn't nearly as fun as making things up, and so began his career as a #1 international bestselling author.

Andrew is also a contributor to the Chicken Soup for the Soul books, where he's written about his two battles against cancer and the struggle to redefine his life and become a recognized author.

For more information about his books, please visit www.andrewekaufman.com or follow him on Facebook at: www.facebook.com/andrewekaufman/ and on Instagram at: https://www.instagram.com/author.andrewekaufman/

Made in the USA
Monee, IL
16 January 2024

928b56d9-ea43-44f4-8715-77f9aad45d6dR01